BULLETS AREN'T KOSHER

EZRA BARANY

Dafkah Books

ALSO BY EZRA BARANY

Books in The Torah Codes series

The Torah Codes

36 Righteous: A Serial Killer's Hit List

Deborah's Number: A Bank Heist Mitzvah

Other books by Ezra Barany

6 Short Stories of Suspense

Plan Your Novel Like A Pro: And Have Fun Doing It!

ISBN #978-1-944841-23-2

To each of my students.
Keep striving to discover your true self.

NOTE FROM THE AUTHOR

From the opening of the movie "Dark City," to "The Fifth Bullet" episode in the Castle television series, to "Bourne Identity," the stories that used the amnesia trope always grabbed me by the throat and wouldn't let go. I loved them so much, I had to try incorporating that trope in one of my books.

It was exciting to see how my main character worked at figuring out who he was, and especially interesting to discover his inner struggle at determining if he was a good person or not.

I sprinkled in other characters: ones requiring redemption, and others who society deemed to be "bad people." I poured this concoction of characters into a thick plot and stirred in a good helping of danger. Coming up with danger required dreaming up things. Disturbing things. Things like murder. And kidnapping. And romance.

This book has all those things, so be forewarned.

BULLETS

AREN'T

KOSHER

1

OUCH. MY HEAD.

One of my temples pounded like a hammer. A hammer hitting bundles of dynamite.

Where the hell was I?

The cold wooden floorboards pressed against my cheek, my whole body flush to the cool surface.

Why was I on the floor?

Mariachi music blared nearby. Was I in Mexico?

I wanted to go back to sleep. My head fogged with no lighthouse in sight. I would have fallen back to sleep if it weren't for the other body lying on the floor. She lay face down. I could only see her blonde hair and ponytail.

Damn, I hoped she wasn't dead. That would suck.

I struggled to push myself off the ground but my muscles whined, so I gave up. For some reason, my waist felt colder than the rest of me, I felt wet there. The small pool of blood answered some questions.

Also explained the sting. I was bleeding from the hip. Was that even a thing? I've heard of bleeding from the side, or shooting from the hip, but bleeding from the hip? Odd. And not very heroic. Surviving with a black eye, a broken nose, or a fractured rib sounded heroic. A bloody hip? Not so much.

The light at the window clued me in that it was still daytime. What was this place? Looked less of a home and more of an apartment by how small it was. I lay in the living room by the sofa.

What day it was, I had no idea. The clock on the wall read 4:40.

What month was it? My head blurred away the answer.

I decided to start easy. What year was it? The fog wasn't letting me in on that one, either.

Okay. What was a simpler question? How about this: Who was I?

I ran through the database of names in my head, but there wasn't a single search result in that thing.

Terrific.

I tried introducing myself by muttering, "My name is…" No name came to my lips, not even at the tip of my tongue.

Whatever. First things first. I had to patch myself up.

With all the strength I had, I pushed myself off the floor and nearly fell back down, clutching onto the side of the couch. Damn wound, making me weak.

The woman on the ground wasn't moving, but she

wasn't bleeding. Either she was dead or asleep. Whatever she was, whether I helped her now or later probably wouldn't make any difference. And unless I helped myself first, I might fall unconscious. What use would I be to her then?

While leaning on the couch, I tugged my slacks down a bit and checked my hip. Still bleeding, but the wound didn't seem to be too big. Just a couple millimeters wide. Made a mess of the side of the off-white couch, though. Felt sorry for whoever owned the couch. Maybe I could pay the owner for damages once I got back on my feet. If I could afford it. Was I rich? No idea. I left that thought for another time.

I stumbled to where the bathroom might be. Found it. Unbuckling my belt and tugging down the side of my pants, I snagged some toilet paper and wiped off the blood. I made a note of the slacks, dress shirt, and tie. My clothes ruled out the possibility that I lived on the streets. I checked my reflection. Didn't recognize the man. At least I wasn't hideous to look at, just average. Brown hair, brown eyes, but a long neck. I saw how fast a guy could get bored of seeing that face over the years. Forgetting it may not have been due to a bout of amnesia.

I searched the medicine cabinet, found some rubbing alcohol. I explored the drawers and cabinets, taking a strange comfort in the way the sounds of the drawers and cabinets resounded off the tiles of the bathroom. I pictured the sound waves floating through the bathroom. Was it normal to think about such things?

Under the sink, I found a first aid kit. Leaning against the sink, I splashed a sharp dose of the rubbing alcohol on my bloody skin, despising the stinging pain of it, and taking comfort in seeing the skin clean around the wound. After taping a bandage on the spot, I already felt better. Still foggy, but the pain was less. I found headache meds in the kit. Swallowed a couple of those with some gulps of water from the sink.

With my pants back on, I moved to the living room to see how the woman on the floor fared.

My fingertips at her neck confirmed a pulse.

"Hey, lady! Wake up!"

No response.

"Your pizza's ready!"

No response.

"*Donde esta la piñata?*"

No response.

Oh, well. If I was in Mexico, and she only understood Spanish, that was all the Spanish I knew.

She wore jeans and an olive-green t-shirt.

Who was this woman? Better yet, who was I?

I stood and checked my pockets. No wallet. That would have been too easy. The only thing in my pocket was a set of keys.

There was a wedding ring on my finger. I was married. My chest warmed to know that. But where was my wife? Crap. Was this woman on the floor my wife?

Think positive. Maybe my wife was at work or in our house, wherever that was.

I sat on the couch, inched off the ring, and examined the inside. It was engraved. "SP + NY."

My head clouded as I worked on what it meant. Either those were two states—like New York plus, uh, Southern Pennsylvania, or whatever—or those were our initials. I was either S.P. or N.Y. Figuring the woman always went first, it was a good bet that N.Y. were my initials. So what was my name?

Norman? Neil? Norbert?

God, I hoped it wasn't Norbert.

I slid the ring back on and sunk onto the soft couch. Sure felt good. Made me want to float away, let the curtains of my eyes close. A feeling nagged at me that I was in trouble, but there was so much smoke in my head I couldn't see the forest fire for the flames.

I took a breath and sat up straight. Had to stay awake and fight gravity in case I was in trouble.

Who was the woman on the floor? Maybe she had a wallet. Of course, that meant digging into her pockets. I don't know how my wife would feel about that. But then, maybe that was my wife on the floor. The way her left hand was tucked under her body, there was no way to tell if she was married. Best to find out. At this point, any clue as to who the hell I was would be welcome.

I nudged her petite frame over so that she lay face up. The young twenty-something face still didn't ring a bell, if I even had a bell to ring.

Her hand didn't have one. A ring, that is.

I dug into her bulging pocket and pulled out her wallet.

Strange. No credit cards, no health care card or other cards, just a driver's license and hundreds of dollars in cash.

I checked the name on the driver's license.

Holly Sampson.

Didn't remember the name from anywhere, but it was more evidence she couldn't have been my wife. My wife was S.P.

There was something in her other pocket. I reached in and removed a fold of leather. Another wallet? I opened it and sighed with relief.

It was a badge. The Berkeley Police Department. So I wasn't in Mexico. That's good. I was in Berkeley, California and better yet, this woman was a police officer and could help me with figuring out who I was.

I tapped her cheek, hoping light slaps would wake her.

"Officer, wake up. You've been promoted to Captain."

No response.

"Officer Sampson?"

Her eyes fluttered, thank goodness. I kept repeating her name. She squinted. I stopped tapping her cheek.

I smiled. "I'm glad you're okay."

She shoved me away and jumped to her feet, fists up, eyeing me with daggers, dirks, and all sorts of pointy objects.

"I'm not going to hurt you." I raised my palms up in surrender.

She scanned the room and jumped at something

that lay on the floor in a corner. A hunting knife! I hadn't noticed it.

She raised it, pointing it at me.

"Officer, please! I'm not going to hurt you."

"Got that right," she barked. "I'm going to be the one doing all the hurting."

She lunged and swung the knife at me. I ducked out of the way. She staggered and leaned against the wall, as though too dizzy to stay upright.

"What's this all about, officer? Did I do something wrong? If so, arrest me. I'll come in peacefully."

She saw her wallet and badge on the floor and scowled, still trying to make sense of what was going on. Keeping the knife aimed at me, she eased to a crouch and grabbed her wallet and badge.

"You're not going anywhere." She pocketed her belongings. "You're going to die here."

Damn, that sounded depressing. What about all the sandwiches I'd miss out on eating?

"You know, dying is damn inconvenient," I said, inching to the front door. "Could you at least tell me what I did, or what you think I did?"

"You know damn well what you did." The knife wavered. I couldn't tell if she was nervous or fatigued. "I'm Richard's daughter."

"Who's Richard?"

"Why you—" She lunged at me again.

I dodged and knocked her arm away.

She countered with a punch to my wounded hip.

I screamed out the pain.

I may not have known my name, but I knew when I overstayed my welcome. I dashed out the door and came upon flights of stairs. How high up were we? Four floors or forty, didn't matter. I had to get down all of them.

Her steps echoed in the stairway chamber, as if stomping on me from above. I tried running down two, then three stairs at a time.

That was a mistake.

I fell down onto a landing right on my wounded hip.

You know, getting chased by the police with pain drilling in your side is a great way to take your mind off of such trivial questions as who the hell you are.

Her clomping was getting close. Pushing myself back up, I descended down the remaining stairs. Turned out to be only about ten flights.

I exited the building into a chilly day. A lake lay before me, and beyond the lake a slew of high-rise buildings. Dollars to dipshits, that was a downtown. There wasn't a lake near downtown Berkeley, was there? Couldn't remember.

For now, I needed to find a safe place to hide. Preferably a public place. A place where witnesses were a deterrent against stabbers.

I ran against the wind and passed a grocery store, a Korean BBQ joint that smelled of cooked pineapple, and a pedicure place whose acidic cleansers smelled like they were trying to hide a dead body.

I checked behind me. Good. The officer wasn't

there. I ducked into a nineteen-fifties-themed diner, Skylight Diner, and hid in the back corner booth with red seats. With all the customers in the way, my table was hard to see from the front door. Plus, I had a good vantage point.

Just to be safe, I examined the back and, sure enough, there was a back door I could run out if necessary. It had an alarm warning across the handle, but I had plenty of emergency in me to warrant opening that door.

I slunk low and moved the napkin dispenser, sugar jar, syrup, ketchup, and mustard bottles in front of me. I was still too tall for the items on the glitter-dust table to hide my face, but I felt safer.

A wailing toddler sat with her parents in a booth on the opposite side of the restaurant. The father murmured something to quiet her, but she wasn't listening.

Ugh. That kid had a loud set of pipes.

I better not have any kids of my own. I could never tolerate a family life.

The waitress in her uniform, a dark green dress, approached. "Heya, Ed. You're here early."

I started. "You know me? My name's Ed?"

"What are you talking about?" She put a hand on her hip and smiled. "I've had just about enough of you pushing away my advances, I don't need you to pretend you never met me."

She winked. That confirmed it. She knew me. I must have been a regular at this diner.

"Miss," I read her name tag, "Alessandra, I need your help."

"You act like you don't know me, and now you need me. You are one confusing player, big boy."

"I don't remember who I am." I shifted in my seat and winced at the pain at my hip. Thankfully, it hurt much less than before, and the headache was gone. "I hit my head, I think. Is there anything you could tell me about myself?"

"What sort of game are you playing, Ed? I have seven other customers waiting for me. I don't have time for games. Are you going to order, or what?"

I had to convince her I needed her help. If that meant ordering something to have more time to extract what I needed from her, so be it. "Fine. I'll order something."

"The usual?"

"Sure." Whatever that was.

After scribbling something down on her pad and putting in my order, she tended to the other customers.

I squeezed off my ring and examined the engraving inside. SP + NY. If one of those initials were mine, how come she called me Ed? What if the ring wasn't really mine? What if it was stolen?

If I was wearing someone else's ring, then perhaps I wasn't married after all. My gut sank at that thought. A part of me really wanted to be married, and I didn't know why.

Alessandra returned with my order. It was two eggs sunny side up, hash browns, bacon, and sourdough toast. She said I was early today? It was around five o'clock in the afternoon. That meant I normally ordered breakfast for dinner.

"Are you going to eat it or stare at it?" Alessandra asked.

"I'm serious, Alessandra. I have no idea who I am, where I live, what I do for a living, how I got here, who my friends are, and why a cop is trying to kill me."

Alessandra leaned back, "What do you mean a cop is trying to kill you?"

I showed her the bandaged wound at my hip, the result of Officer Sampson's blade skills.

"You're serious? You really don't remember who you are?"

"I'm dead serious." I waited for her to complete her evaluation of my expression.

Alessandra sighed and sat in the seat across from me. "All right, I think I can spare a few minutes to tell you what I know. But I'm afraid it's not much."

———

Carl and Sarah Best's Residence
Amsterdam, N.Y.

SARAH BEST FELT a kick in her belly. She paused from emptying a trash bin and rubbed the spot the little foot kicked. Being without Carl during the entire nine months of her pregnancy was not how she wanted her maternity leave to be like.

"I hear you, Little One. I miss him too."

She had tried everything she could think of to find Carl. Searching under both Carl Best and Nathan Yirmorshy, she'd found nothing on the Internet, and she'd received no help from the police. She purposely didn't tell WITSEC about Carl's disappearance. Ignoring their warnings of leaving the city was a major no-no and could end their protection services.

Yes, she understood why he left. When she had been tortured by that crazed cop who wanted to know where Carl was, it'd put her life in danger. Carl wanted to make sure she wasn't in harm's way anymore, so his goal was simple: stop the cop. But Carl left without letting her have a say, dammit. He didn't even know that she was pregnant.

Outside, she shook one of the rarely-used bins into the dumpster and a loose paper towel fell to the ground. She bent to pick it up and paused from throwing it in the trash. Carl's handwriting was on it, and read, "Master artist," and had a phone number.

She returned inside to study the napkin.

Whose phone number was this? Carl never kept secrets from her. Perhaps this had something to do with where he went?

She sat at the kitchen table, threaded a strand of her blonde hair behind her ear, and called the number.

"This is Brian."

She didn't know a Brian. "Brian who?"

There was a pause.

"Who is this?" Brian asked.

"This is Sarah Best, Carl Best's wife. There was a napkin with your number on it. Something tells me you know where he is. Now who is this?"

The line went dead.

What the hell?

2

Skylight Diner
Oakland, CA

As the sky darkened outside, I leaned toward
Alessandra, eager to hear what she knew about me.

"Okay," Alessandra said. "Here it is. Your name is
Ed. You come here every evening at six thirty and order
the same thing. You always dodge my flirts by praising
your wife." She lowered her voice imitating mine. "She's
so great at this, she's so great at that."

"So I do have a wife."

"Sure do. You talk about her all the time."

I tried to picture her. Couldn't.

"What did I say about her?" I wrung my hands.
"Did I tell you where she is?"

"I asked you to describe her one time. You said she had blonde hair."

That Berkeley cop had blonde hair. But she couldn't have been my wife. Her initials were all wrong.

"She also had a dimple on one side of her mouth." Alessandra touched her cheek. "Said it made her look... what did you call it? Asymmetrical! You said her face was asymmetrical because of that one dimple on her cheek."

"I used that exact word? Asymmetrical?"

"Yep. You said she was a tarot reader. A good one, too."

"That's weird."

"What's weird?"

"I don't feel as if I'd believe in tarot. But I guess I do."

"You also said she was as smart as a whip who got her masters in whipping."

"She whips people?"

"No, you were just making a joke. I remember that because in my line of work..." She smirked. "Well, I just remember you saying that."

"Did I say where I live?"

"I asked. You said you lived in the big apartment building down the block next to Lake Merritt Grocery Store."

That was the building I had just come out of. That was my apartment building? I laughed.

"What's funny?"

"I'm the poor guy who has to deal with the blood on the couch."

"The cop attacked you in your apartment?"

"Seems that way."

"Why would he do that?"

"She."

"What?"

"The cop was a woman."

Alessandra tilted her head as if figuring something out.

"There a problem?" I asked.

"I bet you she found out you had a wife and went ballistic on your ass."

"You think I had an affair with her?"

She frowned. "On second thought, I don't think so. You love your wife too much, and you always turn me down. And let's face it. Who in his right mind would turn down this?" She ran her hands down her sides with ample curves upstairs and downstairs.

I sunk in the booth's seat. If my name was Ed, why did the ring say SP + NY? Was it someone else's ring I wore? Was I pretending to be married? Was it my way of turning down Alessandra's advances?

I studied Alessandra. She had a point. Who in his right mind would turn down that?

"What's wrong?" Alessandra asked.

"I'm not completely sure I'm married." I showed her the ring and explained my reasoning about the initials not matching my name Ed.

"But if you're not married, then why pretend?"

"I don't know. Am I some undercover agent who has to pretend he's married? What if I work for the cops and have to pretend I'm a white collar criminal? What if I work for the FBI or the CIA?"

"All right, Mr. Bourne." She glared at me and stood. "While I can't say for certain you're not a spy, you are definitely married. Unless you're more of a sausage boy than an egg boy."

"What?"

She propped her foot on the seat beside me, hitched her dress to expose and offer her knee like a can-can dancer, and raised an eyebrow.

"Oh, I'm an egg guy," I said. "Definitely an egg guy."

"Then if you can pass this up, you're married. Now eat your food to get your head on straight while I tend to the other customers."

She moseyed off.

How did I like to eat my eggs? Did I mix the eggs with the hash browns? Did I eat the meal one item at a time? I had a bite of the hash browns. It tasted good, but bland. I snagged the salt and sprinkled the plate. The hash browns tasted better.

Then I gulped down a heavy thought. I didn't have any cash or credit cards to pay for it.

———

Carl and Sarah Best's Residence
Amsterdam, N.Y.

SARAH SAT at the kitchen table, stared at her phone, and punched the number again.

After the seventh ring Brian answered. "Yeah?"

"Listen, you want me to go to the police and have them make inquiries about you?" She pressed her palm against the table, ready to slap it. "Tell me where Carl is now!"

"No deal. You want to turn me in to the police, you go right ahead. But my customers trust me. They need to be able to trust me. I will not betray Carl."

Damn. That was the wrong approach.

"I'm sorry, Brian." She huffed out a breath, put a hand on her belly. "Obviously, I don't want anything bad to happen to Carl either. He's my husband, but that's why I need your help."

"No can do. He left clear instructions for me not to tell anyone where he went. Especially you."

Damn it, Carl.

She rubbed her belly. *We'll find him little guy.*

"Can you at least meet me face-to-face?" she tried. "I just want to talk about it with you. I promise. If you convince me to drop this pursuit, I will drop it."

The silence on the other end felt like waiting for a roulette wheel. Would it land on her number?

"You won't talk to the police?"

"I promise."

"All right, then." Brian told her where and when to meet her and hung up.

Excitement sizzled through her body. She patted her belly. She might see Carl soon.

3

Skylight Diner
Oakland, CA

No wallet. How was I going to pay for this dinner?

Alessandra returned. "I just remembered. You asked me to lock something up for you in the staff locker room. Wanna give me the key and we can see what it is?"

"Sounds good." I handed her my set of keys. She studied them.

"None of these keys are for a locker. Do you have another set?"

"No. You think it's something important?"

She shrugged. "All you said was that you couldn't

keep it in your apartment. I assumed it was just some kinky porn."

Oh, geez. My cheeks burned. "I don't think I need that right now."

She chuckled and ran a hand across my cheek. She eyed my plate of eggs, hash browns, and bacon.

"You're eating a lot slower than usual," she said.

"I am? Probably because I forgot to tell you I have no money."

She laughed. "Oh, darlin'. You almost never have your card with you. We have it on file. I just ring you up, you sign it, and we're good to go."

That didn't make sense. "Why didn't I carry my wallet?"

"You always went home first. Said you liked to have your pockets free when you were out and about in the afternoons. Eat up, Ed."

That explained why I only had keys in my pocket.

I looked at my plate.

She sighed. "Now what's wrong?"

"Do you remember how I ate it? I mean did I mix it up or what?"

"You used to mash it all together."

"Yeah?"

"And then snort it up your nose with the straw."

I eyed the straw. Looked uncomfortable.

"Relax, Ed. Enjoy this opportunity of discovering yourself all over again."

I smirked and took a bite of the eggs.

"I still don't get why the cop was trying to kill you," she said.

I was really getting into the egg yolks mixed with the hash browns. My stomach must have been hiding its hunger. "I don't know. Maybe she thought there was a spider on my hip and wanted to cut it off."

"Cute."

"Hold on a sec." I held the fork in the air as if it were a wand to conjure the truth. "She said she was Richard's daughter."

"Richard? Who's Richard?"

I shrugged.

"If only you knew his last name."

I snapped my fingers.

"I do! It's Sampson."

She sat down. "She said she's the daughter of Richard Sampson?"

"No, it's just that her name was Holly Sampson, so I imagine her father has the same name."

"Assuming she's not married, you mean."

"I didn't see a ring."

"Have you done an Internet search on him?"

"Can't. Don't have a computer on me."

"Your phone?"

"Don't have one. I suppose I leave that with my wallet at home, too."

"Here." She took out her phone and turned it on. "Do your worst. I need to check on the other customers."

She left me alone and I first checked a map application to see where I was. East 18th Street, Oakland, California, near Lake Merritt. Oakland was Berkeley's neighbor city.

I dove into the World Wide Web to find the reason a police officer wanted me dead.

It was amazing how many Richard Sampsons there were.

Officer Holly Sampson had said her father's name was Richard, as if that were an excuse to attack me. So trying to figure out who he was seemed a reasonable next step.

On the social media sites I found as many as fifty-seven Richard Sampsons. I was willing to bet the farm, if I had one, that none of the Richard Sampsons in the social media sites was her father. Didn't seem like an old folk's place to hang out.

I tried the white pages online and got even more results. Three hundred and eighty-one to be exact. Fortunately, I could narrow it down to state and city. In Oakland, there was only one Richard Sampson listed.

I wanted to check with Alessandra to see if it was okay to call him with her phone, but she was busy. I called the number.

"Si?" a man said.

Did I get the wrong number? "May I speak with Richard Sampson?"

"Si, this is Ricardo. You want a good tan?"

"I'm sorry, I'm not sure I have the right person. I'm

looking for a Richard Sampson. Is your last name Sampson?"

"Technically, it is Gonzales. You want a good tan?"

"So you're not Richard Sampson?"

"At tanning salon, I am Richard Sampson at Richard Sampson's tanning salon. You want a discount?"

"Excuse me, but do you have a daughter named Holly?"

"Thank the good Lord, I have no children."

"I see. Out of curiosity, why do you name yourself Richard Sampson?"

"Would you go to Ricardo Gonzalez's Tanning Salon?"

I got the point. Even people who believed themselves not to be racist exhibited racist behavior.

"So you want to come in? I have availability for a great tan at ten o-clock and eleven o-clock tomorrow morning."

"No thanks. I'm trying to bleach my skin as pale as possible."

"Okay. Have a beautiful day!"

Dead end.

I tried an Oakland search for the name "Ed Krieg" on the white pages website.

Nothing came up. Then I saw a picture of myself in the news.

Well, not me, exactly, just a police artist sketch. But it looked a hell of a lot like me.

I straightened. The day-old headlines read:

"California State Senator-Elect Stabbed 17 Times."

"Murderer of David Deutsch Still On the Loose."

"Police are On the Hunt for State Senator-Elect's Killer"

Crap.

4

Skylight Diner
Oakland, CA

If I was the killer, why had I been in my apartment when I should have been on the run?

Perhaps because they only had a drawing of my face and not my name. Not enough to find me.

I had a sudden craving for sunglasses and a hat.

A dream of a memory came to me. A monster reached out at me, reaching for my pockets, his face a horrible fly-looking creature.

In the dream, I was thinking, "Not that key. Not that one."

He took it anyway, a silver-colored key with a deep nick in the side.

Why had I been so worried about losing it?

The memory couldn't have been real. There were no such things as fly people.

Alessandra stopped by my table with the bill. "Find anything?"

Best I kept quiet that I was a suspect of a homicide. A Senator-killer.

"Couldn't find our Richard Sampson," I said.

"So what's next?" She took back her phone.

"I'm thinking of going back to my apartment and getting my phone and wallet. If I have a computer, even better. I should be able to find some answers there." If it wasn't swarming with police.

"Good idea."

I signed the bill and handed it to her.

She smiled and I did a double take.

"Could I see the bill again?" I asked.

"Relax, Sweetheart. I didn't over-charge you."

"It's not that."

I examined my signature. The scrawl was illegible, but the initials were clear. The first name started with an N, the last name started with a Y. So my name wasn't Ed Krieg.

"I really am a spy!" I said. Why did that feel so cool?

The waitress examined the first letters on my signature. "N and Y, just like your ring."

"That must be my real name. I must have signed my name all these years that it's second hat for me now. Or old nature. Or whatever."

"Hold on a sec. Let me see if I can find yesterday's bill you signed." She left the table.

I exhaled. What a relief to know the true initials of my name. Even more relief knowing that my name wasn't Ed Krieg. The initials spelled EK, the sound someone makes when accidentally swallowing a bug.

I studied the signature closer. The last name was impossible to read, but the first looked like something worth guessing. There were four or five letters after the "N," a couple of "A"s and a "T" between them. Was it Nathan? It didn't look like anything other than Nathan.

My name was Nathan.

Good. I like that name.

Alessandra came back with one of my past bills. We checked the signature. It was clearly Ed Krieg.

"Weird," Alessandra said comparing the signatures. "Why do you have two names? And which one is your real one?"

"That one." I pointed to Nathan's signature.

"How can you be sure?"

"I wasn't paying attention to what I wrote. I just scribbled what felt natural. Only years of doing that over and over will make that happen."

"Okay." She scowled. "So why are you pretending to be some guy named Ed Krieg?"

"Wait one sec. I think I have the answer to that written on the back of an old receipt in my pocket." I pretended to search my pockets. "Darn. I must have thrown it away."

She did her hand on her hip stance again. "You know, you're pretty funny for a guy who doesn't know who he is."

"Then maybe I'm a comedian." I scooped a final fork of hash browns. "Better yet, I'm a spy posing as a comedian." I ate the last of the delicious crispy potatoes.

"I could believe that."

"Yeah?" I paused my chewing and looked up at her.

"Sure. You're funny, but not comedian funny. You're more government official funny."

"Ouch."

"What's your next step?" She turned to the diner's front door where a chuckling pair of teenage boys entered, her next customers.

"I'm going to see about recovering my wallet and phone." I wiped my mouth with a napkin. "That should have answers."

5

Riverlink Park
Amsterdam, N.Y.

IN THE EARLY EVENING, THE SKY WAS A LAVENDER
dusk and, as instructed, Sarah went to Riverlink Park
and sat at the designated bench and waited. The river's
waters meandered past her with a babbling sound.

A man in his fifties, sporting a dusty auburn fedora
and matching coat, sat beside her.

She almost explained that she needed the seat free
because she was meeting someone, but he said, "It's like
a secret meeting in an espionage film, isn't it?"

His teeth were crooked, but there was no reason to
judge his character by his teeth.

"You're Brian?"

"Pleased to meet you, Sarah." He turned to face her and held out his hand.

She shook his calloused palm.

"Carl didn't tell me you were pregnant."

"He didn't know."

Brian's eyes widened with surprise.

"He still doesn't know," she said. "I found out the day he left over eight months ago and I've been unable to get a hold of him."

He closed his eyes and massaged the bridge of his nose. "Now I understand why you're so eager to find him."

"So you'll help me?"

He studied her and frowned. "You're not going to stop until you find him, are you?"

"I can't."

He looked out at the river. She followed his gaze. A boat drifted along, lit up with a string of lights in the shape of a trapezoid. Was it called a cabin cruiser? She didn't know her boats. Two teenage girls held drinks aboard. They wore jeans and sported bikini tops even though the air chilled all exposed skin.

One playfully threatened to push the other overboard. The one losing her balance shrieked, but managed to remain on her feet and threw her drink in her friend's face. They were so carefree.

Sarah wrung her hands. What would Brian's decision be?

He returned his attention to her. "Are you able to travel by plane while you're this pregnant?"

Her heart pumped faster. "Yes."

He nodded. "Okay. Carl's in Boise."

"Boise, Idaho?"

"Yep."

"What's he doing there?"

"That's all he told me."

She reflected on what she would do once she arrived in Boise. File a missing person's report? No. Being in WITSEC, it was better to not have his picture plastered everywhere.

"I can help you with getting new documentation," Brian said. "That could help you get on the plane without alerting WITSEC. That sort of thing."

"That's what Carl came to you for? For fake IDs?"

He chuckled. "There's quite an art to it, more than just typing a fake name over your own. I use my special skills to create practically undetectable replicas of identifications, passports, driver's licenses, you name it."

"So Carl has a whole new identity again?"

"That's right. I couldn't do my best work because it was a rush job."

She smirked. How many times had he changed his identity? First Nathan, then Carl, and now...

"What's his new name?"

"Carey Larkinson. I can give you a new identity also, if you like."

"Sold." Hold on a second. "How much does it cost?"

"It's on me. You're pregnant, you should be with Carl, so I'll help make that happen, free of charge."

Her heart thumped. She hugged him and thanked him and kissed his cheek. She was going to see Carl again.

"What do I need to do?" she said.

"Give me your current driver's license."

She yanked open her backpack purse and scrounged for her driver's license.

"I'll disassemble it, copy your picture, use it to make your new ID, then I'll reassemble your old ID to look as good as new."

Wait a minute. Giving him the only ID she had? Was that safe? She had only his phone number and knew his first name. It wasn't quite enough to trust him.

"Do you have a card," she said, "or some way to get in touch with you in case the phone number doesn't work?"

"Certainly." He pulled out a business card. His name was Brian Santana. His work address was on the card.

She smiled. "You're also a watch repairman?"

"That's right. Feel free to stop by anytime when you return from your trip, and I'll repair your clocks, wrist-watches, pocket watches, or any other timepiece you need fixed."

Now she had enough information on him to contact the police if need be. She gave him her driver's license and more words of thanks.

He stood and helped her up. "Come back here tomorrow morning at eight. I'll have your documentation in tip-top shape."

Sarah felt lighter on her walk home, and warm in the dark, chilly night.

6

Skylight Diner
Oakland, CA

I PEERED OUT THE DINER WINDOW. THE EARLY evening sky was purple. No sign of Officer Sampson. Good. I hastened back four blocks to the apartment building and examined every face on the way. No undercover cops seemed to be loitering nearby, except for this one young guy in an Oakland A's baseball cap and beard. He leaned against the wall of my building and was reading a newspaper. I checked his ears for one of those curly listening wires but could only see one side of his head. No curly wire on that side.

He yawned and his eyes drooped from reading the paper. That didn't seem like proper surveillance behavior. An undercover cop would pretend he's doing his own thing, but he'd be alert.

I kept my gaze downward as I stepped into the apartment building and took the elevator to the twelfth floor, the top floor. Couldn't remember what floor I lived on, but it didn't matter. Going a few floors above my own was a good strategy for checking floor by floor for hostiles.

"Hostiles?" That was a military term, wasn't it? More of an indication that I was a spy.

I decided to test my knowledge of spy jargon as I poked my head from hallway to hallway before descending one level and repeating the process. What was the code for a hostage situation?

Couldn't think of any number, word, or phrase an agent might use as a code for a hostage situation.

How about a major hub for dealing drugs? Did I know a code for that?

Nope. Nothing.

A bank robbery? Serial killer? Bomb threat?

Nope, nope, and nope.

If I were truly with the FBI or CIA, wouldn't I know some codes for those things? At least some jargon, right?

But I didn't. Unless the amnesia made me forget those things, chances were I was not a secret agent.

Bummer.

At the ninth floor, I landed at a hallway that looked familiar. At least, the cheap posters of famous artwork looked familiar. They were posters of Italian masterpieces.

Posters. Of masterpieces.

Might as well take a picture of a beer and ask how it tastes.

I found the apartment I had raced out of. The door was wide open. I had run out of the room, and Officer Sampson followed me. No one closed the door?

"I suppose I don't have a butler," I muttered.

I entered, leaving the door open. Was Sampson hiding in one of the rooms, waiting to attack me?

First the living room, my blood still on the side of the couch and on the floor. I touched my bandaged hip. My hip was sensitive, but the pain was gone.

I had a nice-sized TV. I must like television. I hoped I didn't like soap operas, because if I did like soap operas, I'd have to watch a lot of them. The thought made me sick.

I moved to the bedroom, as quiet as I could. No one in there. No one in the kitchen or bathroom, either. My bed was a single bed, too small to share. So if I had a wife I adored, why wasn't she living with me?

Something caught my attention. I checked the bedroom and living room again.

Odd.

No pictures.

No wonder I didn't realize this was my place when I first woke up. There were no pictures of me anywhere. I let out a sigh of disappointment. I had hoped to see what my wife looked like.

So why no pictures? Was I, or rather was Ed Krieg, posing as an unmarried man? Then why keep the wedding ring on? And why tell Alessandra about my wife?

Only two answers came to mind. Either I posed as Ed Krieg, a married man whose wife no one would ever meet because there was no true woman in my life, or I posed as a single man, removed all traces of who my wife was, but couldn't bear parting with the ring.

The inexplicable connection I had for the ring made my heart heavy knowing I did indeed have a wife and missed her something awful.

I scanned the living room again. Nothing more than a bloody couch, a TV shifted at an angle, and a memory of that recent scuffle. I moved to the bedroom again. Nothing out of the ordinary aside from it being very sparse. I checked the closet and drawers. I had what amounted to three different ensembles to wear. I must have done the wash every two or three days.

These slacks I had on were bloody and uncomfortable. I changed into blue jeans and a white T-shirt.

I looked under the bed.

There it was. A laptop.

I flopped it on the bed and turned it on. This had to hold answers.

Dammit. It asked for a password. I tried "Nathan" nothing. I tried "wife." Nothing. I tried "Up crap creek without a paddle." Nothing.

I shut it. Perhaps I could find a hacker to get me in.

Where were my other things, my wallet and phone?

In one dresser drawer, I found an envelope, and in it a letter. I removed the letter.

"Meet me at the Vistavolt Hotel, room 722, at 7:30 a.m." The signature was illegible.

Silly girl. I must have been quite the charmer.

I checked the return address on the envelope. Odd. The return address was San Francisco's Vistavolt Hotel address, but the postmark was the city of Marin, across the Golden Gate bridge from San Francisco.

Why was the letter mailed in Marin for a meeting at a San Francisco hotel? I hoped she wasn't married. The last thing I needed to worry about was a jealous husband.

I returned the letter to the drawer.

In the dresser drawer, I shoved aside the three bundles of black socks. My phone and wallet were underneath.

Finally!

I flipped open the wallet and checked the cards. Only two credit cards, both under the name Ed Krieg. A photo of a woman. Was that my wife? She had a single dimple on her cheek, just as I'd described to Alessandra before I lost my memory.

She was quite a beauty. I was a lucky guy. So where was she? Damn, I hope she didn't break up with me. Or worse, I hope I didn't break up with her. What an idiot I'd be for leaving her.

Of course, I had no idea what kind of a woman she was. Was she a bad person? Did she leave pens uncapped? Did she eat people without their consent?

I checked the money. Ones and fives. All small bills. Nothing as bizarre as Officer Sampson's wallet, which had a slug of hundreds inside.

I checked the driver's license. Next to my picture was the name Edgar Krieg. Was this real? It had to have been a fake.

I held it to the light. It had the stripe on the back and all the intricate colorful patterns embedded in the card. But nothing reflected in the light, no DMV insignia or numbers, or anything like that. Driver's licenses had image overlays visible at certain angles, didn't they? There could be only one reason this driver's license didn't have such an image.

Impressive. This was one hell of a forgery.

That was all the wallet held, but just to be sure, I felt for any hidden pockets. The ridges of a card stood out. I found the pocket and removed the card.

Another driver's license. This one from New York. Whose would this be? Ed's or Nathan's?

I checked the name next to my picture. It read Carl Best.

Dammit.

———

SEAMUS CREAMER SCREAMED as Aiden flogged him. This time, Aiden had used the fifteen flails instead of the more painful thirty. Damn, it felt like there were cuts all along his back.

If only his infantry division at basic training army

could see him now. They'd think twice about calling him "Seamus the Wuss," and all those other nicknames.

Aiden struck him again and again. The flails whooshed and landed on his back with a thud. Damn it all to hell!

Seamus jerked against the shackles as if it would help him get away.

Aiden yanked Seamus's hair. "How does that feel? Share the pain."

Seamus cursed. "Feels like I've been stabbed with a fountain pen."

Aiden chuckled and, by the sound of it, set down the flogger. "Let's try a little punching practice."

He threw a powerful punch into Seamus's shoulder. Seamus sucked in a breath. The punch burned into a spot of pain.

Aiden pummeled him in the same spot, again and again.

Seamus longed to cry out "Mercy," but he wouldn't allow Aiden to have the satisfaction.

So he let Aiden use him as a punching bag, transforming his upper arm into a splotch of dark colors, just like Aiden had done to his other arm the day before.

When Aiden finished, Seamus commended himself for not begging for mercy.

Aiden wiped his sweaty self off with a towel, donned his shirt and tie, and vacated the room locking the metal door behind him.

Seamus panted. So close. Just a few more days of this and Seamus would have all he coveted.

7

Ed Krieg's Apartment
Oakland, CA

WHO THE HELL WAS CARL BEST? I CHECKED THE
New York driver's license to see if it was real. The whole
shiny part of the DMV logo lit up when held in the
light. It was real, as far as I could tell.

How was that possible? Was Nathan my real name
and Carl Best some secret identity of mine? Or was my
real name Carl Best and I spent so many years as that
Nathan guy that even my wife didn't know my true
identity?

I returned the license to the wallet, pocketed the
wallet, and turned on the phone. Another code needed.
Thankfully, it was based off of facial recognition. I lined

my eyes up to the dots and the phone unlocked. The screen's background was an image of a ewe with tired eyes wearing a party hat. The caption read, "Nappy Ewe Here!"

What other pictures did the phone hold? I clicked on the photos icon.

Image after image displayed me smiling next to the one-dimpled woman, goofing off next to her, laughing with her, kissing her. My heart broke apart. Whoever she was, I felt like I came home.

From the hallway outside the apartment, Officer Sampson came charging at me.

Dammit, what hole had she come out of?

I dodged her and ran into the bathroom with the laptop and phone, fumbling with the door to shut and lock it.

She lunged at me again. I closed and locked the door.

"Open the door, Nathan." Her voice was calm.

She knew my name? My real name?

"Not until you say pretty please with a cherry on top."

She kicked the door. Crap. The door wasn't going to last long under her barrage.

As she kicked, I looked for an escape. Fortunately there was a small window I could squeeze through. That was it. I'd climb out and go down the fire escape!

I opened the window.

Damn. No exterior fire escape. Just straight down several stories.

She pounded harder, kicking the door so hard it shook my chest.

I pocketed the phone and estimated the drop to the window of the apartment directly below. Checked out the pole that held up the shower curtains.

Good. The bar was easy to remove.

I yanked it off and fed the curtains — still attached to the pole — through the window. It was like a flag's fabric hung out the window while the flagpole stayed inside. I positioned the pole so that both ends of it pressed against the wall and couldn't get through the window. No way the rings of the shower curtain could slide off.

Sampson kicked the door open. I squeezed myself through the window and fell clinging to the curtain with one hand. The shower curtain's bar at the window frame prevented me from falling further. With the other hand, I struggled to keep hold of the laptop.

No good. The laptop slipped from my hand, fell several stories to the ground, and busted into pieces.

Damn.

Sampson peeked out from the window above. She sneered and sawed at the shower curtain with her hunting knife.

I clung to the curtain and dangled beside the lower level's window, the one on the eighth floor.

I kicked at the window. It did nothing except propel me from the wall.

My heart raced with the dread of stopping. I knew full well it wasn't the falling that kills you, it was the stopping — the splat on the ground. With each cut Sampson made disconnecting the shower curtain rings from the curtain, I dropped a few more inches.

I pushed against the window to swing far from the wall and get more momentum. It was enough. I kicked the window, breaking it open.

I squeezed through — ouch! — and cut my back on a slice of glass. Stinging pain seared through me. Still, on the scale of one to ten where one is complete bliss and ten is death, I suppose getting sliced by a piece of glass was no more than a three.

The shower curtain drifted down the side of the building.

A voice called out from inside the apartment "Mary? That you? The cat's got your teeth again."

I rushed out of the bathroom and came face-to-face with a man whose wrinkles around his eyes suggested more years of happiness than of hardship.

He scowled at me.

"You're not my wife."

"Thanks. Every bit of information helps."

I sprinted for the front door and passed an old woman asleep on the couch. A cat lay on her lap with dentures dangling in its mouth.

8

Lakeshore Avenue
Oakland, CA

I CLATTERED DOWN THE STAIRS AND OUT ONTO THE
night street with no incident. I had to get back to the
diner and Alessandra. Right now, she was the only one I
could trust to help me with whatever was going on.

I rushed past the grocery store and some people
yelped behind me. I glanced over my shoulder. Damn!
In her pursuit of me, Sampson shoved people out of
the way. At least I had close to a city block's head
start.

I circled the block and veered back to the large
grocery store. Grabbed a line of several shopping carts
and pushed them. It took a bit to get the momentum
going. Sampson spotted me and sprinted closer. As I

steered the metal chain of shopping carts into the store, a man in a cap held the door for me.

Once inside, I angled the carts perpendicular to the entrance, barring the door from opening.

Sampson pushed on the door, ramming into the carts. The carts were too heavy for her. I got a bunch of complaints. You know, people whining about how they couldn't get out of the store, but I didn't care. It wasn't like they would go hungry.

Sampson and some customers struggled with the chain of carts blocking the door. I dashed to the back of the store.

In the employees-only area, I pushed through swinging doors into the grimy, stinky warehouse of stacked foods and kept going until I found the open-air delivery area.

I hurried by the delivery trucks, circled around the grocery store, passed the Korean BBQ and pedicure place, back into the Skylight Diner.

I wanted my now-usual spot in the back but it was just after 7:30 p.m. Peak dinnertime. The place was packed. My seat was taken.

Alessandra pointed to a corner seat at the counter, hard to spot from the front entrance. Just what I wanted. After making her rounds with customers, Alessandra leaned across the counter. "You look as cheerful as a drenched cat in the rain."

"Thanks. I bet you say that to all the guys."

"Oh my Lord, your shirt's got blood on it!"

"Oh, yeah. Either I cut myself going through a

broken window, or I challenged a rhinoceros to a dance-off and lost."

She scowled. "Why'd you go through a broken window?" She eased my collar up to examine the wound on the back of my shoulder.

"Ms. Copsie Daisy was upset," I said. "I didn't bring her flowers."

"That cop again? Well, come with me and let me put a bandage on it."

I wasn't about to refuse her offer of applying the bandage. After all, putting a bandage on your own back is about as simple as stuffing tea down a volcano.

She took my hand and led me into the women's locker room. No one was inside. She opened a first-aid kit and flipped through its contents.

"Take off your shirt," she said.

Felt more like a nurse giving orders than an intimate suggestion.

T-shirt off, I faced the wall of lockers and listened to her rip open the bandage packaging. She pressed the bandage to my shoulder, putting more attention on the sticky edges to make sure it stayed on.

"Done," she said.

"Thanks. I'll wash up in the men's room."

"I'll do the same." She stepped into the woman's restroom and I heard her turn on the water.

I spent the next five minutes in the men's room washing the blood off my shirt. When I returned to my seat, Alessandra poured me a cup of coffee.

"So tell me," she said. "Find out anything at your apartment?"

I showed her my two driver's licenses, pointed out which one was real and which one was a forgery.

"So you're not Ed Krieg. But I thought your real initials were NY. Who's Carl Best?"

"I don't know, but at least I know where he lives."

I took out my phone.

"What are you going to do?"

"I'm going to call my wife."

I did a search for "Carl Best" along with the address on the driver's license. Nothing came up.

I found the number for New York's Amsterdam Police Department and called them.

A lady answered, "Amsterdam Police."

"Hi, I wonder if you could help me locate someone who lives in Amsterdam."

"Sir?"

"Yes, I'm good friends with a man named Carl Best and I've lost touch with him. Do you think you could look up his phone number for me?"

"That's what social media sites are for. Good day, sir." Click.

"Hello?" No response. "Hello?" There ought to be a law against hanging up on people.

I had to try a different approach. I just hoped I didn't get the same person.

I called the police department again.

A man answered, "Amsterdam Police."

"This is Captain Grover with the Fresno police

department and we've got a bomb set to go off in nineteen minutes. We're convinced a guy in Amsterdam knows how to diffuse it, but we need his phone number. Goes by the name of Carl Best."

"Sir, the penalty for crank calls is two years in prison under the Telecommunications Act."

"Dammit, we've now got eighteen minutes. You want us to blow to smithereens, or are you going to save the day and give us his number?"

"Why don't you just look it up in the system?"

"I'm standing at the bomb site, away from my desk, and thought it would be faster contacting you, but apparently I could have written a request via snail mail and got a speedier reply. You gonna help or what?"

No response.

"Damn you to hell!"

"All right. Fine. What's the name again?"

"Carl Best." I waited and heard typing.

"Here he is." He gave me the phone number. I memorized it. "Do you also want his criminal record?"

I blinked. "His what now?"

"His criminal record. Says here he was arrested for grand larceny."

"Grand larceny?"

"Yes, sir. Robbed from a bank electronically. But the charges were dropped."

Why didn't I feel relieved? Was I really the kind of guy who would rob banks and kill people running for senator?

"Who is this really?" he asked.

"What?"

"There is no bomb, is there?"

I hung up.

Did my wife leave me because I was arrested for grand larceny?

Only one way to find out. I called the home phone number.

9

Skylight Diner
Oakland, CA

THE PHONE PURRED ITS RING TONE. WHAT SHOULD
I say if my wife answered? Would the conversation go
like this?

Hi, this is Carl. Who is this?

*This is your beautiful wife with the one dimple. I miss
you and love you and want to go trick-or-treating
with you.*

No one picked up. A part of me was relieved.

Got my own voice on the answering machine,
instead.

"This may be me or it may be a recording. Either
way, leave a message after the 440 hertz tone." *Beep!*

I hung up. Now what?

I examined my phone, flipping through the photos of my wife. Damn, I wish I remembered her name. I should have asked that Amsterdam cop her name.

Alessandra stopped by.

"What did you find out?"

I told her about getting my home phone number in Amsterdam, New York and not reaching anyone. I skipped the part about having been arrested for grand larceny.

"This is quite the mystery!" she said. "Don't give up. I want to know how this mystery ends."

After she stepped away to assist other customers, I checked the phone's address book. No numbers or addresses listed. I tried the call log.

There was one phone number I called a lot. I dialed the number.

A woman's voice answered. "Caldwell for California State Senator. May I help you?"

Hmm. "This is a campaign office?"

"Yes sir. Would you like some information on Mr. Caldwell's platform and his stance on the current issues?"

Why did I call this place often? My gut sank. Did I kill a senator-elect to help this guy get voted in?

"May I speak to Ed Krieg?" I said.

"He's not in the office today. Shall I transfer you to his voice mail?"

"Yes, please."

I waited until the connection was made and heard my own voice say, "You've reached Ed Krieg, financial analyst. Leave me a message and I'll get back to you before the end of the election."

I very much doubted that.

I hung up. So I worked for this guy Caldwell who was running for a state senate seat. The idea that I killed his competition answered the question of why I would kill David Deutsch in the first place.

A chill crept through me.

"Whatchya looking at?" Alessandra asked. She leaned over to look at the phone display and placed her hand on my shoulder.

I sucked in a breath and arched my back, wincing from the pain.

"Oh! Sorry!" Alessandra jerked away her arm.

"You know, I'd take a warm, relaxing bath to soak my wounds, but it's hard to relax in a tub when a cop is trying to kill you."

"Tell you what. Stay the night at my place. I have an extra set of keys." She took out her keys and detached a pair of keys from the key ring.

"No, that's not what I meant. I wasn't trying to get you to offer me your place."

"I know. You're not that kind of guy. Which is exactly why I feel comfortable doing this."

She held out her house keys.

"You can go straight there and I'll be over once my shift ends," she said.

I stared at the keys. If she had known about my being mixed up with grand larceny and political murder, she would think twice before handing me her keys.

"Take them before I call that cop on you."

I shrugged. I had no plans to kill Alessandra. I took the keys and she gave me her address.

10

Alessandra Westbrook's Apartment
Oakland, CA

I MADE MY WAY TWELVE BLOCKS DOWN EAST 18TH Street to Alessandra's place under the night sky. The cut on my back didn't hurt so much in the cool air, and I didn't feel any pain on my hip. Good things come in small packages, but if I were offered a choice of a small package or a lack of pain, the choice wouldn't be a hard one to make.

Alessandra lived in a gated apartment complex on the corner of 12th Avenue and East 18th Street. Not the prettiest part of Oakland, but if I got shot here I wouldn't complain about the view.

I opened the building's front gate with one of the

keys. An old lady was leaving at the same time I entered. She eyed me suspiciously. Her horn-rimmed glasses and huge hair bun made her look like an Aunt Bernice.

I nodded hello.

"Do you live here?" she squeaked.

I adopted a dreamy, stoner smile. "Babe, do any of us live anywhere? Or do we live everywhere at once?"

She huffed and marched down the sidewalk.

I climbed up the outdoor steps to Alessandra's apartment, 208. I unlocked her door and stepped inside.

Wow. Shelves full of traveling souvenirs were aligned and ordered in a fashion as if to define the term *neat freak*. My apartment was pretty clean but only because it had nearly no furniture or anything to clutter the space. Alessandra's space was full of paintings, goddess figurines, animal statuettes, crystals, miniatures of fantastical creatures, and other knickknacks. If I were to pick one up and return it to the shelf, she'd probably notice it had been moved. I bet she had obsessive-compulsive disorder.

I sat on the couch. Ouch. The cut on my back didn't like how fast I sat down. I eased against the soft cushion. Soon, the wound stopped whining and I sighed.

No television? No books? This was going to be a long wait.

Feeling a bit hungry, I stepped to her kitchen. Inside her fridge was a pizza box. What kind of pizza did she like?

I opened the box and wrinkled my nose at the appalling sight of anchovies. Who in their right mind ruins a perfectly good pizza by covering it with a layer of fish?

"Calm yourself," I mumbled. Perhaps I'd actually like the taste.

I lifted a slice and took a healthy bite, cheese, sauce, and fish. I spit it out into the sink, turned on the faucet, cupped my hands, and gargled the offensive salty fish tang out of my mouth. Just like a person could never reach the speed light, there should have been a law of physics where pizza could never reach the taste of fish.

I panted, recovering from the trauma. After cleaning up the sink and returning the pizza box to the fridge, I wandered the apartment. There were two bedrooms. The one with the vanity mirror? Likely her bedroom. The other, as pristine as the living room, must have been the guest room. So this was where I'd spend the night.

I checked the closet. What I saw made me doubt my safety. Inside were chains, handcuffs, and clamps. My mouth dried. Did she have plans to lock me up? Then I saw the whip, straps, and dildos. That explained it. Sort of.

She had a wild side. But in the guest bedroom? What did she have hiding in her own bedroom closet?

The front door clicked with the sound of keys. I rushed to the living room sofa, plopped down, hissed at the sharp pain at my back, and struck a bored pose.

Alessandra strode in and glanced at me. She did a double take. "You looked inside the closet, didn't you?"

My face burned with a blush.

Here I was, late at night, sitting on the couch in the apartment of some kinky woman who expected me to spend the night. Did she have plans to cuff me to her bed? Plans for me to cuff *her* to the bed? Was she going to force-feed me anchovy pizza?

"Relax. I'm a dominatrix," she said.

That was supposed to relax me?

"Men and women hire me to act out their fantasies. I'm not going to do anything to you unless you pay me and your request is within reason."

"So you're a..." how to say this? "Courtesan."

She laughed.

"Not quite. I don't have sex with my clients. Keeps it legal."

Gosh. A real live honest-to-goodness dominatrix. So many questions.

"You said your client's request always needs to be reasonable?" I asked. "What do you mean?"

She shrugged.

"Women often come to me to act out rape fantasies." She grimaced. "Those I don't do."

"Ah. Better they get therapy instead."

"No. Nothing wrong with rape fantasies. What matters is consent. Anything done without consent is wrong. Rape fantasies are different. Can't have a rape fantasy against your will."

"Yet you still won't accept such a request?"

"I don't like pretending I'm a rapist." Her gaze drifted away, perhaps to a place she didn't want to remember. She stepped to the kitchen and called out, "Want a beer?"

"I don't know. Do I like beer?"

"Beats me. You always ordered the eggs and hash browns. Of course, we don't serve beer at the diner."

"Bring it on then."

From the kitchen came a few puffs of sound, bottles opening under pressure, their caps tinkling on the kitchen counter.

She returned with two open bottles and handed me one.

"Heineken." I tasted it. It was good. More than tasting good, I recognized it. "This is Heineken!"

"Good." She smirked and sat beside me still wearing her waitress uniform. "You can read."

"No, I mean I remember liking this. This is my favorite beer."

"Your memory's coming back?" She pivoted to face me better. "Do you remember anything else?"

I scoured my mind. That man with the face of a fly popped in my head. Why was I thinking of some impossible fly-faced man?

I then managed to remember my wife's beautiful, cheerful face, but nothing more. I shook my head no.

She patted my knee. "Well, at least your memory's coming back. Have some patience and you'll remember everything."

I took another sip. The fizz settled down my throat and calmed my gut. I held up the bottle. "I needed that."

She leaned into me. "You need a lot more than that, hon."

I bit my lip. Was she hinting at something between us?

"Don't get any ideas, sailor." She winked. "All I'm saying is even if it will take time to get your memory back, you need to find out who you are and fast. I bet your wife's worried sick about you."

From my wallet, I took out my beautiful wife's picture. It was strange having a wife, being attracted to someone I didn't really know. On the one hand, I felt more of a strong connection with Alessandra for helping me out. On the other hand, this wife of mine was hot.

"That your wife?"

"Mm-hm." I said.

"She sure is a cutie. Just as you described her."

I gulped down more of the cold beer.

"So what's your next step?" she asked.

"I need to go to Caldwell's campaign office. That's where I work."

"You know where you work? That's great!"

"Yeah. Now all I need to do is look up where it is."

"It's in the city." She straightened her panty hose at her calves.

"San Francisco?"

"That's right. On days you came late to the restaurant, you said you just missed the bus."

"So I took the bus to work and back."

"That's one way to do it."

"What are the other ways?"

"There's the BART train." She smoothed down her dark green dress. "That gets you there fast, but can add up to quite a tidy sum, and it's always crowded in the mornings during rush hour."

"What else could I have done to get to San Francisco?"

"The bus is cheaper, but slow. Are you okay with going slow to work?"

"I don't know."

"Are you a morning person or a night person?" She adjusted her dress at the shoulders, lowering the neckline a touch.

"My gut says I'd prefer to sleep in as long as possible." I scratched the back of my neck. Was I really wanting her neckline to fall lower?

"Okay, so let's say you take the fast way."

"The BART train?"

"Right. But there is one more fast way to get to San Francisco without paying a cent."

"What's that?"

"The casual commute."

"What's the casual commute?"

"You stand in line at a designated spot, people pick you up and take you to downtown San Francisco for free."

"If it's free, what do they get out of it?"

"They get the carpool lane. Less traffic."

"Ah." I had another sip.

"There's a casual commute line just off Lakeshore Avenue."

"Maybe I should go there and see if anyone recognizes me." On the other hand, what if they recognized my picture from the police sketch? Best to wear sunglasses and a ball cap, just in case.

Overall, it was a good plan. Maybe the place would trigger some memories.

11

Riverlink Park
Amsterdam, N.Y.
Friday morning, February 3rd

At Riverlink Park, Sarah shivered in the grey morning and smiled as Brian handed her the new driver's license as well as her old one. He nodded.

Everything looked perfect. She couldn't tell the difference between the two aside from her new name: Scarlett Bronson.

She thanked him and hugged him, making room for her big belly.

Back home, Sarah packed in haste, making sure she included a spare bottle of Carl's meds. She left her phone in her sock drawer to make WITSEC think she never left home.

She whistled the Beatles tune "I'll Be Back" as she snatched her keys, picked up her coat, and coaxed her luggage and excitement out the door. The taxi ride took a shorter amount of time than expected.

At the Albany International Airport, she stood in line to buy a ticket. The next plane out to Boise was in four hours with two layovers. It didn't matter. She'd waited this long, she could wait a few more hours to be with Carl.

Many people glanced at her pregnant belly. Most of them smiled with love for her future family. A television in the corner was broadcasting the news. She ignored it.

The question was, once she got to Boise, what could she do to find him? She'd have to look for Carey Larkinson, Carl's new identity. With enough poking around, she should be able to find him.

"Next," the airline attendant called out.

Sarah approached the counter. "I want a ticket to…"

The television flashed a sketch artist's rendition of Carl. That had to be Carl. What the hell? He was wanted in San Francisco? He was a suspect in murdering a senator-elect?

"Miss?" the airline attended coaxed.

"I need to be on the next plane to San Francisco."

12

Alessandra Westbrook's Apartment
Oakland, CA

IN THE MORNING, AFTER A BREAKFAST OF strawberry yogurt and cereal, Alessandra gave me a man's leather coat to stay warm. One of her clients had left it and never returned to claim it. I checked myself out in the mirror. The coat looked good on me.

I thanked her and walked the near twenty blocks to the casual commute area. Lake Merritt sparkled in the morning light. My breath fogged. I tugged the coat closer around me.

My back's scrape was healing into a good clean scab. The pain was gone, but the thing itched like a flea discotheque.

At the casual commute, the line looked relatively long.

"Is that him?" A woman pointed at me, whispering to another.

"I think so," the other woman said.

Damn, they thought I was the murderer.

A bearded man wearing a yarmulke and suit called out to me. "Hey!"

I turned and strode back toward Alessandra's place. The Jewish guy ran after me.

What the hell? Since when is it a good idea to chase after a suspected murderer?

I picked up the pace, turned a corner and ran. What was he going to do to me? A moment later he came around and rushed after me.

This was ridiculous. I stopped running, hands on my knees, and panted a tornado. He caught up to me and held on to my arm to keep himself up as he caught his breath.

"Why were you running, Ed?" he asked.

He knew my name. "Why were you chasing me?"

"Are you kidding?" He scrunched his brow. I must have known him. I guess I did take the casual commute. "Last time I saw you, our driver gassed us to sleep. When we didn't see you at the casual commute line these past few days, we got worried."

Gassed? What? "Who's we?"

"Me and Ranelle. She's waiting at the casual commute with her friend."

The name didn't sound familiar.

"Did you hit your head or something?" the man asked.

I nodded. "I don't remember who I am."

He frowned in sympathy. "Let me introduce myself. My name's Yitzhak Budnitz. You and I talk all the time at the carpool commute. Let me take you back to Ranelle. Ever since she and I recovered from the crash, she's been awful sick about you."

We walked back the block and a half to the casual commute line. The two women were near the front but as soon as they saw me they stepped out of line and rushed toward me. Yitzhak pointed out which one was Ranelle.

"Thank goodness you're all right," she said. "We were so worried about you. Nice jacket, by the way."

"Thanks. I'm fine. I just don't remember anything."

"You're lucky," Ranelle said. "I've been trying to forget my last two husbands."

"He's serious," Yitzhak said. "He hit his head and now he can't remember who he is."

"But you know how to speak," Ranelle's friend said. "How can you speak if you've forgotten everything?"

I shrugged.

Yitzhak stepped in. "I'm familiar with this type of memory loss. There are different types of amnesia. This is a sort of retrograde amnesia. He's forgotten his more recent memories, but his childhood skills have stayed with him."

"Do you remember what happened to us in the car?" Ranelle asked.

"No."

"It was the three of us," she said. "I was sitting in front wearing my navy blue office dress suit. The two of you were in back. Yitzhak was wearing what he always wore."

She gestured to his suit. Why was she telling me what we wore?

"You were wearing navy blue slacks with an ivory button up shirt and a narrow maroon tie. The most important guy was the driver. Boy, was he a cutie. He wore jeans, a T-shirt, and a denim button up over it. He had a dimpled chin and auburn hair."

What was up with all the clothes talk?

Her friend asked, "Was the collar thin or wide?"

Really?

"It was a wide collar," she said.

I shook my head. "Get to the point."

"Anyhow, we were crossing the Bay Bridge from Treasure Island into San Francisco when he put on a gas mask."

"A gas mask?"

She went on to describe how the driver had punched in the cigarette lighter, which released some sort of sleeping gas.

My body tensed. A full memory of the carpool ride flashed in my mind's eye: The driver hadn't looked familiar. When we got into the car, Yitzhak had sat in the back seat and closed his eyes.

Up in the front passenger seat, Ranelle had said to

the driver as he pulled away from the curve, "Hi, Mister. You single?"

The driver let slide a smile and didn't reply.

"I don't see a ring on your finger," Ranelle said. "You know, you've got cute dimples."

The driver didn't respond.

We drove across the first part of the bridge where Oakland connected to Treasure Island. The Bay waves were white-capped and choppy, the sky grey.

"So where do you work, Mr. Mysterious?" Ranelle kept trying. "Uh… What's that you got there? A mask?"

Lights lit up the tunnel as we punctured through Treasure Island. We came out the other end onto the bridge connecting Treasure Island to San Francisco. The driver was putting something over his head. A gas mask.

"Oh, I get it," Ranelle said with a melody in her voice. "You're getting ready for some kinky San Francisco morning show, aren't you?"

The driver pressed the cigarette lighter in. Smoke wafted in the air. The door locks clicked shut.

"What the hell?" Ranelle said, alarm in her voice.

I tried to lower the window to get the smoke out but the controls didn't respond. Ranelle wrestled with the button to lower her window too, with no success.

He must have ignited something with the cigarette burner. At the time, I thought maybe it was a cyanide pellet or hemlock.

Ranelle hammered at the window with her flat palms, "Help! Smoke!"

Cars whizzed by on their way to the city. No one on the freeway could hear her, of course.

My eyelids grew heavy, wanting to close. I reached for the driver's gas mask at his neck and struggled to yank it over his head. He gripped the edge and managed to keep his mask on.

Holding my breath, I unbuckled Yitzhak's seat belt.

He woke up confused. "Are we there yet?"

I wrapped the seat belt around the driver's neck and yanked as hard as I could. The driver struggled, gasping for breath.

Ranelle hunched unconscious against the window. Yitzhak slumped beside me. The driver swerved nearly hitting the car next to us. The bridge ended and he steered toward the first exit but missed. We crashed into yellow plastic trashcans of water by the exit.

I had floated on the surface of unconsciousness long enough to see him stumble out of the wrecked car, long enough to notice the door beside me open, long enough to feel him search my pockets and find my keys, long enough for him to remove one particular key from the chain and throw the rest in my lap.

I had pleaded with him, "No, not that key. Not that one."

Now — standing with Yitzhak, Ranelle, and her friend — Ranelle summarized the rest of her version of the story.

"The driver veered off," she continued, "and crashed into barrels of water, I heard, but by that time I was unconscious, and I think so were you. I woke up in the hospital."

"As did I," Yitzhak said. "Since we ended up with only minor bruises, we went back to our regular lives, reconnecting here at the casual carpool line."

"So what happened?" I asked. "Did the driver take anything?"

"That's the odd part," Yitzhak said. "Nothing was taken. Ranelle and I still had all our belongings. We just had our nerves shaken up, that's all."

"Sure nothing was taken?" I asked.

"Nothing," Ranelle said. "That's why we were hoping to talk to you. Did he take anything of yours? Do you remember?"

There was no man with the face of a fly. His fly face was the gas mask.

"He took a key of mine," I said, but what was the key for?

"What did it open?" Ranelle asked.

"The gates of hell," I said feigning concern.

They looked confused.

"I have no idea," I said. "All I remember is that he took my key and I desperately wanted him not to."

"Maybe it was to all your money or your wife's jewels, in some safe," Ranelle said.

I shrugged.

She checked her watch. "I've got to get to work."

Her friend checked her smart phone. "Me too. Will you be here tomorrow?"

"I doubt it," I said. "I'm still trying to figure out

everything. That might be awhile before I get back into the swing of things."

The women said their goodbyes and good luck. They got back in line for the commute.

"I'll stay with you and fill you in on everything I know. The nice thing about being a software engineer? Flexible hours. I don't have to be at work right away," Yitzhak said. "Have you eaten breakfast?"

"Nothing worth celebrating."

"Come with me, Ed. I know a good diner."

13

Dolly's Trolley Café
Oakland, CA

I THOUGHT YITZHAK WAS GOING TO BRING ME TO
the Skylight Diner, but he took me to a different one,
one right next to the lake called Dolly's Trolley Café.
This diner was the shape of a long trolley car. We were
shown to a booth with a window that looked out over
the calm water of Lake Merritt.

Yitzhak ordered a hard-boiled egg, a bag of barbecue-flavored chips, and bottled water. I ordered two
eggs over easy with bacon, hash browns, and sourdough
toast.

"That's an odd breakfast," I said. "A hard-boiled egg,
chips, bottled water?"

"All prepackaged, so I know it's kosher. Or at least,

as kosher as I can get when dining out. What about your order?"

"My order?"

"Bacon, eh?" Yitzhak asked.

"What about it?"

"You do know you're Jewish, don't you?"

I thought about that. "That would explain Mr. Happy's cosmetic surgery down there."

Yitzhak smirked. "Most baby boys are circumcised, you know."

"True."

"You told me why you're not religious."

"I did? Did I say why?" I sipped my water.

"You said you've seen proof of Genesis being written by God," Yitzhak said. "But that there was no proof that the other books of the Bible were Divinely written."

"Did I actually use that word, 'proof?'"

"Yes. Now, *Kashrut*, the laws of what to eat and what not to eat, are in the book of Leviticus, one of the other books of the Bible. Since those laws were not in Genesis, the book you believe was Divinely written, you felt keeping kosher wasn't a legitimate set of laws to follow."

"Why would I think there was proof that God wrote the book of Genesis?"

"I don't know. Something about codes in the Torah. I never pressed you about it. Your relationship with God is your own choice."

I glanced at his yarmulke.

"So what's the reason behind wearing the midget Frisbee?" I asked.

Yitzhak smirked.

"Humility," he said. "The reason we wear *cippot*, which is Hebrew for *yarmulkes*, is to remind ourselves that even though we are all made in the image of *Ha'Shem*, we are separate from Him."

"Or Her."

He smiled. "Or Her. We are not gods."

"Is that from the Old Testament?"

He shook his head. "A custom, not from the Bible."

Meh. Customs. Never trust a word that's also used at airports.

The waitress served our meals to us. Now I felt conscientious about eating bacon in front of Yitzhak.

He must have figured me out because he said, "Relax. I don't break out in hives if I see someone eating bacon."

I nodded and crunched into the salty, oily wonder.. "Why do you keep kosher, anyway?"

He smiled and peeled the shell off his egg.

"See what you did there? You asked, why keep kosher? Your behavior is the reason why," he said.

"What do you mean?"

"Everyone has their own reason, but mine? When I saw those *kashrut* laws in the Bible, I did the same thing you did. I asked why the heck did *HaShem* care what I ate? Why keep kosher? I realized I was questioning the Almighty Himself."

"Or Herself."

"Yes," he chuckled. "Or Herself. Point is, the Bible trained me to question God, and, in doing so, trained me to question authority. These kosher laws in the Bible? I believe they were put there to teach us to question authority."

Hmm. That was a twist.

"I became grateful," he said, "for learning how not to be a blind follower. So, as a way to express my gratitude, I keep kosher."

Uh, wouldn't it be more in line to question authority by *not* keeping kosher? Whatever. Enough of this.

"What else do you know about me?" I asked.

"Yes. Let's get down to that."

"Let's start with my name." I mixed the eggs and the hash browns together.

"What do you mean?"

"On the one hand, people are calling me Ed. On the other hand, I have an out-of-state driver's license that says my name is Carl Best. And on yet another hand, my true initials seem to be N.Y."

"The truth is, Ed, your real name is Daniel Frost."

I dropped my fork. It clanked to the floor. "What the hell?"

"You're working under cover for the CIA in a drug smuggling sting operation that went wrong when you lost your memory."

Holy crap!

"That key that was stolen?" he said. "That was for a

suitcase which contained three point seven million in unmarked bills."

"How do you know all this?"

"Allow me to introduce myself. I'm your handler. We've been looking for you for quite some time, Daniel."

I collapsed back into my chair. I really was a spy.

Yitzhak smirked, then laughed, patting his belly. "Naw. I'm just messing with you."

I blinked. What the—? Then smiled. "That's cold," I said. "You are one cold Jew."

"Come on, I had to say that. If I hadn't taken advantage of your memory loss, then I'd have been breaking some sort of commandment." He smirked and bit into his hard-boiled egg..

I picked up the piece of bacon and bit into it staring at him as if saying, "Take that."

The waitress gave me another fork and I shoveled in a bite of the egg and hash browns mix.

"Here's what I know," Yitzhak said. "You work for Mr. Caldwell."

I grimaced.

"What's wrong?"

"Here's something I don't get," I said. "You seem like a pretty smart guy who's with the times. If you're so 'with it,' then how come you don't know about the death of that other guy running for senator?"

"David Deutsch? Oh, I know about his death. Horrible thing, that. Why do you bring it up?"

"Have you seen the police sketch of the suspect?"

"No, I get all my news as text emails, so no images."

I pulled out my phone and showed him the image of the suspect who looked very much like myself. "Look familiar?"

"What the—? Is that you?"

"I hope not. According to the news," I pointed to the sketch on the phone's screen, "this guy is the prime suspect."

Yitzhak sighed and looked off to the side, deep in thought.

"So what do you think I should do?" I asked. "Go to the police. Explain everything and be completely upfront?"

"No. The reality is the police have their own version of what happened and no matter what you say, they'll work out a way to twist it to their scenario." He stroked his beard and wrapped his hand around his bottle of water without taking a sip. "You should get a lawyer and turn yourself in, but don't say a word. Maybe you can make a deal or negotiate with the D.A."

"Where am I going to get a good lawyer?"

Yitzhak laughed.

"What's so funny?"

"There must be a joke somewhere about someone getting in a car accident outside a synagogue, surrounded by doctors and lawyers. The point is I know a few lawyers who go to my synagogue. One of them is a criminal attorney and has quite a good rep. Stay here. I'll give him a call."

Yitzhak stepped outside to where it was less noisy

and called. He paced on the grass. The water of Lake Merritt reflected the sun whose light glinted in my eyes. Was Yitzhak really trying to help me? Or was he going to call that cop Holly Sampson to arrest me? Something about the way he held his phone close to his ear was evidence enough of him wanting me dead.

I studied his handling of the phone more closely. No. Logic dictated that phone handling was no basis for a measurement of how much someone wanted you dead.

He came back in. "His calendar's full but he keeps his lunches free for emergencies. He can see you today. I hope that works for you." He handed me a yellow note ripped from a notepad. The note had the lawyer's address in San Francisco.

"Sorry, but I'm a part of the Rockettes chorus line and we have a show," I said around a mouthful of eggs.

Yitzhak chuckled. "At least you haven't forgotten your sense of humor."

Good to know.

"What do those barbecue-flavored chips taste like?" I said. "Any good?"

"You want to try some? Here, I'll open the bag."

"Anything else you know about me?"

"Lately you've been more in your head. Concerned about something." He snapped open the bag of chips. "I asked you what was troubling you, but you just said it was a work thing."

I bit into a chip. I spat it out. There should have been a commandment against barbecue-flavored chips.

14

Lakeshore Avenue
Oakland, CA

JUST AFTER NINE IN THE MORNING, YITZHAK AND I returned on foot to the casual commute. The cars had stopped coming, so we took a Transbay bus into the city. I had a lawyer to meet. The seats were roomy and comfortable, larger than the ones on the local buses. Glancing out the window showed the Oakland ship-yards with their horse-shaped cranes.

"Anything else you remember about me?" I asked.

"You confided in me that you actually have more than one wife."

"What?" I was incredulous.

"Oh, come on, Ed. You keep setting yourself up for

that one. I honestly don't know anything else significant about you." He chuckled.

"What did I bring to work?"

"A suitcase."

"I don't suppose I had any secret weapons in it."

"Nope. I saw you open it once to work on a file in the carpool. Just boring spreadsheets with numbers."

We crossed the Bay Bridge toward Treasure Island, the man-made island between Oakland and San Francisco. The waves covered the bay in wisps of white foam. So I was just a typical businessman with a typical nine-to-five job.

"Sorry, Ed," he said. "You may not be an exciting guy, but for your sake, I certainly hope that's the case. I don't want to be able to say I knew a murderer."

Yeah. Being boring, having a boring life, that actually sounded... awful. It should have been appealing, because no one wants trauma and emergencies. But me? There was something inside that wanted to live a different life, whatever form that took.

Dammit, what if I was the kind of person who got a kick out of killing someone? What if it gave me an adrenaline rush, something I thrived on? What would that say about me?

"Yitzhak?"

"Yeah?"

"What if I turn out to be a bad person?"

"That's a tough question. Partly because that presumes there's a proper definition of who a good person is and who a bad person is."

The San Francisco skyscrapers became steel giants the closer we came to them.

"What does Judaism say about it?" I asked.

"There's a Hasidic story about a master teacher who said God created atheists to teach us the most important lesson of them all — the lesson of true compassion. When atheists do acts of charity and kindness, they aren't doing so to find favor in God. They're not hoping for a reward. Their kindness comes from their inner sense of morality." He studied my face as if making sure I understood the message. "So when someone comes to you for help, you should become an atheist in that moment, imagine there is no God, and assist them simply because it feels right."

I nodded.

"Does that help?" he asked.

It really didn't. Maybe I needed to restate the question.

"What if I did murder David Deutsch? What if I find out that I enjoyed it?"

Yitzhak stroked his beard. "How would you feel if you found out you did kill him?"

My stomach capsized.

"Just awful."

"You're a good person, Ed."

15

SARAH HAD TO CONVINCE THE LADY AT THE TICKET counter that her pregnancy was low-risk so she could fly, and then she had to wait four hours at the gate of Albany's noisy International Airport for the San Francisco flight.

Had Brian lied to her?

He'd said, *I will not betray Carl.*

Even though she was pregnant and needed to reconnect with Carl, Brian still didn't betray his customer. He lied to her about Carl's whereabouts. And when she had admitted to doing all she could to find Carl, he offered his services for free. He didn't do so out of the goodness of his heart, but to stop her pestering and send her on a wild goose chase.

"I bet there is no Carey Larkinson," Sarah muttered. She didn't care if her voice drew looks from the people sitting nearby. "I bet Carl's new name is something else entirely."

Well, Brian sure fooled her. But there was one last card to play.

At the local shop in the terminal, she bought a burner phone and called Brian. She rubbed her pregnant belly as she waited for him to pick up.

"This is Brian."

"You gave me bad information." Her voice quivered as she worked to contain her anger.

No response.

"Carl isn't in Boise, Idaho. He's in San Francisco."

"Why do you say that?"

"Never mind how I know it. I also know that his fake name isn't Carey Larkinson, is it?"

"Look, Sarah. It's like I told you. I don't betray the trust of my customers."

"Goddammit, what's my husband's new name?"

No response.

"I don't care what I said before. I will get the police to your little watch and clock store to investigate you unless you tell me his name."

"Those business cards are just to build trust with my clients. They see an address, they feel like they can trust me better. And while they can trust me, there is no way I'm giving people my real address."

"You little—"

"Now before you start a tirade about getting the police to trace this number, you're not the only one who uses burner phones, you know. I go through one every several months. This number will be dead by the end of this call. Speaking of the end of calls, you've just reached yours."

He hung up.

She cursed and threw the phone into her purse.

16

Jerry Rothblatt's Office
San Francisco, CA

IN THE LATE MORNING IN AN OLD BUILDING, I found the office suite of that lawyer Jerry Rothblatt. The door had all brown paneling with the name etched in and resembled the kind of office door that opened to private dicks in noir detective films waiting for shady clients.

The secretary was a young, clean-shaven guy that looked like an advertisement for a soap commercial. He stopped typing on his computer keyboard and looked up. "Are you Mr. Krieg?"

"That's right. Is Mr. Rothblatt in?"

"Yours truly." He stood up and offered his hand.

This young kid was Mr. Rothblatt? "You go to the same synagogue as Yitzhak?"

"Sure do."

Clean-shaven, no yarmulke.

"Ah!" He stroked his clean-shaven cheeks. "Just because I go to the same synagogue doesn't mean I'm as religious as Yitzhak. Let me get my coat and we'll have lunch. Do you mind eating at the park? There's a good food truck I know of, if you like Mexican."

"Well, considering my picture is plastered everywhere on 'Wanted' signs, staying out of the public arena will probably be best for me right now."

"Good idea. I have a bag lunch, mind if I eat it?"

"Do your worst."

"Okay, Mr. Krieg. Tell me your issue and I'll see if I can take your case."

As he chomped on his smelly tuna fish sandwich, I told him about waking up next to a cop who then tried to kill me. I explained how Alessandra filled me in on my marital status and eating habits, how I worked as a financial analyst for Senator-elect Caldwell, and how Yitzhak suggested I might not be the killer after all, considering the remorse I felt. The whole time he ate, he nodded, and took notes on a yellow legal pad.

Sandwich done, he wiped his mouth. "Okay. The best thing we can do to prove you're not the perpetrator is to alibi you out at the time of the crime. You'll need a solid one for it to hold up against prosecution."

"How do we go about that?"

"Do you have any receipts, any calendar events marked, social media pictures, anything like that?"

"All I have is my phone and wallet."

"Let me take a look at those."

I handed him both.

He checked my wallet's pockets. "No receipts there." He looked at the cards. "Carl Best? I thought your name was Ed Krieg."

"Oh, yeah. That's something else you should know. Apparently my real name has the initials N.Y. I'm not sure what they stand for, but I apparently have a lot of pseudonyms."

"That's not going to help you much. We'll need to get clear on why you have so many names."

He checked my phone. "Here's your calendar. Have you checked this already?"

"I don't even know if I use online calendars."

He flipped the screen with his finger. "Uh, oh. This isn't good."

"What? What did you find?"

He showed me the screen. The previous Sunday morning note read, "Meeting with David Deutsch at 7:30 a.m."

"If I'm not mistaken," he said, "that's around the time Mr. Deutsch was murdered."

Crap.

17

S.F. International Airport
San Francisco, CA

SARAH'S FLIGHT WAS EXHAUSTING AND uncomfortable. She'd fidgeted the whole six-hour flight and had to get up to use the restroom so many times. Planes were not designed to seat pregnant women.

As soon as she deplaned, she bought a pair of sunglasses and a big blue sun hat at the nearest shop. If Carl had come here to find Holly Sampson and somehow make sure she was no longer a threat, then it made sense that Holly was in this city. Sarah didn't want another run in with Holly. The last one nearly killed her. Even though Holly wasn't expecting her to be in San Francisco, there was no point in risking being recognized.

Also, her friends and relatives believed her to be dead. Her faked death was part of a plan to keep her safe. If she were to run into an old friend, that could upset them horribly. Herself, as well.

Past baggage claim at the exit, Sarah approached the car rental booth.

A young lady with a crimson ribbon in her hair and several rainbow bracelets on her wrists said without any sincerity or enthusiasm, "Welcome to San Francisco. How can I help you?"

The lady accentuated her disinterest by not making eye contact. Her name tag read Trish.

"I want your cheapest car."

"You're in luck. We're out of economy cars. I can give you a mid-size SUV for the same price."

"Uh, okay." An SUV? What was it like to drive one of those?

Like an automaton, Trish pulled out the paperwork, X-ing all the lines that needed signing.

Uh, oh. Sarah didn't have a credit card under her false name to pay for the car.

She signed all the documents as Scarlett Bronson. That's what her license said, which Trish barely looked at. Now to pay for it. She couldn't use cash. Even if she had enough cash on hand, Trish would demand to record a credit card.

The only credit card she had was her Sarah Best card, the one WITSEC gave her. Would that trigger an alarm to WITSEC that she was out of Amsterdam? She wasn't sure.

Oh, well. There was really no time to debate it. She was here in San Francisco and there was no going back.

She handed the Sarah Best credit card to Trish. Thankfully, Trish mechanically ran the card without analyzing the name on the card.

She signed it Scarlett Bronson.

Trish gave her a key and instructions on where the car was, a Jeep Compass. She said to check for dents, and to fill it up with gas before returning it.

Sarah thanked her and darted away before Trish had a chance to see the name on the credit card.

At the royal-blue jeep, she took a deep breath. *Relax. Trish will never scrutinize the credit card on file.*

Still, there was the good possibility that the marshals would find out that she was in California.

That meant she had to act fast before they found her and took her back to Amsterdam, New York.

18

Jerry Rothblatt's Office
San Francisco, CA

I STUDIED THE DAMNING EVIDENCE ON MY PHONE. "What do you suggest I do?"

"You're not going to like it," Mr. Rothblatt said.

"Tell me."

"I suggest we go to the San Francisco police station and you turn yourself in. The sooner we do so, the better a deal we can work out with the DA's office."

My head spun. Did he want me locked up? Or was he really on my side? "You want me to cooperate with them?"

"Absolutely not. You have the right to remain silent. Enforce that right. I'll drip feed information to them and investigate all angles to get you limited jail time."

"I have to do time?"

"I'm not going to sugar coat it for you. It doesn't look good. Considering you had plans to meet Mr. Deutsch at the time of the murder, and there's a strong resemblance between you and the police sketch of the suspect, the evidence is stacked against you."

"So if you think I did it, what's your angle going to be?"

"Your amnesia may be a blessing. Neither of us knows if you really committed the crime, so as long as there's an absence of solid evidence, the DA may feel uncomfortable charging someone of a crime he can't remember committing. Meanwhile, I'll double check if there are any mentions of you on the Internet. You know, pictures of you taken at a brunch or somewhere during the time of the crime. I recommend you do the same."

I must have been somewhere else when the crime took place. Me stabbing someone seventeen times? It seemed absurd. Why would I do such a thing?

"All right," I said. "Let's go to the police. I just want to make a phone call first."

In the hall outside Mr. Rothblatt's office, I checked my phone, found Caldwell's campaign number on the Internet, and dialed.

"This is Lance Meyler at Vote for Caldwell."

I didn't recognize the name or the voice. I wasn't sure how to play it. I decided to check for the reaction.

"This is Ed Krieg."

"Ed? Thank goodness you're all right. We were worried sick about you."

"How come?"

"First you don't show to work, then I see this crazy news about someone looking like you killing David Deutsch."

"You don't think it was me?"

"Of course not. You would never do that. Why don't you come in and get back to doing your work while this whole murder thing gets sorted out. The financial analysis of the campaign budget needs to be completed by the end of the week. Since you've been gone, Jimmy has been assigned to the job and, though a fine analyst, you know how prone Jimmy is to making mistakes."

"Good old Jimmy," whoever that was. "Has as much mathematical focus as a squirrel on cocaine."

"So get back over here."

"Tempting as that is, my lawyer advised me to turn myself in."

He took some time before replying.

"What is it you plan to do, Ed?" He sounded concerned.

"Once I make a deal with the DA, I'll tell them everything I know."

"That's not a good idea, Ed. Trust me on this. Cops just twist everything around and put words in your mouth. You don't deserve that treatment."

I liked how supportive he was, but what were my

options? Follow the advice of a campaign worker I didn't know or of a lawyer I just met?

"Thanks for the vote of confidence, but I'm going to follow my lawyer's advice."

"Who is your lawyer?"

"You mean, do I know him well enough to trust him?"

Lance didn't say anything.

I wished him goodbye and returned to Mr. Rothblatt's office. "I'm ready."

19

Highway 101
San Francisco, CA

Sarah pulled out of the San Francisco International Airport in the Jeep Compass. When she tapped the gas pedal, the machine responded with power. Another fun thing, she was perched higher than most regular cars. She could get used to this seductive gas-guzzler.

She put on her sunglasses and adjusted the navy-blue sun hat. First stop should be the old haunt. She drove across the Bay Bridge through the crawling traffic. She'd forgotten about the traffic. She didn't miss that. She inhaled the fresh ocean air. But how she missed that air. With a glance to the side she had a breathtaking view of the Maya-blue skyline resting atop the azure water. She got off the bridge, crawled through more freeway traffic, then took surface streets into Berkeley, and parked a few blocks near her old apartment building on the cross streets of Durant and Telegraph.

She walked up to the busy corner, a block from the University of California, Berkeley campus. It was strange being back. She loved this spot, its combination of Berkeley's college students and hippies and artists decorated the streets. The streets themselves were lined with old record stores and health food restaurants and pizza joints. On the one hand, she felt like she'd come home to where she wanted to be. On the other hand, her life had been turned upside down and everyone walked past as though nothing was different. She wanted to shake each and every person on the street and yell, "Wake up! Something is wrong. Something is very wrong!"

Hiding her face from the passersby in case one might recognize her, she buzzed the intercom to her old apartment. Maybe Carl had stopped by.

A voice sounding very much like her own answered the intercom, "It's cold."

"Excuse me?"

"It's too cold."

Whatever. "My name is, uh, Scarlett and I used to live here. I was wondering if—"

"It's too cold. It's too cold." The voice that sounded like her own screamed the words.

There was crackling on the speaker. Was someone on the other end? No one spoke.

She cautiously approached the intercom, half expecting it to jump at her throat. "I, uh…"

The door's lock buzzed open as though challenging her to enter.

She bit her lip and stepped into the building.

She climbed the stairs to her old apartment door. A TV blared from within. It was some horror film, by the screams. So *that's* what she had heard downstairs at the intercom. She took a deep breath and knocked.

"Just a minute," a gruff man's voice called from behind the door. The TV turned off. The man grunted, then growled as he yanked open the door. "Sorry about that. This darn door sticks, so I need to put in a little elbow grease to open it."

She smiled. She had spent years wrestling with that very same door.

The man was an overweight fellow, mid-sixties, in an undershirt and tan slacks. Behind him piled a clutter of belongings making it impossible to see much of the floor. She wasn't too surprised. The apartment was so small, it always took her a good deal of time figuring out what to let go of to keep a clean apartment.

"Hi, I know all about the door. I used to live here."

"You did?"

"That's right."

He spoke with good cheer. "Did you want to come in and see how I ruined the place?"

She chuckled. "No thanks. I just have a quick question. Did this man stop by?" She pulled out a picture of Carl.

He scrutinized the photo and shook his head. "Doesn't look familiar. How long ago might he have stopped by?"

"In the last couple of months."

"Then definitely not."

She sighed.

"I'm sorry I couldn't be of any help."

"No, that's all right."

"He your beau?"

"What?"

"He your boyfriend?"

"Oh." She gazed at Carl's picture and took a good long gulp of the photo. "Yeah. He's actually my husband."

"The father?"

She rubbed her belly. "Yes."

"Then I hope you find him soon."

At least before the marshals find me and the police arrest him.

She wished the man a good afternoon and headed down the stairs, leaving one of her favorite places behind.

20

Telegraph Avenue
Berkeley, CA

SARAH STROLLED DOWN TELEGRAPH AVE AND stopped by People's Park in Berkeley to get her bearings and come up with a plan.

What was that whole incident of hearing her own voice say "It's too cold" through the intercom? Could that have been the *Shekinah* giving her a clue? Supposedly, the *Shekinah*, the female aspect of God, reached out to those whose lives were twice as important as other lives. Sarah knew she wasn't more important than anyone else, but there were indeed times in the past when some *entity* communicated with her, helping her in some way.

It was too cold? What did that mean?

Whatever. She'd have to think about that another time.

Maybe she could spot something in the news about the crime and Carl as a suspect. She pulled out her phone but it was a basic burner phone and didn't have access to the Internet. She stepped to a newspaper dispenser and bought a copy of the *San Francisco Chronicle*. She walked back toward the car smelling her favorite pizza and falafel restaurants.

She wanted answers first, but her appetite and the needs of the little one in her belly convinced her those answers could wait.

Pizza won out.

At the restaurant's counter, she sat on a barstool. She took a few bites of the vegetarian slice and flipped through the newspaper and spotted an article on the murder.

According to the article, Senator-elect David Deutsch was stabbed seventeen times in a crime of passion and last visited by a man who looked very much like Carl. So awful. And so unbelievable.

Even if Carl wasn't taking his meds for his bipolar disorder and had hallucinations, he couldn't go this far and stab somebody. Could he? Seventeen times?

She pictured herself in front of her most dangerous enemy, Holly Sampson. If Sarah had a knife, yeah. She might blindly thrust the knife at Sampson over and over.

But there was a big difference. She would only stab blindly if she felt threatened and couldn't escape. It took a lot to get Carl to feel threatened. He was so good at taking care of himself, of taking life on calmly and dispassionately.

Sarah finished the pizza slice and washed it down with water and used her napkin to wipe her mouth.

She needed someone to help her investigate the case, someone who knew her and knew Carl, someone she could trust, and someone who knew about them being under Witness Protection.

She used 411 to find the number she needed and dialed. The tone purred then someone picked up.

"This is Detective Graff."

Sarah's heart pounded. "Hi Detective Graff, this is Sarah Best."

"Please don't tell me that doppelganger sketch of Carl is the real Carl. You're both in Amsterdam, right?"

"Actually, I'm at People's Park in Berkeley."

"Dammit, Sarah. What is your problem? We had you all set up in Amsterdam and chased away the trouble. Please tell me Carl is still in New York."

"I honestly don't know where he is."

"That's good news. Otherwise I'd have to arrest you for obstruction of justice."

"But you know him, Detective. You know he wouldn't kill that man."

"Yeah, but keep in mind, I worked side-by-side with a partner, believing she was a good person, too. She ended up kidnapping and torturing you. So I'm not the best judge of character."

A college kid dressed in a maroon tie-back halter

top and faded blue jeans sat next to her. Sarah turned away from her and spoke quietly.

"I'm worried, Detective. If they catch him, they might convict him because of the police sketch and everything." Sarah rubbed her belly.

"Relax. The police sketch is used to rule out suspects, not identify them. But there are a number of other things that could incriminate him."

"Like what?"

"If his handwriting matches that of the signature in the visitor's book, if witnesses can place him at the scene, if his fingerprints are found on the knife. Many things can determine if he's guilty or not."

"Can you investigate the crime scene and see if it was him?"

"Out of my jurisdiction, hon. You need to talk to the SFPD. I know someone who could help you out."

"I don't want anyone else. I want you. You're the only one I know won't investigate while thinking he's already guilty."

There was silence on the line.

"Okay," Graff said. "I'll see if I can make a few calls. But afterward, you must report to the San Francisco Police and tell them everything you know about his possible whereabouts."

Sarah sighed out a breath of relief. "Thank you."

"And call me tomorrow morning at eight."

"I sure will."

Her heart warmed. She was no longer alone.

21

Berkeley Police Department
Berkeley, CA

DETECTIVE BOBBIE GRAFF LOGGED IN TO THE National Data Exchange System and searched for the case number of Senator-elect David Deutsch's homicide. After jotting it down on a yellow sticky note, she called her friend she had met at Police Academy six years ago who now worked with the San Francisco Police Department.

"This is Sergeant Cheung."

"Hey Elizabeth, it's Bobbie. Got a minute?"

"Hey, Bobbie. How's it going in Oakland?"

"I transferred to Berkeley PD about two years ago."

"Let me guess. Fewer homicides to deal with."

"Don't you know it. Listen, I got a favor to ask of you."

"Name it."

That's what she loved about Elizabeth. Always a yes from her. Still, the best way to ask for the favor was to ease into it. "I wonder if I could get a look at the file for one of your cases."

"Sure. What's the case number? I'll pull it up and send copies to you via CLETS."

The California Law Enforcement Teletype System wouldn't be a clandestine way of seeing the file. "Yeah, maybe you'll want to meet with me and hand-deliver it."

"Why's that? Want to see if I turned out okay? I promise you, I've been clean and sober since you met me."

Elizabeth wasn't an alcoholic, but before signing on to the police academy, she was a constant drunk. Doctors labeled her as an alcoholic and after a few meetings, Elizabeth realized she was the only AA member who had no difficulty staying off the sauce. A misdiagnosis, thank goodness.

"You'll see why I want it hand-delivered." Graff gave her the case number.

"Let me pull that up."

Any moment now, Elizabeth would see that it was a high-profile case. Graff waited for her response.

Elizabeth gasped. There it was.

"Why are you asking for David Deutsch's homicide file?"

"It's a long story. Tell you what. Meet me in person with a copy of the file and I'll explain the whole thing. If you're not satisfied, don't give me the file and we'll part ways, no hard feelings. What do you say?"

After a short pause, Elizabeth said with good cheer, "Copy that. I look forward to seeing you again, Bobbie. It'll be good to catch up. Our old hangout?"

Graff smiled. "Our old hangout it is."

22

S.F. Police Station
San Francisco, CA

I STUDIED THE INTERROGATION ROOM AS MY lawyer Mr. Rothblatt stood in the doorway. The room contained a table with two empty chairs on one side and me sitting on the other. Had I been in one before? Was I the kind of person that police would greet me by saying, "Well, well, well. If it isn't old Ed Krieg again."

The San Francisco Police Station near Market Street resembled a brick fire station on the outside, and a zoo with cubicles instead of cages on the inside.

Mr. Rothblatt asked me, "You sure you'll be okay if I leave you here?"

He had reminded the police that they could not

interrogate me without him being present. They placed me in an interrogation room, anyhow.

"They'll probably come in and say all sorts of things to get you riled up." He put a hand on my arm and squeezed to comfort me. "Don't say anything. Don't let them get to you."

"I'll be fine."

"I'll be back at the end of the day after my other appointments. It may be as late as seven."

No problem. "I'll see you later."

He left. Meeting with the police could actually be informative. Maybe they could tell me some things about myself that could trigger memories of who I was.

Less than a minute later, two officers came in and sat across from me at the table. One lumbering, burly male, and one thin, grimacing female.

"Good afternoon, Mr. Krieg," the burly one said. "I'm Officer Mickey and this is my partner Officer Bonnais."

I nodded in greeting.

Mickey and Bonnais. Did Officer Mickey become a policeman because he hated being called Mickey Mouse? Did Officer Bonnais get a lot of crap as a girl being called Boney or Boner?

She frowned at me. Officer Mickey didn't look at me that way. He just looked tired.

"How are you this afternoon, Mr. Krieg?" he said.

I didn't say anything at first, but the uncomfortable silence got to me as they waited for an answer. After some time, I gave in and said, "Fine."

"Good," he replied. "As you know, we won't be asking you any questions about the case without your lawyer present so we're just going to chat. That okay?"

Officer Bonnais looked like she wanted to chomp my head off.

"Sure," I said.

"Excellent," he said. "Now you know what you're being charged with, correct?"

I nodded.

He didn't say anything as if waiting for me to vocalize my answer. Was the conversation being recorded? They were playing me, just like Rothblatt warned.

I decided to play along.

"I do."

"Good." He cracked a tired but kind smile. "So we're just going to run by what we know so far. If we're missing anything, feel free to fill us in on any details."

"Got it."

"So you live in Oakland on East 18th street near the lake, is that right?"

"No."

Officer Mickey raised his eyebrows. "No?"

An odd memory surfaced.

"I live in Oakland on the cross street of Bellevue and Grand Avenue."

He scowled and wrote down the cross streets. "Address?"

"I don't remember."

"Right," Officer Bonnais sneered. "The amnesia."

"That's correct." When would they discover I gave them the location of Fairyland, the theme park for toddlers?

"Where do you work?"

"I work for Carpet Investment Assessments."

He wrote it down. "What do you do there?"

"We assess high-valued carpets in peoples' homes. Have you heard of us?"

"I haven't, but I have a sister who bought an oriental rug when she traveled to China. Do you think that's worth anything?"

"Our company goes around the globe, so if she lives in another state or country, it would be no problem for us to fly over with a camera, take some shots, and if necessary, bring the carpet in for assessment."

He forced a smile, so I dropped the rest on him.

"We don't usually go by our full name," I said. "We just go by C.I.A."

He dropped his pen. He leaned over to Officer Bonnais. "Let's just show him how dire his situation is."

She nodded. "Let me do this first part." She opened the file in front of her and shoved in front of me a picture of the body. "Here's David Deutsch, the man you murdered."

I cringed at all the blood. No movie portrayal can match the disgusting reality of a dead body.

"Look at the picture, Mr. Krieg." She inched the picture closer to me. "Admire your handiwork."

I couldn't look. Damn, I hoped I didn't do that.

The officers exchanged puzzled expressions. I wasn't

sure what they were expecting. Did they think I'd enjoy seeing the photo?

Officer Mickey took away the photo, to my relief, and replaced it with another one. It must have been taken from a camera on the ceiling because it was a picture of me leaving a hotel room.

"This places you at the scene of the crime," he said. "Interesting thing is, no one else entered or exited the room at the time of death. You had to have been there during the crime."

Crap, was that true? Or were they playing me?

Bonnais crossed her arms. "What do you have to say to that, Mr. Krieg?"

They *had* to be playing me. I pointed to the photo.

"I'm afraid that hotel carpet isn't worth very much."

"Lock him up," Officer Bonnais said. "Give him a taste of what to expect."

Mickey stood and picked me up by the arm. "Come with me, Mr. Krieg."

"Wait a minute!" My gut sank. "You can't put me in jail without arresting me, and you don't have enough to arrest me."

"I've got some news for you, Smarty-pants," Officer Bonnais said. "We can detain a murder suspect for up to ninety-six hours."

Ayatollah granola! How would I clear my name while locked up?

23

Oakland Hills
Oakland, CA

Under the darkening sky, Sarah drove through the Oakland hills to the remote duplex where Carl once lived back when he was Nathan Yirmorshy. Would Carl go to his old home? Checking there was as good an idea as any. It actually wouldn't make sense for him to come back to the place, considering how terrible his experience had been living there. But right now, it was the only idea she had.

She pulled into the gravel driveaway and stopped. She stepped out of the car, taking the path leading to the front door. A biting wind snuck under her coat collar and she shivered. The lights were on in the living room in the apartment where Carl had lived.

Sarah knocked.

A forty-something year old woman wearing a pink apron answered the door. High-pitched voices of children playing behind her filled the space. Sarah's heart warmed.

The woman wiped her hands on the apron and eyed Sarah's big belly. She smirked, "Whatever you're selling, we have enough of them running around the house."

Sarah smiled. "Hi, I hope I'm not interrupting anything. My name's Scarlett."

The name was growing on her.

The woman shook her hand. "I'm Amy. What can I do for you, Scarlett?"

"My husband used to live here. I'm wondering if you've seen him."

Amy peered at the photo of Carl Sarah held up. "Wish I did, lucky gal. Don't tell me that sweet-stick up and left ya."

"No, he didn't." Sarah glanced over Amy's shoulder. "I mean, not in the way you think. He wanted to make sure I was okay." The inside of the house looked so different, warm tones and messy with toys.

Amy caught her inspecting the house and scowled.

"I'm sorry," Sarah said. "This place has changed a lot since my husband lived here."

The baby kicked. Sarah winced, clutched her belly, and leaned against the doorframe.

"Maybe you should come in and sit down. Take a load off," Amy said.

"I'll be fine."

"Get your butt in here, Scarlett." She waved her inside. "It's as cold as a glacier's personal ice chest out there. Unless you've got an important meeting with Tom Cruise, you're gonna rest a bit. Look at it this way, you'll get to see all the changes we made to your husband's poor interior decorating decisions."

"I don't want to impose."

"Should have thought of that before you showed me that picture of your handsome missing mystery man." Amy gently pulled her inside by the arm. "Now get out of the doorway. You're scaring all the heat away."

Sarah welcomed the warmth of the home and the greeting.

She entered Amy's home and barely recognized it from when Carl lived there. Sure, the position of the rooms was the same, but now they had a woman's touch. The warm pastel colors were a stark contrast to the dark shades Carl preferred. The arrangements were also different. The TV now faced the door leading to the mudroom. Two love seats and a comfy chair made a square with the TV.

Sarah followed Amy into the living room.

"Greg, we have a guest."

The lanky man named Greg groaned in his comfy chair dramatically. "Not again."

He stood.

Amy gave the introductions to her husband.

"Greg Miller." He outstretched his hand with a genuine smile. "It's a pleasure to meet you, Scarlett."

She pointed to the two boys playing on the floor,

yelling and laughing. "That slave is Remy. He's eleven. And that slave is Chris. He's five."

"I notice they're not playing on their phones," Sarah said.

"No phones until after dinner," Amy said.

They stopped their loud play and stood straight like proper little gentlemen. Sarah shook both their hands.

"Are you famous?" little Chris asked.

Remy snickered.

"More than I want to be," Sarah said honestly.

"All right Remy," Amy said. "Why don't you prepare the salad while your father and I give Scarlett the third degree?"

"Okay, Mom." Remy raced to the kitchen.

"Chris, you can set the table," Amy said.

"Okay, Mom." Chris skipped to the kitchen.

Greg pointed to one of the love seats. "Have a seat, Scarlett."

The mini-couch was nice and soft and perfect to take a load off her tired legs. She took out her picture of Carl.

"Have you seen my husband? I thought he might have come here." She tried to lean in to hand the picture to Greg but was too far away from him.

Greg stood and stepped to her, reaching for the picture. He studied it, then shook his head and handed it back. "I don't think I've ever seen him before. I can say for certain that I haven't answered the door to this fine-looking man, if that helps."

Drat.

"Thank you, anyhow." Sarah admired the soft color palette of the living room, the yellows and powder blues. "When my husband lived here, this house was a duplex. Is that still the case?"

"The entire duplex is ours," Greg said. "The other side is rented out to a travel writer who, at the moment, is out traveling. She is the perfect neighbor."

Must have been nice not having a neighbor that spied on you all the time, like Carl's neighbor had done when he lived here.

"I'll let you get to your dinner." Sarah stood with a grunt. Moving around with this extra weight was tricky and something she still wasn't used to. With her luck, she'd probably get used to it just in time to have her baby, then she'd have a whole new world and baby being to get used to. Would that be without Carl? She held her belly.

Greg put out his hands as if to catch her should she fall. He looked at Amy, concern on his face.

"I'm fine," Sarah said.

"Nuh-uh," Amy said, "You're not leaving until you get some food into that big belly."

"Oh, I don't want to impose," Sarah said again, though dinner sounded good.

Remy rushed in. "I made extra salad for Scarlett."

"See that?" Amy said. "You don't want to disappoint Remy by leaving without tasting the salad he made for you, do you?"

Sarah smiled. "I suppose not." *Bless that boy.*

"Come to the table." Amy went to the kitchen.

Greg extended his arm inviting Sarah to go to the kitchen before him. Sarah followed Amy.

Amy said over her shoulder, "I hope you like eating cyborg parts. We like eating machines."

Remy sang out of embarrassment, "Mo-om!"

Amy's humor was wonderful. It reminded Sarah so much of Carl's.

God, she missed him. Where was he?

24

High Horse Club
San Francisco, CA

IN THE COLD, LATE EVENING, DETECTIVE BOBBIE Graff stepped to the door of the High Horse Club and paid the pricey entrance fee. The tall man who looked like he'd stepped out of a GQ fashion magazine stamped the back of her fist and gave her two tickets for two cocktails.

As she walked down the humid, darkened hallway, sounds of women screaming with delight grew louder. The smell of sweat blanketed the place. By the time she reached the main hall, the joyful screaming arrived at a near ear-piercing pitch.

Chatting with Sergeant Elizabeth Cheung was going

to be a challenge with all the noise, but talking was never the reason they'd come here before.

The male stripper on stage sported a cowboy hat, jeans, and chaps. He'd already taken his shirt off. It would probably be another fifteen minutes before he reached his full Monty.

A voice pitched above the crowd called out, "Bobbie, over here!"

Graff followed the voice. Sitting at a booth, Cheung grinned with more reasons than just seeing her again.

Graff smirked. Naughty Cheung, braless in a plunging V-neck party dress. The dress may have been red, but it was hard to tell in the dim room. The only light came from the stage spotlights.

Graff sat down at the booth beside her and they hugged. They had to yell into each other's ears to be heard.

"You look...great," Cheung said and scowled at Graff's white office blouse and loose tan dress pants.

"I'm thirsty." Graff snagged Cheung's drink and sipped. Club soda.

"That was almost sneaky enough for me to not realize you're checking up on what I'm drinking."

Graff laughed. "Guilty."

"What's new?" Cheung asked. "Any boyfriends?"

"No, still single. You?"

"Me too." Cheung then howled at the stripper on the stage who ripped off his chaps.

"How about your downstairs girl? You keeping her happy?"

Cheung laughed. "I once hired a carpenter for a job. I was so impressed with his drilling skills, I had him keep on drilling after he finished the job. He comes over whenever I get the itch."

"Nice."

"How about *your* downstairs girl?" Cheung gave her a pointed look.

"She's happy. But I had to switch to rechargeable batteries."

"Copy that!" Cheung said. "So what's the story?"

Graff looked around at all the women. Though they probably wouldn't hear, this booth wasn't the best place to yell out Carl's situation.

"Can we go upstairs?" Graff asked.

"Sure." Cheung glanced at the stage. "Oh, hold on a sec."

After a few more beats in the music, the stripper yanked off his jock strap and threw it into the din of the screaming and cheering women.

Cheung hollered her approval, then picked up her backpack. "Okay, let's go."

On the way up the narrow staircase, they crossed paths with a woman in a little black strapless dress in heels and a tilted martini glass. In a struggle to take the next step down, the drunken woman teetered, spilled the martini, and collapsed into Cheung's arms. The woman giggled, apologized, and staggered down the rest of the stairs mumbling something about wondering who drank her martini.

Graff followed Cheung up the rest of the way to the

mezzanine. One of the walls was made of thick glass, allowing the guests to watch the show without all the noise. The mezzanine was also better-lit with a few tables.

At a side bar, Cheung used her second ticket for another club soda, and Graff got a light beer.

Cheung chose a back table, resting her backpack on the floor beside her chair.

"So here's the situation," Graff said. "There's a man I know who has helped with solving a few cases of mine, and has also been in some trouble through no fault of his own."

"Is he single?"

Graff smiled. "No. In fact, I spoke with his wife this morning."

"I promise not to hold that against him. Continue."

"He and his wife should be in New York, but it seems they're both in the Bay Area."

"How is that a problem?"

"This is what my friend looks like." Graff held up her phone, showing Cheung the police sketch of David Deutsch's killer.

"You're kidding me."

"I wish I was."

"But if you know where he is, you need to bring him in so we can question him."

"That's the thing. I don't know where he is."

"How about his wife? Do you know where she is?"

"I promised her I'd talk to you first before bringing her to you for questioning."

Cheung looked away.

"What's wrong?"

"That's not following protocol, and you know it. If we have someone we can question, that's priority."

"You're right." Graff sipped her beer. "It's just that she asked me to get more evidence to prove it wasn't him. I am convinced he's not your guy. I just thought that if I could see the evidence, I could help out by excluding him from your list of suspects."

Cheung massaged the bridge of her nose as if wiping away her disappointment. "What's his name?"

"Carl Best. His wife is Sarah Best."

Cheung took a sip of the soda water and licked her lips. "I can't do it. I can't give you the copy of the file. I cannot be implicated in all of this."

Graff sighed. "That's fine. I'll go through the public channels and the next time I talk to Sarah, I'll bring her in to my precinct for questioning and send you her statement, or I can send her over to you if you want to question herself."

"You've always been the better interrogator. Besides, she knows you and trusts you. Better that you do it."

"Thanks."

"I'll be back. I just want to go see the dancers up close. That might take a while." She glared at Graff. "It might take a good long while."

Cheung walked off leaving her backpack behind. Graff got the hint.

25

Amy and Greg Miller's Duplex
Oakland Hills
Oakland, CA

SARAH WAS SERVED DINNER, AND IT WASN'T CYBORG parts. Dinner was succulent chicken in tomato sauce with fried cut potatoes and steamed and buttered broccoli. Remy's salad of romaine lettuce hearts, sliced tomatoes, and grated carrots with a Thousand Island dressing also tasted scrumptious. She told him so. He beamed with pride.

As everyone ate, Amy made an announcement. "Sarah here is going to entertain us with the story of her missing husband. Go ahead, dear. But save the naughty parts for after my slaves have gone to bed."

Her sons Remy and Chris didn't react to being

called slaves. They must have been tired of rolling their eyes at the remark. If only Carl were here. He'd feel right at home with all of this sarcasm and irreverent comments.

The kitchen looked lived in and functional and warm. Chris kept vying for Remy's attention, saying, "Hey, Remy, look!" Chris would then make a face or use a fork to conduct an imaginary orchestra. Remy always seemed uninterested. Amy and Greg put their attention on praising their sons while setting limits.

Here was a good and safe and comfortable place to reveal her dilemma. "Carl and I live in New York. He worked at a bank, I work at a grocery store."

"One second." Amy held up a palm for her to stop. "What do you mean he worked at a bank? Past tense?"

"Yeah," she said. "He was arrested for robbing the bank—"

"Oh, cool!" the boys said together.

"—But the charges were dropped. He didn't really rob the bank."

"Aw," the boys said.

"Still, the bank has no interest in rehiring him anytime soon."

"I'll bet," Amy said. "Go on."

"Anyhow, during the whole bank fiasco, there was a woman who tried to kill me and Carl."

"Really?" Remy asked.

Sarah nodded.

"Cool!" the boys said.

"Guys, settle down," Greg said. "There's nothing cool about someone trying to kill you."

An uncomfortable silence fell across the table, then Greg chuckled and shook his head. "Sorry. I can't say that and keep a straight face."

Amy whispered to Sarah, "Not to belittle your trauma, but we don't get much excitement around here."

Sarah couldn't keep a straight face either, chuckling as she took another bite of the delicious dinner. There was something genuine about Amy and her family, relishing her sticky situation. Pompous folks might cluck at how awful Sarah's experience was, but they were often disingenuous.

Greg stabbed a piece of chicken with his fork and raised it to his lips. "So they caught this wicked woman, I'm assuming?"

"No, she's still out there."

He stuffed the chicken into his mouth and talked around his chewing. "In New York?"

"No, actually. I'm pretty sure she's in the Bay Area."

"Awesome!" the boy chorus said.

Amy dabbed her lips with a napkin and motioned with a finger for Sarah to lean close to her. "Can you open your mouth, please?"

"Excuse me?"

"Just open your mouth."

She played along, opened up, and felt like she was at the doctor's office. Amy peered inside.

"Nope. It seems your brain has not fallen into your

throat. So if you still have something upstairs, then maybe you can understand this little lesson." Amy gestured with slow measured movements. "The way it works is this — if someone is trying to kill you, you move *away* from them. Not closer."

Sarah smirked.

"Never mind," Amy said. "Your husband robbed a bank, a wicked woman tried to kill you and your husband, and now she's here in the Bay Area. Please continue."

"So Carl left me because he wanted to find the woman who tried to kill us and somehow make sure she was no longer a threat."

Remy said with wonder, "He's gonna kill her?"

Amy scolded him. "Remy!" She turned to Sarah and whispered, "Is he going to kill her?"

"I'm sure he won't, but there's another problem."

Greg cut a piece of chicken with fervor. "This keeps getting better and better."

"I saw Carl on TV," she said.

"Your husband's famous?" Little Chris asked.

"I mean, a picture. I saw a picture of Carl on TV."

"A naked picture?" Amy bit her lip.

"It was a drawing, really," Sarah said.

Greg scowled. "I'm confused. You saw a naked drawing of your husband on TV?"

"Gross!" Remy said.

"He wasn't naked," Sarah said. "It was a police officer's sketch."

"I'm not sure I follow," Amy said.

"You know that Californian senator-elect that was murdered recently?"

"David Deutsch," Amy said.

"They think Carl did it."

"Whoa!" the boys said.

Amy and Greg just stared at the table as if trying to process that.

"Please, Mom," the boys said. "Can we check it out? Please?"

Amy nodded.

The boys took out their cell phones.

"What was the senator's name again?" Remy asked.

Greg spelled the name for Remy.

Remy told Chris, "I'll check the news about David Deutsch's death and you look for videos on it."

"Okay." Chris bent over his phone.

Greg said to Sarah, "You don't think he did it, do you?"

"Carl's been accused of a lot of things, and every time he's been innocent. I know he wouldn't hurt anyone except in self-defense."

Amy tapped the table in thought, then said, "Do you think there might be a situation where he mistakenly is in self-defense mode and accidentally hurts an innocent man?"

Sarah's gut clenched.

"You don't look so good. What is it?" Amy asked.

"Carl has bipolar disorder." She fiddled with her wedding ring. "If he doesn't take his meds, he might get delusional and think people are after him."

"You think he hasn't taken his medication?" Amy said.

"I don't know. All I know is that he's good at defending himself." How to say this? Sarah took a deep breath, sighed, and spoke softer. "I just hope he's well enough to know when it's appropriate and doesn't fight random people he meets."

Amy and Greg studied her with expressions of concern.

"Here's something," Remy said, reading a news story. "David Deutsch was staying at the Vistavolt Hotel and his body was found by the maid just after ten a.m. The coroner placed his time of death between seven and nine a.m. that same morning. The senator-elect had only one visitor that morning and though the visitor is thought to have left a false name at the visitor's desk, the clerk was able to give a police sketch of the suspect."

Oh, Carl. I hope you've been taking your meds.

Amy put an arm around her. "I'm sure it's all a big misunderstanding."

"It can't be a misunderstanding," Remy said. "The man in the police sketch was the only one to visit David Deutsch. It had to have been him."

"Remy!" Amy said.

Greg wiped his mouth with a napkin. "Remy, the news doesn't necessarily report the full story, only what the police tells them. Maybe there are missing details."

Amy squeezed Sarah's arm. "Maybe the killer just looks like your husband and isn't him at all."

She wanted to believe that, but that sketch looked too much like Carl.

Chris's phone screamed.

She jumped, startled.

He laughed and held up his phone for all to see the video he was watching. "Screaming goats! Ha, ha!"

For heavens sake!

Remy snatched the phone out of Chris's hands. "That's not funny."

26

High Horse Club
San Francisco, CA

DETECTIVE BOBBIE GRAFF HAD A GOOD VIEW OF
Sergeant Elizabeth Cheung dancing up a storm near the
front of the stage where a stripper in a fireman's uniform
was swinging a piece of fire hose in creative and sugges-
tive ways.

Graff picked up Cheung's backpack, unzipped it,
and found the Deutsch file. Standing over the table, she
took pictures of every page with her phone. When the
font was small, she took multiple pictures of each part
of the page to make sure she'd be able to read it off her
phone. The file was thick, but only because it was a
senator-elect that was killed. More pages didn't necessarily mean the case was any easier to close. A lot of the

pages were likely witness statements that said the same thing: they didn't see anything. It didn't matter. Each witness was at a different location at the time of the homicide. A map of their every location could eliminate possible escape routes the killer took.

When she finished photographing the files, Cheung was still dancing. She had the fireman's yellow trousers wrapped like a boa around her neck.

Graff slipped the file into Cheung's backpack and placed it back on the floor. As she waited for Cheung to return, she flicked through her phone's pictures. Thank goodness they came out clear. Cheung trotted up the stairs singing loudly.

Graff shoved her phone into her pants pocket. "Had a good time?"

She dangled the yellow slickers. "You bet. Did you see how well that guy swung his hose around?"

"Before or after he stripped?"

Cheung laughed. "It's getting late. I've got a carpenter to call before his bedtime."

"All right, young lady. Have a blast."

At the club's front door Graff embraced her friend again and promised to talk soon.

———

Amy and Greg Miller's Duplex, Oakland Hills
Oakland, CA

Sarah wiped her mouth with her napkin. "Thank you for the delicious dinner. I should be on my way."

"What's your plan?" Amy asked as she collected the dirty plates with Greg.

"I'm not sure. Maybe I'll take a look at the hotel where David Deutsch stayed and see what I can find."

"No, I mean what do you plan to do now?"

Sarah shrugged. "Stop at a motel for the night?"

"Nuh, uh." The dishes clacked as Amy placed them in the sink. "You are not staying at a motel. I don't want to wake up tomorrow and see a news report, 'Pregnant lady murdered by wicked woman. Graphic pictures at eleven.' You're staying here."

"That's very kind of you, but doesn't my being here put you in danger? I mean, I don't want your boys to be in harm's way."

Amy and Greg laughed.

Greg said, "Woe unto those who try to fight Remy and Chris."

"What my husband's trying to say is our boys can take care of themselves," Amy said. "Now settle in. We've got a luxurious guest room."

"She means the couch in the living room," Remy said while playing on his phone a beeping and shooting and cheering video game.

"It's luxurious," Amy insisted and returned to her seat next to Sarah at the dining table. "The pope gave our couch five stars when he did his Bay Area tour as a bassist in a punk rock band."

Sarah smiled. "A bassist."

Amy muttered, "Hidden talents, that one." She squeezed Sarah's hands in her own. "You're spending the night. Is that clear?"

"Yes ma'am," she said. "Um…"

"What is it?"

"I've been here before, remember? Carl used to live here. I don't remember there being two bedrooms, so where do the boys sleep?"

"You must have been here back when there was a mudroom and garage," Greg said. "We had that remodeled into a second bedroom. They sleep in there."

Sarah asked the boys, "How do you two like sharing the same room?"

Remy rolled his eyes and Chris said, "It's great!"

Sarah smirked. Spending the night was going to be fun.

She turned to Amy.

"Thanks for having me."

27

S.F. Police Station
San Francisco, CA

THE POLICEMAN BROUGHT ME TO A HOLDING CELL
with five other guys. Big guys. Guys I wouldn't want to
share a pizza with, much less a cell.

I had to think fast. How could I make sure I wasn't
turned into one of their girlfriends? Hopefully, this
leather jacket made me look tougher than I felt.

They stared at me, wolves sniffing out my weak-
nesses, hungry for the kill.

Who was the alpha male?

One of the smaller ones was young and had a man
bun. He looked relieved I was locked up. Maybe he,
too, was trying to figure out how to avoid getting
married to one of the bigger guys.

He smiled and spoke with a stutter. "What are you in for?"

I had to think. Was the alpha the bald guy with the muscle shirt and tattoos on his bulging biceps?

"Killing someone," I replied, half-lost in thought. Was the alpha the tall guy in a leather jacket?

The small man-bun man said to me, "You mean, like defending yourself from someone who attacked you?"

"No. They got me in for killing David Deutsch," I said.

Or was the alpha the guy with the Mohawk and studded jean jacket?

"But he was murdered," man-bun man said. "Not just killed. Wasn't he stabbed, like, fifteen times?"

"Seventeen," I said.

Was the alpha the guy lying down on the cot, not leaving anyone anywhere else to sit? Why were the standing ones inching away from me?

"You didn't do it, though. Did you?" man-bun asked.

Ah. Now I got it. *I* was becoming the alpha.

"Maybe I didn't." I peered at him. "Maybe I did."

He backed away as did the others, spreading themselves along the walls. The guy on the bench stood up and avoided eye contact with me.

I lay down on the bench and got some sleep.

28

Amy and Greg Miller's Duplex
Oakland Hills
Oakland, CA

THAT EVENING, SARAH NESTLED ON THE SOFT AND warm futon. Crickets sang outside. Close by, Remy and Chris in their room whispered to each other.

The older boy Remy said, "Know what? What if someone else broke into David Deutsch's room and killed him? Just because someone goes into a hotel saying he's gonna see somebody doesn't mean he'll only see that one person."

A bed squeaked. Maybe Chris was sitting up.

"Whatchya mean?" Chris said.

"What if the real killer went into the hotel saying he

wanted to see Mr. Smith, but was really sneaking in to kill David Deutsch?"

"Who's Mr. Smith?"

"I made him up."

"Well, if you made him up, doesn't that mean the people at the front desk would know the guy was made up?"

"No, what I mean is, pretend there really is a Mr. Smith... Never mind. The point is, maybe someone else killed him and not Scarlett's husband."

Scarlett? Oh, yeah. The family knew her as Scarlett, not Sarah. Her heart warmed at hearing Remy defend her husband.

Chris said, "What if Scarlett's husband is a cop? Like an undercover cop? What if he was supposed to stop the killer, but didn't get there in time?"

"Yeah, maybe. Maybe he didn't tell Scarlett about being under cover." Remy said. "What if he isn't just under cover, but under deep cover, like a CIA agent, and he can't tell anyone who he really is or what he's doing?"

"Oh, I know! What if he's, like, this alien from outer space who finds people in trouble and stops bad things from happening."

"That's stupid."

"Why?"

"Aliens can't get here. Do you know how much fuel it would take to cross space that far?"

"How much?"

"Like, a lot," Remy said. "Like picture a football stadium filled with rocket fuel."

"Wow!"

"Then double it," Remy said. "No, quadruple it!"

"Wow! That's a lot of fuel."

"Yep."

Chris said, "What if Scarlett's husband is actually an alien who came here and ran out of fuel? What if he was asking the senator for some fuel and then the killer came, and killed the senator, and then saw the alien and said, 'Awesome! An alien!' and put him in the trunk of his car."

"Come on, Chris, why would a killer kidnap an alien?"

"To show his friends."

Sarah chuckled. Her head got heavy on the pillow, and she drifted off to sleep.

———

IN THE MORNING, Sarah woke up before the others did and wrote a note thanking the family for their hospitality. With the sun rising behind her, she drove down the street toward downtown Oakland.

No time to worry about breaking laws regarding making calls while driving. She called Detective Graff.

"I have the file for us to look over," Detective Graff said. "I'll print out everything at home and then I can meet you to discuss it."

"Thank you so much. Where shall we meet?"

"I'd bring you in to the station, but we'll be talking about some pretty sensitive stuff."

Sarah held her breath to hear what alternative Detective Graff might suggest. Going to a police station where she'd get looks from the officers for being a suspected killer's wife? No, thank you.

"Let's have breakfast," the detective said. "I'm buying. I know a place not too crowded." She gave Sarah directions and said, "Meet me in the produce section."

It was an odd place to chat, but still, much better than a police station.

29

S.F. Police Station
San Francisco, CA

I HAD TO BE CAREFUL.

Around me, the trees and thick plants rustled. Was something nearby?

Here in the humid jungle, all sorts of animals could be ready to pounce on me. They all wanted me dead.

In the clearing ahead, a koala bear hobbled out. So cute. But could I trust it?

It seemed to smile with kindness. Why did it carry two crowbars?

It clanged the crowbars together as if they were drumsticks clicking out a rhythm. I studied the effort the koala bear put into banging the crowbars against each other. The bear's smile now looked like a sneer.

Dammit! The bear's goal was to distract me!

At my side, a gorilla in a police uniform attacked me.

I woke up in the holding cell.

"Ed Krieg." A San Francisco police officer rapped on the bars with his baton. "Come on out."

I wiped the sleep from my eyes.

Leaping lepers, what a dream! Now what? Was my lawyer Rothblatt here to visit me?

I eased off the cot. By the way all eyes were on me as I sauntered out the jail cell door, I felt like royalty.

The officer slid the cell door shut and pointed down the hall. I headed toward the visitor's area.

"Not that way." He pointed to the right. "That way."

I walked down this unfamiliar hall and he stopped me at one of the doors, a solid metal door.

He unlocked the door and opened the creaky vault. The space was the size of a closet. Its amenities included a porcelain object that may have been a working toilet, but I wasn't getting my hopes up. Even the one light bulb on the ceiling was in its own cage.

"Why the upgrade?" I asked.

"Our high profile criminals get special treatment."

Did I dare ask? I dared.

"What do you mean by *special?*"

"Get in the goddamned cage."

I held my hands up in surrender and stepped in.

He closed the cell with a clang. All these clangs. It

was like the police department's personal soundtrack was made up of clangs.

The clang's echo died down. The light bulb inside wire mesh buzzed and barely gave off enough light for me to see my maybe-toilet less than an arm's length away.

A few minutes later, a key rattled in the lock and the door squeaked open. Already free to go? That was a short lockup.

The light from the hall was bright.

A young man in a black business suit jumped me wielding a knife. I blocked his arm, grabbed his collar, and used his momentum to smash him into the back wall. He bounced off and charged at me again. I ducked and grabbed his wrist. With my free hand, I punched him in the windpipe. He gasped. I clenched my fist around his windpipe, dug my fingers in, and squeezed. He dropped the knife and clawed my fingers at his neck. His fight weakened. He passed out from the lack of oxygen. I let him drop to the floor.

What the hell was that all about? The cops want me dead? And did I really use some sort of super spy martial arts? I had to think about that one later. Right now I had to save my hide.

The cell door was ajar. I peered out. The officer that had put me inside stood with his back to the door. I wasn't sure if he was my attacker's lookout, or if he couldn't bear to witness me being murdered.

"Is it done?" he whispered, keeping his back to the door.

I gurgled and struck the walls a few times to make it seem like the fight was still in progress. He said nothing more.

I had a few seconds to sort out what happened and form a plan before the guard got curious enough to turn around. First, who attacked me? My attacker, a heap on the floor, looked no older than twenty-five. I searched his pockets and found a large plastic bag with a familiar phone and set of keys. My belongings?

What was he going to do, plant my phone somewhere? Check what I had stored on it? I pocketed my phone and keys.

Who was this guy? No ID. By the way he dressed, he didn't come across as an experienced fighter. But what did I know? A moment ago, I didn't even know I knew how to fight. I *did* know that boxers don't wear suits in the ring. This kid must have been following orders, doing a job he clearly wasn't an expert at. That meant I wasn't a super spy trained in martial arts. I was just a guy fighting an inexperienced kid.

The knife was not a hunting knife or kitchen knife. It was a handmade shank made of glass, wood, and duct tape. Why a shank? He must have planned to leave the shank behind, make it look like one of the other prisoners got me.

I wasn't safe here. I had to escape the jail, find a safe place, and hide from the police.

The officer just outside the door still faced away, probably waiting for the kid to finish setting up the crime scene.

After removing my leather jacket, I pulled off the kid's blazer and tie and put them on. The fit was a bit tight, but at least I didn't look like my grungy self when I had first come to jail. I carried the leather jacket in my left hand to keep my right free.

The officer turned to face me. "You done?"

I punched him in the gut. He doubled over. I grabbed his keys. Down the hallway at the only exit, it took me three keys to figure out how to unlock the door. That opened to another hallway, which led me to a cop at a desk. The cop was talking on his cell phone. A sign-in sheet for visitors was in front of him.

If I wanted to get out of here quietly, I'd need to play it cool. I stood there for a minute.

"No, honey," he said. "It's nothing like that. You're completely misunderstanding me. Just a second." He tapped on the clipboard's *Time Out* box and said to me without looking up, "Sign out, please." He turned away from me to have some semblance of a private conversation in a police station while on duty. "Honey, you have to understand, there's a difference between a goodbye kiss and a hot and heavy kiss. She was just saying goodbye. That was it. I swear."

There was only one free box to write the *Time Out*. I traced the line on the ledger with my finger. The printed name said "Howard Lichtman." Howard Lichtman, eh? Hopefully, he was too dumb to use a false name.

Time In said 6:33 am. Whatever happened to my lawyer Rothblatt? He said he'd check in on me last night. Oh, well. No *Yom Kippur* holiday edible gift basket for him.

I checked the clock, 6:55 am, and filled the *Time Out* box.

I exited the one-way exit door without saying anything and entered the police department's workspace, a sea of cubicles.

There were cops all sorts of busy. Some were on the phone, some were studying their computer screens, some were chatting to their neighbor, some were listening to visitors and writing reports, too busy to watch who was leaving the hall of the holding cell. Perfect. I ambled out into the room and crossed towards the station's exit. So close to getting outside. Unfortunately, Officers Mickey and Bonnais were sitting at their desks along the beeline to the exit. I took a more circuitous route through the bullpen, scratching my eyebrow, hiding my face.

Officer Mickey stood up and greeted a woman who had just entered the police station. They stood together chatting, blocking the exit.

I plopped down at a cubicle, one whose occupant was away. How long until Mickey was clear of my exit path? I peered over the ledge. They were still there discussing some matter.

I grit my teeth and sat. Someone shouted in the distance. Then another. The officer that had stuck me in solitary confinement must have staggered out and let the others know I'd escaped.

"He's changed into a black blazer and tie," the officer announced.

I checked the exit again. Officer Mickey stopped his conversation and eyed the commotion at the jail's entrance. He said something to the woman, probably excusing himself, then strode with the other officers toward the jail to find out what was going on.

I tugged off the tie, removed the blazer, and my leather jacket back on.

My eye caught a picture on the desk near where I hid. It showed two female police officers in their dark blue uniforms. Presumably this desk belonged to one of them. They were wearing smiles of the genuine article, like they were sharing a day too wonderful for words. The two women in the photo seemed to be close friends. I recognized one of the women. Just a glimmer of a memory, really. Feelings of safety and comfort bubbled up. She was my ally. I was certain.

The desk was decorated with a *Back to the Future* movie postcard and a picture of singer Michael Jackson on the cubicle wall, a Rubic's cube, and a plastic figurine of ET. A stack of business cards lay squared beside her computer terminal. According to the cards, her name was Sergeant Elizabeth Cheung. If I could trust one woman, I could probably trust the other.

I pocketed one of her cards, jotted down a note on a yellow sticky note, and slipped it into her drawer.

The commotion frothed into chaos with some shouting. Officers darted to the jail. I moved to the exit with a brisk step.

"There he is!" An officer shouted.

Crap.

I sprinted out of the police station.

30

Piedmont Grocery
Oakland, CA

IN THE MORNING, SARAH ENTERED PIEDMONT Grocery store on Piedmont Avenue. She passed the cleaning supplies and the ammonia smell soured in her mouth. At the produce section, the fresh citrus scent filled her lungs with welcome relief.

There by the potatoes stood Graff. Ah, a friendly face. Her heart warmed.

Graff shifted her mint green canvas tote bag to the other shoulder. "Whoa! You didn't tell me you're smuggling a baby across the border." There was a sadness in her eyes. What was that about?

Sarah smiled and rubbed her belly. "Yeah. Carl doesn't know either."

"You're kidding. We need to fix that. But first, let's eat." Graff led her to the salad bar with plenty of choices. The choices were more appropriate for lunch, but that was okay.

From the roasted chicken to the home-fried red potatoes to the selection of olives and macaroni and cheese, everything looked and smelled delicious. Sarah filled her plate with macaroni salad and potato salad. Graff served himself a square of lasagna.

A cashier with the nametag of Claudia said to Detective Graff, "Haven't seen you in a while."

"Changed to the Berkeley Precinct."

"Traitor," she joked. "Who's your friend?"

"Another traitor," Graff said. "No longer lives in the Bay Area."

Claudia rang up their purchases together.

Graff was going to pay for everything? "You don't have to do that," she said to Graff.

"Don't worry about it," Graff said.

Claudia glanced at Sarah's belly. "Boy or girl?"

"I don't know yet."

"It'll be a girl." Claudia said. "I have a sixth sense about these things."

"Really?" Sarah asked.

"I'm often wrong." Claudia tapped her temple. "But even when I'm wrong, I'm very good at it."

Sarah laughed. Graff paid for their lunches and they walked a block to a place called Glen Echo Creek Park, a hidden and petite slice of greenery beside a nearby creek. They sat on one of the scattered low, wide boulders and Graff set her tote bag beside the rock.

Sarah dug into her potato salad and sighed. "Delicious."

"It's all grade-A stuff at this store. Before I give you the file, fill me in on what exactly happened starting with Carl's move to California."

Sarah explained that Carl left her nine months ago, and how his only goodbye was in the form of a note explaining his desire to keep her safe and make sure Holly Sampson was out of the picture. Throughout, Graff kept glancing at Sarah's belly without any indication of joy.

"Why didn't you call the marshals?" Graff asked.

"Even if the marshals found Carl and brought him back, they'd just move us somewhere else and Holly would probably find him again."

"True," Graff said. "I know Holly Sampson's detective skills. She would find you quickly. With the marshals on his tail, she'd find him even faster."

Sarah went on, explaining how she found the man who'd forged documents and provided Carl with a new identity, and gave her another identity of her own to follow him. When she saw the police sketch on TV at the airport, she decided to make the trip to San Francisco.

Graff finished her lasagna. "What's your new identity here?"

"Scarlett Bronson."

"Nice name."

"Yeah. Sounds like it belongs to an author of regency romance novels." She smiled and took another bite of her amazing, creamy salad.

Graff set down her empty plastic container, pulled out a manila envelope from the bag, and extracted a pile of papers.

"I looked these over just before coming here," Graff said. "It doesn't look good."

"Can I see them?"

"I can't let you. Only citizens involved in the incident can request access to the file."

Her heart knotted. "And I'm *not* involved?"

Graff didn't reply.

"Please," Sarah said. "Let me see those files."

Again, Graff did not respond.

"Maybe I can see something — some detail about Carl that no one else knows about — that will clear his name."

Graff nodded and handed some documents from the file to her.

Sarah bit her lip and stared at the documents. Did she want to know the details of the murder? Yes. She had to know.

The pictures resembled pictures of pictures.

"These documents look odd," Sarah said.

"They're printouts from my phone," Graff said. "The vic was stabbed seventeen times by a kitchen knife, found at the crime scene. They're still working the prints, but since it's a high-profile case, the prints are being processed quicker than usual. That will either clear him or incriminate him."

"It has to clear him." She wiped her sweaty palms on her knees. "His prints won't be found on the knife. Even if he were to kill someone, he's smart. He wouldn't just leave the murder weapon lying around."

"What you're saying is that even if his prints are found on the murder weapon, he couldn't have done it?"

"Yes. You know him." She gripped the pictures tighter in her hand. "You're hearing me, right?"

Graff took a deep sigh. "What I hear is a devoted wife desperately supporting her husband. And that's what the jury and the world will hear, too."

Oh, no.

Graff showed her a photo of the hotel's guestbook. "But here's something. The suspect who requested to see Mr. Deutsch signed in with a false name. Take a look at the signature and tell me what you think."

Sarah gasped. Not only did it look like Carl's handwriting, but also the name, Antoine Prioré, was the kind of name he'd write. Antoine Prioré, an Italian scientist, was a hero of Carl's.

Graff whispered. "So he *was* there."

"He couldn't have killed him. Maybe someone else inside the hotel went to David Deutsch's room and Carl came up after him. Or maybe Carl left the senator-elect alive and someone who had a room at the hotel went in after."

"No, Sarah, that can't be the case."

"Why not?" Her throat choked.

"It can't, because of what the police kept from the press."

"What? What did they keep from the press?"

"Now you have to promise not to share this information with anyone."

"I promise."

"I'm serious. If this picture of the suspect were to get out, all sorts of nut jobs would get hair cuts, buy outfits, and claim to be the killer."

"I promise. What the hell is it?"

"It's this." Graff pulled out a photo taken from an overhanging camera that revealed a hotel hallway. A man frozen in mid-step was exiting a hotel room. It was Carl.

"This still from the video footage was taken at the time of the murder," Graff said. "This has to be the killer leaving David Deutsch's hotel room."

Oh, God, no. "It has to be self-defense. Maybe David Deutsch attacked Carl. Couldn't that have happened?"

Graff shook her head. She showed pictures of the crime scene. Thank goodness there was no dead body.

"Look at the furniture," Graff said. "Nothing is toppled over. All the chairs are in place. The table hasn't been shoved over. There are no signs of a struggle."

"Maybe Carl was just in a daze and put things back in order before he left."

"There are no defense wounds, Sarah."

"What does that mean?"

"It means that when he was stabbed, he didn't put up a fight. Whoever killed him, might as well have been killing a defenseless man."

"Let me see that."

Graff offered her the pages and the empty manila envelope. "I'm sorry about what I said earlier. You are directly involved. I'll let you keep the file. Feel free to look it over and see if you can spot something that would justify Carl's innocence. Call me if you find anything, okay?"

Sarah nodded and took hold of the pages, but Graff didn't let go.

"You have to promise me not to share this file with anyone," the detective said.

She gulped. "Of course. I promise."

Graff let go the papers.

There had to be an explanation for why Carl was in David Deutsch's hotel room that morning.

She studied the blood work. It made little sense to her. What about the crime scene photos? The living room looked clean. An aquarium on one wall, a couch and two lounge chairs by another wall, a television at another wall. The dining room was just as neat as the living room, no toppled chairs. The floor of the dining room was another story. The body lay face up in a pool of blood. She shivered and put everything away. It would be better to examine everything later in private.

"I'm sorry, Sarah. It looks like Carl was at the crime

scene and stabbed David Deutsch. Maybe he had a good reason. But if that's true, you might want to look into getting a lawyer. I do know a few good ones that under certain conditions will do pro-bono work."

Graff kept talking, but Sarah tuned her out. Carl couldn't have murdered the senator-elect, could he?

31

S.F. Police Station
San Francisco, CA

I RACED OUT OF THE SAN FRANCISCO POLICE
Department into the busy street, chased by a wave of
blue uniforms. The sunlight was bright and the cold air
had a bite to it. The cops yelled, some giving
commands, others ordering me to stop. Thankfully, they
wouldn't shoot in a public place.

I scrambled down Eddy Street. Maybe not the best
move, as it made my destination of Market Street a little
too predictable. Only one way to go, easy to cut me off.
I zigzagged across the car-infested intersections to turn
corners and switch streets. Downtown San Francisco
was perfect for that.

At the intersection of Powell and Sutter by the Sir

Francis Drake Hotel, an electric bus sat, stalled. Its metal trolley poles were disconnected from the electric wires above the street, ones that ran along the street like telephone lines. With a long, hooked pole, the bus driver was manipulating the bus's poles to reconnect with the electric lines.

Police were scrambling towards me on Sutter Street. More police were racing toward me from the other side of Sutter. Powell Street seemed my best option. I could race down the steep street or I could sprint up it. The choice would have been a simple one if the downhill part of Powell were cop-free.

It wasn't.

From the bottom of Powell, several cops dashed toward me. Running uphill would have been my remaining option, but nope. Police were up there, too.

The street vibrated beneath my feet. It was the rattling of the underground cable for cable cars going up and down Powell Street. If only there were a cable car passing by, I could jump on and make my getaway.

Or...

I jogged to the bus driver and snatched the hooked pole out of his hands.

"Hey!" he said, but didn't chase me.

Perhaps he was flummoxed. He never had to worry about pole muggings before.

From thirty feet away, police officers surrounded me.

"Don't move!" A few had their guns drawn, but

pointed to the ground. They yelled at the bystanders, "Everybody get down!"

I plunged the metal pole into the thin hole that sliced the road where the cable car's cable ran underneath. I worked at it a bit and got lucky. The hook caught on the cable, yanked me off my feet, and dragged me up Powell Street.

I rode the street face down like a fisherman pulled by a fish trying to get off my fishing pole and I wouldn't let go. I must have been going over ten miles per hour.

Damn, that hurt.

Thankfully, the jeans and leather jacket protected my skin from the friction.

Up the hill in front of me the cops reached for me but missed. I tensed all my muscles, trying to minimize the pain of the pull at my arms and lay to distribute my weight evenly. Less friction of the road on my chest that way. I then turned on my side.

The cable dragged me up Powell, higher and clear of all the police. From the friction across the asphalt, my side burned. At the next intersection, the light was red for me, but I had no brakes. The cable dragged me across the street in front of oncoming cars whose drivers, thankfully, had quick reflexes and screeched to a stop.

It was human nature. When you see something you don't understand, like a man being dragged across the street, you step on the brake.

At the top of the next block, I let go and slid to a

stop. The pole flung forward, then sank through the slit and clattered beneath the street.

I stood. Ouch. My biceps ached, my arms felt like they were ready to fall out of their sockets. Out of sight from the police, I ducked into the Fairmont Hotel's café, Caffe Cento. Geez. It was like stepping into a king's palace, what with all the chandeliers and columns. The piano player in a tux was playing some classical piece. Chopin? Bach? Ray Charles? I didn't know music history.

I rubbed at the ache in my shoulders. A thin man in a trench coat carried a briefcase to one of the tables. Crap, there was a bomb in the briefcase! I had to warn everyone. I had to stop him!

If I could snatch the briefcase from him, I could perhaps find a laundry chute and dump it down there. Or maybe I could shove the briefcase into a mailbox outside.

I strode to the seated man with the briefcase. Dammit, he was opening the briefcase on the table. Was he going to detonate it and sacrifice his own life?

I yanked the open briefcase from his hands. Some papers fell to the floor.

"Hey!" the man said.

Where was the bomb?

I scrounged through the briefcase.

"Give that back!" He stood.

No bomb. Not even a laptop. Why did I think he was carrying a bomb?

"I'm sorry." I placed the briefcase on the table and helped him with picking the papers off the floor.

"Why did you do that?" He glared at me.

"I—I don't know." First, I had suspected Yitzhak wanted to kill me by the way he was holding his phone, and now this. What was wrong with me?

I shook it off, apologized again, and stepped to the café's doorway to look outside.

Where to next?

I wasn't safe at home with that police officer Holly Sampson after me. I wasn't safe in the city what with the San Francisco police after me. I couldn't go to Alessandra's apartment. It felt wrong to hang out there during the day while she wasn't there. Besides, I had given back the key to her and didn't like the idea of having to go to the diner and ask her for it again. Why put her in trouble for harboring a known suspect?

I peered out the window. Cars and pedestrians passed by with urgency. They had their own places to be. How long had it been since I came in, ten minutes? The police would be near soon. I had to keep moving. I had to find someone that would willingly hide me.

I opened a browser on my smart phone and checked the address for Caldwell's campaign headquarters. My next stop.

32

S.F. Police Station
San Francisco, CA

SERGEANT ELIZABETH CHEUNG RETURNED TO THE
S.F. Police Department after following a dead-end lead
for a liquor store burglary case. Almost lunch time. In
the break room, Officer DuPont poured himself a cup
of coffee.

"Hey, Cheung," he said. "You'll never believe this.
You know that suspect we've been searching for with the
David Deutsch case?"

She nodded.

"We had him in lockup last night."

"You did?" Had Bobbie Graff come through with
helping get him arrested?

"Yeah. Guy by the name of Ed Krieg. His lawyer, Mr. RothSplat, brought him in."

She knew Mr. Rothblatt the attorney. Heck, everyone in the department knew him. He'd successfully defended a sixteen-year-old suspect accused of pushing his younger sister out a twenty-story window, hence the nickname.

"He escaped," DuPont said. "Can you believe it?"

"What? How?" She peeked into the coffee carafe. Empty. Figures.

"Krieg assaulted the guard and escaped by latching on to an underground cable car cable."

"Unbelievable." She pointed to his full cup of coffee. "Thanks for not leaving any for me."

"Look on the bright side. Instead of this stale crap, you'll have a fresh brewed cup of crap."

She snorted. "Funny guy."

At her desk with a fresh cup of coffee, she flipped on her computer. As it buzzed to life, she opened her drawer to pull out the file on the liquor store burglary. She caught a scribbled message on a post-it. It read, "Howard Lichtman tried to kill me."

Who wrote this? Who was Howard Lichtman?

She tapped the man's name into the Internet and found on the Career Connections website that Howard Lichtman was a security guard employed by a security-guards-for-hire company. Who was this guy? Why was his name on this unsigned and mysterious post-it in her desk drawer?

Who would go into a police station, sneak to her desk, write this note, then leave?

Hmm. When two odd things happened at the same time in the same vicinity, they were often related. One, Ed Krieg escaped his cell, and two, someone left a note in her desk. Whoever wrote the note might not have snuck into the police station. They might have snuck out.

If Krieg left the note for her, then maybe he was trying to find an ally. Or a sucker.

Cheung called Davis, the officer in charge of booking and holding. "Did Ed Krieg have any visitors?"

"Mr. Lichtman, Krieg's attorney."

The low-level security guard?

She did a search for Howard Lichtman on The State Bar website. "I thought Krieg had a different attorney." Zero search results.

"No law against having more than one lawyer."

Cheung hung up. No law against having more than one lawyer, but there was indeed a law against having a lawyer that doesn't have a license to practice.

33

Mountain View Cemetery
Oakland, CA

Sarah needed a quiet, relaxing space to think. She walked a few blocks from Piedmont Grocery to Mountain View Cemetery, where a few people visited the acres of grassy hills filled with lost loved ones.

Sitting on a marble bench under the cold sky, she spent the rest of the morning pouring over the pictures and information in the crime file Detective Graff lent her. The more she read, the more she found Carl in the little things. Not just signing the hotel guestbook as Antoine Prioré, but also the suspect's escape path, down the servant elevator instead of the main elevator and through the underground staff parking lot. That sounded like something Carl would do. He'd done it before. Also, the picture of Carl leaving David Deutsch's room showed him wearing a tarot sweater, one she had given him for his birthday, one that showed the card of the lovers. There was no way the man was anyone other than Carl.

Did Carl really kill Mr. Deutsch? He wouldn't do something like that, but if his back were up against the wall?

Her throat clenched to think of him in so desperate a situation that he'd feel forced to kill.

Maybe it was time to ask Graff for a list of good defense lawyers, but something still nagged at her about the file.

What she needed was some fresh eyes to look at it. But she had promised Graff to not show the file to anyone else.

That promise be damned. Carl had to be innocent, and if it meant breaking promises to prove it, so be it.

From the pile, Sarah removed the photo of Carl leaving Deutsch's hotel room and the disturbing photo of Deutsch's body and set them aside. She returned the rest of the documents to the manila envelope and placed the envelope and the two photos in her backpack purse.

There were two very creative investigators who would be perfect for the job. Hopefully, they were available to give her their insight.

She hiked out of the cemetery, climbed in her rental car, and drove back into the Oakland Hills.

34

Outside Caffe Cento
San Francisco, CA

I STRODE TO CALIFORNIA STREET AND, MAKING sure the coast was clear of cops, I stood at a bus stop beside an elderly couple carrying shopping bags. They spoke Chinese. I called Lance Meyler at the campaign office, the one who questioned whether I could trust my lawyer Rothblatt. When he picked up, I identified myself as Ed Krieg and said, "I'm coming over. I'm hungry."

"I'm so glad to hear that," Lance said. "We'll have some lunch ready for you. You didn't say anything to the police?"

"I enforced my right to remain silent."

"Smart move. Can I make a suggestion?"

"What's that?"

"Once you hang up the phone, remove the SIM card and battery. The police will probably trace your phone."

"I'll do that. See you soon."

———

S.F. Police Department
San Francisco, CA

AT HER CUBICLE, Elizabeth Cheung called Jerry Rothblatt, Krieg's lawyer on record.

"Good afternoon, Sergeant. I heard about Mr. Krieg's escape and I assure you, I have not heard from him since. I intended on visiting him at the station last night but got caught up in an emergency."

"That's all fine and dandy, Mr. Rothblatt, but I'm calling about his other lawyer, Howard Lichtman. Can you tell me about him?"

A pause hung on the line. "I was not aware that Mr. Krieg had another attorney. Was he assigned one?"

"No, but Lichtman was the last man who visited him and claimed to be his lawyer. I'm beginning to believe he was not a lawyer at all."

"Why's that?"

"His online record lists him as a security guard. I

also checked the California State Bar and his name wasn't listed."

"Why are you telling me this?"

"Because this Lichtman guy may have tried to kill Krieg."

A deep breath on the other end of the line. "That would explain why he escaped."

"I know it's not exactly protocol, but off the record, do you think Krieg is innocent?"

"Nothing is ever off the record, Sergeant, but if I were to study a hypothetical case where the suspect was the last one to be with the victim while the victim was alive, it would seem to me, hypothetically, that the suspect was guilty. As for the quality of a man's character? I've met wonderful, righteous men, and I've met cold killers. Honestly, when I have conversations with my clients, I am unable to tell the difference."

"Thank you, Mr. Rothblatt."

After spending an hour on the liquor store burglary case researching the criminal files of suspects, Sergeant Cheung started a fresh batch of coffee in the break room. A man and woman dressed in black suits approached her with a stride that said they meant business of the Federal government variety.

"Sergeant?" The woman showed her a badge. "I'm Aarika Kelly. This is my partner Khalil Hakimi and we're with the marshals. I wonder if you can answer a few questions."

Yep, Federal.

"What do you need?" Cheung set down her hot coffee mug.

"We're here to inquire about the arrest of Carl Best."

"Maybe you can jog my memory. Is this about some burglary? When was the arrest made?"

"Homicide. A few hours ago."

Cheung shook her head no. "You must be in the wrong place. The only homicide arrest wasn't named Carl Best."

Kelly pulled a photo from the file she carried. "Was this the man?"

Cheung sighed. "He was arrested as Ed Krieg. Let me guess. He's some killer from the mafia who ratted on his boss, that right?"

"We need to speak to him right away," Kelly said.

"I'm afraid you're too late. He escaped about an hour ago."

The marshals glanced at each other.

"Who's in charge of the case?" Kelly asked.

If someone was truly trying to kill Krieg, best to find out more about him from these marshals. Fortunately, no other officers were in the break room at the moment.

"We're all in charge of that case." Cheung stretched the truth. "It's a high-profile case. Why don't you come sit and talk to me about it."

She led them to some extra chairs by her cubicle.

Kelly placed her file in her own lap. "What was he charged with?"

"He wasn't officially charged with anything. But he's

a suspect in the homicide of Senator-elect David Deutsch."

"That doesn't sound like him," Kelly muttered.

Graff had said the same thing.

"Can we see the evidence?" Hakimi asked.

Cheung extracted a copy of the case file from the drawer and handed it to Hakimi.

"Do your worst," she said.

Hakimi opened the file and flipped through its contents as Kelly scanned over his shoulder.

Cheung leaned back in her chair and reviewed leads in the liquor store burglary case file.

"Excuse me," Kelly pointed to the picture on Cheung's desk. "You know Detective Graff?"

Her gut clenched. Did they know she had shared the David Deutsch file with Graff?

"We're good friends," Cheung said. "Why do you ask?"

"Graff has been closely connected to Mr. Best. It might be a good idea to get her help in the case."

"You think so?" Cheung worked on hiding her excitement by staying reclined in her seat. If the marshals dragged Graff in on the case, then Cheung couldn't be blamed for sharing the file with her. "Do you know how to find this Carl Best again, or at least how to contact him?"

"We know some of his routines and habits," Hakimi said. "Any word from his wife?"

"Who's his wife?" she said, pretending not to know.

"We'll take that as a no."

"Do they love each other?" Cheung asked. "Enough to stay in contact?"

"They're pretty close," Kelly said. "They got married at our headquarters."

"How romantic." There was no way to hide her sarcasm. "Have you contacted the wife?"

"No answer. Are there any other leads we might have in locating Mr. Best?"

Cheung shrugged. "I'm afraid I can't think of anything. It may take some time before we get any leads on his whereabouts."

Cheung's phone rang. "This is Sergeant Cheung."

"Sergeant? This is Ed Krieg. Did you get my note?"

San Francisco Hills
San Francisco, CA

SERGEANT CHEUNG SOUNDED PLEASED TO HEAR
from me. Well, pleased may have been the wrong word.
More like stunned. This was the last call I needed to
make before taking apart my phone.

"You got my note?" I asked again. I had an amazing
view from the top of Powell and California Street.
Standing at a bus stop along with the elderly Chinese
couple and others waiting to ride helped to blend in.

"Mr. Krieg," she said. "You need to come back to
the police station."

"And get a replay of someone trying to kill me in
jail? No thanks."

"All right, let's start from the beginning, Mr. Krieg. Or should I say Mr. Best?"

She knew my other name. The one on my driver's license.

"How did you hear about that name?" Cars whizzed past.

"I have two marshals here with me who say you should be under their protection. They know you as Carl Best."

Marshals? "Why are the marshals after me?"

"You're supposed to be in the Witness Protection Program. Why are you acting as if you didn't know that?"

"Because I *didn't* know it. I have amnesia. The only reason I left that message with you is because I saw a picture of you with that woman on your desk."

"Detective Graff?"

The name was unfamiliar at first. I tried saying it quietly a few times. A memory of her helping me out in a tight spot at an airport came to me. "Isn't she with the Oakland police?"

"Used to be. Now she's with the Berkeley Police. We know each other from doing the same Oakland Police Academy training. So you don't remember why you're in the Witness Protection Program?"

"No, I don't."

"Usually it's because someone wants you dead."

"So far, that's the story of my life."

"As much as we want to get you back here, let me ask you this. Why did you call me?"

The question was tougher to answer than I thought. I spoke off the top of my head hoping what came out would make sense. "I want to know who I am. I want to know if I'm the kind of person who would really kill."

"Hold on a second."

I overheard her speak to someone, hopefully one of the marshals.

"Mr. Krieg, I'm going to hand you to one of the marshals."

"This is Marshal Kelly," a woman said.

"Kelly what?"

"No, Kelly's my last name."

"Oh. Sorry."

"Many people make that mistake. Mr. Krieg is it?"

"Today it is."

"We know you as Carl Best, but as you might guess, that was not your birth name."

"Are my true initials N.Y.?"

"We aren't allowed to give any information to anyone about who you used to be," she said, "and saying it over the phone could compromise your identity."

For some reason, I took comfort in her paranoid behavior. So much like my own, as I was coming to learn.

She continued, "What you should know is that you never killed anyone before coming into our program. You're not a killer."

I gulped. Relief curled up in a ball and lodged itself in my throat. I didn't know how much I needed to hear those words until that moment.

"Please, Mr. Best or Krieg or whatever you wish to be called, you must understand that your life and your wife's life are in danger. As soon as we get the two of you back in our protection, the sooner you can return to a normal life."

I thought about it, drying my eyes.

"Mr. Krieg?"

"That's a very big and delicious carrot you're holding in front of me. How do I know this isn't all a ruse to get me to turn myself back to the police?"

"How would it be if we didn't meet at the police station? What if we met in a public place?"

I tried a question that could be construed as either positive or negative. "And when I meet you there, you'll take me in?"

"Tell you what, Mr. Krieg. We can meet and chat, and we'll tell you everything we know about your past. If, afterwards, you don't want our protection, well, then we can't force it upon you."

"And I can just walk away?"

"You can just walk away."

Sounded too good to be true. But in my heart, I trusted Detective Graff. And if Elizabeth Cheung was a good friend of Graff's, then maybe I could trust her and these marshals, too.

"Sergeant Cheung has to be there also," I said.

"That's fine. Where do you want to meet?"

The bus stop had a map of the city. I examined it. There was an enormous park at the edge of the city. "The entrance to the Japanese Tea Garden in Golden

Gate Park. Tomorrow at, say, four p.m. I've some things to do first."

"We'll see you there."

I hung up. The bus arrived and the elderly couple boarded.

Thank God, I wasn't a killer.

———

Sergeant Elizabeth Cheung studied Marshal Kelly's face.

"You're not really going to let him go, are you?" Cheung said.

"I was partially truthful," Kelly said. "If he doesn't want our protection, he's free to go. What I meant was, free to go straight into your cuffs for when you take him back in as a suspect for your homicide."

"So you're giving him to us?"

"Chances are he'll choose our protection over getting taken in by you. Besides, since he escaped jail, he can now be charged with something, I imagine. Even if it's as trivial as assaulting a guard on the way out."

"I would hardly call that trivial."

"The point is, we set up a meeting with him and he isn't going to disappear anymore."

Cheung nodded. That *was* good. "I'll tell my captain the three of us are going to pick him up."

36

San Francisco Hills
San Francisco, CA

AFTER DISASSEMBLING THE PHONE BY REMOVING the SIM card and battery, I took the next bus to Caldwell's campaign headquarters downtown.

I'm not sure if it was the best idea I ever had, but Lance Meyler sounded like he had genuine faith in my innocence, and I needed that.

My stomach growled for lunch. I needed that, too.

Ten minutes later, I arrived to a glass store front with campaign signs of a cheerful Senator-elect Aiden Caldwell smiling or waving, a middle-aged man in a suit and red tie. The signs said, "Vote for Aiden Caldwell, because change is past due."

I entered the building. Dozens of casual-dressed

employees at cubicles chatted up constituents on phones, no doubt soliciting promises of votes. I took a step back when I saw Caldwell standing in the doorway of a large corner office.

Logic stated that Caldwell had that office. The head honcho always got the corner office.

He was speaking with one of his employees. He was here? Impressive. I thought he might be traveling all across the state talking to his constituents. Guess I was wrong.

He saw me and strode over.

"Ed! I'm so glad to see you." He shook my hand. "Let's move to the back."

No complaint there.

Getting out of sight was priority on my to-do list. Did he know he was harboring a fugitive?

He didn't act like it. He draped an arm across my shoulder and led me through the cubicles and past the conference rooms on the side wall to the rear of the spacious, busy room.

"It's good to see you, Ed. I was worried something happened to you, or," he chuckled, "or someone bribed you into revealing my little secret."

He didn't know I had amnesia. He didn't know I had no idea what he was talking about. He had a secret? I'd have to learn what it was all over again.

"Your secret's safe with me," I said honestly.

"I knew I could count on you." He checked his watch. "It's about time for my workout. You willing to do your usual job?"

Did he mean balancing the books? "Sure."

Maybe I could find some secret expenses he didn't want the public to know about, something that could lead to who might have killed his competitor, David Deutsch. On more pressing matters, maybe I could get the lunch Lance promised.

He led me past his corner office to a door with a sign that read NO ENTRY, AUTHORIZED PERSONNEL ONLY. What had I done to get authorized status? Whatever I had done, at least this area would have fewer people around, more private. Caldwell walked ahead of me to a back stairwell and down the all-cement stairs and walls. At the bottom of the steps there was a hallway lined with a few doors. One of them was made of steel and stuck out like a sore nose. He led me to that one.

He unlocked the door. "It's good to have you back, Ed."

Was he going to lock me up in there? I let him walk in first.

I followed him in. The room was cement walls, no windows. In the corner, a bearded man sat hunched on the floor, his shirt off, and his arms and legs red and striped with scabs. His wrists were chained like leashes to the wall.

What in the hell?

Aiden Caldwell unbuttoned his shirt. "Time to get to business."

37

S.F. Police Station
San Francisco, CA

Sergeant Cheung entered the captain's office. "I've got good news and bad news."

"Go ahead, Sergeant." Captain Williams rubbed the dark circles under his eyes.

"The good news is I've got a lead on Krieg's location and he's going to meet me tomorrow."

"That *is* good news." He picked up his prize baseball with all the San Francisco Giants baseball team players' signatures and squeezed it in his hand.

"The bad news is he may be out of our jurisdiction."

He bore his gaze into her. "What do you mean?"

"He's in the Witness Protection Program. I've got a

couple of marshals here ready to take him into protective custody."

"Goddammit. Don't they realize we're investigating a homicide?"

"They're pretty convinced he's not our guy, but they haven't seen all the evidence. They said they're willing to cooperate with us to the full extent of the investigation. We can question him as much as we want, but they'll be holding him for us."

Captain Williams grumbled something she couldn't decipher. His gaze went to the Giants pennant hanging on his office wall, but he seemed more lost in his thoughts than interested in the pennant.

"If it's any consolation," she said, "there is one benefit in all this."

"What's that?"

"If he chooses not to be protected by the marshals, we get to take him in ourselves."

"The chances of him making that decision are as likely as my son cleaning his room."

"That doesn't sound so unlikely."

"You haven't met my son."

38

Amy and Greg Miller's Duplex
Oakland Hills
Oakland, CA

SARAH PARKED OUTSIDE CARL'S FORMER DUPLEX, approached the front door, and knocked. She rubbed her arms against the cold. She *had* to figure out how to prove Carl's innocence.

Amy answered. "Not dead yet? Good. Come on in. I just made some apple cider and I need a taste tester before I give it to my other victims."

Sarah laughed at Amy's Carl-like humor and relaxed her shoulders a bit. She stepped out of the freezing air and into the warm home.

From the couch, Greg stood and shook her hand,

"Good to see you again, Scarlett. Did you find your husband?"

"I'm afraid not. I came to ask for your help."

"No can do." He pointed to his wedding ring. "I'm taken."

Amy lightly punched him in the arm and handed her a glass of cider. "As you can see we're a very spicy household. Hopefully, the cider is the same." She gestured to the couch. "Have a seat. What can we do?"

"Hi Scarlett!" Remy ran out of his room and grinned. His little brother Chris followed him into the living room.

"Who do you think would win in a fight?" Chris asked. "Pokémon Pikachu or Beast Boy from Teen Titans?"

Sarah sat and considered what Carl would say. "Is Pikachu wearing a laser gun on his back?"

Chris's eyes widened. "Yeah!"

"Then Pikachu. Definitely."

"Why don't you two go to your room?" Greg said. "Scarlett wants to have a boring adult conversation with us."

"Okay," Remy said. "Come on, Chris."

"Actually," she said, "I was hoping Remy and Chris would be the ones to help me."

Remy brightened and Chris gazed up at her with excitement.

"How so?" Amy said.

"I have a copy of the police file on Mr. Deutsch's

murder and I was hoping they could look at it and spot any ways that Carl could be innocent."

"Cool!" the boys said in unison.

Inevitable scowls of concern formed on Amy and Greg's faces.

"I made sure that the file is rated PG by removing any disturbing photos." She patted her purse.

Amy glanced at Greg. "Some free training into becoming detectives? I suppose that's okay."

"Let's see what you got there." Greg held out his hand.

She handed him the manila envelope and he flipped through the pages, handing them one at a time to Amy, who then handed each page to the greedy fingers of Remy and Chris.

The boys scattered the pages on the floor as if putting together a puzzle. Chris studied the pictures of the crime scene and Remy read the reports silently.

"How do they know Carl was in the room?" Remy said. "Couldn't a bunch of guys go to the man's room during the time he was murdered?"

She pictured the photo of Carl in the hallway leaving the hotel room, the one Detective Graff most insisted she not share with anyone.

"One of the pages not here is proof of Carl being the only one who entered and exited his room at the time of the murder," she said.

Remy scrunched his lips to one side and examined the reports further.

"He has a neat aquarium," Chris said. "The rock looks like it's floating."

He was talking about the large and decorative coral rock.

"This is weird," Remy said. "He had super high levels of ATP."

"Let me see," Greg said. Remy handed the report to his father.

Amy explained to her, "Greg's a pathologist."

"That is rather odd." Greg returned the report to Remy. "The ATP levels are quite high."

"What's ATP?" Sarah glanced at the graphs Remy pointed to.

"Adenosine Tri-Phosphate," Greg said.

Sarah cycled through her memories from high school. "Isn't that something to do with providing energy in the body?"

"Yep," Remy said. "But also, in my biology class, we learned that ATP slows the rate of rigor mortis."

"Okay. What do you think that means?" Sarah asked.

"Well, nothing, really. I mean the heat was blasting at its highest setting. So they cancel out. It's just... Let me check something."

Could the body have decayed more slowly because of the ATP?

Remy pulled out his smart phone and tapped the display like a virtuoso. In an excruciating minute of waiting for him to discover something key to Carl's innocence, he finally said, "Yeah, this doesn't seem very likely."

"Don't keep us tied in knots. What did you find?" Amy said.

"The dead guy's levels of ATP were high, as if he were super relaxed when he was killed." He held up the chart to show his mother. "But the levels were not only high, they were much higher than normal." He let go of the chart and it fell to the floor. "Let me see if I can find anything else."

More relaxed than normal while being killed? How was that possible?

Over the next fifteen minutes, Remy sifted through all the documents a second time. Chris got bored and played with Legos a few feet away.

"Sorry, Scarlett," Remy said. "I can't find anything. It was like the high ATP slowed down rigor mortis, but the heat in the room sped it up, so the ATP and heat cancelled each other out. Sorry."

"That's okay, Remy. You did a great job and it was nice to feel supported." She helped Remy gather the papers together. "Who knows? Maybe that weird ATP thing will help."

She turned to Amy and Greg. "Thanks for everything."

"No trouble at all," Amy said. "Greg married me on the condition that if we were ever visited by a pregnant lady whose husband was wanted for murder, we would let our future children study the crime scene."

Amy embraced her. Sarah's heart clenched. Still no proof of Carl's innocence.

She returned to her car. If the photos couldn't prove Carl's innocence, maybe she needed to see the crime scene in person.

39

Caldwell's Campaign Headquarters
San Francisco, CA

Aiden Caldwell handed me his shirt and ordered the prisoner to stand and face the wall.

The prisoner complied, his chains limp attachments to the wall. From a side table, Caldwell grabbed a flogger.

Was I just going to let this happen? No way. Caldwell placed a hand on the prisoner's back and got ready to flog him.

I stepped forward, "Mr. Caldwell."

"What is it?"

The prisoner peered over his shoulder at me. Was that a shake of his head? Was he telling me to not intervene and let this happen?

The prisoner made the secretive signal again.

On the table other tools of torture awaited. "You sure you don't want to start off with something else?"

"I always start with the flogger, you know that."

"Never mind. Go ahead."

I couldn't believe I was saying that. Why would I let him torture someone? Why did the prisoner not want me to stop Caldwell?

Only one answer came to mind. I must have tried to stop Caldwell before and it just led to more painful punishment for the prisoner.

The prisoner cried out in pain at Caldwell's ministrations. First the flogger, then a cane, then a whip. The whip nearly cut into the poor guy's back. So many times I wanted to stop him, but the prisoner caught me and signaled me not to say anything.

At last, Caldwell had enough. He let the whip fall to the ground, stepped to a water basin, and washed his face.

"Towel."

I grabbed a clean, folded towel from beside the torture instruments and tossed it to Caldwell. He wiped his face with a hard rub to dry off.

"Shirt."

I handed him his shirt. He buttoned up. "Excuse me, Ed, but I have to get to the conference room for a meeting with the governor. You'll lock up?"

"Sure." I guess one of my keys did that job.

Caldwell whisked out the door.

The prisoner grunted, "What took you so long?"

40

Bay Bridge
San Francisco, CA

SARAH DROVE ACROSS THE BAY BRIDGE INTO SAN
Francisco. She navigated up to the Vistavolt Hotel on
Nob Hill, parked in a pay lot, and entered the hotel.
The elevator required a card key. No wonder Carl had to
sign in.

Near the front desk, she hung around the display of
brochures advertising local attractions — Pier 39, Fisherman's Wharf, Ghirardelli Square, Grace Cathedral.
San Francisco had to a lot to offer.

A man asked the front desk clerk, "I'm expecting a
package. Did one come for me?"

"I'll be happy to take a look, sir. Room number?"

"Room five-seventeen. Mr. Cronenberg."

"I'll be right back."

After a few seconds, the clerk returned with a package and handed it to the guest.

Across the lobby, Sarah strolled to the hotel restaurant and examined the menu. After enough time passed, she returned to the front desk.

"Excuse me, I have a meeting with Mr. Cronenberg in room five-seventeen."

"Of course." The gentleman presented her with a binder opened to a sign-in sheet. "Just sign here for a visitor key to the elevators."

She signed it, "Scarlett Bronson," and was given a card key.

"You can leave the key in the return slot over there when you're done with your visit."

"Thank you."

At the elevators, she used the card key to call the elevator. David Deutsch's room was 722. She took the elevator to the seventh floor and made her way to the hotel room door.

Now what?

Carl had shown her how to open bolted doors with a bump key and how to open certain hotel room doors. During his previous paranoid episodes, he trained himself on how to sneak around. Showing her the things he learned had been just a fun way to spend time together.

With some strain, she got on her knees — not easy to do nine months pregnant — and examined the bottom of the lock. Yes! This was one of those simple locks she could open the way Carl had shown her.

She took the elevator back down to the lobby and headed for the hotel gift shop, but it was closed. At the front desk, she approached a different clerk, avoiding the clerk she had already spoken with.

"Excuse me, I'm making a card for my son's birthday. Do you happen to have any felt tip markers?"

"Sure, hon. Let me see what I can find." The woman searched behind the desk and came back up with three felt tip pens. "I could only find red, orange, and black. Is that okay?"

"That's perfect, thank you."

Now she had direct access to the truth.

————

IN THE VISTAVOLT HOTEL LOBBY, Jayden Fitch studied his tablet. According to his video connection piggy-backed to the camera just outside David Deutsch's hotel door, the pregnant lady was sneaking around. Was she even pregnant at all? Or was she trying to smuggle something to or from the room?

On the one hand, calling in his boss to apprehend a pregnant lady would get him in hot water if she turned out to be innocent. On the other hand, if he didn't call it in, he'd be out of the Jacuzzi's hot water and thrown into some freezing-cold ocean instead.

Jayden called his boss. "You should know, there's a lady that went to David Deutsch's room, looked at the door handle, then came back down. She's at the front desk right now."

"What's she doing?"

"Hard to say. Looks like she's asking for something."

"Keep an eye on her and let me know if she does anything more than just look at the door handle."

"You bet."

He studied her. What was that lady up to?

He leaned to put his phone away and knocked his hot coffee onto his lap.

Yeowch!

He let his tablet drop to the floor, stood, and shook out his wet pants.

Damn. Damn. Damn.

He tucked the tablet into his briefcase and went to dry off in the restroom.

41

Vistavolt Hotel
San Francisco, CA

SARAH RETURNED UP TO DAVID DEUTSCH'S ROOM. Choosing a color at random, she uncapped the red marker and tugged at the felt tip until it was about an inch out of its holder. At the bottom of the lock mechanism, underneath the door handle, was a rectangular hole. She pushed the long, red tip in the hole and pressed. At the sound of a click, she turned the door handle and opened the door.

Closing the door behind her, she flicked on the light with her elbow and examined the room. She was in.

JAYDEN FITCH RETURNED to his chair in the lobby. It looked a little wet from his spilled coffee. The wet splotch on his pants resembled another kind of accident.

Terrific.

In the lobby, he found another chair that had less of a view of the front desk, but still had its advantages. At least it was dry.

He studied his tablet and examined the camera feed of David Deutsch's room. No one was there, and the door wasn't blown off by some explosives. The lady probably tried the door handle again, gave up, and left.

42

Caldwell's Campaign Headquarters
San Francisco, CA

"What took me so long?" I stared bewildered
at the prisoner in Caldwell's dungeon. "What do you
mean? Were you waiting for me?"

He shifted his stance and winced. "Do not jest with
me. You were supposed to assist me in escaping days
ago."

My stomach sank. A major fail on my part. I apologized and explained my amnesia predicament. I added,
"Who are you? Why is Caldwell doing this to you?"

"I'll relay my tale soon." He gestured with his chin
to the corner of the room. "There's an ice pack in that
chest. Please apply it to my contusions."

"Of course." I wrapped the cold ice pack in a clean

towel and pressed it against the dark splotches on his back. "Fill me in on what this is all about."

His shoulders went limp, as if hope deflated out of him.

"The abridged version is this. My name's Seamus. While Caldwell claims to be an everyman candidate, with wholesome family goodness, the truth is he's a sadist. He takes pleasure in inflicting pain. Perhaps what happened was he required a prisoner as a puppet for him to release all his sadistic itches. One night, two weeks ago, I was returning to my parked car when some of his henchmen snatched me. They hauled me here to be his whipping bag."

"What the hell?" I adjusted the ice pack to other parts of his back and kept an eye on his facial expressions to confirm he was telling the truth.

"What they are unaware of is that I work freelance as a journalist. With my connections and the evidence you compiled from the times I've been tortured, we can ruin his chances at becoming senator and my article will be plastered across the Internet."

That put a positive spin on things. "So you're happy to take the beatings as a sacrifice for your legacy. Is that why you didn't want me to stop Caldwell just now?"

"With the secret photos and videos you took, Caldwell can kiss his votes goodbye. And that Lance character..." He shook his head.

Lance Meyler? He was the guy on the phone who recommended I come to the campaign office once I disassembled my phone. Well, as long as Seamus and I had the evidence, we were in great shape.

Then Seamus froze. Was he thinking the same thing I was?

"You don't recall where you stashed the evidence, do you?" he said.

"I'm sorry about that."

He chanted a string of curses so long, I thought he might have set a record.

"The key!" I said.

"What key?"

"A key that mattered a lot to me. It must be the key that unlocks the evidence, for a safe deposit box or something like that."

"That's a good start. Let me see the key. Perhaps I can identify the kind of lock it opens."

How to say this? "Someone stole the key."

His string of curses extended into a new national anthem.

"Look," I said. "I'll get the key back, so you won't have to put up with any more torture."

I don't know why I made a ridiculous promise like that, but the alternative of letting him endure more pain just to get more evidence was not allowed in my personal rulebook of choices. Good thing to know about myself.

"How do you propose on doing that?" he roared. "Hire a magician?"

"There are lots of options," I said, hoping one would

come to me on the spur of the moment. "I could hire a detective, for example."

He gritted his teeth, then relaxed with a look that read all was not lost.

He didn't need to know that I was wanted for murder and probably couldn't get a detective willing to take me on as a client.

"In the meantime, I'll try to get you out of here." I set the ice pack on the floor and took out my keys.

Seamus shook his head. "You attempted that already. None of your keys work."

What were my choices? I studied the thickness of the slack chains around his wrists connected to the wall. The links were about a quarter inch thick.

"I'm going to need a hacksaw."

"That was your conclusion the last time I saw you. Then three days passed."

"I promise, I'll come back to get you out of here."

"I'll believe it when I see it. For now, ransack your office. See if the evidence is concealed there. I think your office is somewhere on this floor."

I nodded. That was a sensible next step.

I returned the ice pack back to the ice chest, and exited the room. Caldwell had asked me to lock up when I left, so I must have had the key. Sure enough, on my second try, a key fit and locked the door. My stomach turned along with the sound of the heavy bolt turning, imprisoning Seamus.

43

Vistavolt Hotel
San Francisco, CA

SARAH STUDIED DAVID DEUTSCH'S ENORMOUS hotel suite. It was bigger than the Berkeley apartment where she had once lived. The entrance led to the space that doubled as a dining room and living room. If she considered this similar to a one-room apartment, then at first glance, nothing seemed out of the ordinary. The burgundy banquet chairs surrounded the square mahogany dining table right where they should have been, the TV and burgundy sleeper sofa and matching loveseat formed neat right angles to each other right where they should have been.

She moved from corner to corner gazing at every inch of the place, then entered the kitchen. From the kitchen counter, she used a paper napkin to open the cupboards. Deutsch just had a standard supply of health foods, fruits, and vegetables. His refrigerator held milk and juice, cottage cheese and cheddar cheese, sliced bologna and bread.

She moved back to the living room.

What was she doing here?

She plopped onto the couch and slumped, chin in her hands.

What could she expect to find that the police couldn't? There had to be something to prove Carl's innocence. Had to be.

The flat screen TV looked high end. Carl would have liked it. The aquarium beside the sofa had four goldfish. The coral rock didn't look like it was floating. It lay on the bottom of the aquarium. Sarah removed the manila envelope from her backpack purse and extracted the pages. She found the picture of the aquarium. Chris was right. In the picture, the rock looked like it was raised a bit and seemed to lay on something. Was that ice?

Couldn't have been ice. Why would someone put ice in the aquarium? Especially if they had the heat on so high?

Sarah stepped to the aquarium. There was something tied to the rock, like a piece of twine.

She reached in and lifted the rough and heavy rock out of the aquarium, letting it drip over the surface of the aquarium water. Twine was tied around the rock.

One of the ends of the twine hung down one or two feet, a fishing hook at the end.

Why was a fishing hook tied to the rock? It seemed like a very odd way to decorate an aquarium.

Sarah spotted the thermostat above the aquarium, installed upside-down. It was an older style with a lever instead of a digital display. Its lever currently pointed to seventy-two degrees. The police report stated the thermostat was at its highest setting. Since the thermostat had been installed upside down, that meant the lever would have been all the way down at a temperature of ninety degrees. The police must have reduced the temperature after processing the crime scene.

What had the female voice said over the intercom of her old apartment building? She'd said, *It's too cold. It's too cold.*

"It's too cold," she muttered. Could it have been the *Shekinah* at the intercom who'd said those words?

Sarah moved to the air conditioner at the window. It was turned on at its highest setting, yet no cold air came out. Was it broken? Maybe it was unplugged.

She put her hand on her belly and eased herself down to her knees to examine the outlet. There was none. The wire went straight through the wall. By the smears of white on the wall, it wasn't hard to tell that there was some kind of plaster job around the wire. She went to the kitchen, found a knife, and carried it back to the living room, careful to hold it with the napkin. Under the air conditioner, she poked the knife into the wall and carved at the circle of plaster around the wire. The plaster gave way easily. She tugged at the wire. An entire electrical component came out of the wall. A timer?

So inside the wall, the air conditioner's plug had been plugged into a timer, which was plugged into the outlet. She memorized the timer's settings. So *that* was the error the police made. She'd found it.

With her smart phone, she took pictures of everything she found, the rock with the fishing hook, and the upside-down thermostat, and the air conditioner's settings, and the timer embedded in the wall. She placed everything back the way she found them. Carl couldn't have been the murderer. With the freezing temperatures outside? The room had been too cold. Now she could prove his innocence.

———

JAYDEN FITCH YAWNED and glanced around the lobby. No sign of the pregnant lady. Motion from his tablet's screen caught his attention. The lady was *leaving* David Deutsch's room. How was that possible? How did she get inside in the first place?

He reached into his wet pocket and extracted his phone. He had to call his boss, but then the phone slipped from his hand and landed on his leg, and fell to the floor.

Dammit!

The lady was out of sight on the screen. Probably at the elevators.

He picked his phone off the floor and made the call. "The lady went in and out of David Deutsch's room."

"Did she do anything inside?"

"Not sure. No cameras inside."

"Take care of it."

"You got it."

He tucked his phone back into his wet pocket. Where the hell was this lady?

There she was, strolling away from the elevators and returning felt tip pens to the front desk.

He followed her out of the hotel.

44

Caldwell's Campaign Headquarters
San Francisco, CA

Outside Seamus's cell, I nearly collided with a clean-cut blond-haired guy in a gray suit carrying a tray of food. Presumably for Seamus.

"Ed," he said. "I'm glad you came."

"Glad to be back." I hoped I didn't let on that I had no clue who he was.

"Did you remove the SIM card and battery?"

Ah! It was Lance Meyler.

"Yeah, I'm safe."

"Good. Stay low until they find the guy who did it. We'll take care of you if you want to stay the night."

The idea made me sick. I must have glanced at

Seamus's dungeon cell because Lance chuckled. "Not like that. There's a guest room on the second floor."

How could he let Seamus be in so much pain?

"What are your thoughts with all of this?" I gestured to Seamus's cell.

"I'll be the first to admit, I get a bit queasy thinking about it. But we have to consider the greater good. We have to remember all of the great things Caldwell has done and can continue to do as long as he has the power to do so."

I wished I knew what those great things were.

He continued. "So if you're asking, is the welfare of the state and country more important than the wounds of one man? I'd have to say yes. Thinking about the big picture is something we all have to do."

I nodded, only to avoid making him suspicious of my loyalty than to agree with him.

"Does that make Caldwell a bad person?" Lance shrugged. "I hate to drag out that old German saying but it applies. *Gemeinnutz geht vor Eigennutz.* The welfare of the nation takes precedence over the selfishness of the individual. In this case, the needs of our country do outweigh this one life."

I wanted to punch him. The saying had been engraved on Nazi currency and wasn't true if one of the options was to save everyone's lives. Not sure how I remembered that, but then amnesia was a fickle affliction.

"I've left a sandwich for you in your office," he said.

"Thanks," my stomach convinced me to say.

"Can you get the door? I need to feed this guy before Caldwell's meeting finishes at five o'clock." Still holding the tray of food, he tilted his head at the door to Seamus's holding cell.

"Of course." I unlocked the door and let him inside. "You got a key to lock up?"

"I should hope so. I'd be pretty ill-prepared as a campaign manager if I didn't have all the keys."

I shivered and went down the hall to find my office.

Unlike Seamus's cell door, the rest of the doors in the hall were your standard don't-give-a-damn kinds of wooden doors. One of the doors had my name on it. I tried it. Locked.

This downstairs hallway for authorized personnel only was private enough to not worry about getting caught struggling with the keys.

After a few tries with my set of keys, I figured out the proper one and stepped inside.

Aside from a brown-bag lunch on my desk, the room was clean. Too clean. My sparsely furnished apartment was messier than this. Just an office chair and a desk decorated with a calculator, a desktop computer, and a printer. The trash can beside the desk hadn't been emptied recently, probably because it looked like I hadn't used it much. The desk's surface had no papers, no pencils, no rubber bands or paperclips. Did I ever use the space?

I sat down. The ergonomic chair was so soft it felt new. The brown-bag lunch held a soggy sandwich in plastic wrap, a bag of salt and vinegar chips, and a bottle of water.

I started the computer. With a low hum, the PC whirled its spinning drives. What kind of sandwich was it? Bacon, lettuce, and tomato. If I were Yitzhak, I'd probably follow the kosher laws and remove the bacon as a way to express my gratitude to the Almighty. Well, I wasn't feeling grateful. I ate the sandwich and chips, and washed it all down with the bottle of water.

While the computer finished booting up, I opened one of the desk drawers.

There it was. A huge mess of papers piled haphazardly. Had someone else done that?

No. In my heart, plopping piles of papers in a drawer seemed more my speed. Hide the mess.

The computer's main screen blazed, raring to go. No password needed? Worked for me.

Time to find out more about who I was.

I started with the contact database. Names I didn't recognize showed up, all of them having phone numbers with the same three digit prefix. These were likely fellow employees in the building.

Just to confirm, I called a random number with the same prefix as the others.

"This is Jimmy with Caldwell for Senator, how can I help you on this beautiful day?"

"Hey, Jimmy. This is Ed Krieg. Can you get me a chicken casserole and a cup of golden monkey black tea?"

"Wha—? Dammit, Ed. Get your own damn tea."

He hung up.

Yep. They were all coworkers. So the database was of no help.

Let's see what the pictures had to say.

I opened the pictures folder.

Empty.

I tried a search for all image files on the computer. Nothing but logos of the campaign popped up.

I hoped I wasn't the good employee who kept his personal files separate from work, but it sure seemed that way.

There had to be something, some trace of me floating as ones and zeros on this computer's harddrive.

I used the computer's camera to take two pictures of myself, one attempting to smile, the other realizing that a smile just didn't sit right. I found a website that did online facial recognition, searching through all major profile images on the Internet. As I let the results run, I removed from my wallet the picture of the woman likely to be my wife.

My heart's tempo went up a notch. So beautiful. I wanted her with me and I didn't even remember what her voice sounded like.

I glanced at the printer. Printers have a number of handy features. I scanned her picture onto my computer, opened a fresh tab on the browser, and ran another facial recognition search using her picture. The website guaranteed a response within a half hour.

That was okay. I had other things to work on in the

meantime. Knowing I could learn her name in the near future was enough to lift my spirits.

I opened a file that read: Paychecks.

Just as I imagined, the file was a spreadsheet that contained the employees' names and their monthly paycheck amounts.

For fun I rearranged the order of employees by top salaries. Aiden Caldwell had an absurd amount of income, but that was no surprise. In fact, it appeared lower than what I expected most senator-elects got. Second to him was Lance Meyler. Also reasonable, considering he was the campaign manager.

I eyed the others. I wasn't much further down on the list. Made me wonder where I kept my money. Which bank? Or was it all hidden in my apartment somewhere?

Further down still, I spotted a name I was not expecting.

Howard Lichtman. The young man that tried to kill me at the police station.

45

Vistavolt Hotel
San Francisco, CA

SARAH GOT OUT OF THE COLD AND INTO HER JEEP.
She drove from the top of a San Francisco hill down
Broadway, a steep street. Most of the hilly streets were as
steep as those with cable cars. It was as if the city had
planned to have cable cars on all San Francisco streets.
But there were no cables running underground or any
cable cars, just steep streets leveling off at the intersections, then steep again with a sweeping view of San
Francisco and the bright blue bay. Oops, she was turned
around, heading toward the ocean instead of
downtown.

The car behind her bumped into her own.

"Hey!"

Sarah eyed the rearview mirror. A balding man she had never seen before was hunched at the wheel.

He accelerated and his car bumped her again.

Oh, no. Bump me once, it's an accident. Bump me twice, you're trying to get me off the road.

Sarah put one hand on her belly, gripped the steering wheel hard with the other, and sped down the steep street so fast the car was air-born coming off the intersections. The jolts couldn't have been good for the baby. He followed her, close on her tail.

She leveled off at an intersection and turned onto Hyde Street and drove faster. Maybe that would help lose the guy behind her.

Who was he? Why was he trying to kill her? Could it be that Holly Sampson found her and this man worked for Sampson? She climbed higher and higher of one of San Francisco's precipitous slopes. The car persisted behind her in strong pursuit.

She turned at the next street and cursed her luck when she realized she'd turned onto the top of Lombard Street, famous for being the crookedest street in the world. A winding, brick road and she was about to head downward on it, Coit Tower in the far distance.

The man's car sped at her. Dammit. She was stuck behind a line of cars waiting their turn to drive down the snake of a street. Probably tourists.

She rubbed her belly. "Don't worry, Little One. We'll get out of this mess." They had to. She had to save her child. She had to find Carl. She had the evidence to clear his name.

Her pursuer drove at her. Her heart froze.

To avoid being hit, she steered onto Lombard Street's sidewalk, crushing gardens and crashing down sharp drops, on and off the street.

Her rental clattered and jerked, sideways, up and down. She held her breath and gripped the steering wheel tighter. Metal crunched beneath her. What was that? Her tail pipe?

She tried steering straight down. The steering wheel seemed to have little effect. Did the steering mechanism break? The jeep shifted its angle, facing left without actually changing the direction of its fall. Panic lodged in her throat.

She left the winding part of Lombard and continued straight down the hill. Control returned to her steering, thank goodness. She peeked at the rearview mirror. Her pursuer was no longer in sight. Driving straight down Lombard Street? Apparently, he wasn't having any of her crazy ideas.

She let out a sigh of relief. Good. She had managed to get rid of him.

She pressed the brake to slow down. No response.

What the hell?

Fear flooded her chest.

She pumped the brake again, but the pedal was already flat on the floor.

Faster, her jeep rolled down the steep hill. She swerved around the car crawling in front of her. At the intersection, she swerved onto the cross street. She moved too fast. Her jeep spun into a near one-eighty.

She pulled on the emergency brake and the car screeched to a halt.

She panted. The hood of her car steamed white and black smoke. She held her belly.

"Please kick. Please kick for me."

46

Caldwell's Campaign Headquarters
San Francisco, CA

I SCOWLED AT THE COMPUTER SCREEN. AIDEN
Caldwell wanted me dead? That's the only way I could
put it together. Howard Lichtman tried to kill me,
Howard Lichtman worked for Caldwell, ergo Caldwell
wanted me to push up daisies.

Why? Either Caldwell liked daisies, or he knew
about Seamus's plan to expose him.

If Caldwell knew I had evidence that could ruin his
career, he'd want that evidence to vanish. And perhaps
me along with it.

I did some further research in my computer's office
records, finding out everything I could about Howard
Lichtman. His address, date of hire, his birthday. Geez.

Some guys were as old as a fine wine. This kid was no older than a fine milk.

I checked his former employment. He'd been a security guard at some small grocery store. Did security guards have any fight training? If so, this one didn't have enough to stop me.

In the carpool car crash, I had lost the key to Seamus's evidence to the man in the gas mask. Perhaps stealing the evidence wasn't enough. Howard Lichtman must have been hired to stop me from revealing the evidence as well. Silencing me required killing me.

Hmm. They had the key, but probably didn't know what it opened. They may not have the evidence, after all.

I had to get the key back. With any luck, I could figure out where the evidence was locked up. Best place to check for the key had to be Caldwell's office.

One of the websites pinged. I checked the results of my face. Nothing. I checked my wife's results. The webpage revealed a page full of women's profile pictures. Many of them resembled my picture of her, but only one looked dead on.

Sophia Patai.

I tugged off my ring and checked the initials on its inside edge. It read, "S.P. + N.Y." This had to be her.

My heart raced with excitement. I found my wife. I could quickly find her contact information and go see her. I could finally hear her voice. Hold her in my arms.

I searched her name on the Internet. In a half second, a link to her social media profile popped up.

I clicked on the page. My gut sank to my chest as I read her friends' posts.

"I miss you, Sophia."

"I know you're in a better place, and miss you so much."

"Rest in peace, Sophia."

47

Lombard Street
San Francisco, CA

SARAH EXTRACTED HERSELF FROM THE WRECKED
rental jeep and waved down a car.

Please, Little One. Please kick.

A white car stopped and through the open window,
she said to the female driver, "I need to get to a
hospital."

"Hop in," said the young woman with medium-
length auburn hair. "Are you having the baby now?"

"No." But that was all she wanted to tell the driver
as she eased into the passenger seat.

Please, Little One.

The driver kept quiet, thank goodness. She drove
with caution, always checking her mirrors, yet not too

slow. Good. That was the best way to assure her arrival at the hospital would be fast and safe.

Please.

The driver wore a T-shirt and jeans. The laptop backpack in the back seat suggested she was a college student, but chatting with her about it was not a priority.

A lump lodged in Sarah's throat and she rubbed her belly. *Please, Little One. Give some sign that you're still alive.*

The driver dropped her off at the nearest hospital. "I hope everything works out," she said.

In the emergency room, Sarah filled out a bunch of forms and turned them in. The patient admissions representative told her to have a seat.

Maybe she wouldn't have to wait long. The only others in the room were a coughing teen boy on one side of the room, and a middle-aged man and toddler, probably father and daughter, sitting on the other side. She sat across from the father and daughter.

"When is Mommy coming back?" she tugged her father's slacks and held a raggedy cloth doll in the other hand.

He picked her up and placed her on his lap. "She'll be fine. She just has to finish seeing the doctor." His distant expression belied his words.

Sarah rubbed her belly. *Please, Little One.*

A nurse called on the coughing teen boy. Good. She must be next on the waiting list.

Two men and a woman entered the emergency room. They all wore leather and looked to be in their twenties. One had a bag of ice over his bloody cheek and his white T-shirt was splattered with blood. Holy cow!

His friends helped him with the paperwork and they sat where the coughing teen had once been.

The toddler clung to her father.

The father held up the raggedy doll. "Tell me about your Madeleine doll." He had to ask a second time to successfully distract her from the whimpering man with the bloody cheek and shirt.

The nurse called on the wounded man, and his friends stayed in the waiting room. Calling on him before herself made sense. He needed urgent care.

Still. Either her baby was dead or it wasn't.

Her chest became heavy. Knowing the truth may not have been urgent, but the fact that her child might be dead hurt so damned much.

Finally, after twenty more minutes, a nurse escorted her to a hospital room.

The nurse said, "The doctor will see you shortly."

Sarah grabbed the nurse's sleeve to stop her from leaving. "How shortly?"

The nurse gasped and stared wide-eyed at her snagged arm. "The doctor is finishing a patient's stitches, but she should be with you soon." Her voice wavered as if in fear.

Sarah released the nurse's sleeve and the nurse hastened out the room.

There had to be something here to determine if her baby was okay. A stethoscope! That's what she needed.

She opened the drawers and cabinets. No, no, and no. Dammit!

She plopped on the hard bed covered in crinkling paper. While waiting for the doctor, she rubbed her belly, pleading, "Please kick."

The doctor came in, an Asian woman with a ponytail.

"You are concerned about your baby, is that right?"

Sarah snagged the stethoscope off the doctor's neck and listened for the baby's heartbeat. "Where is it?" Her lungs felt crushed. She couldn't breathe.

"Please, Ms. Bronson." The doctor gave a forced smile. "Allow me." She gently took the stethoscope out of Sarah's hands and placed the stethoscope's tips in her ears. She held the cold plate to Sarah's belly. She searched one side, then another.

The doctor sighed. Keeping the metal plate on Sarah's belly, she removed the plugs from her ears and placed them in Sarah's ears.

Sarah heard the bubbling thub-dub coming from her belly.

"Your baby's going to be just fine," the doctor said.

Sarah let out tears and clung to the doctor, thanking her.

"Well," the doctor said. "You may not thank me years from now when your child asks for a sports car."

Sarah laughed.

48

Caldwell's Campaign Headquarters
San Francisco, CA

I POUNDED THE DESK.

Dammit all to hell!

My wife was dead. My throat constricted and I couldn't swallow.

Perhaps this was the second time I had discovered it, the first time would have been before the amnesia. How had I reacted the first time? Now I felt as if a knife had been plunged into my gut.

The air tasted sour, the computer looked icy, the hum of the electronics sounded like a dentists' drill.

How was I supposed to speak to people? What was I supposed to say when they asked me how I was?

"I feel like shit, because my wife died, someone I don't even remember, but my heart misses."

This was how it felt when your left hand got amputated from your body, and you didn't know how much you needed it until it was gone.

I had to move forward. I had to get Seamus out of here. After that, I didn't care what the police did with me. Whether I killed that man or not, they could lock me up for the rest of my life.

The first step? Find the key. If Aiden Caldwell was behind this, I needed to rummage through his office and find it. He was at a meeting. His corner office upstairs should be empty.

I exited my office and climbed the one flight of stairs.

The office windows were dark. That made sense. He was out meeting with the governor. I approached the office door. Caldwell's copper nameplate was on the door. Further proof. I tested the doorknob. Unlocked. Guess he trusted his employees, at least during the day when the headquarters were busy.

When no one was looking, I slipped in. I left the lights off.

I flipped on his desk lamp and checked the agenda book next to his computer. His meeting would end at five o'clock. Only two minutes from now. That plus the couple of minutes it should take for him to get from the conference room on the far side of the campaign headquarters to his office, I probably had about five minutes.

I checked the left-hand column of desk drawers

first. I opened the top drawer. Fortunately, the lamp was one of those with a bendable stem. Manipulating the lamplight, I pointed its spotlight on the drawer's contents. In a tray of many compartments, there were staples, paperclips, and other office supplies. Nothing worth examining.

The middle drawer was locked. I tried the bottom desk drawer. Hanging files were tagged for locations, strategies, speeches, and supporters.

On the right-hand side of the desk, was a column of two other drawers. I tried the top one first.

Bingo.

In a ceramic red dish was an assortment of keys on a plain key ring. I sorted through them.

Anti-bingo.

Not a single one was the key I remembered. The one with the nick on the side.

Perhaps the key was too important to leave in the drawer with paperclips and other loose keys.

I shined the lamp at the clock. I had two more minutes before Caldwell returned.

Where would he leave something important?

Someplace hidden or locked.

The locked middle drawer.

I'd need a key to open it. He wouldn't do the obvious, would he?

I snatched his key ring of keys. Two of them looked small enough to be drawer keys. The first one unlocked the drawer.

My mind had a little mental celebration, samba

music, piñatas, the works. I loved mental celebrations. Its confetti and streamers were always easier to clean up.

I opened the drawer. Nothing but a manila file folder.

I returned the battery I'd stowed in my pocket to my phone and turned it on.

One minute left.

"Come on, come on."

The phone finished booting up. I opened the camera app and snapped pictures of the contents in the file. After taking a picture of one of the pages, I turned it over to ready the next page. My hands shook from nerves.

It seemed never-ending, page after page, but there were only six of them. Didn't read any of them. Didn't have the time.

Once done, I glanced at the clock. I was wearing out my luck. Caldwell should have been back by now, if he came straight from the meeting. Perhaps he was chatting with someone before returning. Perhaps he got a call and was making his way back slowly. Perhaps he turned into a snail and was waiting for his fairy godmother to turn him back into a human.

I returned the file to his desk drawer and locked it. After placing his keys in the top right drawer, I peeked out the door and scanned the busy room of employees making phone calls to get support for Caldwell. No sign of the candidate.

I still didn't have my missing key, the one that

would unlock evidence of Caldwell's cruel treatment of Seamus, the key with a nick on the side.

Checking the locked middle drawer may have been a waste of time. It's just that locked places look like signposts that say, "Looking for something valuable? Check here first!"

The locked drawer may have been a diversion from finding the missing key. The remaining option was a hiding place. Was Caldwell a high person or a low person?

I considered how he thought of himself. A high-powered person. Getting on his knees to tape a key to the bottom of a drawer might be too beneath him. I felt the ridge of the door's lintel just above the door. Only dust and neglect. On the right side above the door was something metal. A key. Bingo.

I took it down and examined it. A silver-colored key with a deep nick on its side.

This was the key taken from me. I exhaled a breath of relief.

The door opened. The overhead light turned on.

Caldwell stood at the door, surprised to see me in his office. His gaze dropped to the key in my hands.

With calm, he opened his hand to me.

"Mr. Krieg, please return the key."

"Of course, Mr. Caldwell. Just answer me this one question."

He let his hand drop. "What might that be?"

I rammed my body into him, knocking him to the floor, and sprinted toward the exit.

"Lance," he said. "Stop him! He has the key."

The various employees peeked up from their desks to see the drama.

Lance mumbled something to Howard Lichtman. I raced past them. If only I had heard what their conversation was about. How to kill me, I presumed.

Both chased after me.

49

Berkeley Police Department
Berkeley, CA

DETECTIVE BOBBIE GRAFF PICTURED SARAH BEST'S large belly. The image triggered unwanted memories of her time in college, the night she had been raped. Though the perp had been arrested and convicted, working with the police and lawyer wasn't the hard part. The hard part was going against her friends' advice by choosing to go through with the pregnancy. But the miscarriage made the issue a moot point.

Her ringing phone brought her back to the present. She answered.

"I got it!" It was Sarah Best.

"Got what?"

"I figured out why it can't be Carl."

That would be a miracle.

"I'm listening."

"In David Deutsch's hotel room, the thermostat was upside down. That means when the lever was fully up, the thermostat was at its coldest setting. The body was found with the thermostat at its hottest setting."

"So?"

"So that made the body look like it decayed quickly."

True. Bodies decayed faster in hot environments.

"You think the room was originally not hot?" she asked Sarah.

"I found a timer next to the air conditioner. The air conditioner was set to its coldest setting and, according to the timer, blasted cold air from one a.m. to five a.m."

"And yet the thermostat was set on high heat?"

"I don't think so. You know the aquarium underneath the thermostat?" Sarah asked.

"I remember that from the crime scene photos."

"There was a piece of coral in the aquarium that had twine tied around it, and a fishing hook at the end of the twine."

"I don't follow."

"In the crime scene photo, the rock looked elevated, like it was sitting on a block of ice. When I sneaked to the room, the rock was on the bottom of the aquarium."

"Hold on a second. You went into the hotel room?"

"Stay with me," Sarah said.

"For Chrissake, Sarah. You were at the crime scene?"

"Detective—"

Shit.

"Were you at least accompanied by a police officer?"

"Please, Detective. Just listen to what I have to say."

Shit. Shit. Shit.

"Fine. What in the hell do you have to say?"

"If that ice was originally a large block of ice, then the rock was elevated. The fishing hook could have been hooked onto the lever of the thermostat when the thermostat was all the way up in its off position. Then as the ice melted, the rock would have lowered, and the hook would have pulled the thermostat's lever down."

"Making the room heat up."

"Yes," Sarah said.

"So you're saying the room was originally cold, then became hot after five a.m."

"Yes. And that's not all. The reports showed high levels of ATP."

"And?"

"ATP slows down decay. In fact, it turns out there's no way to have as much ATP in your body as David Deutsch had. He must have been injected with ATP or, I don't know, something that caused him to produce a lot of ATP."

Hmm. Maybe Sarah had something. "If that's true, that means he was injected with it before he was killed, so that the fluid could circulate in his system."

"Works for me." Sarah sounded excited.

"Let me talk this out." She moved to a quieter part of the station where there were no nearby officers listening in on the conversation. "With the room so cold, and with that much ATP in his body, the time of death couldn't have been between seven and nine in the morning. It had to have been earlier."

"And Carl wasn't seen going into his room before seven in the morning," Sarah said. She wasn't grasping at straws, after all. Sarah had a genuine defense for Mr. Best.

Now the question was should she have Sarah arrested for trespassing into a crime scene? Or should she pursuit justice?

She viewed the framed picture of her father on her desk. His killer had never been caught.

"I'll let the SFPD know to check David Deutsch's body for injection wounds and to check the room for the air conditioner's timer," she said. Justice won this round. "They'll need to reevaluate the proper time of death with these new variables. Good detective work, Sarah."

"Thanks."

"But understand, I also have to let my friend in the SFPD know you went into the hotel room. I'll leave it up to her on whether you should be arrested or rewarded."

Sarah blew out an audible breath. "I understand. Thanks so much, Detective."

Graff called the SFPD. Hopefully, Cheung would be supportive.

Caldwell's Campaign Headquarters
San Francisco, CA

FROM CALDWELL'S CAMPAIGN OFFICE, I RUSHED onto Market Street, Lance and Howard on my tail. Pedestrians on the busy sidewalk screamed. Dammit, was that a gun Howard waved about?

I dodged between tourists. Would Howard shoot into a crowd? The police wouldn't, but he wasn't police, he was a security guard.

With the majestic Ferry Building on my right, I raced across the wide Hyatt Regency Plaza, and dashed past a fountain that looked like Picasso's cubism version of worms mating.

I hustled up the steps of the Hyatt Regency and pushed into the lobby. The ceiling lofted high above and the walls were ringed with floors and floors of hotel rooms. Ivy draped the walls, probably plastic.

I bolted around an indoor fountain, past the shops and the front desk. I reached the elevators, stumped. They required card keys.

An elevator door opened for the guests waiting next to me and I stepped in with them. The elevator was a cylinder with glass walls. As I ascended, the elevator's windows gave a view of the hotel lobby. Down below, Lance and Howard stormed into the lobby and scanned the indoor plaza. Lance pushed against Howard's arm, coaxing Howard to lower his weapon.

Lance glanced up and spotted me in the elevator. He grimaced.

I got off the twelfth floor with the others. Where could I go to get away?

I jogged along the walkway that lined the wall. I got as far as the walkway on the opposite side, the hotel lobby lay below like in a canyon between me and the elevators.

Running away from the elevators was a mistake, really. The only way down was the elevator.

On the opposite hotel wall, I had a view of Lance and Howard rising inside one of the elevators. Probably got in the same way I had.

They saw me through the elevator's glass window and stopped at my floor. They took opposite directions, flanking me on both sides.

I had two ways to escape. One, run into one of them, knock him down like a linebacker, and get to the elevator. If I did that, I'd go toward Lance. He didn't have a weapon.

Problem was I'd have to wait for an elevator.

They eased closer to me, Lance on my left, Howard on my right. Howard pointed his gun at me with a steady hand, chest level.

"Ed," Lance said, "just give me the key and we'll let you go. You can go home and live peacefully."

I escaped the second way.

I climbed over the railing, clung to the plastic ivy, and slid down from one level to the next.

Interesting thing about the ground. Unlike predators, it looks a lot scarier the farther away you are from it.

I dropped down clinging to a vine. The vine ripped out, putting me in freefall for a split second until I snatched another vine. My heart jumped to my throat.

I descended that way, level to level, dropping and catching vine after vine. I reached the second floor: the first level of hotel rooms just above the lobby floor. The drop from there would have been too far, about thirty feet. I climbed over the ledge to get onto the second floor's walkway. My feet touched the solid floor. My legs felt like jello — watered down jello. And my arm muscles ached.

I scampered to the elevators. Waiting for the elevator seemed a horrible option.

That's why God made stairs.

The stairwell did indeed exist, right next to the

elevators, it turned out. How had I missed the stairs when I was on the higher floor?

I raced down the one flight and pushed open the exit to the street to the blessed brisk fog.

I'd escaped the building's beautiful trap and I didn't stop running, even as the pain built up in my side, until I reached the bus terminal.

Inside the bus station, I caught my breath. I'd managed to get out. Now the only question was, where should I go?

51

Lakeshore Avenue
Oakland, CA

HOLLY SAMPSON CURSED. A FULL DAY CHASING down Carl, her father's killer, and she still hadn't found him. Stomping down East 18th Street, the busy thoroughfare away from Lake Merritt, she retraced yesterday's steps past the stores Carl had run by, and glanced at every man in the vicinity.

She had been so close to capturing Carl, and then she lost him. The thought of it made her clench her jaw.

She entered a Korean BBQ and showed Carl's picture to the customers. "Have you seen this man?"

All she got were no's.

"Ma'am?" It was a guy in a tan suit and yellow tie,

matching the colors of the servants' aprons. He was probably the manager. "What you want?"

"Have you seen this ma—?"

"No, now get out. You disturb my customers."

"You didn't even look at the picture. Look at it."

He didn't look.

"Get out," he said, "before I call police."

She grabbed his collar and brought his face to the picture. "Look at it, damn you. Do you recognize him or not?"

He lifted his chin in bravado, but his eyes showed his fear. Eyes don't lie. Staring at the picture, he said, "No. I not see him before."

Holly let him go and rushed out the restaurant. Her next stop was a diner on the corner of East 18th Street and 3rd Avenue.

The female host said, "Table for one?"

"I'm not here to eat. Have you seen this man?"

The host examined the picture. "Sure. He was in the back this morning. He and my coworker talked up a storm."

Holly put on a smile. "I'm so glad he's all right." She flashed her badge. "I'm with the Berkeley Police and he just left our department and forgot his wallet."

"Oh, I see. You didn't try calling him or his house?"

"He isn't answering his phone, and he isn't home at the moment. I'm at the end of my shift, so as soon as I get his wallet back to him, I can go home and get some rest. Do you think you can help me locate him?"

"You can try calling Alessandra."

"Alessandra?"

"The waitress. She might know where he is. In fact, I think I overheard her offer him to spend the night. I can give her a call if you'd like."

"You know what? Why don't I just stop by her place and ask her in person? That way I can see if he's there, and if he isn't, she can tell me where he might be."

The host scowled. "Not sure how that's easier, but I'll get you her address."

"Thank you so much."

Another step closer to putting Carl in the ground.

52

S.F. Bus Depot
San Francisco, CA

I HAD TO GET OUT OF SAN FRANCISCO. GET AS FAR away from Lance and Howard as I could. There was only one place I felt comfortable going. Using some of the small bills I had in my wallet, I hopped a bus to Lake Merritt, a bus that would get me closest to Alessandra's place.

On the bottom level of the Bay Bridge, the bus motored toward Treasure Island — the island halfway between San Francisco and Oakland.

A memory flashed. I remembered driving along this very road at night in a van, my wife beside me. We were scared, not sure how to stop the van.

I remembered the van stopped inside the tunnel in

Treasure Island. As Sophia and I walked the rest of the way to Oakland through the chilly air, we held hands.

Hands I'd never hold again. I sighed, my chest heavy.

The bus now passed through Treasure Island's tunnel toward Oakland, toward Alessandra's apartment, a woman I barely knew. I sighed again.

What did I know so far? From my running around Oakland and San Francisco the last few days and memories popping like popcorn, I'd re-pieced a fragment of my life. I wasn't sure how I felt about it all. But I did know I worked as the financial analyst for Mr. Aiden Caldwell's campaign.

Seamus was a prisoner to Caldwell's hidden vice, tortured for Caldwell's pleasure. Seamus trusted me to help him expose Caldwell's sick side. Seamus must have given me the evidence for safekeeping. I'd locked up the evidence somewhere and kept the key. Then, a couple days ago on my way to work, someone attacked me and my carpool mates during the carpool ride and stole the key. Caldwell must have been involved in that theft because he had the key in his office.

Now that I had the key back, Caldwell's team was trying to retrieve it. The only reason would be that they didn't know what safe or drawer the key opened, so they were unable to recover the evidence.

Unfortunately, I didn't remember what the key opened either. Or where.

When I'd returned to the campaign office earlier today, they could have held me hostage and asked me what the lock opened, but instead, they didn't grill me. They had taken the key and treated me as if they never knew of the key in the first place. Perhaps they wanted to pretend they didn't know of the evidence and key's existence. They wanted me to think it wasn't them who took the key. And after that failed attempt to kill me in jail, they probably figured there was no point in killing me as a fugitive. No one would believe what I had to say.

That was their plan. Had to be.

Befriend me, help me out from this mess with the police and the supposed murder, and from the goodness of my heart, I would be happy to help them by making sure the evidence didn't go public. If that plan didn't work, they could always blackmail me. Either I keep the evidence private, or they turn me in to the police. And who would believe a murderer who claimed Aiden Caldwell was a sadist?

My stomach churned. I was stuck between a rock and a harder rock.

We crossed to the Oakland side of the Bay Bridge, the part of the bridge that looked like a giant sail.

What about David Deutsch's murder? Did I really do it? Or did they set me up to get leverage against me from exposing Caldwell? That seemed more likely.

What evidence I was holding — somewhere — must reveal what a creep Caldwell was and would end his campaign and his entire political career and land him in jail.

If they had indeed set me up, that was a pretty neat

trick. Based on what the police showed me, I was the only one who left his room after he died. The only way I could be innocent of that was if the killer was also in the room, and if I witnessed the murder. If that were the case, the killer must not have left until much later. Unless he was Spider-Man and crawled out the side of the building.

The bus rumbled toward the end of the bridge. The waves of the bay roiled, white caps rippling. I suddenly remembered how when Sophia and I held hands walking on the bridge, the waves sounded like they were clapping to celebrate my love for her.

She was the one woman I needed the most. And she was gone.

Dammit all to hell.

I wiped my cheeks.

53

Alessandra Westbrook's Apartment
Oakland, CA

As the sun set, Holly waited outside the gate in the freezing cold until an occupant exited the apartment complex to slip inside. She climbed a flight of steps, found Alessandra's door, and knocked hard.

"Who is it?"

She held up her badge to the peephole. "Berkeley Police, ma'am. I just have a few questions."

There was a pause. "Are you Holly Sampson?"

Dammit. She knows who I am. What did Carl tell her?

"That's correct, ma'am. We're concerned about a gentleman with delusions of persecution. That may have included me. Could you open the door, ma'am?"

Another pause. "He seemed rather convinced that you were trying to kill him."

"Yes, he believes a number of people are after him. We're just concerned that he may pose a danger to others. Do you have any idea where he might be?"

"Where's your partner? Don't you come in twos?"

"He's in the police car waiting for me."

"I'll tell you what, Officer. If you come back with your partner, I'll let the two of you in and tell you what I know."

Dammit all to hell. "All right, I'll be right back."

Holly stomped away, then on tiptoe returned to Alessandra's door. After a few seconds, she tapped lightly on the door and hid on the side of the wall, out of view of the door's fisheye.

"Alessandra?" she said, adopting a high voice with a Spanish accent. "I can see you?"

Silence. Then the door opened a crack. She rammed into it, slamming it open. She tackled Alessandra to the floor and held her hunting knife to the woman's throat.

"You scream, and I'll cut your throat. Where is he?"

Alessandra gasped, her eyes wide with fear.

"Tell me where he is!"

Alessandra arched her head back, glancing at the closet.

Holly hissed, "He's here? Hiding in the closet?"

Alessandra didn't say anything.

"Don't move." She eased off Alessandra and marched toward the closet.

Alessandra lunged for the closet ahead of her.

What did Alessandra hope to accomplish? Did she plan to warn Carl? Did she plan to hide there?

It was amusing to watch Alessandra desperately work the knob to open the closet door.

54

Bay Bridge
Oakland, CA

THE BUS APPROACHED CLOSER TO LAKE MERRITT,
closer to where I had the run-in with that Berkeley
police officer. She had attacked me in my apartment.
Her badge ID revealed her as Officer Holly Sampson.

Why did she want me dead? She thought I killed
her father? I had no memory of him. And where
was she?

At this point, all that mattered was getting Seamus
free. I'd worry about Sampson later.

The bus stopped at MacArthur and Lakeshore
Avenue. I hopped out and strode under the lamplight to
Alessandra's place. An occupant was just leaving the

apartment complex, so I caught the gate and slipped in. She eyed me suspiciously.

"I'm here to see Alessandra."

She jerked her head away with a disgusted frown. Right. Alessandra's side job was a dominatrix. Her neighbor must have thought I was a client.

I climbed up the steps two at a time to her room, number 208. At the door, I knocked.

There were some muffled pleading sounds. Uh, oh.

"Alessandra?" I put my ear closer to the door. "It's Ed."

The door opened.

Alessandra stood carrying her whip. She had her hands at her hips and her legs wide apart like Wonder Woman. "You're just in time. Look who came for a visit."

In the middle of her living room, Holly Sampson sat hands and feet bound to a chair. She was gagged, and growling.

I grinned. Things just got interesting.

"That's Officer Holly Sampson," I said to Alessandra. "But I get the impression she's not really an officer."

Holly protested behind her gag.

I ignored her and asked Alessandra, "What happened?"

Alessandra explained how she'd been attacked by Holly and managed to overcome her with her special whip skills.

"Normally I save the rough stuff for my special clients." She waved the whip toward Holly. "But Ms.

Sampson here was asking for it. What do you know about her?"

"Nothing more than what I already told you. She says she's Richard's daughter, but I don't remember any Richard Sampson."

Holly wriggled and huffed through her gag.

Alessandra frowned at her. "Could be she was lying."

"Let's ask her." I crouched down to eye-level with Holly. "I'm going to take off your gag. There's no use screaming for help. If you do, we'll just put the gag back on. Do you understand?"

She didn't move, just glared.

"Besides," Alessandra said. "my neighbors are used to hearing screams coming from my apartment. Most of them think it's cute."

Holly glanced from Alessandra to me, defeat in her eyes, then nodded.

I tugged down the gag and Holly took a moment to breathe regularly.

"It's stone," she said.

I scowled. What did she mean?

"Not Richard Sampson," she explained. "My father's name was Richard Stone. Now you get it?"

I shook my head. "No. Should I get it?"

Holly cursed, and kept cursing.

"Should we put the gag back on?" Alessandra asked.

"Let her finish her creative word poop. I'm going to check my phone." The Nappy Ewe Here background on the phone was an amusing juxtaposition to Holly's swearing.

"What are you looking for?" Alessandra asked.

"I want to see if I can find out who Richard Stone is."

"What the hell?" Holly yelled. "What's wrong with you?"

I opened the browser and punched in "Richard Stone."

"You want to find out who he is?" Holly said. "Don't you mean who he was? My dad is dead. You killed him."

Questions of whether I was a good person crawled back inside my skull. Did I really kill her father? Why? And did I really kill David Deutsch? For fun? Was I a killer before my amnesia?

"I honestly don't remember," I said. "Amnesia. I think I hit my head in our bout of fighting at my apartment, if that's what we were doing. I don't remember that, either. Was your father a police officer, too?"

She sighed with frustration. "He worked for the Department of Defense at the Pentagon."

I pocketed my phone and turned to Alessandra. "I think I'm understanding what happened to me. If I had killed someone so important, I must have been running from not just the police, but also the FBI and any other government agency eager to catch me for killing one of their own. That's probably why I changed my name. To make running away easier."

Holly said nothing.

Alessandra paused, then shook her head. "I still don't think you're capable of doing such a thing."

"Then why would I change my name?"

"Actually," Holly said, "there *is* something wrong with your theory."

"What's wrong with it?"

"I was the only one hunting you down. No one else."

"I don't get it. Why would no one come after me?"

"Everyone thought my father died of a heart attack."

"I made it look like a heart attack? What did I do, inject him with air or something?"

"I don't know. All I know is you were the one who killed him." Her eyes welled, so unlike a police officer who had seen so much. Was there something she wasn't saying? Something more than losing her father?

"How did you find out?" Alessandra asked.

"Jonas, my godfather, told me."

Alessandra scowled. "How did *he* find out?"

"I don't know, but he's high up in government. Higher up than my father was. So if anyone had the resources to find out, he would."

Jonas was in the government with access to intel? I wasn't sure whether to be impressed or suspicious. Could be the intel was bad. "So now you want your revenge."

"I gotta say, revenge isn't very fun if the guy you're killing doesn't even know he's committed a crime. Are any of your memories coming back?"

I remembered holding hands with Sophia as we

walked across the Bay Bridge and the waves clapped for our love. But I didn't remember much else about her. I loved her deeply and I couldn't remember why. My heart clenched.

"Slowly, but surely," I said.

"Then if I ever get free, you'll be the one strapped to this chair, and I'll hold you until you remember what you've done."

"I'm not into that kink," I said.

Alessandra pulled me aside and whispered, "What do you think we should do with her?"

Hmm. If we kept her tied up, someone would need to watch her all the time. Alessandra had better things to do, and I needed to free Seamus. If we let her go, who knew what sort of trouble she'd stir up without anyone watching her?

Holly had just said she'd hold me hostage until I remembered killing her father. Trying to free Seamus would be rather difficult while tied to a chair.

And then there was the whole plan of freeing Seamus in the first place. How was I going to swing that? I needed help.

"I have an idea." I turned to Holly. "How would you like to help me free an innocent prisoner?"

"I just tried to kill you," she said. "Why would you expect me to help you?"

Alessandra glared at me. "Yeah, Ed. Why would you expect Holly to help you?"

"Because I sense something brewing inside of you.

Maybe you're doubting whether I truly killed your father."

"What gives you that idea?" Holly frowned, glanced away, not able to hold my gaze.

"You said yourself that you were the only one after me, that most everyone else was convinced that your father died of a heart attack."

"So?" She shrugged awkwardly with the restraints,

"You said it's not much fun killing someone who doesn't know what he's guilty of." I struggled to untie the knots Alessandra had so skillfully tied. "So you're not in a hurry to kill me, not until I remember actually killing your father. So for now, I feel safe around you."

Weird logic, I knew it, but so what? It made sense to my amnesiac brain.

Rope free, Holly rubbed her wrists. She bent down and whipped out a small gun from an ankle holster.

Crap! Alessandra and I ducked.

"Relax, Nathan." She checked the gun's clip. "I'm not going to shoot you until one of these bullets has your name on it."

That didn't make me feel any better. But Holly yawned, showing no sign of needing to be hyperaware of her surroundings.

Alessandra stood at ease and turned to me.

"If Holly did want to shoot us," she said, "she would have done it by now."

"Yep. Let me guess," Holly said. "Once you do remember killing my father, you'll still pretend you don't remember."

"Ed doesn't kill people," Alessandra said.

"You mean Nathan," Holly hissed. "His name's Nathan."

"Whatever," Alessandra said. "He's not the type."

"Even if I did remember killing your father," I said, "you're right. I'd act as if I didn't remember. But I bet you're skilled enough to know if a person is lying."

"Perhaps." Holly tucked the gun back in its holster. "What do you need help with?"

I told her about Seamus, the journalist that Aiden Caldwell held prisoner for his sadistic pleasures. The whole time, Holly frowned in disgust.

"I want you to help me free him," I said.

"Okay," Holly replied without hesitation.

Alessandra studied me as if my face were changing into a catapult. Okay. Maybe it *was* a bad idea to untie Holly.

Alessandra sighed, as if giving in to the idea of making Holly an ally.

"So how did it go in San Francisco, Ed?" she asked.

"Oh, I nearly forgot!" I searched my pocket and retrieved my prize. "I found the key hidden in Aiden Caldwell's office."

"That's the key to one of the lockers in my diner," Alessandra said.

"You sure?"

"Sure, I'm sure. Every locker key has that notch on the side. Want me to go there and get the envelope you asked me to lock up for you?"

"Later. Let's free Seamus first." I stepped closer to Alessandra. "Do you have a set of handcuff keys?"

She put her hands on her hips.

"Hon, I have a set of keys for *every* kind of handcuff."

Bay Bridge
San Francisco, CA

ALESSANDRA DROVE US THAT NIGHT IN HER SMALL electric car, a pink BMW i3, across the Bay Bridge into San Francisco to Caldwell's campaign office. I rode shotgun with delicious-smelling pizzas stacked on my lap, a half a dozen boxes of heaven.

"What is my full real name?" I asked Holly who sat in the back.

"Nathan Yirmorshy," she said.

The engraving on my wedding ring. "S.P. + N.Y." The N.Y. stood for Nathan Yirmorshy. A flash of a memory hit me. I gasped.

Alessandra glanced at me, then returned her focus on the road. "What's wrong?"

"I'm remembering things."

"Like what?" Alessandra had a look of concern.

"I worked for Google as a computer programmer and lived in a duplex in the Oakland Hills."

"What's the address?" she said.

I waded through a wall of webs in my head. Nothing.

"I can't remember an address, but I have some sense of where it is." Just thinking about the place brought up feelings. I lived alone. Back then, I relished my solitude. Now, the idea of being alone was revolting to me. Did Holly know about my married life? Did she know the answer to what happened to my wife? How had she died? I wanted to ask, but I didn't want to trigger a memory and feel the pain of her loss all over again.

On California Street in Downtown San Francisco's Financial District, Alessandra pulled up in front of the campaign office and dropped off Holly and me.

"I'll give you a two-minute head start," I said to Holly.

"Give me one." She stormed inside Caldwell's headquarters.

I ticked off a minute in my head, the boxes of pizzas heavier with every second. By the end of the minute, Holly should have crossed the bullpen to the back of the headquarters, waiting for my part.

I strode in.

The evening crew was busy cold-calling constituents during the dinner hours. Holly stood in the back and nodded to me. She was ready.

"Pizza, everyone!" I said. "We've got cheese, veggie, and non-kosher pepperoni."

I set the pizza on a table near the entrance. The bees came to the honey, thanking me.

"What's the occasion?" one of the volunteers asked.

"Aiden Caldwell knows you could be doing something with your lives and yet you chose to be a volunteer here, so this is his way of expressing his gratitude."

Joy spewed from their happy faces. Two ladies gave me a hug. One guy also gave me a hug, holding me tighter than was comfortable. The security guard, Howard Lichtman, stood a few feet away from me and spoke into a walkie-talkie. Lance Meyler, Caldwell's right-hand man, appeared at the back and strode toward me.

Holly slipped through the AUTHORIZED PERSONNEL ONLY door stairwell without Lance noticing. Howard approached me, a red welt on his windpipe where I had punched him in jail. He kept his hand on the hilt of his gun. Would he actually use his gun around all these people?

If Holly was following the plan, she was downstairs using the key I gave her to get into Seamus's cell, using the keys Alessandra gave her to unlock Seamus from his cuffs, and was bringing him back up.

Side by side, Lance and Howard approached me. If Howard got close enough, he could hold the muzzle to my chest and fire and the surrounding employees would be none the wiser. It might even be possible to carry me away from the scene before anyone noticed I'd been shot.

The backdoor alarm sounded. Good. Holly had taken Seamus out the back exit.

Lance gestured for Howard to stick with me, and he raced to the back.

From the stack of pizza boxes on the table, I yanked at the bottom box, like removing a card from the bottom of the deck.

I held the pizza box vertical. There was no pizza in this box. Instead, it held a large-sized metal pizza pan I had bought from the store. Howard was close to me and had his gun drawn at his hip where no one could see it unless they were looking.

I crouched behind the pizza box. He fired. The bullet clanged against the metal pizza pan. No standard bullet could penetrate over an inch of durable aluminum.

People screamed.

"Get down," Howard shouted.

Some crouched to the floor, others ran to their desks. I hustled to the front door, still crouched behind the pizza pan.

Howard fired another shot at me. PING. The strike of the bullet against the pan jarred my arms.

I scurried out the front door to the sidewalk. Seamus and Holly were already in the back seat of Alessandra's car.

Lance turned the corner, having exited the back way, and charged at me.

The front passenger door of Alessandra's car swung open. I tumbled in.

Alessandra peeled away as I was closing the door. Howard fired shots at us. We ducked. A bullet struck through the back windshield, shattering it. Alessandra turned at the corner and sped us away.

———

SEAMUS LOOKED TRAUMATIZED in the back seat as we crossed the Bay Bridge to Oakland. He didn't say anything, just stared out the window at the Bay. Maybe he was in shock.

From my wallet, I pulled out Sophia Patai's photo. My wife. A vision of cards came to mind. Not playing cards. Tarot. She read Tarot cards. Well, that was hardly scientific. Did I ever tell her Tarot couldn't make accurate predictions? Did she prove me wrong?

I put away the picture and asked Holly, "Did you know Sophia Patai?"

"No," she said.

I didn't say anything.

"Did she die?" Holly asked.

"How did you know?"

"You asked me 'did' I know her, not 'do' I know her."

I nodded. "I saw her social media page. Everyone posted things like rest in peace."

All those sorrowful farewells posted on Sophia's

profile page... Losing someone I didn't fully remember but my heart longed for? Damn, that still hurt.

"Sorry," Holly said.

Sounded like she meant it.

Caldwell's Campaign Headquarters
San Francisco, CA

LANCE STORMED BACK INTO THE CAMPAIGN headquarters. How could he have let Seamus escape? What was he going to say to Caldwell? What would happen if Seamus talked? Nothing good.

Should he go to Ed's apartment in Oakland? Not yet. Ever since Ed had been in jail accused of murdering the Senator, chances were he stopped hanging out at his home. Way too many police kept an eye on it.

Perhaps he should check Seamus's home. Seamus wasn't accused of anything. There were no cops outside his home, ready to arrest him. Then again, Seamus wouldn't go there. Both Seamus and Ed had to have known that Seamus's place would be the first place Lance looked.

Still, better to leave no stone unturned. He would send a two-man crew to watch Seamus's apartment building, just in case.

Now, where to find Ed?

Lance headed downstairs to Ed's office. Inside, he scanned the room. It was an odd space. Why so empty? No posters, no pictures, no books, no shelves, just the bare bones of an office.

There had to be something here, something that could tell him where Ed might be.

Lance punched the computer's "on" button and checked its history. Two photos were loaded into the computer that day. He opened them. The photos were of Ed and some woman.

The history revealed that Ed had been on facial recognition websites. For some reason, Ed's own face didn't turn up any names, but the girl's face did. The girl was dead, from the looks of her social media.

Lance didn't know what to make of it. Ed had never talked about a girlfriend or a wife.

What about the printer? He checked the printer and printed a list of its history. Just the scan of an image. The printer hadn't been used for anything else in the recent weeks. With a flick of the switch, he killed the printer's power.

Lance sighed. His gaze dropped to the floor. What else was there to do? The trash can. Inside, there was a receipt to a diner in Oakland. The Skylight Diner.

He seared the restaurant's name to his memory.

Alessandra Westbrook's Apartment
Oakland, CA

AT ALESSANDRA'S APARTMENT, I DID THE FORMAL
introductions.

"Seamus, this is Alessandra, a waitress and dominatrix. Apron by day, catsuit by night."

Seamus squinted as if Alessandra was too bright to
see. "Pleasure to meet you?"

"And this is Holly. She's a police officer with the
Berkeley Police Department."

"Thank goodness," Seamus said.

I added, "She's going to kill me once I remember
that I killed her father."

Seamus laughed and shook her hand. "I didn't
realize Ed had a sense of humor."

"He's not kidding." Holly crossed her arms. "I'm going to kill him. Pleasure to meet you, Seamus."

His laughter died.

"Alessandra, Holly, this is Seamus," I said. "He's a journalist willing to let himself be whipped and tortured for the sake of a good story."

Alessandra and Holly studied the exposed bruises on his arms.

"Ah, yes," Seamus said. "Now I see how who we are can sound a bit bizarre out of context." He faced me. "Tell me you have the key."

"We have the key," I said.

"Tell me you know what it opens."

"We know what it opens," I said.

"Thank goodness. Let me see the key."

I showed it to him. He snatched it from my hand.

"See the nick in the side?" I said. "That's the standard marking for the staff lockers at the diner."

"Ed told me to lock up an envelope for him," Alessandra said.

"It's in your locker?" Seamus asked Alessandra.

"No one gets my locker key, big boy." She put a hand on her hip. "I selected a different locker."

"What was the locker number?"

"Two-oh-eight."

"Okay. Where's the diner?"

She told him.

He clenched the key in his fist.

"I'll be back," he said and ran out of the apartment.

"Wait!" I said at the open doorway, but Holly grabbed my arm and stopped me from following him.

"Think about it," she said. "Caldwell knows you have the key to the incriminating evidence against him, and knows you were the one who locked it away. If anyone's going to retrieve the evidence, they're going to think it's you. They're going to look for you, Carl. Not Seamus."

"Actually, Holly," I said, "Seamus has more credibility than me. He's a reporter. I'm a fugitive accused of murder. Caldwell is probably looking for Seamus, not me." Then it sunk in. I glared at Holly. "You just want dibs in killing me first."

She shrugged.

I closed the door. Maybe it was best to let him be in charge of taking down Caldwell considering what the senator-elect did to him. Besides, he had said he was going to come back.

Hopefully, he meant it.

Alessandra studied my face. "What are you thinking?"

"Do you have a towel or cloth or neck?"

"What do you mean?" Alessandra said.

I just wanted something to wring.

"Never mind." I went to the kitchen. "Any more beer?"

58

Skylight Diner
Oakland, CA

SEAMUS LOLLOPED TO THE SKYLIGHT DINER IN THE night, key in hand, sucking in breaths every time the welts on his back came in contact with his clothes. Damn, that stung!

Didn't matter. Here it was, the day he had pined for so long. He had spent the past month flogged and whipped.

He entered the diner.

"Sit anywhere you want, sir." The hostess at the cash register exhibited an air of indifference by the way she placed her attention of the contents of the till.

"Thanks."

He made a beeline for the back, ignored the EMPLOYEES ONLY sign, and marched into the back room.

It always stupefied him how pristine the customer areas looked and the EMPLOYEES ONLY section looked like a place for rats to congregate.

Where were the lockers?

He scanned the large area. Just boxes of inventory, and signs directing to the men and women restrooms.

Peering in the men's restroom, he saw an anteroom of lockers. Since this key was Alessandra's, it had to belong to one of the lockers in the women's restroom.

Seamus perambulated into the women's locker room and searched for locker 208. He spotted it.

"Sir, what are you doing in here?" declared a woman in the waitress uniform.

Seamus smiled, "Alessandra requested that I procure an item from a locker."

"I don't care what Alessandra said. You can't just waltz in here. This is the ladies locker room. We change here."

"I understand. In fact, I expressed those very same sentiments, but she insisted."

"Give me the key and I'll get it for you while you wait outside."

"But it's just…"

She held her palm out with her other hand on her hip. "Now."

No reason to cause a scene. He handed her the key.

"What am I looking for?"

"It should be an envelope."

"Fine. I'll get it for you. Now leave."

Seamus stood outside the restroom door, biting his nails. One benefit of being imprisoned for weeks, he didn't have the opportunity to practice his foul habit of biting his fingernails, so now they actually appeared healthy.

He listened in. The locker squeaked open. Silence. The silence lingered. Oh, no. She better not be perusing through the pictures. If she regarded the images of him being tortured by Aiden Caldwell, all sorts of potential reactions might occur. She might be disgusted and demand he leave without the pictures, she might call the police, she might — The locker squealed closed.

She returned and handed him the manila envelope. "Here you go. Cute pics. Just remember, no going into the ladies locker room."

Cute pics? He opened the envelope and inspected the images. None of them showed Caldwell with Seamus. In fact, none of them had Caldwell or Seamus in them. Just pathetic pictures of Ed and some woman. What the hell kind of joke was he playing?

Dammit all to hell, shit, hell, damn shit, shitty hell, damn sucking hell shitter, hell sucker, dammit!

Ed better have a good explanation.

As he stormed out of the diner, he passed by a customer reading a newspaper. A sketch caught his eye. What was Ed's picture doing in the newspaper?

He plucked the paper out of the customer's hands.

"Hey, I was reading that!"

Seamus scanned the article.

No. No, it couldn't be true.

He stomped the floor, "No, no, no, no, no!"

The fantasy of his fortune burned to ashes.

59

Alessandra Westbrook's Apartment
Oakland, CA

IN ALESSANDRA'S LIVING ROOM, I SAT ON THE couch nursing a beer with Holly. I tapped my knee anxiously awaiting Seamus's return. Alessandra paced. At least nursing a beer was better than nursing a friend back to health.

"Where's your girl?" Holly sat in a cushy armchair.

"What do you mean?" I asked.

"Sarah. The one I threatened back in New York. Where is she?"

I shook my head trying to work that out. Did I move on from Sophia's passing and find a girlfriend in New York? A glimmer of hope returned that I wasn't alone.

A loud knock hammered at the door. Alessandra peered through the peephole, then opened the door. Seamus barged in. Good. He made it safe and sound. Alessandra closed the door behind him.

"What the hell is this?" He threw something on the coffee table.

"It's an envelope," I said. "It holds documents. Pronounced, en-veh-lope."

"What was it doing in the locker?" he shouted.

Alessandra cocked her head.

"It's not the evidence you were looking for?" she asked.

"Is this supposed to be some mean-spirited gag?" He pointed at the manila envelope. "You're scheming against me, aren't you?"

"I swear, Seamus. That should have been the evidence." I reached for the envelope to see what the problem was.

"Fine, then explain this." He slapped a folded newspaper onto the coffee table. The police sketch of my face filled the top of a column. The headline read, "Senator-Elect David Deutsch Stabbed to Death."

"Why didn't you tell me he became a homicide victim while I was a prisoner?" he yelled. "No wait, don't tell me. You didn't say anything because you were the one who committed the crime. What was your motive? Were you hired to kill him? Or did you know that he hired me to get the dregs on Caldwell, so killing off my money-maker was just your way of antagonizing me?"

"David Deutsch hired you?" I asked.

"Damn straight he hired me. I didn't endure all of this torment just for an exclusive."

"How much did he offer you?" Holly asked.

His gaze bore into me as he answered Holly.

"Ten. Million. Dollars."

Holy crap.

"But I won't see any of that, thanks to ol' Amnesia Brains here." He turned to Holly, "What about you? I had the impression you were a police officer. Why don't you arrest him?"

Holly stood, approached Seamus, and patted the air gesturing for him to calm down. "I have no intention of arresting him. I'm going to kill him, remember?"

He threw his hands up in the air. "Lunatics. I'm dealing with lunatics." He turned to me. "Where's the authentic key? Tell me, dammit."

"I have no idea. I thought that *was* the real key." I opened the envelope. "I'm as surprised as you." What else was so important for me to lock up?

"So help me," he said. "I'll procure that money one way or another."

He marched out of the apartment and slammed the door behind him.

I peered inside the envelope and shook the photos onto the table. They were pictures of me and my wife, Sophia Patai. In one we were at a carnival. I had a dollop of chocolate ice cream on my nose and she wore a sinister grin while holding the offending weapon on a sugar cone. Another picture was a selfie of us as we sat in a restaurant booth I didn't recognize. The rest were similar fond souvenirs. Some memories flooded back, memories of us enjoying the carnival, sharing delicious dishes at a restaurant, gazing into each other's eyes in the bedroom.

I had even taken Sophia to my house in the Oakland Hills. I think that was the day we met. Remembering her more clamped my heart in a vise and squeezed my love for her into my blood. This unfamiliar woman, suddenly a part of my memories. It was so strange.

I had been so afraid when the thief in the gas mask assaulted me. I thought, "No. Not that key. Not that one."

But it wasn't the evidence of Aiden Caldwell's activities I had been so frightened of losing. It was the pictures of my time with Sophia.

I studied the pictures again. Her impish act of dotting my nose with chocolate ice cream warmed and relaxed me.

"I don't get it," Alessandra sat beside me on the couch. "If that wasn't the key, is there a key?"

I shrugged.

Holly returned to her seat.

"Let's just talk this out," Holly said. "Suppose, Carl, that you did kill Deutsch."

"He didn't," Alessandra said.

"Fine, but let's just play out the scenario. So Carl, you help out a journalist with gathering evidence to put away Caldwell, your boss, or at least to push him out of the race. Caldwell gets wind of your collection of evidence, so he hires someone to steal the key from you. Later, with no key and no access to the evidence, you kill Deutsch. If you were paid to kill Deutsch, then your motivation would be money."

Alessandra crossed her arms and stared stonily at Holly. This scenario of me being a killer bothered her, bless her soul. But something Holly said earlier nagged at me.

Holly continued, "The day after Deutsch's death, I tracked you down and we fought in your living room. You hit your head and got amnesia. Maybe that was the day you were supposed to free Seamus to expose Caldwell and ruin his chances at becoming the senator. Caldwell and Deutsch were the only two left in the California Senate race. Those actions suggest that your true goal was to kill off both candidates and clear the way with no one to vote for in the Senate race."

I was only half-listening.

"That makes no sense," Alessandra said.

Holly leaned back in her chair, defeated.

"No, it doesn't," she said.

"Now let's run the scenario as if Ed didn't kill anyone," Alessandra said. "Ed works at Aiden Caldwell's campaign to make sure people see the politician's eccentric side. That way, Caldwell loses his chance at the Senate. Meanwhile, let's say someone sets up Ed as the killer for David Deutsch's death. Why would they?"

Holly scowled. "If someone knew he was planning to discredit Caldwell, maybe setting him up as a murderer would cut Carl's credibility and he'd be unable to use the evidence against Caldwell."

My head fogged trying to answer Holly's question. Sarah?

Alessandra nodded. "I think that's it. What do you think, Ed?"

I looked up from the floor. "I don't remember having a girlfriend in New York."

60

Lakeshore Avenue
Oakland, CA

On Lakeshore Avenue, Seamus purchased a
burner phone and called the campaign office.

"Caldwell for Senator. This is Jane."

"Good afternoon Jane, could you connect me with
Lance Meyler?"

"Hold please."

Seamus pictured Lance's worried face, desperate to
do anything Seamus wished. A palpitating pleasure
stirred inside.

"Caldwell for Senator. This is Lance."

"Good afternoon Lance, this is your conscience
calling to collect."

"Seamus?"

"Indeed. It might interest you to know that I have some captivating footage of what Caldwell and you did to me," he said. Lance didn't need to know that he didn't actually have the footage.

The reply was flat. "What do you want?"

"Let us set an appointment to negotiate the terms."

"Fine. Come on in to my office and we can discuss it."

"Not an option. We're meeting at a public place."

There was some hesitation. That was a good sign.

"Where?" Lance asked.

"The Ferry Building."

Lance muttered a curse. Seamus smiled.

"When?" Lance asked.

"Tomorrow morning, seven-o-clock, on the center steps that face Market Street."

"I'll see you then, Seamus."

The heady return of his dream bubbled up. His dream mansion and several Bugattis and Maseratis in the large garage warmed his chest.

———

Alessandra Westbrook's Apartment
Oakland, CA

I PICKED at the stitching of the couch. A gust of dusk wind outside struck the living room window. The window shuddered.

I said to Holly, "Tell me about this Sarah in New York."

"Like what?"

"What does she look like?"

"Are you kidding? You keep looking at her photo."

What was she talking about?

I pulled out Sophia's picture from my wallet, stood, and brought it close to Holly.

"This one?"

"That's her."

"This is Sophia," I said. "Not Sarah."

"Nope."

I studied the picture half expecting it to turn into a photo of someone else. Alessandra stepped beside me and gently took the photo from my hand.

On my phone, I pulled up Sophia's social media profile and showed Holly the condolences.

Holly peered at the profile. "Well, I'll be a puckered pumpkin. You know what this means, don't you?"

"What? What does it mean?"

"Your wife is alive. She only pretended to be dead."

Alessandra embraced me from behind. Good thing, too. My knees weakened and I might have collapsed on the rug if she hadn't held me up.

"Oh, Ed. Isn't that such great news?" She squeezed me.

"I don't know what to make of it." My head was spinning from hope to fear and back. "Why would she pretend she was dead?"

Holly sipped her beer, then said, "Probably for the same reason you changed your name to Carl."

"What reason was that?"

"I don't know," she said, "but it's one of two reasons. Either one or both of you killed someone and you're running from the law, or someone is trying to kill you and you knew about it, so you ran away."

"The latter makes sense," Alessandra said to Holly, "considering you're the one trying to kill him."

"No, it would have been someone else. I didn't try going after Carl until after he changed his name. And considering I found marshals at your home in New York, you were probably in WITSEC — The Witness Protection Program."

"The marshals said I never killed anyone," I said. Speaking of which, I had an appointment with them tomorrow by the Japanese Tea Garden.

"What marshals?" Alessandra said.

"Long story," I said. "Point is, whatever the reason Sophia and I had for changing our names, it was because of Sophia, not me. Otherwise, there would have been no reason for her to pretend she was dead."

"True. You would have just changed your names," Holly said. "It's as if someone wanted her dead, and WITSEC set it up so that whoever wanted her dead thought she was dead."

"Okay," I said. "But who wanted her dead?"

Holly shrugged.

"If she is alive," I said, "then her life is still in danger and she has to stay in hiding."

"What's next?" Alessandra asked.

I plopped onto the couch and lay down.

"After getting some shut eye, let's go to where I once lived in the Oakland Hills and see if we can find any clues there. Holly, you can take the guest room, a.k.a. dungeon of pleasure."

"Just in case you get any lethal ideas," Alessandra said to Holly, stepping to her closet of sex toys, "I've got some comfortable fuzzy handcuffs to make sure you stay in bed."

"I get it." Holly put her wrists together. "Fine by me."

61

The Ferry Building
San Francisco, CA
Saturday morning, February 4th

SEAMUS PURCHASED A BAG OF SMOKED ALMONDS from a vendor by the steps in front of the Ferry Building. A light fog from the early morning hung overhead.

The Ferry Building was a hangout for tourists and locals alike. The perfect public place. Inside, a handsome mall of high-end stores — gourmet chocolates, organic salamis, cooking ware, local cheeses, and small farm vegetables — filled the old, renovated building.

Outside, while sitting on the cold steps facing Market Street, the foot traffic in and out of the Ferry Building was bustling, just what he counted on. It was safe being surrounded by so many innocent civilians.

He reached under his sweater and retrieved his phone from his shirt pocket to check it. Good. It was still recording.

He ate one of the almonds. The smoky taste was potent, stronger and bolder than store-bought brands. In just a few days, he could buy all the gourmet almonds he wanted on a private beach on Spectabilis Island.

Where was Lance? It was already a quarter past seven. He was fifteen minutes late. That didn't seem like the behavior of a desperate man. Something was wrong.

Ten minutes later, Lance still hadn't showed. Why would Lance risk exposing Caldwell's sadistic nature? Though Seamus didn't actually hold the video and photo evidence to blackmail Caldwell, the threat should have been enough. Had he misjudged Lance?

He hiked a few yards, stepped into a café, ordered a cappuccino, and sat at an outside table that kept the wide front stairs in his vantage point. He winced from his body's souvenirs of welts. At least he had an agreeable view of Market Street, the passing trolleys, and the passersby coming and going. The fog, like a dream, started to vaporize.

There was Lance. Seamus flagged him from the café table.

Lance strolled over and settled in the chair across from him.

Seamus leaned back. "Good morning, Lance. I trust you're doing well."

Lance crossed his arms. "Get to the point."

Seamus chuckled. "Here's how the affair will proceed. I possess footage of Caldwell flogging me, whipping me, and enjoying the hell out of it. I also possess footage of you doing those sick things, and me begging for mercy. Ed holds a copy, too. You get Caldwell to cough up ten million dollars, and I will retire all the evidence."

Lance stood and stalked to Seamus's side of the table.

Seamus flinched. "What are you doing?"

Lance put his arm around Seamus and patted his chest. "Now what could this be, I wonder?"

Lance reached his hand down Seamus's sweater and lifted the phone from his chest shirt pocket.

His heart sank.

"You see, Seamus. It's things like this that make me think you don't have any footage and just need me to say something to create actual evidence."

The cell phone in his grip, Lance returned to his seat, smug, and crossed his arms. At least he was out of arms reach should he intend to inflict harm. But that did nothing to calm Seamus's pumping heart.

"Let me tell *you* how this works," Lance said. "Go ahead and light him up."

"What?"

Lance nodded to Seamus's chest. Seamus looked down. He started. A red dot wavered at his heart. Shit.

"If you do happen to have footage, you have five seconds to tell me where it is. If you don't tell me, I'm going to call your bluff and let my sniper here show you his skill at sharpshooting. Five... Four..."

Seamus jumped away from the table.

"Fire," Lance said.

The wall beside Seamus splintered into bits. A bang echoed. His breath quickened. He bolted for the Ferry Building. Splintering of dust puff after puff followed him.

Screams drowned out the sounds of the shots fired. Women screamed and cradled the heads of their children as they carried them away. Men crawled, hiding behind vegetable stands.

Seamus's hip burned. A bullet had grazed him and sliced his pants. He dodged the tourists and kept sprinting.

With a final turn, he made it inside the Ferry Building. He retreated down the long and crowded passage, his heart racing to pump as fast as his legs demanded.

Lance chased after him, gun in hand.

Shit.

Seamus swerved toward the bayside exit. He limped along the wooden planks of the dock. He checked behind him. Lance had followed him onto the dock. In front of him, a ferry was boarding its final passengers.

Lance fired. Seamus lost his footing and stumbled.

Shit and dammit. At least, the shot missed.

He got back up, then ran through the open chain-link gate to board the ferry. He jumped aboard.

"Hey," the ferry crewmember shouted. "Where's your ticket?"

Seamus thrust a couple twenties at the ferry worker. "I must ride this ferry. Keep the change."

The worker's face lit up. He signaled the ferry operator. Rigging released, the ferry powered up, and the boat motored away from the pier.

Where was Lance? There he was, at the gate on the dock.

Seamus sighed his relief at the narrow escape, his heart pounding.

Lance looked side to side. Was he seeking someone? No one was near him on the dock. He raised his gun and fired.

Seamus clutched his bleeding chest and fell over. Cries for help circled him.

Oh, no! This can't happen.

His pounding heart pumped the blood out of him.

This can't be happening.

He reached for the onlookers that crowded him. "Assist me."

He became sleepy. Any help that came was too late.

62

Skylight Diner
Oakland, CA

From her apartment building, Alessandra walked the several blocks to the Skylight Diner, the morning sunrise on her back. As she stepped into the diner, she called out a "hi" to Jim and Mary, the cook and hostess.

Mary said, "The next time you're going to send someone into the ladies locker room," she leaned in close and whispered, "make sure he's handsome."

"You got it, babe." Alessandra chuckled. "Lord knows we could use some handsome men in our locker room."

"Check out the knockout punch in that corner," Mary said.

Alessandra eyed the handsome fellow, his azure suit and bedroom eyes matched. If only she had more customers like him.

She tied on her apron and made her way to the back.

"Excuse me," the gorgeous man stopped her. "Do you happen to know my friend?"

He showed her a picture. She smiled.

"How do you know Ed?" she asked.

"We actually go back a long way. My name's Andy, by the way."

She shook his hand. It was strong.

"Pleasure to meet you, Andy."

"Do you have a second? I'm just on my way out, but there's something I have in the car I've been trying to get to him. Will you be seeing him?"

"He comes in here all the time," she said. "I'm a little late for my shift, but I can start a bit later. How far's your car?"

"It's just outside."

"Lead the way." She called out to Mary, "I'll be back in a few. Can you cover me?"

"I've got your back, dear, unless someone else does." Mary winked.

Alessandra smirked and followed Andy out the door. This would be a great opportunity to get information about Ed's past.

"So how do you know Ed?"

"I've known him since before he came to San Francisco."

"And where was that?" She loved his azure eyes.

"Oh, it was in a small town actually. You wouldn't have heard of it."

Uh, oh.

"Do you also know Carl?" she asked.

"Carl?" He stopped near a parked Audi. "Don't think so. Was he also from Ed's early years?"

She put her hands on her hips.

"You aren't a friend of his, are you?" she said. "Who are you?"

He glanced side to side, then struck her in the face. She winced at the searing pain in her nose, closed her eyes, dizzy.

He shoved her in the car. She toppled into the back-seat clutching her shattered nose. The pain took her over and under to blackness.

63

Amy and Greg Miller's Duplex
Oakland Hills
Oakland, CA

THROUGH THE EARLY MORNING FOG OF THE Oakland Hills, I drove Alessandra's car to my old home, Holly in the passenger seat. It was strange remembering the turns in the roads and the surrounding trees without a memory of the street names and my address. The farther I went into the hills, the more memories I had of my old landlord watching me there.

"Holly, you're quiet."

She sighed. "When I was in upstate New York looking for you, I ran into a couple of marshals."

"You mentioned that."

"Dammit, I just—" Her voice cracked. Then she said nothing.

I knew better than to prompt her. Sounded like she had a tough time talking about it. Better to let whatever she had to say brew to readiness.

"I killed them," she said.

What in the hell? I pulled over.

"What are you talking about?"

Holly yelled, "I killed them, okay?" She wheezed out strange high-pitched cries. She doubled over and shook. "Oh, God. I killed them."

She killed the marshals?

"I killed them." She repeated herself, chanting like a mantra as if saying it enough would finally make it true. Perhaps she denied killing the marshals for so long, she hoped her past would go away.

Maybe forgetting my past was a blessing in some ways.

"I'm so bad," she said over and over, rocking in the passenger seat.

I said nothing. No condolences, nor any words of sympathy. She killed marshals? If what she said was true, then yes, she committed the worst crime. If a jury found her guilty, she'd get the death penalty. It wasn't a question of whether or not she was a bad person. She was. The only question was what could she do about it?

Would saving two lives cancel out the killing of two lives?

I couldn't imagine anyone would agree to that. An accidental death was the bane of medical doctors. They helped, comforted, and sometimes saved the lives of hundreds of people, and the one time they made a bad mistake and a patient died, they lost their license to save any more lives.

I pulled away from the curb and continued following the familiar trees and houses up to my old place.

There it was. The driveway to my former home. A gravel road weaved through a forest.

I turned onto it. The gravel crunched loud as if we were breaking the stones into smaller pieces.

We came to the one-story duplex, and I parked in front.

The light was on in my old place. Someone was there. The trip may have been a waste of time, but maybe the person or people who lived there now could give me some information about myself.

"I'm going in," I said. "You don't mind staying behind?"

"I'll wait for you." Holly sniffed, her face a mess of tears and snot.

———

IT WAS WHAT, eight o'clock? Hopefully I wasn't intruding too early in the morning.

The house looked familiar, but off. What happened to the garage? In place of the garage was a full wall with a regular door on the side, like a back entrance.

I knocked on the front door. The wooden door and

metal knocker looked the same as when I had lived here.

A woman wearing an apron answered. "Carl! So good to see you. Have you been in touch with Scarlett yet?"

Hmm. Who was Scarlett? "Have we met before?"

"Don't you remember? I keep showing up in your fantasies," the woman said with a straight face.

I cracked a small smile.

A man's voice came from the background, "Now, Amy. Play nice."

Amy grabbed my forearm, "Come in, Carl. Let's catch you up on all you missed, starting with your wife Scarlett."

I stiffened.

"What's wrong?" Amy asked.

"I better not have two wives."

"Oh! Now that *is* very interesting." She grinned and introduced me to her husband Greg and to her two sons, Remy and Chris. "Have a seat, Carl."

I sat on the sofa. The boys flanked me, sitting beside me.

"I have a ton of questions for you," I said to Amy.

"And we have many questions for you," she said.

"I know!" the little guy named Chris said. "Let's play a game. We can, like, go in a circle. We go in a circle and ask questions."

"That wouldn't be fair," Remy said. "We'd be asking Carl a bunch of questions before he'd have a chance to ask one."

"Then let's take turns," Chris said. "First I go, then Carl goes, then you go, then Carl goes, then Mom goes, then Carl goes, then Dad goes. Like that."

"I'm game," Greg, Amy's husband, said. "How about you, Carl?"

I right away saw the flaw with the game. Considering I had amnesia, there was likely going to be a bunch of times when I'd reply, "I don't know."

"On one condition," I said.

"What is it?" Chris asked.

"Each person who asks the question has to first try answering it themselves."

"That's weird." Remy scowled.

"Okay," Chris said. "I go first. Ready?"

"Ready." *Please say something about who this Scarlett woman is.*

"Who would win in a fight? The mountain lion or the stingray? I say the mountain lion."

Remy rolled his eyes.

Hmm. "If the mountain lion has a black belt in karate, then I say the mountain lion."

"Yes," Chris cheered.

"That question doesn't count," Remy said. "Did you kill that senator guy?"

They knew about that? If so, why did they let me into their home?

"What do you think?" I asked.

"I say no," Chris said.

I grinned.

"So did you?" Amy asked.

"I honestly don't know."

Greg scratched his head. "How do you not know something like that?"

"My husband's right," Amy said. "A recipe? That's forgettable. A dream during the night? Easily forgettable. Killing a man running for senator? Not so much."

I explained about my amnesia, waking up in my apartment. I left out the part about a cop trying to kill me.

Amy laughed, "That's quite a pickle you're in. Your turn, Carl."

"Who's Scarlett?"

Amy smiled, "Who do you think she is?"

"You said she's my wife. But this is my wife." I showed her the picture of Sarah.

Chris and Remy peered over her shoulder.

"That's Scarlett," Chris said. "She's really cool."

My wife was alive! I tried to sort it out. We started as Nathan and Sophia in Oakland. We went into WITSEC as Carl and Sarah in New York, and now we were Ed and Scarlett in Oakland. Were we running from our WITSEC identities? And where was my wife? I had to see her!

"What are you thinking about?" Amy asked. "I can smell the burning oil from here."

"One wife. That's a relief."

"I want a turn," Greg said. "What was it like getting arrested for robbing a bank? I'm thinking you were scared. Especially waiting in jail."

Ah, yes. When I had crank-called New York's

Amsterdam Police Department to get my old phone number, I learned of the grand larceny charge in my criminal file. "How'd you find out about that?"

"Scarlett told us about that incident," he said. "But don't worry. You were framed. Do you remember anything about it?"

I shook my head.

Remy slapped his knee. "Aw, man."

"But I do remember my recent experience in jail."

Greg's eyes widened. "Your recent experience?"

"Yes," I said. "I turned myself in to sort out the David Deutsch murder."

"How did you get out?" Amy asked.

"I escaped."

"Cool!" the boys said.

"How did you escape?" Remy jiggled his legs. He couldn't sit still. I had to smile at that. Was I like that as a kid? I didn't remember.

"You already had your turn," I said. "My turn." I asked Amy and Greg, "You met Sophia? Scarlett, that is. Is she okay?"

"She's pregnant," Chris announced.

What the—? My stomach did a somersault.

"Chris!" Amy scolded. "I'm sorry, Carl. You should have found out directly from her."

"She's pregnant?" My head spun. I was going to be a father? What kind of man was I to leave my wife knowing she was pregnant? "Is she.... How far into the pregnancy is she?"

"She's really big," Chris said. "She's gonna explode at any moment."

I glanced at Amy and Greg to verify Chris's words.

Greg cocked his head at Chris. "What *he* said."

I was going to have a kid? I couldn't see myself doing that. Raising a kid? That had to be really hard, like harder than doing jail time.

"My turn," Amy said. "What have you been up to, besides waking up with amnesia and escaping from jail? Have you been running from the law?"

I was going to have a kid?

"Carl?" Amy said. "Open mouth, flap tongue, make sounds resembling words."

"Right. Sorry. Mostly I've been trying to remember who I am. I've had the help of a waitress and a Berkeley police officer, but I'm not sure why I'm here in Berkeley instead of New York."

Greg pouted. "Well that wasn't very interesting, was it boys?"

They both nodded.

Chris held up a finger. "Next time, if you don't have a good answer, make one up."

I kept a straight face.

"My turn," I said. "Is the baby a boy or girl?" Time to guess. "I'll say a girl."

"She didn't tell us," Amy said. "I think it's because she didn't know."

"My turn!" Chris said, bouncing in his seat. "How did you escape the police?"

"How do *you* think I did it?"

"I bet you put sleeping pills in all their drinks."

"Clever idea!" I leaned forward with playful interest. "I must remember that the next time I'm arrested. The truth is, I would have been fine staying in jail, but the officer guarding the cell turned his back and let in a guy to kill me."

"Whoa!" the boys said.

"As he attacked me, the cell door was slightly open. I took that opportunity to run out of the police station."

I told them how I used the underground cable car cable to escape.

When I was done, they were silent, with dropped jaws and wide eyes.

"That is so... cool!" Remy jumped up and punched the air.

"What's Sophia — Scarlett doing here?" I asked Amy. "Is she looking for me?"

"That's exactly what she's doing here," she said.

"Do you like tangerines?" Chris asked.

"I'm not sure. I don't remember eating tangerines, but that doesn't mean I don't like them."

"Hang on," Chris said. "I'm gonna get you a tangerine."

"That counted as a question. My turn," I said. "Is there anything else Scarlett said about me?" I asked. "Billionaire? Extra home in the Cayman Islands? That sort of thing?"

Greg laughed. "She said someone was trying to kill you in New York. You left her to keep her safe. When you left, you didn't know she was pregnant."

I didn't know she was pregnant when I left her? What a relief!

"Remy?" Amy said. "Can I have your turn?"

"Sure, Mom," Remy said.

"Carl, how come you haven't called her? Scared of what she might think about you being a suspect in David Deutsch's death?"

"Most of the time I thought she was dead. Even when I found out she was alive, I couldn't call her. I still don't have her phone number."

She rolled her eyes. "Oh, for all the frozen bunnies on Mars. Really? Is that the only reason?"

I nodded.

"Greg?" She prompted.

"I'm getting the phone now." He retrieved the cord-less home phone and handed it to Amy.

She pulled a folded piece of notepaper from her apron pocket. "She gave us her phone number."

My stomach froze. I was going to talk to my wife? I was going to hear what her voice sounded like?

She dialed, then held the phone to her ear. A part of me hoped Amy would be the mediator between us, relaying what we said to each other.

"Hi hon, it's Amy. I've got someone here who wants to talk to you." She handed me the phone.

The phone handset felt heavy. Heavier than I remembered phones weighing. My wife on the other end of the line.

Amy gestured for me to talk to her. Greg smirked

like this was a clever joke and he couldn't wait to see my face at the punchline. Remy glared at me as if telling me to hurry up. I must have been committing some form of injustice by keeping Sophia waiting.

Chris ran in. "Here, Carl. Here's a tangerine. I peeled it and everything."

Amy shushed him and pulled him into a side hug.

I held the phone to my ear. What should I say? Was there a standard greeting for amnesiacs talking to their wives for the first time since their head injury? Probably not.

I said the first word that came to mind. "Hello?"

Amy and Greg Miller's Duplex
Oakland Hills
Oakland, CA

I LISTENED TO MY WIFE'S TEARFUL, JOYFUL VOICE.

"Oh, Carl," she cried, "I found you."

A clump of sweet pain wedged in my throat. She was my key. She unlocked my past. Memories flooded in. How we met in Emeryville, how she helped me through my trial of having no place to call home, how we escaped a never-ending attack on her, how she helped me understand who I was by simply asking what I wanted and what having that would do for me. I still felt pieces of the puzzle missing, but at least I had the frame to work with.

She asked me what had happened to me. I explained

how I woke up with amnesia and followed clues to figure out what happened. I didn't mention Holly Sampson, Alessandra, Seamus, nor my arrest and escape from jail. There would be plenty of time for the heavy stuff later.

"I'm calling from a hotel in San Francisco," she said. "Listen, Carl. If you have amnesia, then you probably haven't been taking your meds."

"My meds? What's wrong with me?"

She laughed. "Nothing's wrong with you. You have bipolar disorder. Without your meds, you might get delusions or hallucinations."

That explained a lot. No wonder I got suspicious over Yitzhak's phone call to the lawyer at Dolly's Trolley Café. No wonder I thought the suitcase at the Fairmont Hotel held a bomb.

"Carl, there's something I need to tell you, show you, in person."

"Chris already told me."

She laughed. "Of course he did. I'll be right over. Oh, and Carl?"

"Hm?"

"You didn't kill David Deutsch. I know how they set you up."

I was set up? That fit Alessandra's theory of someone knowing my plan to discredit Caldwell and discrediting me by making me the scapegoat for Deutsch's murder.

Tension spilled out from my shoulders. I was set up. I didn't murder him.

Wait a sec. Sarah knew I was a suspect and she didn't distance herself from me?

Wait a sec. She knew *how* I was set up?

"How?"

"Now what would be the fun in telling you over the phone? I'll be there soon."

I hung up and returned the phone to Amy. "Sarah's on her way."

"Excellent." Amy cradled the phone back in its home. "So what does an adventurer do while waiting to re-meet his wife?"

"He introduces you to the woman in the car parked outside."

She eyed me suspiciously. "I thought you *don't* like the idea of more than one wife."

I chuckled.

———

City Hall Hotel
Van Ness Avenue, San Francisco, CA

JUST BEFORE NINE A.M., Sarah checked out of the hotel. She didn't have her car anymore, but she had something better. Reuniting a healthy family.

She requested a rideshare. In three minutes, her designated car pulled over and the passenger door swung open.

She leaned over to look into the car. A gray-haired woman in the driver seat.

"My goodness gracious, dear," the driver said. "You look ready to replicate. Going to the Oakland Hills?"

Sarah got into the passenger seat. "Yes. I'm meeting my husband."

"How lovely. Buckle up."

Amy and Greg Miller's Duplex
Oakland Hills
Oakland, CA

WITHIN FORTY-FIVE MINUTES, SARAH AND THE
kind woman pulled up at Amy and Greg's house. Sarah's
heart pounded with joy. She gripped the door handle.

"Is this where your husband is?" the woman asked.

"Yes." Sarah opened the car door.

"No wonder you're all smiles."

She thanked the woman and extracted herself and
her belly from the car with a grunt.

"I can walk you to the front door, if you like."

"That won't be necessary. I'm fine."

"Well, okay then."

Sarah shut the car door and crunched across the

gravel to the porch. The kind woman didn't drive away until Sarah was at the front door. Sarah waved and the woman drove off.

Butterflies fluttered in her stomach. Would Carl still be attracted to her? Was that something amnesia could erase?

She took a deep breath. Enough worrying.

She knocked.

Carl answered. He stood there, drinking her in with his eyes, as a man too long in the desert. She grabbed him and kissed him with all her pent-up passion. The eight and a half months she spent missing him, the days she spent needing him, the nights she spent desiring him, fused into a bottle uncorked and overflowed into that one kiss.

He kissed her back, matching her fervor and need, holding her tightly, as if he didn't quite believe she was real.

When they broke from the kiss, Carl stepped back and examined her belly, giving it a loving rub. His smile made him glow with love.

"You're gorgeous," he said.

"You're not so bad yourself, kiddo." She rustled through her backpack purse. "Here. Take one of these."

He studied the small, plastic canister of medicine. "If this will make me stop imagining bombs inside briefcases, I'm all for it."

He swallowed one of the pills and pocketed the bottle.

"Come in," he grabbed her hand and led her in to the duplex.

She stepped inside and froze when she saw Holly Sampson sitting in one of the chairs. It couldn't be!

She grabbed Carl's arm. "We have to get out of here." She pulled Carl toward the door with all her strength. "She wants to kill you. She'll do anything to see you dead. Do you understand?" Her voice sounded hysterical even to herself, but she couldn't help it.

Carl resisted, standing firm.

"We have to get out of here before she kills us," she screamed. "She wants to kill you!"

"I know," he said calmly, with no trace of concern. "I know she wants to kill me."

What the hell was he talking about? He knew but he didn't flee?

"She thinks I killed her father," he said. "But I don't remember that. As long as I don't remember killing him, she has no interest in getting revenge. I know that sounds odd, but the truth is she's proved very helpful to me."

"How is that possible? That woman tortured me trying to get to you, Carl. She killed two marshals, for heaven's sake!"

Amy pulled her boys close to her and studied Holly who was sitting relaxed, legs crossed. "*You're* the woman that tried to kill Scarlett and Carl?"

Holly raised her hand in the air. "Guilty."

"Wait a second," Carl said to Holly. "You tortured her?"

Holly opened her mouth but stopped herself from saying anything. She was probably going to say how the methods of torture were waterboarding and "mere threats." She was probably going to defend herself by saying she did nothing to permanently harm Sarah. She was probably about to put her foot in her mouth and thought better of it, the bitch.

"So why are you as calm as a kitten now?" Amy asked Holly.

"Like he said, I don't get much of a thrill killing someone who doesn't remember deserving it."

"What are you talking about?" Sarah screamed. "Carl never deserved any such thing."

"He killed my father. Richard Stone."

"No, he didn't." She tugged at Carl's arm to leave. "Richard Stone was trying to kill me, so we got him arrested."

"Yes," Holly said. "He died of a so-called heart attack. But he didn't have a heart attack. He had no history of heart problems. My godfather Jonas is high up in the political chain, and he says my father was killed by Carl."

"Did your godfather say how Carl did it?" Amy said.

"He said Carl must have injected Succinylcholine in him."

"Wait a sec," Remy said. "Carl was the last person to see your father alive?"

Everyone looked at the boy, surprised he would join such a heated discussion.

Amy took Remy and Chris's hands. "Remy, maybe you and Chris should go to your room while we discuss this."

"Wait," Remy pulled his hand away and asked Holly again, "Was Carl the last person to see him?"

Sarah embraced Carl's side. No harm had better come to him. "Carl was with me when Richard was in his holding cell. There must have been other guards who saw him last."

"What does it matter?" Holly asked.

"Because Succinylcholine acts on the body right away," Remy said.

"He's right," Greg said. "The only one who could have killed him that way was the last person who saw him."

Holly looked in a daze. "That would mean…" Her lips tightened. She balled her fists. "Sarah, why was my father trying to kill you?"

"He thought I was one of the thirty-six righteous. For some reason he wanted to destroy all the thirty-six righteous to cause some huge end-of-the-world thing."

Holly cursed.

"What's wrong?" Carl said.

"My godfather was the last to see my father alive. They were always super religious. They put the 'mental' in fundamentalists. I wouldn't put it past either of them to do absurd things for the 'greater good,' even if it meant killing each other."

"So I didn't kill your father?" Carl said.

"Excuse me." Holly stormed out the front door,

slamming it behind her. Her sobbing outside was audible.

All of this was so strange.

Sarah hugged Carl from behind, holding him tighter. This had better not been a dream.

"Why is she crying, Mom?" Chris said.

"It's okay, Chris," Amy said. She stepped close to Sarah and asked with a quiet voice. "If she knows who killed her father, why is she upset that it wasn't Carl who killed him?"

Sarah replied with a whisper, so the boys might not hear. "In the process of trying to get to Carl and me, she killed two others. Innocent marshals. Before tonight, she must have thought she had a reason for killing them to get to Carl." She squeezed Carl in her arms. He squeezed back. "Now she knows there was never a reason to kill those marshals. She has to own up to the fact that she's a murderer."

"She confessed the same thing to me." Carl turned to face her. "Now tell me how I can't be guilty for killing Deutsch."

Baby kicked. She sucked in a breath. "I need to sit," she said.

"Remy," Amy said, "get a pillow for Scarlett."

"On it." He raced out of the room.

In moments, she sat on the couch with them in the living room, a cushy pillow rolled up at the curve of her back.

Carl held her hand, cozied up to her. "Dear wife, please tell me how I can't be guilty for killing Deutsch."

She nodded, loving his warm body next to hers, and explained how the timer for the AC in the hotel suite made the cold temperature delay the body's decay. The injection of a substance that increased the body's ATP slowed the decay even further. The melting block of ice in the aquarium pulled the thermostat's lever with a fishhook, increasing the room temperature to stage hot conditions. When the coroner came to estimate the time of death, his conclusion was based on a constantly hot temperature of the room, not on a changing room temperature.

Carl listened leaning in. Amy and Greg had their mouths open, slack-jawed. The boys accompanied her explanation with "Whoa!" and "Cool!"

There was something else in Carl's look of wonder. It was loving admiration. She got goose bumps and grinned. Her family was back together. Now she needed to ensure it stayed that way.

Amy and Greg Miller's Duplex
Oakland Hills
Oakland, CA

How did I get so lucky to marry such a smart, gorgeous woman? What were the chances?

A flash of a memory hit me: A long string of letters and numbers from when I started working at Caldwell's campaign office.

I squeezed Sarah's arm.

"I think I know where the evidence of Aiden Caldwell's brutal fun is."

"What are you talking about?" she said.

That's right. None of them, except Holly, knew what Aiden's extracurricular activities were.

I told them I worked at Caldwell's campaign office

and witnessed his hidden, cruel nature. Because of the evidence I had on him, he wanted me out of the picture, even if it meant sending someone to my jail cell to kill me. I explained how the amnesia was a blessing to my safety because I'd forgotten all about Caldwell's horrid hobby and had forgotten that I kept a stash of evidence against him. Then after I figured out where I worked, I returned to the campaign headquarters and witnessed Caldwell torturing Seamus. When Caldwell left, Seamus told me about the evidence I'd been accumulating.

"Why would Aiden Caldwell let you see him torture Seamus again if he counted on your amnesia to keep it a secret?" Greg asked.

"I don't think he knew I had amnesia, so he kept it business as usual."

"But if he knew you were holding evidence against him," Amy said, "why would torturing Seamus in front of you be safe? Wouldn't he risk you going against him all over again?"

She had a point. Caldwell's actions didn't make sense. I tried to see how having me witness his brutality could benefit him, but no sensible reason came to light.

I shrugged. "I really don't know."

"Anyhow, continue your story," Greg said.

I told them how Holly and I saved Seamus, and that the key I thought would lead to the evidence didn't.

"But now I think I know where the hidden evidence is," I said. "If we get our hands on it and release it,

Caldwell will have no more reason to hurt me. The evidence will be out there."

"Where is it?" Sarah threaded a strand of her blonde hair behind her ear. "Do you need a key to unlock it?"

"The answer to your first question, it's right here." On my phone, I showed her the picture of the ewe with the caption, "Nappy Ewe Here."

She scrutinized the image, then turned to me. "Are you trying to be funny?"

Chris twisted my wrist to get a closer look at the image. "A sheep?" he asked.

"It's a ewe," Remy said.

"No, it's not," Chris huffed. "That looks nothing like me."

Remy rolled his eyes.

"Not 'you,' " Remy said. "A ewe. E-W-E. Ewes are female sheep."

Amy put her hand on her hip. "I hate to break it to you, but that's not Aiden Caldwell. Though I do see the resemblance."

"It's steganography," I said. "Hidden text is embedded in an image. The more text there is, the bigger the image. I coded this image with text that will help us find the evidence we're looking for." Evidence made up of disturbing pictures and video footage.

Sarah scowled. "How are we supposed to find the text that was encoded in that image?" she said.

"I have an app that does that." Remy hopped from foot to foot, excited. "You can convert text into an image, then convert the image back into text. There are also online sites that can do it."

"Would you do the honors?" I handed Remy my phone.

"Cool." Remy grinned and tapped one-handed all over the screen.

Chris sidled beside him and watched with wonder.

"I don't understand," Greg said. "How is this evidence? Is it a transcription or something?"

"Done." Remy held up the phone. "It's a web address."

"To what website?" Sarah said.

"To an online storage site," Remy said.

The website address was a long string of letters and numbers, just as I remembered in that flash of a memory I had moments ago.

Sarah peered over my shoulder, Amy looked over my other shoulder, and Greg held back the ravenous boys who were eager to see what they were not allowed to see. I copied the long website address from the text and pasted it into the web browser. The online file storage page came up and asked me to login with a username and password.

Terrific. This I didn't remember. Thanks amnesia.

"What do I do?" I asked to whoever was open to giving a suggestion.

"Try the link that says 'lost username or password.'" Sarah said.

I did. The screen said, "Your password has just been sent to your email."

"There you go," Amy said. "Check your email and Bobina's your transgender aunt."

"What's my email?"

"You don't have an email," Sarah said. "You were always too paranoid about people tracking us down that way."

"Yeah, well, it's not hard to track someone down based on when they last used their email," I said in my defense.

"I thought you had amnesia," Amy said.

"I never forgot the how-stuff-works info."

"So where are we going to get the user name and password?" Sarah asked.

Hmm. What would I do if I were me?

Before my amnesia, I must have had a system for setting up online accounts. If I avoided getting an email account unless absolutely necessary, why would I give in and set one up? Only one answer came to mind. For work.

I checked the website of Caldwell's campaign.

"What are you doing?" Sarah asked.

"Checking the format of email addresses for Caldwell's contacts."

Under the staff page, the pattern was the same: the first initial and last name. On the sign in page for the campaign site, I typed in the email:

ekrieg@Caldwellforsenate.com

"Now the password," I mumbled.

"Give me the phone," Sarah said. "I think I can guess it."

"How?" I handed it to her.

"You're a romantic, Carl. You may not think so, but I know it."

"So what do you think the password is?" Amy asked.

"My real first name and the year we met." She typed, then frowned. "Didn't work."

"I probably wanted odd characters in the password. Try the full date we met, the day, month, and year divided by hyphens."

She tapped the screen, waited, then shook her head.

Wait a sec. I had it. "Try Sophia again, but zero instead of o, one instead of i, and the at sign instead of a." It would read s0ph1@.

She typed. "Yes! We're in!"

She gave the phone back to me and there was the storage site's username and password reminder at the top of the email messages list. I opened it and shook my head. My user name was "end-of-pi."

I never would have guessed that.

I reset my password, navigated back to the online file site, and logged in. "I'm in," I said. There were two folders, one marked Caldwell, the other untitled.

I opened the Caldwell folder. Images of Caldwell torturing Seamus came up. There were also videos I didn't care to watch.

"This is it," I said. "This is what we need to stop Aiden Caldwell."

Amy and Greg Miller's Duplex
Oakland Hills
Oakland, CA

I reassured Sarah and the others of their safety when Holly returned to the house, washed up in the restroom, and sat silent in the living room's large armchair. In my hand, the phone buzzed. I checked the display. It was Alessandra.

"Who's that?" Sarah asked.

"The pizza I ordered."

"You ordered pizza for breakfast?" Chris cheered.

I shook my head no. "It's Alessandra."

"Then why didn't you just say that?" Remy rolled his eyes.

"Hi Alessandra."

"Hello, Ed." A man's voice. Not Alessandra's.

The voice sounded familiar but I couldn't place it. "Who is this?"

"It's me, Ed. You're helpful hand, your team worker."

I got a chill. "Lance? What have you done with Alessandra?"

Holly scowled and mouthed, "Who's Lance?"

I shook my head and quieted her by holding up my hand.

"Tell you what, Ed," Lance said. "Seamus told me you have certain images that might not help our friend Caldwell in his race for Senator. Now that Seamus's no longer around to cause trouble, that just leaves you."

What happened to Seamus? Did he go on a trip?

"Where's Alessandra?" I asked.

"What happened, Ed? Did you have a girl named Sophia Patai who died and now Alessandra's your new girlfriend?"

Even if his information was skewed, how did he know so much?

"I don't have a girlfriend," I said.

"Then you won't mind if I take out Alessandra's tongue with a carving knife."

I clutched the phone. "Christ, Lance, what is it you want?"

"I want the end of the existence of the evidence. None of this 'here's a copy' crap. I want it gone from this world — destroyed. Is that clear?"

"I don't know where it is," I lied.

He paused. "What the hell is that supposed to mean?"

"I just forgot, okay? I have amnesia and now I don't know much of anything."

"That's a strange card to pull, Ed. But I think I know what you're asking."

Asking? I wasn't asking anything.

"I'll give you more than just an hour. I'll give you the rest of today to get the evidence and I'll meet you at Fort Point."

"You'll bring Alessandra?"

"Of course. I'll need her easily accessible to extinguish the life from her if you don't fulfill your end."

Damn him.

"Be at Fort Point tonight at eight o'clock," he said.

Fort Point? That was a National Historic Site. "Won't it be closed?"

"You're resourceful. You'll find a way in."

He hung up.

I clenched my jaw.

"Who was that?" Amy asked.

I explained how Lance was holding my friend Alessandra hostage and wouldn't release her until I met with him at Fort Point that night and coughed up the evidence. I relayed that he intended to kill her if I didn't fulfill my end of the bargain.

Sarah bit her lip and put her hand on her belly. She was due any day now. Having to deal with this threat was probably the last thing she wanted to focus on. "So what are we going to do?" she said.

"I'm going to compile this evidence, first of all."

"And give it to him?"

"No. I'm going to hold a press conference and expose it to everyone."

Amy and Greg Miller's Duplex
Oakland Hills
Oakland, CA

As we sat on the couch, we ate a delivery pizza for brunch. It took a bit of time for me to explain my next steps. I scrutinized Sarah and Amy to see if they understood my plan. Greg, Holly, and the boys were playing a call-and-response guessing game.

Holly's wide eyes expressed excitement. "I spy with my little eye something green."

"Hoppy the Hippo!" Chris retrieved a stuffed hippopotamus from the corner of the room.

"Hoppy's gray, not green," Remy rolled his eyes.

"He's green when he's sea-sick," Chris said.

Holly and Greg looked at each other and laughed. How long had it been since she smiled or laughed?

Sarah took out her phone. "I think we need to bring someone else into this if we want to make sure your plan works." She dialed a number. "Hello, Detective? This is Sarah. Here's the man himself." She handed me her phone.

"Carl?" The voice said.

"Who is this?"

"It's Detective Graff."

I remembered the voice. Memories filled in some missing pieces of who she was and how she'd helped me and Sarah start our new life together with the Witness Security Program. She was the woman in the picture on Officer Elizabeth Cheung's desk.

"Detective Bobbie Graff," I said, filled with relief.

"What happened to you?"

"Detective, it's good to hear your voice. I'm in a bit of a pickle, but I guess you realized as much."

"You know, Carl, being accused of murder is getting to be old hat by now. I've come to expect it. How can I help you?"

I remembered that she helped me get past airport security while armed, she helped me stop Holly's father from killing Sarah, it hardly seemed fair for her to help me again, but when it came to catching criminals, that was what she did.

"I want to hold a press conference today, around two o'clock, and expose Aiden Caldwell."

"Expose the man running for senator?"

"Yes." I explained the evidence we had on Aiden Caldwell's secrets and how much trouble Alessandra was in.

"Once the evidence is out there," I said, "Caldwell and his henchmen will have no reason to keep Alessandra."

"I'm not so sure, Carl. They kidnapped Alessandra. Maybe she's seen their faces. They might kill her to make sure she doesn't testify against them."

Damn, she had a point.

"No," I said finally. "If we out Caldwell as a torturer and kidnapper, and all of us know he's holding Alessandra hostage, killing her would only worsen his sentence. He won't have her killed. He's too smart for that."

"I hope you're right," Detective Graff said. "So you want a press conference. Why all the pomp and circumstance? Why not just have me drop off the photos to the papers? Think the press would spend time analyzing the photos to make sure they were genuine?"

"Exactly. Time is the one thing I do not have. By holding the press conference, the news won't be able to resist a story of myself, an accused killer, accusing Aiden Caldwell of his crimes with photos to back it up."

"I get it. The sensationalism of it all is enough to guarantee the story to be broadcast on most news stations immediately. It'll go viral online."

"Right. The news won't be about the images, the news will be that a suspected criminal is accusing the very senator-elect he once worked for. So will you help me?"

"I'll call the stations for you and set up the meet. Two o'clock this afternoon?"

"That's right."

"That's cutting it close. Where do you want to hold it?"

"Where's the best place to maximize their interest?" I asked.

"You can… Well, no."

"What were you going to say?"

"You can rent out a conference room at the top of the TransAmerica Building," she said. "There's a three-sixty degree view of San Francisco. I hear it's pretty spectacular."

"That sounds good, actually."

"Here's the problem, though. There's no press or video allowed there."

"That strikes that option out." I pictured the press dying to get footage from the top of the building. "No, wait, I changed my mind. Let's do it."

"What do you mean?"

"Just imagine it. The suspect of murdering David Deutsch will reveal all about Caldwell's nefarious acts, but only to select bloggers not affiliated with the press. How do you think the press will react if they heard I was offering that?"

"They'd do everything they could to sneak up there and get the scoop so that they didn't miss out on an exclusive."

"Exactly. How much is the conference room?"

"A pretty penny."

"I'll scrape up the funds."

"A very pretty penny."

Yikes. "I'll get some help with the scraping."

"The office in charge of the building normally wants advance notice to reserve the room, but I know a guy," Graff said. "I'm pretty sure we can get the room today."

"Perfect."

"And I'll leak to the press about bloggers getting a scoop to your story," she said.

"Thanks. Hopefully, Caldwell's campaign crew won't get wind of my news conference. Wouldn't want them showing up and raining on our parade."

"Oh, there's only a slim chance they won't find out. In case they do hear about the news conference, I know how we can be better prepared."

Graff hung up to work on contacting bloggers, and I researched everything I could about the top floor of the TransAmerica Building.

69

A Construction Site
Somewhere in Oakland, CA

ALESSANDRA AWOKE WITH A THROBBING IN HER
nose. Was it broken?

She squinted at the daylight. Lying on cold cement, she glanced around with effort. The airy, skeleton frame of the building was a wreck, like it had been torn down and was being rebuilt. No walls, just the cement ground and ceiling with side beams in the corners. The fresh breeze was welcome. She was on what, the second floor? Third floor? The view without walls looked out upon the rooftops of residential buildings, the kinds of rooftops she'd seen when riding an elevated BART train through Oakland. She was on some high-up floor. But that was all she knew.

Her captor wasn't around. The cute guy — who was now a monster as far as she was concerned — had been replaced by two armed men standing several feet away, chatting, their guns holstered.

Her nose hurt like hell. Did her captors even care?

"Can I get some ice for my nose?" Ugh. Her throat was dry. Perhaps she could suck on a piece of ice.

One of them approached, a guy with eyebrows raised so high, it was like he was asking if something was wrong?

He leaned down. "You have pain in your nose?"

If he had to ask, then maybe the injury didn't look as bad as it felt.

"Yes," she said.

"You need something to take your mind off the pain?"

"Any kind of pain reliever would be great."

"How's this?" He kicked her in the gut. The pain billowed and consumed her whole body. She clutched her stomach "I bet you don't even notice the pain in your nose now."

Damn that sonofabitch.

70

TransAmerica Building
San Francisco, CA

AT ONE O'CLOCK, I STOOD BESIDE DETECTIVE
Graff in the single elevator that climbed to the 48th
floor of the TransAmerica Building — the top floor.
Hopefully, Graff had contacted enough bloggers and
online press so that actual mainstream press heard about
it and showed. The problem was, to look like regular
bloggers, the big-time press would be dressed as if they
weren't press, so I wouldn't be able to tell.

As planned, Sarah stayed at Amy and Greg's house.
There was no point in risking any connection made
between her and myself.

Graff and I were an hour early to plan the presenta-
tion a bit. It cost me an extra wad of cash since the

conference room was priced per hour, but the price wasn't so absurd, after all. I thought the price was going to be like renting Disneyland. Instead, it cost about a quarter of a monthly salary per hour. Greg and Amy were gracious enough to front the money.

At the top floor, I spun around admiring how the Golden Gate Bridge shone bright orange from the height of one of San Francisco's giants. The bay sparkled and its islands waved at me. We were lucky. Most of the time, the city was shrouded with fog, but on this fine winter's day, she was bathed in full sun.

The conference room took up the whole top floor with the elevator and stairwell in the center. The room was already set up audience style, with rows of chairs eight deep. I stood on the podium at the single lectern and tapped the mic to test it. It was on.

I'd play the guy wanting to get the exclusive out on the Internet by addressing bloggers, the "most trusted" source of news today. With some of my thoughts on how news spun their stories to manipulate public opinion, calling bloggers "most trusted" wouldn't feel like much of a stretch.

My jacket was getting hot. Graff didn't look like she was breaking a sweat in hers. She must have been used to it.

As the hour approached, people arrived in casual wear — sweatpants, T-shirts, short-sleeved button ups — but some of them had hairstyles so clean-cut, they looked ready to be on mainstream news. I couldn't say I was dressed for the occasion. I had on a windbreaker. Not exactly what a speaker wears at a press conference.

The room was set up for about sixty people. Over eighty people came. Standing room only at the back.

I adjusted the mic closer to my lips.

"First off, I want to remind everyone that video footage is not allowed in the room." I hid my smile in a grimace. My reminder seemed to be a cue to sneak smartphones at strategic angles to film me without looking like they were doing it.

Then it seemed as if the party was over before it began. Four men in black suits popped out of the elevator, flashed badges, and shouted. "Everyone out. Bomb alert."

Dammit!

One of them rushed to the far wall and threw open the fire door. He waved people out. The bloggers and other news people shuffled toward the stairs. What was going on?

Then I recognized one of the black suits by the elevator. Howard Lichtman, that red welt on his windpipe where I had punched him in jail. He now had his gun aimed at me.

"Don't move, Ed," Howard shouted. The two others standing beside him pointed their guns at me as the last one kept waving the visiting bloggers through the fire door. All four of them wore ear buds.

Graff stood in front of me and held out her badge. "Berkeley Police, what's this all about?"

"You better get out of here, officer," Howard said.

"This man has a bomb rigged to go off here somewhere."

"I've been privy to his whereabouts for the past week, and I've been with him for the past twenty-four hours. He hasn't been anywhere near here since an hour ago. I've been with him the whole time."

Howard touched his ear bud, as if listening carefully to instructions. "But sir." Howard paused, then said, "Yes, sir."

Howard shot Graff in the chest. She gasped, crumpled to my feet, clutching her chest. No!

My legs shook, urging me to run.

"Hold your fire," Howard instructed the other men. "We're taking this man alive." He said to me, "Now just relax, Ed." He slowly holstered his gun. The others lowered their weapons. "We're not here to hurt you."

"Good." I ran at him and punched him in the wind-pipe again.

The other men rushed at me. I outpaced them to the stairwell in the center of the room. As soon as I passed through the door, I cursed. The stairwell only went up into the hidden guts of the building.

Up I went.

The stairs were only one flight. At the top, I took the corridor, which led to another corridor, which led to another. I followed the maze and pushed through an exit door. The door opened to the top of the building's pyramid. Crap. Talk about painting one's self into a corner.

Okay. Where exactly was I and where could I go to

get away from Caldwell's men? I had thought the tip of the pyramid was constructed of solid cement, but the pyramidal roof was actually a spacious hollow shell made of aluminum walls. I felt like I was inside a hollow Egyptian pyramid. Two ways led to the tip of the pyramid: a center ladder and a Z-shaped fire-escape-type stairway. The steel Z-shaped stairway lined the angled walls.

I climbed the Z-shaped staircase. Damn, the steps were steep. I had to pull myself up by the handrail to climb each step. The higher I went, the closer I came to the pinnacle of the pyramid, the glass beacon that lit up the San Francisco's night skyline.

I checked below me. I was five or six stories high within the pyramid's aluminum tip. So high up, my head spun. Two of the men in black climbed the center ladder. Howard and one of the goons pursued me up the stairs. Howard eyed me and rubbed his throat. I climbed higher, my leg muscles aching at the workout.

What the hell was I thinking? How could I escape once I reached the top?

"There's nowhere to go, Ed," Howard the observant said. "Just stop this nonsense and come down."

I climbed higher, the walls of the pyramid literally closing in on me the closer I got to the top. Below me was a head-spinning view of the pyramid's inner steel skeleton. I gripped the handrail. Howard and one other were in close pursuit of me on the stairs that lined the wall. The two remaining men climbing up the center ladder kept climbing to get closer to the same height as me. At some point, the ladder would meet with the stairwell I was on, like two converging roads.

Huffing, I heaved myself up and up what had to be the equivalent of about ten stories. I was so close to the top, the stairwell ended and the only way to climb higher was to use the center ladder, the same one two of the men were already climbing. Below me, they climbed closer.

Nowhere to go but up.

The ladder led to a square hole in the ceiling.

I climbed through the square hole and reached the absolute top of the Transamerica Pyramid. The Crown Jewel. The glass beacon was also shaped like a pyramid but was the size of a cubicle. A giant lamp inside occupied most of the room. It was used to light up the tip of the building as a warning for planes. Since it was the middle of the day, the lamp was off.

Maybe I could fight them with something. What was nearby?

I scanned the room.

An open shoebox with wires sat squat against the wall.

Crap, was that what I thought it was?

I checked the device: a digital timer perched on top of multiple bricks of C-4 counted down. A bomb? Really? Did Caldwell tell Howard to scare everyone away by pretending there was a bomb and didn't tell him there truly was a bomb set to go off? Maybe Caldwell considered these men expendable.

The red numbers flashed down one second at a time

as if to mock me. Two minutes left. There was a rainbow assortment of wires whose colors Disney would have been proud of. They might have been trip wires, placed there to detonate the bomb if cut. This wasn't a bomb with simple circuitry.

What could I do?

I'd studied some of the building structure. The good news was that if I jumped out, it wouldn't be a straight drop, it would be at an angle, the angle of the pyramid.

The bad news was the angle was about eighty degrees which wasn't much better than ninety degrees.

The other good news was that the windows of the building could pivot all the way around, so that window-washers inside could just spin the windows to clean the outside of the window.

The bad news was I had no clue whether they were cleaning the windows now. The chances of there being a window partly open on the drop down were pretty slim.

More bad news — before reaching any of the windows, I had to navigate over a hundred feet of a drop along the aluminum side of the top of this pyramid.

Even more bad news, the only way I could get out of here was by breaking this super strong glass that was designed to withstand storms, winds, and earthquakes.

I checked the bomb's timer. One minute and four seconds.

What to do?

If I could find a way to break the glass, slide down the aluminum tip of the pyramid at a controlled speed, navigate toward an open window near the top of the building, then I should be able to get by without too many scrapes.

That was one big if.

I checked for something incredibly sharp and strong to break the glass. The glass had a chicken wire mesh embedded inside it, so once I broke through, I'd need to cut the wire. If I cut a long enough strip of the wire, perhaps I could use it to lower myself down from the top to the first row of windows over a hundred feet below.

Twenty seconds left.

Howard and his team were about two stories below me trudging up the ladder. No way could I cut through this glass and wire mesh in time. Arrgh.

What would Jesus do? Unfortunately, turning the bomb into wine was outside my capabilities.

Ten seconds left.

I picked up the bomb and shouted down at them, "Heads up."

I dropped the bomb down the square ladder hole. Crouched at the other side of the glass-encased room. Closed my eyes and plugged my ears.

The blast shook me. Men shrieked.

The glass sides shattered around me. The steel floor beneath me heated. Crap. I had to get off the floor.

I tucked my hands inside my sleeves. The steel floor got hotter. I stood and clung to the bare wires where the glass had once been. The wind was strong, the wires cool. My sneakers were thick enough to protect me from the hot floor, for now. I lifted my legs one at a time to see how they were faring. The melted soles lifted off gooey like hot cheese.

The cubicle-sized room shifted. It tilted and bent, rolling onto one side. Oh crap. The wall's wire mesh I clung to became the ceiling. The heat of the blast must have weakened the aluminum walls. As the floor tilted further, I clung to the wire like monkey bars on a playground. My fingers couldn't hold my weight anymore. I slid down the steep floor at about an angle of sixty degrees. I grabbed onto the square hole that led to the ladder. Peering through, there was a lot of twisted metal down there. The entire aluminum shell was leaning off to one side. No fire though. The whole place was steel and aluminum, nothing to burn.

Many of the pieces of the pyramid's aluminum wall had blown off. The cold air cooled and hardened the partially melted steel stairs and ladder back to solid. There was no sign of Howard or the others.

This tiny room, the glass beacon known as the Crown Jewel, whined and squeaked threats of twisting and tilting further, opening like the lid of a flip-top lighter. My mouth went dry. I needed to get down before the building had any say in it.

I clambered down the ladder into the pyramid. The ladder leaned more horizontal than vertical and its rungs were monkey bars I had to swing across. I peered deeper below into the darkness, and could make out a few bodies at the base of the pyramid's shell.

Finally my feet could get under me as I reached the part of the ladder that went vertical again.

"Carl, you okay?" A female voice called up to me. It was Graff.

"Yeah. You? You were the one that got shot," I called back.

"I think I broke a rib, but it'll heal."

"Like you said, it's always wise to wear a bulletproof vest when hanging out with me."

"Yep. Think you can make it back down here?"

"Working on it." I studied my progress. About two more flights of ladder to go. Still dizzying.

I finally reached her. Boy, it was hot! I took off my windbreaker.

I then removed the bulletproof jacket. "These things are like a stalker's breathing." She had already taken off hers.

"A stalker's breathing?"

"Yeah," I said. "Hot and heavy. Come on. Let's get out of here."

Felt good wearing just a T-shirt and jeans again. Much cooler.

71

A Construction Site
Somewhere in Oakland, CA

ALESSANDRA SQUEEZED HERSELF IN A FETAL position on the cement floor. The pain from the gunman's kick eased a bit. The two men stood several feet away laughing over some joke the kicker made.

The pain in her nose and gut still throbbed. All that mattered now was ending the pain. What about her clients? Some of them loved pain. They got a rush from it. How had they dealt with pain that was too much? Most of them used the same method.

She tried it. She breathed in and out with deep, steady breaths. She relaxed her body as best she could, letting herself melt on the cold floor. The pain in her gut diminished. She visualized lying on the beach, watching the waves come in, counting them. One, two. The ocean breeze felt real, cool against her face. Three, four. The salty air smelled delicious, refreshing. Five, six.

Counting helped take her mind off the pain. What else could she count?

Lying on the ground, she studied the guy who kicked her, specifically his sneakers. She followed his footsteps and counted the eyelets for the laces.

It was working. She almost didn't feel the pain. It was just a nagging sensation, like a child tugging at a skirt to get her mother's attention.

She pushed herself upright and brushed her hair out of her face.

"Well, hello." The kicker stepped up to her. "Miss Sleeping Beauty has awoken. Does Sweeping Beauty want some wittle pain welievuh?"

She wavered as if ready to fall back to the floor.

Focus on his shoes. They were close now. Count the eyelets.

With her left hand, she touched each eyelet as she counted.

"One, two, three…"

He stood his ground, letting her touch his sneaker. "What are you doing?"

"I'm counting the holes in your shoe. Twelve, thirteen, fourteen. You have fourteen holes." She spoke softer. "You have fourteen holes in your shoe."

He moved his leg back as if ready to kick her again.

She reached to his hip and snatched his holstered gun. He jumped on top of her, flattening her onto the cement, and knocked the wind out of her. The weapon was sandwiched between their bellies, pointed at their feet. If she got a shot off, she might hit herself instead of him. At this point, it was worth the risk. She tried to fire the weapon. The trigger wouldn't budge. Shit. Maybe the safety was on. Where were safety buttons on guns?

He clamped his hands around hers. She ran her fingers around the side of the gun. Something clicked. She squeezed the trigger.

Pop!

The man yelped and clutched his foot.

"That's fifteen," she said.

As Kicker stood and hopped away on one foot, she pointed the gun at the other man. He had a hand on the hilt of his gun.

"Sure you want to do that?" she said. "The good news is that if I do shoot you, I'll shoot you in the leg so as not to kill you. The bad news is I may be a lousy shot and your leg is connected to your crotch."

He put his hands in the air, and backed up to the stairwell.

"Yeah, you better run while you still have feet."

Kicker fell to the ground.

"You shot me!" He held his foot and moaned.

She struggled to stand up, gripping the gun in her hand, and staggered closer to him. "Sorry about that. Do you need help?"

"Yes, dammit!"

She shot his other foot. "That should take your mind off it."

She teetered to the stairwell. First task was to get out of this awful place.

72

TransAmerica Building
San Francisco, CA

I HELPED GRAFF DOWN THE MAIN FIRE EXIT
stairwell and we passed two wheezing firemen marching
up.

"Walk down these stairs as quickly and safely as you
can," the older fireman said to us.

Did he think I had plans to practice somersaults?

We continued our journey. Let me tell you, walking
down forty-eight flights is not an easy task. At the
bottom floor we were met by fire trucks, police cars, and
ambulances. At least, that's what I suspected those
flashing lights came from. It was hard to tell with all the
people hanging around filming the whole thing.

Everyone leaving the building was met by police

officers who pointed to first responders to follow. The officers also waved at the bystanders. "Clear the area. The top of the building could fall."

The office workers who had been inside the building were escorted a block away to safety where they could be questioned for the answers they didn't know and treated for the injuries none of them had.

I went with a couple of firemen to help Graff to an ambulance.

A police officer approached me. "What's your name, sir?"

Giving my Ed Krieg name to a police officer was not the best idea. I was still a suspect for Deutsch's murder.

"Carl Best," I said instead.

He scrutinized me, then relaxed. "Mr. Best, would you mind answering a few questions to sort out what happened inside?"

"Sure." I had the most information of what happened, maybe I could help them shed some light on it. And maybe I could also get their help with getting the word out about Aiden Caldwell's secret since the press conference had been a bust.

"You'll be okay?" I asked Graff.

"I'll be fine. Go. I'll work on confirming Deutsch's actual time of death to clear you. Finish what we planned."

"You betcha." I followed the officer.

The police officer led me to a black Crown Victoria. Probably an undercover cop car.

"I'd like to ask you questions in here, if you don't mind," he said.

A man in a suit held open the passenger door.

My mind was a whirlwind of concerns. Was Graff's injury as minimal as she said? Were Caldwell's goons putting Alessandra through any horrors?

I ducked into the back seat. The man who opened the door for me followed me in. I found myself between two men in suits. The one inside pulled a gun on me.

Damn. Right into a trap. The car steered away from the scene.

"Good to see you, Mr. Krieg."

I had to do a double take because he looked a lot like Justin Bieber, saccharine pop star of the early part of this century.

"I can't say the feeling's mutual," I said.

"We won't take offense. Give me your phone." He held out his palm. I shook it. He yanked his hand away. "Your phone." He held out his palm again.

I handed it over. *We won't take offense?* Strange that he used "we" instead of "I". If he had been in charge of this plan, he would have said "I". Since he said "we," he must have been hired to pick me up.

The car drove past several piers near the bay.

"Let me guess," I said. "You work for Aiden Caldwell."

The one on the other side of me without the weapon said, "How the hell did you—?"

"Shut up, Gabe." The armed guy pressed the muzzle into my arm. As if that would get me to stop talking.

I turned my back on him and faced Gabe.

"So Gabe, when you signed up for this, did you know you'd be kidnapping and be complicit in holding an innocent man at gunpoint?"

"I…" Gabe squirmed. The faux leather squeaked.

"Gabe," I said. "With every mile we go, you get deeper and deeper into trouble with the law. Is that what you signed up for?"

"Shut up," the armed Justin Bieber said.

I saw the wedding ring on Gabe's finger.

"Think about it, Gabe," I said. "You could be the hero. I bet you're one of Caldwell's security guards. If so, you must also have a weapon. You could make your wife proud and help me out."

"What are you talking about?" Gabe asked.

"Don't listen to him, Gabe," the armed Justin said behind me.

"All you have to do," I said, "is point your weapon at the driver, force him to pull over, and let me out."

"Yeah," Gabe said. "That's not going to happen."

"Aren't you worried about what your wife might think if she finds out you're a criminal?"

Gabe pulled out his handgun and pointed it at my chest.

"She cares more about my nice shiny income than she does about what I do on the job," he said.

Crap.

———

AT THE DIRT road three blocks away from the construction site where she had been held, Alessandra patted her dress pocket. Empty, of course. No phone. And no purse. Great. The kidnappers must have thrown it when they took her.

She put out her thumb.

Six cars passed her. So strange. Usually, the first car that passed would stop for her. Didn't matter if the driver was a man or woman, no one could resist "all this."

She looked down at her "all this." Her saffron dress was tattered and soiled. A few drops of blood splotched the fabric. The sight of the blood directed her attention to the pain she was in. She clutched her nose with one hand and her stomach with the other. She was probably not the best depiction of Venus emerging from a clamshell.

When a seventh car came, it pulled over. She went to the car door and peered in to see how honest-looking the face was. Not that her safety barometer was working well, considering how handsome her kidnapper had been.

The driver was a teenage girl, prettier than herself. Way too much mascara, but it worked for her face.

Alessandra climbed in.

"Thank you for stopping."

"You all right, Ma'am?"

That's how it always was. Older men called her miss and teens called her ma'am.

"I just need a hospital and I'll be fine. Know where the nearest one is?"

"Just a sec." She tapped her phone's screen. "Just three point four miles from here."

"Thanks. You drive, I'll sleep."

The vibrations lulled her exhausted body into a grateful slumber.

73

Fisherman's Wharf
San Francisco, CA

AIDEN CALDWELL'S GOONS TOOK ME TO TOURIST-
congested Fisherman's Wharf and double-parked by a
line a taxies and a pier full of ferries.

"If you don't try anything," the armed celebrity
doppelganger said, "we won't shoot you."

They holstered their weapons. I kept my hands
visible and slowly exited the car.

Once outside, I shouted, "Oh my lord! It's Justin
Bieber! Can I shake your hand, Justin Bieber?"

I grabbed both his hands and shook them like I was
happy to see him, when in fact I was making sure he
wouldn't go for his weapon.

"Justin Bieber! What an honor!"

A crowd rushed toward us and joined in the festivities. They delighted in reaching for his hands and asking for his autograph.

In the excitement, I slipped through the crowd and left the two goons to deal with their newfound celebrity status.

Fisherman's Wharf is an easy place to hide among a crowd.

I heard someone say, "Look out! Justin Bieber has a gun!"

Yep, Fisherman's Wharf is an easy place to hide among a crowd, but when Justin Bieber brandishes a gun, people get out of the way. Once Caldwell's men hoisted their weapons in the air, the wave of people split and the armed men chased after me with ease.

I ducked into a street-side attraction displaying life-sized figures of people being tortured. Turned out to be some sort of dungeon attraction.

The lights were low. The only lit areas were the displays of medieval tortures. The horrifying methods of torture on display made Caldwell's treatment of Seamus look like a sweet and loving experience.

Footsteps stomped toward me. I crept further into the maze of darkness.

A face stepped into a body of light. It was Gabe. He pointed his gun at me.

"Don't move."

I dashed around the corner toward other displays.

He fired a shot. The shot sounded like it hit a wall a good twenty feet away from me. Either he had the aim of a donkey drunk on cold medicine, or it was a warning shot.

I raced to the next display — a figure of a man being dunked in a cauldron of simulated boiling water — and found a dark spot to crouch in. Gabe chased after me.

He stood still. Couldn't see me.

The Bieber lookalike came from the opposite direction, flanking me without spotting where I hid.

"You didn't spot him?" Gabe asked.

"No." He glanced around, then faced my direction. "Wait a minute."

Damn.

"We see you." Bieber pointed his gun at me. "Come on out."

"I don't suppose I could request a song, first."

Gabe tugged me out by the arm.

"Yeah, I didn't think so," I said.

"Cuff him," Bieber said.

Gabe spun me around and secured a plastic zip tie around my wrists. Tight.

They took me out of the dungeon tourist attraction with my wrists tied together. The light outside made me squint. They pushed me forward and I got some looks.

"That's right, everyone," I shouted. "If you steal Justin Bieber's girlfriend, he has you arrested."

Bieber pushed me harder.

At the end of the pier, they took me to a private boat. Once onboard, a crew of three men untied the boat and we set off into the bay. It didn't take long for me to figure out where we were headed.

Alcatraz Island. The former prison.

74

Vista Heights Hospital
Oakland, CA

ALESSANDRA AWOKE IN A PASSENGER SEAT HEARING a female voice.

"Ma'am? We're here at the hospital."

She eased her head from the headrest and squinted out the window. A man in scrubs exited the building pushing an elderly woman in a wheel chair.

Her nose drummed sharp slices of pain.

Sonofabitch. That hurt. Would she be able to get to the door without passing out?

"Do you want me to help you inside?" the girl asked.

She waved off her offer. A dominatrix needing help. How humiliating would that be?

"How long have I been out?"

"About five minutes," the girl said.

"Really?" The nap felt like a full day's rest. At least some good news.

She opened the car door and eased out her aching body.

"Thanks for the ride."

"You sure you're okay?"

"Fit as a fiddle. Go on home, now." *Before I can't hold it anymore and scream in pain.*

The nice driver drove off. Alessandra started her journey to the Emergency entrance. Shit. She had to let Ed know she was safe before he put himself in danger.

Don't pass out. Don't pass out.

She navigated her way to check in, clutching her nose.

"If you could just fill these forms out for me." The receptionist handed her a clipboard and pen.

Okay. Once she finished filling them out she could borrow someone's phone to call Ed.

She filled out the paperwork and took deep breaths to reduce the pain.

Don't pass out.

She returned the clipboard with forms to the receptionist. Time to borrow a phone and call Ed.

She found a chair in the waiting room and passed out.

75

Alcatraz Island
San Francisco, CA

As the boat docked at Alcatraz Island, Gabe held my arm, probably to keep me from running away even though there was nowhere to run, and to help steady me as I got off the boat.

Man, it was cold! The wind chilled me further.

Once on firm ground, Bieber said to Gabe, "I'll take it from here."

I didn't like the sound of that.

"Can't Gabe come along? The more the merrier, right?"

"Make sure the boat's tied right," Bieber told Gabe, "and that we're prepared to receive Caldwell."

"Caldwell's coming here?" I asked.

Bieber said nothing. He took me past the blossoming rock flowers and plants. We passed a ranger station, along with all the signs you might normally see for national parks since Alcatraz was now a protected landmark, the only national park with a prison on top. No park rangers hanging around, unfortunately.

Bieber led me to the entrance of the prison, then through long corridors and prison blocks.

"Where are you taking me?" I asked.

"You've been a bad boy, Mr. Krieg. Here's what happens to bad boys."

He led me to a cell with a solid metal door, much like the one Seamus was placed in, but this one was the size of a voting booth. Solitary confinement.

"I'd rather get a spanking," I said.

He pushed me in.

"What if I need to use the gentlemen's facilities?"

He pointed to a hole in the floor and closed the door.

I had thought the dungeon attraction at Fisherman's Wharf was dark? This tiny spot was void of any light.

I sat down on the floor. The only thing to do was wait for Caldwell.

Ugh. Waiting for the time pass was excruciating. There must have been a way to make time pass faster. What if I could literally speed up time? Was that even possible? Slowing down time was possible, using space. Space and time were interconnected.

Wait. That's what I could do to make the time pass faster. Just think about crazy science stuff.

Okay. Space and time were entwined, hence the term space-time. Twist space enough and you could slow down time. Mass and electricity and magnetism all had the capability of twisting space. If gravity bends space in one direction, could we use electricity and magnetism to bend space in the opposite direction to cancel out gravity? Could we bend space so much to make anti-gravity devices?

The door opened. I squinted at the silhouette in the light.

"Mr. Krieg." It was Caldwell. "I am so sorry."

76

Alcatraz Island
San Francisco, CA

I BIT INTO THE CHEESE DANISH PASTRY AND TOOK A swig of the apple juice while Caldwell sat across from me, his guards standing nearby. He had taken me to the ranger's station and made sure I had some food in my belly. He also had his men return my phone.

He sat across from me.

"I wanted my men to find you and keep you until I had a chance to talk with you. I figured Alcatraz was a nice spot to chat without you running off. I never meant for them to actually put you in one of the cells, much less in solitary confinement."

"Yeah, well that's why communication is so important in every relationship. How did you manage to use a place like Alcatraz, anyhow?"

"Some of my friends are rangers here. They've let me hold fundraisers here on occasion." He took a breath. "Lance told me you have some video and images of my little adventures with Seamus. Is that true?"

"Yes, and if something happens to me, if I don't call my contact within two hours, my contact will be giving the information to the press," I lied.

"Now, now. I have no interest in hurting you, Mr. Krieg."

I found it interesting that he kept calling me Mr. Krieg and no longer called me Ed.

"What about Alessandra?" I asked. "Do you have any intention of hurting her?"

"Who's Alessandra?"

"The woman you kidnapped to get me to not publicize your torture games."

He blinked.

"I'm sorry, I'm not following you," he said.

"Don't mess with me, Caldwell. It was pretty cold of you to let your own guards play right into getting bombed at the top of the TransAmerica building."

He eyed me sideways. "Are you pulling my leg?"

"I've had it." I wiped my mouth and threw the napkin down onto the table. "What is it you want, Caldwell? If I give you access to delete the images and video footage of you holding Seamus hostage and torturing him, you'll let Alessandra go?"

"Now hold on a minute. I never held Seamus hostage."

I laughed. "Are you saying there was no one downstairs at the campaign headquarters chained to the wall?"

"No, I'm not denying that. But he wasn't a prisoner. He agreed to be there."

What? That made no sense. No politician as smart as Caldwell would pretend his victim wanted to be a victim.

"All right, amuse me," I said. "Why would he agree to be your prisoner?"

"It's how a sadist and masochist relationship works. We set the limits together, we make sure those limits are never crossed, and we provide each other with what we need in our lives. Safe, sane, and consensual. I thought you knew about this."

I scratched my head. Weren't sadists bad people?

"Allow me to clarify," Caldwell said. "When I was a kid, I accidentally rode my dirt bike over a squirrel. It wasn't completely dead, but it couldn't move. I did the horrific yet typical thing that boys do. I poked it with a stick to see it move. My pokes advanced to trying to break the squirrel's skin. I found myself getting an unusual rush from it and continued poking until it died. I had always had these fantasies of watching things bleed and feel pain."

I shifted in my seat. Didn't help. I was still uncomfortable.

Caldwell continued, "The next day I was so sick to

my stomach about what I had done, I couldn't go to school. I stayed in bed crying my eyes out. My mother asked me what was wrong, but I couldn't tell her. I couldn't tell anyone. Every year that passed, I fantasized more and more about hurting people, and became more and more guilty over my desire to inflict pain."

A desire to inflict pain? I knew such people existed, but it was still hard to believe.

"How did you deal with it?" I asked.

"A friend of mine helped me. He was into domination, was born with it, just like we're born with our inclination to be heterosexual or homosexual or whatever sexual preference one has. My friend said that as much as he had this innate desire to dominate, his wife had an innate desire to submit. He helped me realize that I don't have any wish to traumatize anyone, I only have the desire to inflict physical pain. Knowing that I would never hurt any person who didn't want to be hurt, I reached out to find a masochist, someone who desired to feel pain." His gaze fell to the floor. "I thought I found one in Seamus."

Seamus? A masochist? I saw no indication that he ever enjoyed it.

"Seamus didn't look like he wanted to be there."

"Like I said, we had an arrangement in advance, and, against my wishes but to the advice of my lawyer in case it ever came to court, we even put our agreement down on paper. If he ever wanted me to stop, all he had to do was say 'mercy.' I promise you, I would not have done it if I thought he didn't want it."

I paused. Those locked documents! I took out my phone and scrolled to the picture of the documents I had found hidden in his desk and studied them. The names on the bottom of the multi-paged contract were Caldwell's and Seamus's.

"Is this your contract?"

He squinted at the screen, then nodded. "Where did you get that?"

"In your locked desk. So if you never intended to hurt anyone, why did you keep this hush-hush?" I realized the answer to the question as soon as I asked it.

"While Seamus and I may have agreed to it, the public may not be as understanding."

"I get it. But why at the campaign office? Wasn't that a huge risk of being exposed?"

"Seamus's idea. My home is always surrounded by paparazzi. The curtains don't do much for my privacy. The most private room in my house is the bathroom and that's not big enough for our playtime. We considered renting a separate spot away from my house and away from the campaign office, but Seamus wanted to be sure I could spend time with him as often as I could. Lance agreed that the campaign office was the most inconspicuous place."

"You should know," I said, "I don't think Seamus was ever a masochist."

"I don't understand. Then why did he agree to such treatment?"

"He's worse than a masochist. He's a journalist who cares more about money than the truth. He saw the opportunity as a chance to get an exclusive for mucho moolah. It's why he encouraged me to help him get pictures and video footage of him in the first place. He worked for your competition, David Deutsch. He was offered ten million to get the evidence of your sadistic lifestyle. Unfortunately for Seamus, David Deutsch was killed before Seamus had the chance to collect."

Caldwell slumped in his chair, his gaze dropping to the floor, and sat in silence.

At last, he muttered, "So that was another reason why he wanted to be in the basement of the campaign office. The basement was a better place for him to find someone to befriend and claim he was being tortured." He scrutinized me. "Which leads me to ask, if you don't mind, why did you kill David Deutsch?"

"Wait. Why did you let me return to your campaign if you thought I killed David Deutsch?"

"I didn't know you were a suspect until yesterday, after you took the key. Lance never told me he got the key from you. After you took the key, he advised me not to worry about you. He said you would lay low, considering you were suspected for murder. I thought it best to not get involved, play it business as usual. Then, Lance persuaded me to find you and keep you away from the police until after the election. We didn't want to risk you releasing whatever evidence you have of my sadism until after I became senator and could defend myself with the signed agreement I had made with Seamus."

"Whatever happened to Seamus, anyway?"

"What do you mean?" he asked.

"Lance said something about Seamus being gone."

Caldwell scowled and shook his head. He didn't know.

"Anyway," I said, "now that you found me, you feel comfortable hiding me from the police?"

"You're a suspect, Ed, not convicted of any crime. I stand by all people being innocent until proven guilty."

"Especially if it serves your campaign."

He shrugged.

I glanced at the guards on either side of me, their hands on the hilts of their guns. "That's why all the security? Because I've been accused of killing David Deutsch?"

"Didn't you? I mean, let's be honest. You were the only one who was near him at the time of his death."

I filled him in on my amnesia. I also explained everything that Sophia had told me, including the method for changing the room temperature and how Deutsch was injected with a substance to slow down rigor mortis. "Whether or not you believe me, and believe that David Deutsch died before I came to his room, consider who benefited from Deutsch's death."

"That would be me. Without him in the running, I'm the shoe-in to be voted as the senator."

"Exactly, but as you know, I was working with Seamus because I thought you held him prisoner and I tried to get you out of the race. So what would be my motive for killing David Deutsch?"

"So far as I can make out, you have none."

"Exactly."

Caldwell stroked his chin.

"Why did you go to David Deutsch's room?" he asked.

"I found a letter in my apartment. The signature was illegible. It was an invitation to come over. At first I thought it was from some woman wanting a hotel fling. Just wishful thinking on my part."

"Was there anything odd about the invitation?"

"Just that it wasn't mailed in San Francisco," I said.

"What makes you say that?"

"The return address was the San Francisco hotel address while the postmark was the city of Marin, not San Francisco. It had to have been mailed in Marin."

Caldwell's lips formed a grimace.

"What's wrong?"

"Lance lives in Marin. He had to be the one who sent you there."

Everything fell into place. Lance was the puppeteer pulling all the strings. He kidnapped Alessandra, he planted the bomb to kill me and kill off Howard and his team, and he staged me as David Deutsch's murderer.

"Why do you think he would go so far in doing all this?"

Caldwell sighed.

"He has always been devoted to me," he said. "In fact, I had told him that I wanted him with me wherever I go in the ranks. If that meant I would one day be president, I wanted him with me in the White House. I thought he was loyal to me and the campaign, but perhaps he was devoted to the power he could have."

Here was my chance.

"Mr. Caldwell, my friend Alessandra is still in danger. Lance wants to meet with me tonight at Fort Point to do an exchange, Alessandra for the evidence. I had planned to go public with all the images and footage so that his hold on Alessandra would be pointless, but I see you had no part in this whole thing. Still, I wonder if you could help me get her back."

"Of course, Ed. I know just what to do. Too many have died in my name. It's time to stop this." Caldwell brushed the nonexistent dust off his grey blazer and slacks and straightened his matching pocket square.

"Thank you."

"I have to warn you, though. Lance has a friend high up. I'm not sure who it is, but with Lance's help, the police have turned a blind eye several times when I needed them to. If you're going against Lance, one thing you won't be able to count on is the police."

"Understood." I had my own police connections I could rely on.

77

Vista Heights Hospital
Oakland, CA

ALESSANDRA HAD SOME TERRIFIC PAINKILLERS AND drugs injected in her. After patching up her nose and giving her an ice pack, the nurses helped her into the waiting room where she could wait for her friends to pick her up.

Ed still needed to know she was okay.

She sat next to a large, bearded man with a shiny black eye.

"Do you think you could do a gal a big favor?"

"What's that?" His voice growled like a motorcycle engine.

"I need to make a phone call, but I lost my phone. It's a local call."

"Oh, sure." He smiled and handed her his phone. Who could ever have been mad enough at this nice man to give him a shiner?

Alessandra dialed Ed's number.

"Ed? This is Alessandra."

"You all right? Where are you?"

"I'm fine. I'm at the hospital." She gave Ed the hospital address.

"I'll send Sarah and Amy to pick you up," he said. "Stay right there, okay?"

"Happy to."

She hung up, and returned the phone.

"Can I borrow one more thing?"

"What's that?"

"Your shoulder. I'm mighty tired."

He patted his shoulder twice.

"Thanks so much."

She lay her head on his shoulder and fell asleep.

———

LANCE EXITED off the freeway into West Oakland to make a quick stop at the construction site where his men were holding the waitress. Best to check in on her, see if he could get some information out of her. Maybe she knew something about where the evidence against Caldwell was.

He took the stairs up the skeleton of the building to the third floor expecting to see Sean and Felix standing guard over the waitress. Instead, Sean was on the ground clutching his feet. The waitress and Felix were nowhere. What the hell? Did they run off together?

He strode toward Sean.

"Where's the girl?"

"She grabbed my weapon and shot me in the feet. Scared off Felix."

Dammit!

"Quick!" Sean said. "Get me to a hospital."

The tarps hanging from the steel frames fluttered in the wind. Just beyond, the rooftops of all the neighboring residences in the slums formed a landscape of cemetery-gray shingles.

He said to Sean, "What if the public discovered one of Caldwell's employees had been killed?"

"What?"

"Easier to use that death as a way to promote Caldwell's fight against crime and go for the sympathy vote."

"Lance, what in the hell are you talking—"

He shot Sean in the head.

78

Golden Gate Park
San Francisco, CA

IN THE LATE AFTERNOON, THE PRESS CONFERENCE
was held at the Music Concourse in Golden Gate Park.
Nice, cloudless sky, though still cold. Not as prestigious
a place as the TransAmerica building, but when Senator-elect Aiden Caldwell talks, the press shows up to
report everything he says. It was also near where I had
told the marshals to meet me.

Caldwell stood in front of the cameras. I listened
from the back of the crowd.

"Ladies and gentlemen of the press, it has come to
my attention that there have been some sinister and
criminal acts done all in the name of protecting my
chances of becoming senator. I say with a heavy heart

that Lance Meyler, my campaign manager, was behind these horrendous deeds and I must take responsibility for his behavior. It is for these reasons that I am dropping out of the race. I have been keeping my personal lifestyle a secret and doing so has inadvertently gotten many people hurt. It is time for me to step down and make sure no one else gets hurt. In the meantime, I've been in contact with a fine individual to see if they would be amenable to run for senator. Thank you."

A barrage of questions and the light of flashing cameras hit Caldwell, but he ignored them all and stepped down from the podium.

I went to the storage website on my phone, logged in, selected the two folders that held all the images and video footage of Caldwell with Seamus, and hit delete.

Time to meet up with the marshals, deal with Lance, and go back to my normal life of being in witness protection, whatever that normal life was like.

———

TEN MINUTES LATER, within Golden Gate Park, I found a bench near the entrance of the Japanese Tea Garden. As I waited for Sergeant Elizabeth Cheung and the two marshals, I watched tourists get trained on how to ride a Segway. Seemed pretty basic. Lean left, move left. Lean right, move right. Lean forward, move forward. Stick butt out, stop.

Sergeant Cheung approached me with two people dressed in jeans and shirts at her side. I recognized her from her desk picture. Was that what marshals wore? Shouldn't they wear suits or fancy clothes?

Maybe their whole point was not to stand out.

I liked that.

When they arrived, I stood up.

Sergeant Cheung introduced the marshals to me and I shook their hands.

We sat down on the bench, Sergeant Cheung next to me, Marshal Kelly next to her, and Marshal Hakimi at the end. I guess they didn't want me to feel crowded, so they avoided sitting on both sides of me. I liked that, too.

Hakimi and Kelly leaned forward to get a direct line with me eye-to-eye.

I addressed Cheung. "Detective Graff told you about the whole time-of-death idea?"

"She did. She's looking into it now. I haven't told my captain yet, because I want to make sure we have something solid to show him. He'll need strong evidence to be convinced, so in the meantime, it may be best to keep you out of the police department's radar."

"She's out of the hospital already? I mean, that bullet struck her vest pretty hard."

"She's a trooper," Cheung said. "I picked her up from the hospital. She was itching to get back to work. You don't need to worry about her."

I nodded and addressed the marshals.

"Can I ask who I really am, now?"

The marshals gave Sergeant Cheung a pointed stare.

She nodded, showing she got the hint.

"It sure is nice out," she said. "Think I'll take a quick stroll."

She strolled down the path, out of earshot.

"Your name was Nathan Yirmorshy," Kelly said. "When there was a risk of someone trying to kill your wife Sophia, we worked at convincing her attackers that she wasn't worth going after."

"By staging her death," I said. So far I knew all this, but it was good to hear it from multiple sources.

Kelly nodded. "But that didn't mean she was free and clear, so we gave you new IDs and a clean slate."

"I guess that means you also wiped my criminal record clean."

"You didn't have a criminal record," she said. "Just a grand larceny charge that happened after you got your new identity, but it never stuck. Now you are Carl and Sarah Best. You live in Amsterdam, New York. Then you vanished and not even your wife knew where you were."

"You know why I left?" I wanted to see how much they knew.

"Probably to stop the woman who came to kill you."

"Holly Sampson."

"Yes," Kelly said. "Have you seen her?"

"I woke up on the floor next to her when I first had my amnesia. She tried to kill me." I waved Sergeant Cheung to return. "But Holly and I worked things out."

The marshals shared a bewildered glance. Probably

thought I didn't know Holly had killed two marshals. I didn't want to get into it.

"Have I always been working for the Aiden Caldwell campaign since I arrived in San Francisco?" I asked.

Sergeant Cheung sat back down between Marshal Kelly and me. "I can answer that one. That's correct. And, as far as our records show, you're still on their payroll."

Okay. I came to the Bay Area to lure Sampson near the police district where she was most wanted, so the Berkeley Police Department could arrest her and keep her from being a threat to me. In the meantime, I got a job at Caldwell's campaign to make ends meet, and that's how I got caught up in the whole Seamus mess.

Hmm. I had an appointment with Lance tonight at Fort Point.

"Before I agree to anything, there's some business I need to take care of," I said.

"What business?" Cheung said.

"Later. First, explain to me how this would work. I turn myself in to you marshals people. You put me in a box to hide me from the police who still think I killed Deutsch?"

"It's nothing like that, Mr. Best," Hakimi said. "We'd have you stay at a safe house until we found your wife and can reunite you."

I already knew where Sarah was. She was at Amy and Greg's place. I didn't feel comfortable enough to share that info yet.

"I'd be held in a safe house?"

"Yes."

That sounded good. One problem. I didn't like being held prisoner.

I gazed at the tourists practicing their new Segway-steering skills. That was when the shooting started.

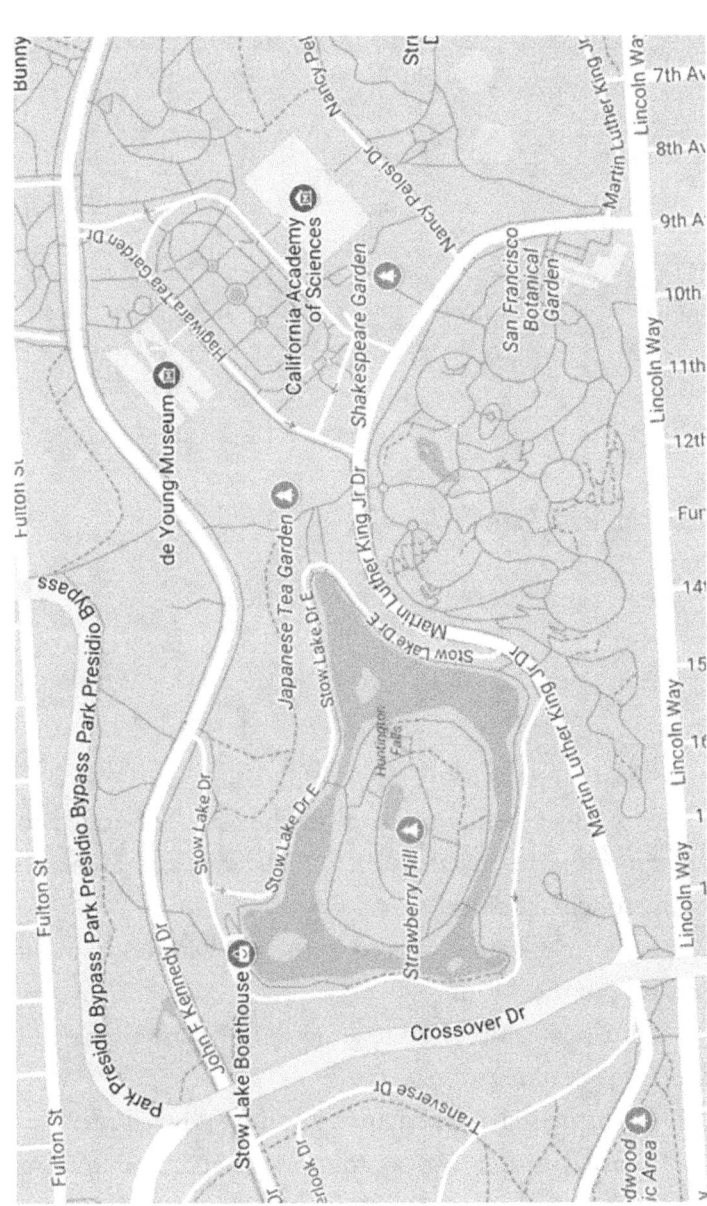

Golden Gate Park
San Francisco, CA

Pop!

Was that gunfire?

Sergeant Cheung got shot in the arm. She rolled to the ground. The marshals drew their guns and fired at a man crouched behind a tree.

Sergeant Cheung winced as she got her gun out and shouted to me, "Run!"

I hustled from the scene and the marshals helped Cheung get cover.

Unfortunately, the enemy's gunfire followed me.

I darted to the Segway tour and snatched one from a tourist. I flicked off the turtle setting, leaned in, and pushed that baby to a clip of over ten miles per hour.

Firing came from other directions. Two men in leather jackets chased after me.

I steered along a rounded path that passed between the California Academy of Science and the de Young Museum.

I looked over my shoulder. Any sign of them? No. I must have lost them.

A rumbling engine noise nearby warned me I wasn't safe. The two of them were now on motorcycles.

Not good. Motorcycles were much faster than what I was driving. But then, these motorcycles were cruisers, big clunky things that would have trouble covering different terrain.

I switched to the grass, steered toward a dirt path, and passed the Japanese Tea Garden.

They got closer. One of them fired a shot. The tree next to me was the victim of the stray bullet.

Hunched, my head between my shoulders, I drove onto Stow Lake Drive and circled Strawberry Hill.

They fired more shots at me. Thankfully the bullets whistled over my head.

Damn, they were close. I went over the rainbow-shaped bridge and followed the hiking trail on Strawberry Hill.

Not the best terrain for Segways, but worse for cruisers.

Up, up, up. Perhaps I could escape them on the bridge on the opposite side of the little island. Fortunately, only one had followed me. Unfortunately, the other attacker had crossed the opposite bridge and was coming toward me. My Segway headed straight at him. A tree swing was along my path. The attacker fired at me. I grabbed onto the swing's rope and lifted my feet off the Segway. The Segway lurched and fell into the attacker ahead of me.

I let go of the rope, landed beside a stream, and followed the stream into the woods. I came upon the top of a waterfall. Dammit. At about fifty feet away, they came after me. I hugged the foliage on the side of the waterfall and let my weight drop, grabbing onto whatever rocks and vines I could.

They shot at me. Bullets cracked into the rocks beside me. We're they trying to miss? I didn't feel like standing still to find out.

I crossed a hiker's trail and jumped into the lake filled with people in pedal boats and rowboats. The gunmen fired at me. People screamed and ducked in their boats.

If I could dive under three feet deep, the water would slow the speed of the bullets.

I propelled myself deeper into the water. Kicking down and down. I couldn't open my eyes in this muck, but I sensed the push of the water made by bullets passing me. A memory surfaced. I remembered seeing action films of bullets passing by the hero underwater. It was cool to watch at the time. Not so cool when you were living it.

My lungs weren't feeling much joy underwater. The lack of oxygen can make anyone grumpy, I suppose.

I felt a thimble-sized punch at my thigh. Had to be

a bullet. Thank you, water, for slowing down the bullet. No thank you for depriving me of oxygen.

I had to surface soon. The choice between getting fatally shot or drowning wasn't my favorite choice. I'd rather have been choosing between Bar-B-Q flavored chips and anchovy pizza.

I remembered that the lake was a donut shape around the island. I swam farther away, towards the general direction of the other side of the donut. Hard to be sure with my eyes closed. Still, had a pretty good sense of direction.

My lungs felt like they'd pop like an overblown ballon. I had to surface, dammit.

There was a mild rumbling sound. Was that an engine? With my eyes closed, I could see as well as a blindfolded jellyfish. I wasn't about to open them.

I followed the rumble sound and surfaced.

An electric boat hummed toward me. The driver navigated across the water fast, frightened by the shooting. More shots whistled past me.

I grabbed onto the side of the boat. It whisked me away. I flopped sideways in the water as I let the boat drag me along.

In a minute, the attackers on the shore were too far to shoot at me.

The helmsman, or whatever boat drivers are called, headed toward the bank. I let go and swam to the edge. I stumbled out of the lake onto the grassy shore panting. My sopping shirt and jeans weighed me down. Didn't matter. I had enough fear and adrenaline to run for miles. I raced past a meadow out of the park to Lincoln Way. Fortune was with me. A bus arrived at the nearby bus stop.

I climbed aboard. The driver glared at me and my sopping clothes. I stood by the front, checking my pockets for cash.

I didn't have any.

The bus driver pulled away and let me search my pockets for change as he continued his route. Thank goodness.

It really didn't matter that I didn't have cash to pay the driver. All I needed was to get a few blocks clear of danger.

At the next stop, he asked, "You got the money or not, sir?"

"Do you take library card?"

He shooed me off his bus.

80

Construction Site
Oakland, CA

IN HIS CAR, LANCE ENDED THE CALL AND CURSED.
Everything was going wrong. His men had the simple
task of killing Ed at Golden Gate Park, but they let him
get away. Idiots!

If what Seamus said was true, there were pictures
and video footage evidence of Lance torturing him. Ed
had that. That couldn't get out. Ed needed to die.

He pounded his fists on the steering wheel. Idiots!

He'd have to kill Ed tonight. But he couldn't
pretend he'd trade the waitress for evidence without the
waitress.

If I were the waitress, where would I go first?

Sean, his wounded guard who was better off dead,

had given him the best clue. He said he needed a hospital. A hospital. According to the map on his phone, the nearest hospital was about three miles away.

It was a quick drive.

Fifteen minutes later, at the hospital, Lance asked the check-in nurse if "his wife" Alessandra had checked in.

The nurse pointed to Alessandra sleeping in a chair in the waiting room. Her pillow was the shoulder of a giant.

"Thank you," he said to the nurse.

How could he get her out discretely? Knocking her unconscious wasn't going to help much. Too many witnesses. She was already asleep, that was a good start.

What about a sedative or other sleeping agent? No. He didn't know how to get his hands on such a thing without snooping around the hospital looking suspicious.

Hold on. What was this?

A woman walked in. The same woman whose picture had been on Ed's computer. She was with a friend.

What could he determine from her? First, she was supposed to be dead, the same one whose profile on the social media page showed friends posting rest-in-peace messages. Second, she wasn't dead. Third, she was pregnant, which meant this was likely the woman that was sneaking around David Deutsch's crime scene. Fourth, since Ed had her picture on his computer, and since she took great pains to investigate the murder, she must have been close to Ed. Fifth, by the way she and her friend were now helping the waitress out of her seat, it was clear they were all together.

He didn't have to kidnap the waitress again, all he had to do was follow them to their lair and use them as leverage before killing them all.

81

S.F. Police Station
San Francisco, CA

SERGEANT CHEUNG WINCED AND SQUEEZED HER bandaged arm, avoiding the wounded area. Squeezing the unharmed part somehow took the sting off the wound.

Damn, that went wrong. Way wrong.

The phone at her desk rang. It was Krieg.

"What the hell happened back there?" he asked.

"We're just as confused as you are. You okay?"

"I'm fine. Got a new burner phone. A dry one." He gave her his new number. "How about you? You're the one who got shot. Jeez, I seem to be saying that a lot today. First Detective Graff, now you."

"I was lucky. Just grazed my arm. All bandaged up."

"Good."

Maybe Krieg could help her determine how the shooters knew to find him there.

"Do you think you were followed to Golden Gate Park?" she asked. "To our meeting spot?"

"Only Aiden Caldwell knew where I was when I came to the park. But he had ample opportunity to deal with me long before. Anyway, it's a good bet no one followed me. If they did, they wouldn't have waited until I had your protection."

"True."

Whoever knew he was coming to the park had to have either known at the last minute, or — a more likely scenario — had to have followed Kelly, Hakimi, or herself.

"Who knew about our plan to meet?" he asked.

"I just told my partner and my captain, the marshals told their headquarters. Do you think there may be a mole in the marshal's headquarters?"

"Maybe," he said.

She didn't know what to say after that.

Krieg didn't speak either.

"Are you sure you weren't followed?" she said.

"I wasn't followed." He sounded offended. "I don't know what my past experience has been with avoiding detection, but for some reason my body has a system of how to move and check my surroundings. I can tell you that not a single face has been the same in all the strolls, buses, and motorboats I took."

"Motorboats?"

"Never mind."

Silence. If Krieg truly hadn't made any false moves to trigger the shootout in the park, then it had to have been someone she or the marshals were in touch with.

Dammit. Had she lost all Krieg's trust?

"Are you willing to stay at a safe-house with Kelly and Hakimi?" she said.

"Gosh, gee." He sounded overdramatic. "I don't want to break your heart or hurt your feelings, but right now I just need my space. It's not you, it's me. And the bullets whizzing past my ears. And the men in leather jackets wanting me dead."

Cheung rolled her eyes. "I get it, I get it."

Krieg didn't hang up. She took that as an invitation to find out more.

"So what's next for you?"

"I don't know, maybe a taco. Maybe a trip to a museum. Maybe stopping some people who keep shooting at me. Whatever takes priority, know what I'm saying? I'll talk to you later, Sergeant."

He hung up. Cheung sighed. Who the hell could have leaked the information of their meeting in Golden Gate Park?

The phone rang again.

"What is it? I mean — This is Sergeant Cheung."

It was Krieg.

"I've had a change of heart," he said. "Meet me at the corner of Marina Boulevard and Old Mason Street. Bring an earpiece, and tell no one other than marshals Kelly and Hakimi."

He wanted to meet at Crissy Field? "You got it."

After hanging up, she snatched her coat and purse, exited the police department, and took her car to Crissy Field.

Amy and Greg Miller's Duplex
Oakland Hills
Oakland, CA

HOLLY SANK DEEPER INTO THE ARMCHAIR AT AMY'S living room as the sun set outside, peeking in the window. She ignored the boys who were playing cards. She ignored Amy's sassy banter with Sarah as they helped Alessandra get comfortable on the couch with two ice packs, one for her nose and one for her stomach. She ignored Greg who hid behind a newspaper with all this female energy going on in the room, though she could relate to him the most. Hiding would be great.

The truth was, she was a horrible person. She had

let her desire for revenge control her and had killed two innocent people in the process.

There was no place in the world for her.

The doorbell rang.

"I'll get it," little Chris said.

The young boy ran to the door and returned holding hands with a man. "Look, Mom. This guy is a real captain."

"Excuse me for barging in," said the tall man with a wreath of salt and pepper hair.

"Show him your badge," Chris said.

He displayed it. A badge for the SFPD. Looked authentic.

"I'm Captain Williams of the San Francisco Police Department, and I understand there's someone here who could help me out with a case I'm working on."

Amy stood. "A pleasure to meet you, Captain." She turned to Chris. "Chris, do you want to practice making the introductions?"

Chris pointed to each person. "That's Mommy, that's Daddy, that's my big brother Remy, that's Scarlett, and I don't know the rest."

Holly smirked.

"I'm Holly, no relation."

Alessandra removed the ice pack from her nose long enough to show her face.

"I'm Alessandra."

"What happened to your nose?" Captain Williams said.

"Funny you should ask," she said. "You might want to sit down for the full story."

"I think," Chris said, "somebody needed a nose and thought hers was... de-catchable."

"Detachable," Remy said.

Amy showed Captain Williams a seat next to Greg on the couch. "The couch isn't seventh heaven, but it'll give your legs a rest."

"Thank you." Captain Williams sat.

Why was the captain investigating a case? That should be left for officers, sergeants, and detectives.

Alessandra explained how she had been hit in the nose and abducted by a man who called himself Andy.

"Remy," Amy said. "Can you take Chris to your room?"

"Okay." He waved for Chris to follow him to the adjacent bedroom. "C'mon, Chris. Let's play Go Fish."

"Good. I think I know how to win this time." Chris raced to the bedroom he and Remy shared.

"What did your captor look like?" Captain Williams took out a pad to take notes.

"Bedroom eyes, a bedroom smile, and a suit so sharp it could cut your heart out," Alessandra said.

"Could you, uh, be more specific?"

Alessandra gave the kidnapper's eye color, hair color, and estimated height. She said that she woke up in a building undergoing construction, described the location in West Oakland, and described the features of the two men with sidearms who watched her.

"You think you can catch them?" Alessandra asked.

"It's not my jurisdiction, but I'm good friends with the captain of the Oakland Police, so I'll pass along my notes and request a rush on it."

"You're investigating a case?" Holly said.

"That's right." He flipped a page over in his notepad ready to write more.

"Shouldn't the sergeants on the case be doing the fieldwork?" Holly asked.

"Normally, yes. And they are. It's just that this is a high profile case and as such requires more manpower on the job. So I'm offering my time to help out."

"That's very captainish of you," Amy said. "Is this about David Deutsch?"

"Yes. I understand someone here has information that can help with clearing up what happened."

Uh, oh. Police officers often had their own agendas. What was this guy's true agenda?

"I was there," Sarah said. "I mean, at the crime scene."

"Watch what you say, Sarah." Holly shifted in her seat. "He's a police officer, remember?"

Sarah gave her a stare of daggers. Even though she was offering good advice, Sarah's resentment was a reasonable response. It's not easy expecting someone to trust your judgment after you've tortured them.

"It's fine," Captain Williams said. He checked his watch again. "Normally, I'd have to bring you in for entering the crime scene, but right now I need all the information I can get."

Sarah explained everything to him, the AC on high

with the timer set in place, the ice cube bringing down the lever of the thermostat to heat up the room, and the injection of something that increased the ATP in David Deutsch's system, all to hide the time of death and make Ed become the main suspect.

The captain checked his watch again.

"So you're saying it could not have been Ed?"

"Exactly."

The captain grabbed Greg, unholstered his weapon, and pressed it against Greg's neck.

What the hell?

Amy screamed and rushed to block the door to the boys' room.

Alessandra stiffened in her seat and winced. Sarah froze.

"It's a shame that it's come to this, but there's no other way," Captain Williams said.

Holly clenched the armrests. "What are you doing?!"

He ignored Holly's question and addressed Sarah.

"You're right, you know. The room was set up to look like it was hot inside on the night David Deutsch was murdered."

"Then why are you doing this?" Sarah demanded.

"Because I can't let the recordings of who entered the room before Ed be seen."

"Let me guess," Holly said. "You'll be the one that people see entering and leaving his room."

"Yes. And that would put me in a difficult position."

"So why?" she said. "Why would you do it?"

"A few reasons. The campaign manager for Mr. Caldwell has some unpleasant documents on me that if they got out, I could land in prison."

"The campaign manager put you up to this?" she said.

"That's right. Blackmail."

"So what are the other reasons?" she asked.

The captain sighed, keeping his gun trained on Greg who didn't peep.

"David Deutsch had plans to cut the budget for the California Highway Patrol. The State Police are a critical unit for solving crimes across county lines, and for some reason he couldn't get that through his thick skull. He kept preaching about preventative measures and restorative justice as alternatives to police action. That's all bullshit. But the left-wing communities were eating that shit up. He wasn't just preaching it, either. He had major support and financial backing from liberal nut-jobs. If he became senator, a lot of police, good people, would lose their jobs."

"You didn't have plans to kill him just for that, did you?" she said.

"Not at all. The unsavory documents pushed me there." He chuckled. "I have to admit, the promise of expediting my path to becoming San Francisco's next Chief of Police didn't hurt any, either."

"It's too late," Sarah said. "Detective Graff is already pursuing the truth, getting the actual time of death estimated. Stopping us isn't going to prevent the truth from getting out."

"I realize she's pursuing it. At least, she will be once her broken ribs have healed. That's why I'm going to make sure her wounds are lethal."

"That's your full explanation for why you're doing all this?" Holly asked.

"Yep."

"Okay. I just wanted to understand your motivation." She drew her gun from her ankle holster and shot Captain Williams in his shooting arm. The captain's arm fell limp and Greg was safe.

Everybody screamed. What a nuisance. She fired another shot between Captain Williams' eyes.

I already caused two deaths, what's one more?

Everybody stared at her, which in itself was no surprise. She holstered her gun.

"He was going to kill us all anyway," she said.

But they weren't staring at her. They were staring just above her.

She heard a click behind her. The muzzle of a gun pressed against her head.

Damn.

Amy and Greg Miller's Duplex
Oakland Hills
Oakland, CA

SARAH STUDIED THE THREE MEN WHO HELD THEM
hostage in Amy and Greg's living room. The one in
charge was called Lance.

Another one was called Felix. Alessandra muttered
something about how she should have shot him in the
kneecaps when she had a chance.

The last one's name was Jayden, and resembled the
balding man who forced her jeep down Lombard street.
He kept farting all the time, and the boys Chris and
Remy, now back in the living room, had trouble
keeping straight faces.

"Shh," Amy said.

Their snickering bubbled up from nervous energy. She'd seen such nervous laughter from her clients when reading tarot cards about their love life.

Carl, where are you?

Alessandra sat beside her on one of the couches. Amy sat on the floor with her boys, Greg sat alone on the other couch, and Holly sat in the arm chair, now weaponless.

There was a ping-pong paddle on the floor. Paddles wouldn't hurt so much in the scheme of things.

Her gaze drew to the fireplace.

A poker would.

She leaned over to Alessandra. "I have a plan."

Alessandra whispered, "Is this an instant good-guys-win-and-nobody-gets-hurt plan, or is it a better-hide-behind-the-couch-to-avoid-all-the-bullet-spray plan?"

"I don't think a single bullet would be fired."

Alessandra grimaced. "You don't *think?*"

"How good are you with a poker?"

She shrugged. "It's been awhile since I played the game."

"No. I was talking about the kind of poker for a fireplace."

"So was I," Alessandra said. "My clients have unique games."

Sarah eyed the wrought iron baton.

Alessandra followed her gaze to the weapon by the fireplace.

"I could do some damage with that," Alessandra

said. "All I need is a distraction. Should anyone else be in on the plan?"

"Yeah. Holly."

"Okay." Alessandra winced as she shifted to the edge of the couch. "Let's give her a look on the count of three."

Huh?

"Why on the count of three?"

"So that we look at her at the same time," Alessandra said.

"We don't have to look at her at the same time, we can just look at her."

"Fine, so let's look at her and try to let her know you're going to do something."

"Good. One, two,"

"Wait a minute," Alessandra said. "I thought we weren't counting."

"What?"

"You said we weren't counting."

"Oh, right. I changed my mind. It's a good idea. One, two—"

"Hey!" Jayden barked. "Stop the secret chatter. What are you talking about?"

"Sorry," Sarah said. "I just have to use the restroom really bad."

Lance pointed to Felix.

"Go with her to the bathroom," he said.

Good. In the restroom she could lock the door behind her, and find something to write with like eyeliner, and write a note to Holly to prepare her for an attack on these men.

"And Felix?" Lance said. "Don't let her go into the bathroom alone."

Darn it.

She went through the motions, and Felix watched her the whole time, not even averting his eyes when she was on the toilet. At least he didn't seem to take any pleasure in watching her. It felt more like he was a rehab lab technician making sure she wasn't faking a urine sample.

She returned to the living room making eye-contact with Holly. Holly scowled as if sensing Sarah had a plan in the works. Maybe the best thing to do was to start the distraction and hope Holly, Greg, and Amy would follow Alessandra's lead on the attack.

"Oh no," Sarah said just above a whisper. She sat on the couch beside Alessandra. "Oh, no. Not now."

"What's wrong?" Alessandra asked.

Sarah clutched her belly.

"It's the baby. I'm having the baby," she cried out.

Jayden said, "What the hell?"

She yelped in pain.

"Damn, Sarah," Alessandra whispered. "Do you think you could hold it for just a bit longer?"

Sarah glared at her.

"Oh, right!" she continued her whisper. "This is the distraction."

Holly gestured to Felix.

"Don't just stand there," she said. "Get some hot water and cloths."

Felix looked confused.

"Don't," Lance said to Felix. "Her water didn't break. It's a trick."

Darn it!

Sarah shrieked again anyway, to keep up the pretense.

"Uh, actually," Greg said, "Women can give birth without their water breaking."

"It's true." Amy rushed to Sarah's side. "I gave birth to Remy in the caul. The sack never broke. Rare, I know, but there you go."

Sarah screamed again, faking pain. Holly scrutinized her. Holly had heard what Sarah's true screams sounded like. She probably knew Sarah was faking it this time. The others didn't move and awaited Lance's next command.

"Fine," Lance said. He nodded to Amy. "Felix, go with her and get water and towels."

Felix pointed his gun at Amy. "Let's go."

Amy and Felix left the room.

Alessandra eyed the fireplace but didn't move. It must have been too far away.

Uh, oh. Jayden was studying Alessandra.

"Alessandra," Sarah panted, "help me lie down."

Alessandra put her arm around her.

"Just lie back, Sarah. Everything will be just fine."

Amy returned with a bowl of hot water and towels.

Holly stood up. "Let me take that, Amy."

Sarah released a piercing scream.

Holly took the bowl of hot water from Amy's hands and "tripped," spilling the contents of the bowl all over Felix and throwing the bowl at him. Felix tried to catch it, releasing his grip on his gun in the process.

Holly grabbed the gun before it hit the floor.

Alessandra leapt for the poker by the fireplace and thwacked it against Jayden's wrist. Jayden dropped his gun. Alessandra struck his shins, one, two. He dropped to the floor, moaning, holding his legs.

Greg snatched Jayden's gun from the rug. Lance shot Holly's hand. She cried out and dropped the gun.

He said to Greg, "Unless you want her dead, drop the weapon now."

Greg gently lowered the gun and raised his hands in the air.

Lance pointed his weapon at Alessandra. She froze wide-eyed. A chill trickled down Sarah's spine.

"Put it down, Alessandra," Sarah said.

Alessandra lowered the poker to the floor.

Jayden picked up his gun, staggered to his feet, and struck Alessandra in the nose and ribs.

Alessandra shrieked and crumbled to the floor. Jayden set a foot back to kick her.

"Jayden, enough," Lance said. "They're useless to us as a negotiating tool if they're broken."

Jayden said, "But afterwards we're just going to—"

"Never mind what happens afterwards. You can do what you like when the time comes. For now, they need to be shiny."

"What do we do now?" Felix asked.

"Tie 'em up and gag 'em. We can't have them trying to escape." He turned to Holly whose hand spilled blood onto the rug. "And get her hand bandaged so she doesn't bleed to death before we negotiate."

"I'll find some rope," Jayden said.

"I'll look for the bandages." Felix headed for the bathroom.

Lance pointed his gun at Sarah. "I have eight bullets left, and there are seven of you. The next time you pretend to have your baby, the first bullet will go into your gut."

Her insides churned. She put a protective arm around her belly. There was nothing she could do as Alessandra remained doubled over, clutching her middle, and Holly contorted over the pain in her bloodied hand. What a fiasco. This stupid plan of hers was her own fault.

84

Fort Point
San Francisco, CA

THE MOON WAS RISING. I HUNG OUT ALONE IN
Cheung's car, a station wagon from the 1980s parked
just outside of Fort Point. The whole shooting incident
at Golden Gate Park had been disruptive, but not
enough to stop me from regrouping with Cheung,
Kelly, and Hakimi at Crissy Field to plan the
rendezvous with Lance at Fort Point.

This was going to be an interesting meeting. I didn't
have the evidence Lance wanted, and Lance didn't have
Alessandra. Purpose of the meeting? To get proof of
Lance's criminal activity.

I spoke aloud for my earpiece to pick up what I
said.

"So what is it with you and the nineteen-eighties, Cheung?"

"My best years growing up before my parents got divorced," she said.

I wasn't sure how to respond to that.

"Remember," Cheung said. "Keep him talking until he says something incriminating."

I drummed a rhythm on the steering wheel.

"Just to play along, I want to hear everyone's voices. Kelly, you there?"

"I'm here, Carl."

"Hack me to pieces?"

"It's 'Hakimi.' Yes, I'm here."

All three were accounted for.

"How about we all have pizza afterwards. My treat." I tended to say crazy things when I was nervous.

"I'm vegan," Hakimi said.

"Really? You don't strike me as a vegan guy, Hakimi."

"It's the buzz cut," Kelly said.

"What about you, Kelly? You also vegan?"

"No way. I'm a carnivore," she said. "Your boys just arrived."

I wondered how Lance was going to play it. Did he kidnap someone else? Was he going to pretend it was Alessandra by putting a bag over her head?

I revved the engine and inched along the road toward Fort Point tucked under the Golden Gate Bridge, an old civil war relic.

At this time of night, the bridge was lit up, its

orange color a beacon to its fame, and named for the many who crossed over it during the Gold Rush to seek their riches.

"Where are they?" I said. "I see the parked cars, but I don't see them?"

"They went into the interior of the fort." Kelly said. "Go inside."

I cut the engine, exited the car, and headed into the fort's center courtyard. Silhouettes of two men in suits stood out. The fort's lights cracked on. Neither of them were Lance. Bodyguards, maybe.

I played the part.

"Where's Alessandra? You know, the one you kidnapped?"

"Give me your phone," the stout bodyguard said, his buttoned suit jacket squeezing tight against his belly.

"What?"

He reached out his hand. "Your phone!"

I had already deleted the files. There was nothing valuable on the phone anymore, so I handed it to him.

He dialed a number on it.

"Lance wants to talk to you," he said.

He held up the phone. Lance's image was there. A video call.

"Hi, Ed. Sorry I couldn't be there in person, but I had some things to attend to."

I could hear him, but could Cheung and Kelly? Was the earpiece sensitive enough to pick up what Lance said?

I gestured for the bodyguard to give me my phone back, but he wouldn't.

"Could you speak up? There's a lot of wind here," I lied. "Where's Alessandra?"

"I'll show you in a minute. But first, show me the footage."

"I don't see what use it is to you anymore, Lance. Caldwell already fessed up to his particular pleasures in public. He's stepping down from the race." Where was Lance calling from? There was a bookshelf behind him, so he was inside some house or apartment. "Where's Alessandra?"

"She's right here." He stepped out of the image and onscreen was Alessandra tied up and gagged next to Sarah, Greg, Amy, and the boys.

My pulse thumped loud in my ears. What the hell?

"Wait, Lance," I said. "There's no reason to do this. Caldwell's political days are over. There's no reason to try to protect him by getting the footage back."

Lance's image came back to the screen.

"Dammit, I'm not talking about Caldwell's footage," he shouted. "I'm talking about the other footage."

"What other footage?"

"You're not fucking with me, are you, Ed?"

Wait a minute. There were two folders listed in the evidence. I only opened the one marked "Caldwell." Was he talking about the untitled folder?

"I swear, I deleted all the files because Caldwell already confessed. I didn't even look at the files."

There was a pause. I could practically feel my beard growing as I waited for his response.

At last Lance said, "I want to thank you very much, Ed. George, take me off speakerphone and listen to my instructions."

The stout man named George put the phone to his ear.

"You got it," he said.

He hung up, pulled out his gun, and aimed it at my chest.

From above, a shot came, and blood sprayed across my chest. George fell over face first. I sprinted to the narrow halls of the fort, its solid cement columns the only place to hide.

The other man, a short guy, chased after me. There was more gunfire from above. Whoa! Those shots struck a column near me. They couldn't have come from Cheung or the marshals.

I glanced above. Two more guys dashed along the top floor. From the looks of it, they were positioning themselves behind brick columns where they could fire at me more easily. I raced down the corridor away from the courtyard.

One shot — I couldn't tell from where — took down one of the men on the top floor. He fell and landed in the center courtyard.

The man on the ground chased after me. I dashed by narrow slits in the walls where cannons once fired.

Gunfire came from above and put down the man chasing after me.

I raced out of the fort. Kelly, Hakimi, or Cheung shot the last gunman on the second floor.

I hopped in Cheung's car and sped away from the fort.

In my earpiece, Cheung yelled, "What the hell happened? Where are you going?"

"Sarah's in trouble, along with the others." My voice broke.

No response.

"I'm headed to my old place. Meet me there."

No reply. I must have been too far out of range for the earpiece to work. They hadn't heard me. And I had no phone to contact them.

85

To Amy and Greg Miller's Duplex
Oakland Hills
Oakland, CA

AT LEAST THE DRIVING GODS WERE WITH ME. I managed a steady eighty miles per hour in Cheung's station wagon across the Bay Bridge without traffic. Fifty minutes after the time I left Fort Point, I made it up the Oakland Hills to Amy and Greg's place and parked on the driveway a couple hundred feet from the house. I got out and approached the duplex. My lungs gulped for breath. I hoped I wasn't too late.

The house lights bathed the front lawn in light, but Lance and his men wouldn't be able to spot the station wagon at the distance I parked. A Cadillac and black

SUV were parked outside in front of Amy and Greg's family van.

How to stop them? First, gather intelligence. How many gunmen were there, and what weapons were they carrying?

I crept across the grass and peered through the living room window. Sarah, Alessandra, and the others were tied up on the couch and gagged. Holly had a bloody rag wrapped around her hand. The gunmen were laying out a tarp and had canisters of gasoline nearby.

Anger thrashed inside me and hammered my heart.

I wanted to barge in there. I wanted to swing my fists. I wanted to rip Lance apart and destroy those other two men.

I wanted to grab Sarah and run, everyone else be damned.

I took a deep breath. It was all a gut reaction. The desire to resolve the problem was good, but acting without a plan would just cause more trouble.

Breathe in.

Breathe out.

There were three of them. Each of them had handguns. That meant they would have to take the time to point and shoot, and not just fire a stream of bullets in the general direction as they would with a machine gun or semi-automatic.

Perhaps I could stop one, then another before a second gunman had enough reaction time to fire off a bullet, but the third gunman would be tricky. The third gunman would have all the time he needed to point and shoot. I've been shot at before. Moving a piano up thirty stories would be more fun.

I checked inside again. Dammit, they were nearly done laying out the tarp.

"Get that other end flat, Felix," one of the men said. He then produced a hefty fart.

"Damn," Felix said. "What have you been eating?"

"I can't help it," the farter said. "There was a cheese platter at the last fundraiser. I love cheese."

If I did take them out all at once, it would have to be Lance first since he'd be the most likely to shoot. It was likely that the others would either wait for orders to shoot or shoot if they felt they were being attacked.

Perhaps I could capture Lance, tie and gag him, then appeal to Felix and the flatulent gunman.

No. What were the chances the gunmen would set down their weapons and say, "You know what, going out for ice cream *does* sound like a good idea."

The better option was to remove them one at a time.

Advantage? I knew the layout of the property.

Disadvantage? No weapon.

I checked the back entrance connected to where the garage once was.

Unlocked. Not too surprising. I had a memory of feeling so safe living here, I had left the doors unlocked.

I opened the door a crack. The garage had been turned into the boys' bedroom.

I had to watch my step because the floor was

covered with toys. I picked up a piece of wooden train track and placed it on the lower bunk bed. That cleared my path better.

A dartboard lay in the corner on the floor, not on the wall. I scanned the shelves. Stuffed animals, toy matchbox cars, books. Well, books could be dangerous, but in a different way. Cards, foam balls.... Here was something: a magician's set.

I scanned through it. Rats. No magnesium or potassium.

Toys these days. Not as dangerous as the days when you could make your own army men out of molten lead or play with ammonium nitrate in a chemistry set, perfect for homemade bombs.

Dammit, I didn't have time for this.

I stepped through the clean mudroom and peeked out the door that led into the living room. No one noticed me. Only Lance was in the room. The other two men were in other parts of the house, and by the sounds of it, they were dousing the kitchen and bedroom with gasoline.

Sarah spotted me and gasped. I shushed her with a finger to my lips.

A can of gasoline lay a few feet away. That could come in handy. All I needed was a distraction. Couldn't get one from any of my teammates, they were tied up at the moment.

I closed the door and took another gander at what I had. Under the bed was a large box. I pulled it out. In big letters it said, *Remy's Box, Do Not Open!*

With a propensity of misunderstanding rules, I opened it.

Yes. The mother lode. There were two paintball guns, a Swiss Army knife, a book of matches — which I pocketed — and many boxes of matchbox-sized containers holding Chinese poppers, teardrop-shaped pieces of paper that held bits of gravel coated with silver fulminate. Pretty harmless as far as explosives go, but with enough of the gravel combined, it could make one big bang.

I spotted a large zip-up sandwich bag that contained toy pieces for a board game. That would be my container.

I carefully unwrapped the poppers and emptied the coated gravel into the sandwich bag. I had to be careful. If the gravel scraped and ignited, the whole bag could blow, the shockwave sending out its supersonic boom for everyone to hear.

The bag was full — ready.

Also under the bed was a remote control dump truck. The bed of the truck wouldn't be effective for carrying liquids, just solids. Liquids would dribble out. That gave me an idea.

I carried the zipped plastic bag of explosive gravel outside.

From the open garage door, I flung the bag at the foot of the SUV.

BOOM!

The armed men's yelps sounded sweet.

"What the hell was that?"

Silence.

"Who's out there?" Lance shouted.

I decided to keep him in suspense.

"I'm going to check it out," one of his men said.

"Don't," Lance said. "That's what they want you to do."

Silence. About ten minutes passed.

"I still want to check it out."

"I can go with him, Lance."

After a minute, Lance said, "Okay. Just stay low."

Lance remained inside as the two men exited in a crouch. They wouldn't find much. Just a torn sandwich bag. The detonated gravel mixed with the driveway's gravel.

The men investigated, guns drawn. Lance stood by the front door and watched.

I slipped back inside the kids' room and crept to the living room. Greg puffed the most through his gag as if trying to say something. He wanted me to untie him.

I shushed him the same way I did Sarah. Who was the most effective in handling stressful and dangerous situations like these? The answer was not my first choice, but it made the most sense. I placed the Swiss Army Knife in Holly's hand, picked up a can of gasoline, and returned to the kids' room.

"There's nothing here," Felix bellowed.

"Get back inside," Lance said.

When the outdoors was clear again, I crept out. Fortunately, the criminal's SUV driver-side door was unlocked. I carefully clicked the door open and dowsed the interior of the SUV with gasoline. There wasn't enough gasoline to cover the other vehicle, but the small amount remaining would suffice for my plan to work.

I lit the inside of the SUV and dashed back to the kids' room.

It took only a matter of minutes for them to notice.

"What the hell?" Felix exclaimed. "Is that my SUV? Jayden, come with me!"

Ah, so Mr. Flatulence was named Jayden.

The two ran outside again. This time Lance stepped out of the duplex and moved closer to the cars.

I filled the bed of the remote control dump truck with the leftover gasoline, then steered it toward Lance. The fluid dripped out, leaving a trail. The truck bumped his foot. He glanced toward the garage entrance to see where the truck came from and spotted me.

"I spoke to Caldwell." I lit the trail of gasoline. "He says you're fired."

The path of fire raced at him and set the truck into a fireball at his feet. His pant leg caught fire. He screamed, patting the fire to extinguish it.

The others shot at me. I fired Remy's paint gun at Jayden.

"Oh, god!" Jayden cried. "I've been hit!"

Both hid behind the Cadillac for cover.

I raced to the front door and heard, "Why is my blood yellow?"

I locked the front door and rushed to the living room. Holly had removed everyone's gags and was cutting the binds off Sarah.

I kept my eyes on Sarah as I helped out with untying the others. She looked unharmed.

"You think you won, Ed?" Lance shouted from outside. "You're not even close. Remember where you are."

A window shattered in the parents' bedroom. A flash of light popped in there. Damn. They just lit up the bedroom.

Smoke already seeped through the hall.

"That's right!" Lance said. "We'll just wait until you come running out for air."

Crap.

Amy and Greg Miller's Duplex
Oakland Hills
Oakland, CA

I turned to Greg. "Fire extinguisher?"

"On it." He raced to the kitchen then to the master bedroom.

I studied our area. The home phone's cord had been ripped out of the wall.

"I'm guessing they took your cell phones," I said to Amy.

"Every last one," she said. "What do we do?"

Best to ask the most experienced of this bunch.

"Suggestions?" I asked Holly.

"Really?" Holly scowled. "You trust me?"

"You're in as much danger as we are." Besides, she

needed this, the opportunity to save the ones she'd harmed.

Greg returned from the bedroom. "The fire's out. We were lucky. It didn't reach the gasoline-soaked spots."

"All right, let me talk this out," Holly said. "They have guns, we don't. But we have numbers. They're just three, we have six."

"You mean eight," Greg said. "Remy and Chris."

"They're children," Holly said.

Amy snorted.

"As long as they're a safe distance away, believe you me," Amy said, "they can still cause a heap of trouble."

"All right, we have eight," Holly said. "Also, we have nothing to lose, and that makes us very dangerous."

"Okay," I said. "If we attack them together, we should use a weapon we're skilled with. Holly, you take the paint gun. Whose good with darts?"

"I am," Greg said. "Best in the local bar. But I've got something better."

"I can shoot rocks with my slingshot!" Remy said.

"Good."

Alessandra grabbed Amy's arm.

"You wouldn't happen to have a whip, would you?"

"Uh, no," Amy said.

"We have a plumbing snake," Greg said. "Will that do?"

"Get it," Alessandra said.

He headed for the basement.

I handed Sarah the keys for Cheung's station wagon, the one I drove to get here. "Take it as soon as you can."

She clutched the keys to her chest.

Amy picked up the poker and gauged the weight of it in her hand.

"I like what you did with this poker, Alessandra," she said.

Alessandra pointed at my body parts.

"The shins, the forearms, the solar plexus, and thighs. Those are the sweet spots."

"Oh, god," Sarah said.

"What is it?" I asked.

"Not to be a Debbie Downer, but my water broke. For real this time."

———

I NODDED TO HOLLY. The bottle rocket was ready. She steadied the paint ball gun through the open living room window.

Lance and Felix stood at the Cadillac while Jayden with the yellow paint ball splattered on his suit, paced in front of his flaming SUV, clearly pissed off and ready to shoot anything.

"Hey!" Holly shouted at him.

He stopped pacing and pointed his gun at the voice.

Holly fired a round of paint in his eye.

He screamed and fell over.

That, my friend, is why you always wear a mask when playing paintball.

"Now," I shouted.

Greg ran out the door firing a nail gun in their direction.

Lance yelped. That had to hurt.

I angled the bottle rocket and lit it. It fired at them making a nice fireworks display in their vicinity. Much chaos and satisfying shouts ensued.

Alessandra strode toward half-blind Jayden. She twirled the metal plumbing snake and struck the man's weapon hand. He cried out. She picked up the gun.

In the confusion, Sarah, Chris, and Amy raced to the station wagon. Felix chased them. Remy raced to hide somewhere in the woods.

Amy stopped to face Felix. "Keep going," she told the others.

Before Felix could aim his weapon, Amy struck him with the poker reciting what she learned.

"Shin."

He cried out and hopped.

"Wrist."

He dropped his gun.

"Solar plexus and thigh."

He dropped to the ground, clutching his leg and his middle.

She turned to run, but the wounded man grabbed her ankle. She tried kicking him off, but he held fast.

Remy used his slingshot to snap a rock at Felix. Right in the temple. Felix let go of Amy. Nice one, Remy.

Amy hopped in the station wagon. The wheels spun in the loose gravel. The car wasn't moving.

"They're getting away!" Lance clutched his nail-pierced shoulder while standing by the Cadillac. Greg fired another nail at him, hit his leg. "Damn it!" He hopped on one leg.

The wheels found traction and the station wagon fishtailed down the driveway.

One-eyed paintball Jayden punched Alessandra in the jaw. She dropped to the ground. He retrieved his gun and huffed across the sizable lawn to cut off the station wagon's path. Arriving at the last stretch of driveway, he faced the approaching station wagon. The headlights shone upon him. He aimed his gun at the car.

I clenched my fists. Sarah was in that car. I had to do something.

As Jayden fired, a well-placed rock smacked the back of his head, throwing off his aim. Remy did it again. Jayden spun.

I launched a second bottle rocket at his gut. He fell over.

The station wagon roared away down the hill.

Alessandra jumped on Jayden's back and twisted his arm backwards.

I rushed over, picked up his gun, and pointed it at him. We weren't out of the woods, yet.

Lance sat on the gravel and raised his weapon at me. A splash of paint struck his temple. He looked dazed.

I hustled to him. He aimed his gun at me with the last of his strength. I fired a round into his shoulder. He dropped his weapon. Was he going to make any last moves? He wavered, then collapsed to the ground, out of steam.

"Look on the bright side," I said. "Where you're going, there is no anchovy pizza."

He grunted and fell unconscious. I snatched his phone and checked it. Facial recognition was required to unlock it. I held it to Lance's face.

"Say cheese."

The phone clicked, granting me access. I turned off the security feature so I could unlock the phone at any time.

The approaching sound of sirens pealed in the distance.

"Come on," Holly said to me. "We need to get you to the hospital for Sarah."

87

CA State Route 24
Oakland, CA

ON THE RIDE DOWN, I SAT IN THE FRONT passenger seat of Greg's family van, a Toyota Sienna.

Was Sarah going to be okay? Was the baby?

I took deep breaths.

Greg did the driving. Alessandra and Holly sat with Remy in the back. Holly clutched the bloody rag around her hand and stared out the window. Memories of my old life returned, the life I had before meeting Sarah. I had worked as a computer programmer and lived alone. How had I enjoyed living alone?

I glanced at the others in the car. Man, it was great to be surrounded by friends. I needed all the support I could get.

On the way to the hospital, I called Yitzhak Budnitz, the guy from the carpool.

"Hey Yitzhak, Ed here."

"Good to hear from you, Ed. Discover more about yourself?"

"I have."

"Let me guess. You didn't kill David Deutsch."

"Correct."

"Did my lawyer help?"

"Not a bit."

"Oh. Sorry to hear that."

"I also found out I have a wife."

"Mazel Tov!"

"Yeah. Want to come join my friends in the waiting room for the birth of my baby?"

"First marriage, now a baby? You don't waste time."

"That's me. Super-fast Eddie. Want to hear another trick?"

"What's that?"

"My real name is Carl Best."

"Oh...okay."

"So will you come to the hospital and hang out in the waiting room for my wife and me?"

"I'd be honored."

After hanging up, I made another call.

"Caldwell, it's Ed Krieg. How would you like to be a guest at my wife's birth."

"I'm guessing you mean in the waiting room and not the delivery room."

"That's right."

"Good. Because as much as I enjoy seeing physical pain, I have my limits."

"Understood."

"But why me? You thought I planned on killing you. That's not exactly someone you invite to so intimate an event."

"True, but everyone's different. Some want no one around, while others want the world to be at the bedside. And you know what they say. Keep your friends close, and your suspicious politicians closer."

Besides, still in Witness Protection, I couldn't invite old friends, but I could invite my new ones.

He chuckled. "See you there, Ed."

When we arrived I heard my wife screaming. "If you don't give me something more for the pain, I will physically maim you and come back for your children."

I hesitated. Then smiled.

That's my Sarah.

I rushed into the delivery room, happy to be nowhere else.

88

Oakland Valley Hospital
Oakland, CA

HOLLY CRADLED HER BANDAGED HAND AND
worked at rubbing the pain away. Damn, it hurt.

She sat in the hospital waiting room with Amy,
Greg, their boys, and Alessandra. Aiden Caldwell had
come in about the same time as the Jewish guy with a
yarmulke. Alessandra held an ice pack to her jaw. A
police officer also sat in the waiting room at the opposite end. He held a bandage over his brow. He must
have had a cut there and was waiting for treatment.

Remy licked his lips. "Can we get some ice cream in
the cafeteria?"

"I'm pretty famished, myself." Greg rubbed his belly.
"How about you, hon?"

"I could eat a leprechaun before stealing his pot of gold," Amy said.

"It's the fight, the adrenaline rush." Holly applied more pressure on her hand. "Makes all your bodily functions run like crazy and increases your need to eat."

Greg stood. "Come on, let's get some food."

"Ice cream," Chris corrected him.

"We'll see," Greg said.

Amy, Greg, and the boys left to get something to eat.

The Jewish guy introduced himself to everyone, then said, "So, Mr. Caldwell. I understand you're dropping from the race. Is that true?"

"That's correct."

"Why is that?"

"I'm into sadomasochism. Not very popular among our constituents."

Yitzhak had an amusing half-smile. It said, "I understand" while simultaneously saying, "I have no idea what you're talking about."

The police officer didn't react at all to what Caldwell said. He sat too far away to hear, about ten seats away.

Yitzhak turned to Alessandra, probably to change the subject.

"How do you know Ed, or Carl, as I hear is his real name?"

"I was his waitress during the day," she said.

"During the day?"

"Yes. I'm a dominatrix for hire at night."

His expression was the same priceless scowl with a

forced smile.

He steered his way to Holly. She got ready for his question.

"How do you know Carl?"

"I came to kill him."

Yitzhak paused.

"I see." He scrutinized her, then her hand. "Are you... still here to kill him?"

She pretended to think about it. Then she shrugged. "Nah."

The police officer studied her face. Not good. There was still a warrant out for her arrest.

"Yitzhak," Caldwell leaned in. "Do you think me a bad man because of my... eccentricity? What does Judaism say about such things?"

"When it comes to being a good person," Yitzhak stroked his beard, "there is a *midrash*, a commentary, which states, people have two sides." He held out his two hands like a balance scale, weighing each one. "We have a *yetzer harah*, a propensity to do bad things, and a *yetzer hatov*, a propensity to do good things. What we want in the heat of the moment is something to satiate our immediate selfish need, like ice cream. What we want for our future often contradicts our selfish need, but is good for us, like eating healthy food."

"It sounds like you're saying I should stop my extracurricular activity. Cut it out from my life like a bad eating habit," Caldwell said.

"Actually, Genesis Rabbah, a book of rabbi's commentary written around the year five hundred, says it's better for both the *yetzer harah* and the *yetzer hatov* to be at odds with each other."

That was strange.

"Hey!" the policeman bellowed at Holly. "Do I know you?"

"No," she said. *You haven't seen my photo on a wanted-for-homicide posting.*

The policeman scrolled through his phone, maybe his email. She maneuvered some strands of blonde hair to hang over and obscure her face.

"Sounds like Judaism supports the yin and the yang," she said.

"Yes and no," Yitzhak said. "If a janitor resists his masochism temptations, it's not such a big deal because other people won't care. But a politician? Every choice a politician makes, in his public and private life, is very important. By resisting your temptations, it's more meaningful because everyone will know you're not giving in."

Caldwell smiled. "Sounds like you're suggesting I get back in the race. Put myself in a position where not practicing S & M becomes commendable."

Yitzhak shrugged. "I would vote for you."

Alessandra laughed.

The police officer tilted his phone in a strange way. Did he just take a picture?

"I've had about enough of this." Alessandra faced Caldwell, "You do realize there's nothing wrong with the S & M lifestyle, don't you?"

"I do," Caldwell nodded. "I just wanted to confirm

my suspicions about how one of my constituents felt about it."

Yitzhak scowled. "I'm not sure I understand."

Holly had to admit, she was as confused as the Jewish guy was. Meanwhile, the policeman went back to tapping on his phone. Did he just send a picture of her to a police department for facial recognition?

Alessandra adjusted the ice pack at her jaw.

"The way I see it," Alessandra said, "there are two categories of bad people. There are those with the propensity to be bad. They're cold-blooded killers, psychopaths, anti-social sons of bitches who don't understand words like regret or remorse."

Holly shifted in her chair, cradling her hand. Did she fit that category? No. She felt remorse. She wished to hell she didn't have a conscience. It hurt too much.

Alessandra continued. "Then there are people like us. We have the ability to discern right from wrong, good from bad. And if that's the case, if we choose to do bad things, then we're bad people because of our choices."

Holly clamped her eyes shut. Alessandra described her well. All the horrible choices she'd made. She was a bad person.

Thank heaven Amy and her family were not in the waiting room. They knew she had killed innocent marshals. Everyone else in the waiting room had no idea of her crimes.

"What if...?" Holly shifted in her seat again and winced at the piercing pain in her hand. She spoke softly, making sure the police officer couldn't hear. "What if someone kills a person and gets away with it? There's nothing they can do to make it up. What should they do? Lock themselves up for the rest of their life?"

"Just to be clear," Yitzhak said, "you're not talking about doing that to Carl, are you?"

Holly shook her head. "No."

Yitzhak released a deep breath. "Good because, you know, bullets aren't kosher." He straightened his chartreuse button-up shirt. "For anyone."

"Understood," Holly said.

"I can tell you what Judaism says, but first I want to make it clear that I'm not interested in masochism, submittance, dominaintenance, or any of that stuff."

Alessandra smiled.

"Okay," Yitzhak said. "In Judaism, when someone wrongs a person, they may repent by asking the wronged person for forgiveness. In the case of murder, the wronged person is dead and, so, is unable to provide forgiveness. A murderer can never be forgiven."

Holly swallowed the lump in her throat but it wouldn't go away. She turned to Alessandra. "What do *you* think?"

"I'm going to take more of a Gandhi approach on that one," Alessandra said.

"What do you mean?"

"Normally we have the obligation to live life to its fullest." Alessandra shook a fist of determination. "We should enjoy all that life has to offer, and we should contribute to the community in some way. If a guy kills someone, he now has two lives to live for. He needs to contribute to the community the way the one he killed would have done, and he needs to contribute to the community the way he, himself, wishes to."

Yitzhak leaned forward, intrigued.

"Not only that," Alessandra said, "but he also needs to enjoy life for two people now. The easiest way to do that is to do fun things with another person. Go to movies together, go to museums together, that sort of thing. Because when you do fun things with a partner, you're not just doing it for yourself, you're also doing it for the relationship."

Now what of the two marshals she had killed? Their lives were set on helping the nation be a safer place for people to live in. She knew all about living a lifestyle of keeping people safe. Could she do such work three times as much? For herself and for the two she killed? What would that lifestyle look like?

She pictured being in charge of National Security. The power to save the nation might satisfy contributing to the community for three people. But getting married? She couldn't see it happening. And how was she supposed to work for the upper levels of national security when there was a warrant out for her arrest for homicide?

There *was* one thing she could do to make the nation safer.

"Excuse me." She stood, keeping her aching hand close to her chest. "I have to make a phone call."

She exited the hospital.

89

Grove Shafter Freeway
Oakland, CA

THE HEADLIGHTS FROM DETECTIVE BOBBIE
Graff's car hit the lane's reflectors guiding her path. She
shifted in her seat as she drove home from work.
Although there was no obligation for staying at her job
as late as she had, the work kept her mind off the pain.
Her ribs, though only fractured, still hurt from being
shot at the TransAmerica building earlier in the day.

Her phone rang. She used the Bluetooth feature to
answer hands-free.

"Bad news, Bobbie." It was Elizabeth Cheung.

"What's up?"

"Two marshals and I set up a meet-and-greet
between Carl Best — or whatever his name is — and

Lance Meyler for a confession, but Lance Meyler didn't show and now we can't get a hold of Mr. Best."

"You think he's in danger?"

"By the way he was screaming at us incoherently via our ear piece, and peeled away in my car? We know he's in danger."

Dammit. Holly must have been behind this.

A click sounded.

"Hey, Elizabeth? I've got someone on the other line. Can I call you back?"

"Sure."

Graff connected the other call. It was her old partner Larry Denton from the Oakland Police Department.

"Thought you should know that Holly Sampson was spotted at the Oakland Valley Hospital."

"Thanks for the heads up, Denton."

Graff turned her car around and made her way to the hospital. Maybe Sarah Best was there having her baby.

Don't you try anything, Sampson.

———

Oakland Valley Hospital
Oakland, CA

GRAFF STORMED through the hospital's emergency entrance. Anyone in the waiting room she recognized? No. Good.

She followed the signs to Labor and Delivery. At the nurse's desk, she showed her police badge.

"I'm here to see Mrs. Sarah Best or Scarlett Bronson."

"Your just in time. They all went to her maternity room three-eleven."

They all? "Thank you."

Hopefully, Sampson hadn't figured out where Mr. and Mrs. Best were yet.

She raced to the maternity room and rushed in.

"Detective!" Carl Best glowed holding his baby in his arms. Sarah Best lay in bed and looked tired. They were surrounded by a smiling crowd: a couple with two young boys, a man wearing a yarmulke, a slender woman holding an ice pack at her nose, and former senator-elect Aiden Caldwell.

"Do you want to hold her, Detective?" Sarah asked.

The baby was wrapped in a white cloth and scrunched her face as if trying to understand the impossible.

"No, thanks," Graff said. "Everyone okay?"

"Couldn't be better." Carl gently handed his daughter to Graff despite her protests. "The head is heavy so keep one hand under it."

Carl apparently knew that she had practically no experience handling a baby. Why did that bother her so much? Was that how people saw her? As someone who didn't know how to raise a child?

Graff cradled the baby. The tiny girl's head was smooth. The baby moved in jerking motions, and her big blue eyes peered straight into Graff's heart, as if to say a baby of her own was waiting to be born. Graff swallowed the stone forming in her throat.

"I can't." She returned the baby to Carl's arms. "I heard Holly Sampson was here."

"She was," the Jewish man said. "Then she said she had to make a phone call."

"In other words, she got away," Graff said.

"You don't have to worry, Detective." Sarah took back her daughter from Carl's arms. "She knows Carl didn't kill her father. She's no longer a threat."

Graff shook her head. "While it's good that she's no longer a threat to you, you don't understand. She's a criminal and needs to be brought to justice."

Graff wished Carl and Sarah a happy and healthy future, then pushed out of the room before their newborn broke her heart any more.

Once out of the hospital, she called her friend.

"Hey, Elizabeth. Mr. and Mrs. Best are fine. I sure could use some company, though."

"Sounds good," Elizabeth said. "Our old hangout tonight?"

Graff smiled. "Exactly."

90

Revivify Café
Washington, DC
Two days later

EARLY AFTERNOON, HOLLY WAITED AT THE CROSS street for her godfather Jonas to show. She sipped her cappuccino. Even in its takeaway cup, the coffee tasted good, soothing.

She checked the clean bandage on her hand. The pain was much less.

Jonas pulled up in a black Mercedes. He had a new car every time she met up with him.

The doors unlocked automatically with a pop. She threw what was left of the cappuccino into a nearby trash can, tugged out the towel in her back pocket, dried her working hand best she could, and slipped into the front passenger seat.

Jonas smiled wide. "It's good to see you, Holly."

They hugged and Holly kissed his cheek.

"It's good to see you, too," she said.

"You hurt your hand?"

"It'll heal."

Jonas pulled away from the curb and drove toward the Italian restaurant they frequented on the rare occasions when they got together.

He glanced at her.

"I'm always amazed at how much you've grown. I only wish your father was alive to see how beautiful you are. He would have been so proud."

Her father had indeed been loving, though he had his other agendas that robbed her of his attention.

"Even alive, he was often too busy to see me," she said.

He parked in the restaurant's parking lot.

"True, he was quite the workaholic."

"Yes, could we just chat a bit here before we go inside?"

"Of course." He turned off the engine and faced her. "What would you like to discuss?"

"My father. He was very religious, wasn't he?"

"That's true. He didn't advertise it much, but he did have a devoted spirit to the faith."

"You could say he was a zealot," she said.

"Well, I don't know about that."

"A lot like you, Jonas."

He eyed her.

"What are you getting at?" he said.

"Allow me to demonstrate. Two days ago I spoke with Nathan and his wife Sophia."

"Sophia Patai?" He blinked. "She's alive?"

She waited for him to catch his own mistake. There it was, the eyes darting away, the drooping of his shoulders, the look that he knew he'd given himself away.

"That's right, Jonas. You never did successfully kill all thirty-six righteous from the list. That's why Sophia went through the Witness Protection Program in the first place, to escape religious fanatics like you."

"Now, Holly."

"Don't." The heat of betrayal seared her cheeks. "Don't try to deny it. If you had no involvement in it, you would have asked about Nathan just now, my so-called father's killer. You wouldn't have asked about Sophia."

She plunged a syringe through his sleeve into his forearm.

He gasped and pulled away from the syringe, but he wasn't quick enough. An ample amount of the solution found its way into his bloodstream.

He looked horrified. "What did you do?"

"Don't worry." She placed the syringe back in her purse. "It's just a paralysis agent. It's temporary. It'll give me a chance to talk to you without you running away."

As his body froze — his eyes stiff in horror — she considered what to say.

"These past several months have been pretty hard. I

set out to kill Nathan and instead ended up killing two innocent marshals."

She removed a hunting knife from her purse.

"I had to reevaluate who I was. I set out to do justice by avenging my father, but I didn't know I was just following your agenda. I thought I was hunting down a killer. Once I realized I had become the very person I was hunting — that *I* was a killer — I felt like I had fallen from grace."

She pushed the tip of the knife into his gut. A drop of blood trickled down. Maybe it was the trick of the light, but it looked like his eyes widened.

"Know what? When I killed those marshals, I think I actually heard angels crying." She remembered the distant sound, like loved ones leaving each other, never to return. She slipped the knife in a bit further, twisting it slightly. Jonas made some guttural sounds. Drool dripped from his lips.

"I met an amazing woman. Alessandra. She inspired me to at least try to become a good person again. I'm not saying I ever will, of course. After what I've done, there's no forgiving that. But at least she gave me an idea. A path to follow."

She pushed further. Now blood dribbled from his mouth.

"I'll have to live for three people. The two innocents, and myself. I'll have to contribute to the community for three people, and help the world, if I can. So I'm thinking about doing some anti-terrorist work, something along those lines, anyhow. What do you think?"

His eyes were glassy, his breaths bubbled.

"Don't worry," she whispered. "I'll live for you too."

She pushed the blade to its hilt. His last breath gurgled out.

She sighed. It was over.

She removed the blade, took out her towel, and wiped the blood off the knife.

"Good talk," she said.

91

Some forsaken road
toward New York

FOR THE FIRST TIME IN MY LIFE, I WAS DRIVING our new family to our new home. Memories continued streaming in as my amnesia lost its grip on me. All those memories convinced me I wasn't such a bad guy.

Sarah sat in the back seat next to our daughter who wiggled and cooed in her infant car seat.

"I have a sandwich for you if you're hungry," Sarah said.

"What kind?"

"It's a BLT."

Bacon.

Yitzhak had said he kept kosher as a way of expressing his gratitude.

I glanced at our daughter in the mirror. A preemie. I couldn't believe the size of her. She must have been as small as a puppy.

When our daughter first came to the world, she did this strange shriek that turned into a giggle. At least, that's what it sounded like to me.

We named her Quincy, short for Quintessence, meaning a perfect example. She brought out the perfect qualities in both of us. In philosophy, quintessence is a fifth substance in addition to the four elements, earth, wind, air, and fire. In physics, quintessence is the unknown source of dark energy that causes our universe to expand.

It's all the things I felt about my daughter, a perfect mystery, one I wanted to spend my entire life trying to solve.

"Well?" Sarah said. "You want the BLT?"

I glanced at Quincy again and admired how she wiggled in her chair. My heart warmed with gratitude.

"No, thanks," I said.

Now that Holly made it clear to the marshals that she no longer wished to kill me, the marshals reluctantly agreed that we could go back to our normal lives.

We didn't know what normal meant. Rather than shock Sarah's friends and family that she was still alive, we decided to hold off with that and continue living as Sarah and Carl Best.

The city of Amsterdam in New York was not the most ideal place for us, considering my rep with the bank, the grand larceny, and all that. So with my substantial donation to the cost of moving us, the marshals set us up in a home in Brooklyn, New York.

Sarah and I were big city people. Based on what Yitzhak once told me, being around many temptations to do bad things would give me the opportunity to overcome them and do great things.

And that was what I intended to do with my second chance on life.

ACKNOWLEDGMENTS

Having a family, a community of people one can rely on, is vital for maintaining health and happiness. Writing and publishing a book requires a family.

I want to thank the following members of my writing family that helped me squeeze this lump of coal into a diamond.

First and foremost, a big thank you to my wife Beth Barany for devoting so much of her time to make this book a quality read due to her edits.

Thank you to my team of beta readers: Matt Posner, Marilyn Lugner, Keri Kruspe, Carol Powers, Mary Van Everbroek, Beth Chapmon, Ien Nivens, and Yale Saiger. Your comments smoothed out the rough edges. Thanks to my cheerleaders George Goodwin and Shyanna Bryan who supported my goal of publishing this book.

And, of course, thank you, member of my reading family. You are the one that keeps me from needing family therapy.

HOW DOES ONE KNOW IF THEY ARE GOOD OR EVIL?

INTRODUCTION TO ESSAYS ON WHAT MAKES A PERSON GOOD

In each of my thrillers, I like to have essays that dive deeper into the topics covered in the story. In this case, many of the characters have some ambiguity as to whether they are good or bad, so the essays will cover what it takes to be a good person. **These essays are mostly my own thoughts on the subject, not the common opinion of Jewish people.** So if you disagree with my thoughts, that's no surprise.

This stuff can be as dry as powdered matzoh, so I'll keep it entertaining for those who really can't be bothered. Be warned, though, I mention some dark, disturbing topics, even within this introduction. As a result, feel free to pick and choose which essays to read and which ones to skip. If you wish to avoid the disturbing content of this introduction, stop reading here and go to the essay of your choice.

I said *stop* reading.

You're still reading, aren't you?

Okay, well, whatever flips your pancake.

Time to get serious.

When I was in fifth grade, I had a kind, close friend who was kind and shared the same interests as me (girls). Let's call him Brian. Brian and I played a game of Trust during one recess where he led me around the playground while I had my eyes closed, then I led him while he had his eyes closed. As a joke, I led him into a metal pole. He hit his head.

Hard.

I laughed and he held his hand against his forehead, looking stunned. I apologized and my laughter turned into nervous laughter, perhaps because I realized I had done something horrible intentionally.

For about twenty years afterward, every Yom Kippur I would pray to God for forgiveness for the horrible act I committed against Brian.

I had done worse things as a child. One example is that while throwing stones at a tree with a friend, I missed and hit my friend. He had to get stitches. That's right, throwing rocks at people can be lethal.

Another example is that when I tackled a classmate in the grass and pressed a feather against his face in fun, the hard part of the feather went into his ear and broke his eardrum.

While I felt horrible for hurting my friends, those two incidents didn't generate as much remorse for me. In the first example, I wasn't aiming for his head. In the second example, my classmate's hair covered his ear, so I had no clue the feather was entering his ear. So they were accidents. Yes, I felt remorse, but not as much as the intended harm I inflicted on my good friend Brian. Thank goodness he and I are still friends.

So I am someone who intentionally caused harm to another. Ever since that time, I've been wondering, how do I know I'm not a bad person?

There are, in my opinion, two sides of what makes a person good. The first is by their acts, the second is by their intentions and beliefs.

A simple example is that the act of killing a person is bad. The act of representing a financially-challenged school at a convention to promote the school's merits is good.

When taking into consideration intention, killing someone to defend one's self and others is good. Using a school's limited funds for an all-expenses paid trip to a convention as a way to travel around the world and be a tourist is bad.

We see people who are good for the most part but do one bad thing and it tarnishes the memory of their entire moral fiber. We've seen a man who enlisted in the U.S. Navy, who earned an athletic scholarship, who was the first black actor to star in a dramatic role on network television, who earned three Emmy Awards, who advanced the status of blacks on television, who produced a kids show with strong positive messages for all children, who delivered a positive portrayal of blacks in a situation comedy show that won several major awards, who was inducted in the Television Hall of Fame, who started a foundation to fund teachers of students with learning disabilities, and who was outspoken about blacks pursuing higher education to support their families. Bill Cosby also has been charged with drugging and raping over fifty women.

There was also a man who is not well-known for: his paintings, his unrequited love for a Jewish girl when he was sixteen, his commitment to being a vegetarian, his taking charge of leading the first anti-smoking campaign in history, his strong support for invention of the blow-up sex doll, his nomination for the Nobel Peace Prize, and his legislation against animal cruelty. Instead, Adolf Hitler is known for the near genocide of the entire Jewish population in Europe.

Can we really equate Hitler with Cosby? No. It would be wrong to put both crimes in one category. Though both crimes are heinous — raping over fifty women and the systematic slaughter of over six million Jewish people — the wicked acts committed are not of equal weight.

Consider the alternate view. I apologize for using a character in a movie, but that's the only example I can think of at the moment. In the film Star Wars, Darth Vader, aka Anakin Skywalker, murdered many people and committed many crimes. Yet he sacrificed his life to save his son Luke Skywalker. In the story, sacrificing his own life is how Darth Vader achieved redemption. However, it is wrong to forgive him for his past atrocities just for doing a good deed in the last seconds of his life. All the crimes he committed in his past outweigh his last good deed. Darth Vader is still an evil man, in most people's view.

If a person's wicked acts outweigh their good deeds, can a person's good deeds outweigh their heinous crimes?

It depends.

How horrible were the crimes? What was the intention behind committing them? Can acts of good be so great they outweigh the crimes? Bill Cosby comes to mind for that question, considering how much of a positive influence he was on television. Or is there no value to their acts of kindness, making the crimes unforgivable? Honoring the victims of Bill Cosby comes to mind for that question. It is worth noting that he has yet to publicly show signs of remorse for his crimes. How can we decide whether or not a man like Bill Cosby is a good or bad person?

If only there were some rubric or check-off list that would objectively evaluate a person's character.

Is there a way society can agree on how to determine what makes a person bad or good? One might claim that the justice system is set up specifically to determine the answer to this question. Keep in mind that two of the current U.S. Supreme Court justices and the current president, Donald Trump, are accused of sexual misconduct. Since I cannot rely on our country's leadership to be unbiased, I choose to educate myself on how Judaism evaluates the goodness of a person.

That is ultimately the intent of the six essays in this appendix.

The first essay will address the Ten Commandments, and rabbis' interpretations of them. The Ten Commandments is the rulebook the character Yitzhak uses to guide his way toward righteousness.

The second essay is an article on the "Top Ten Ways to be a Mensch", by Adrienne Gold Davis, posted on the Momentum Unlimited's Jewish Women's Renaissance Project website. The article is an excellent modern portrayal of how Jewish people pursue the path of ever-loving kindness.

The third essay touches on the definitions of a good person vs. a bad person in Judaism based on the many additional commandments in all the Jewish texts.

The fourth essay will present a possible definition of redemption and if, at all, one may achieve it. The character Holly Sampson inspired the need for this essay.

The fifth essay will cover how sadists can be good people, Alessandra's favorite topic.

The sixth essay will go over how one can decide if they are a good person or a bad person. Poor Carl Best. Having lost his memories, he had to evaluate himself in this regard from scratch.

I will not be including other religions in this appendix because I was unable to find contributors and do not feel well-informed enough to represent them.

THE TEN COMMANDMENTS

One method of determining how good a person you are is to see if you follow the Torah's top ten ways to be a mensch (a good person). The Ten Commandments appear twice in the Torah — the five books of Moses — once in Exodus and once in Deuteronomy. There are slight differences in the wording of each. For example, Exodus says, "Thou shall not covet" and Deuteronomy might have it as "Don't covet while reading an ebook on an airplane." I'll be referring to the Exodus version for no other reason than Exodus is where the Ten Commandments first appear in the Torah.

An overall interpretation of all the Torah's commandments, not just these ten, is that they are divided into three types: the relationship one has with one's self, the relationship one has with others, and the relationship one has with God.

Over the centuries, rabbis and scholars across the world worked to interpret the true meaning behind the words of the Old Testament, especially since much of the work can be considered vague, ambiguous, or presented without any clear reasoning. As a result, I felt it appropriate to check in with many of the commentaries about the Ten Commandments to see what the great thinkers over the years came up with.

Most of the commentaries come from: Rashi, Ramban, Chizkuni, Daat Zkenim, Kli Yakar, Or HaChaim, Rabbeinu Bahya, Rashbam, Sforno, Siftei Chakhamim, and Tur HaAroch. I used the app Sefaria as the main source of this collection of commentaries.

First Commandment (Exodus 20:2)

> "I am the Lord Your God, who brought you out
> of the land of Egypt, out of the house of
> bondage."

This is a commandment? Where's the "Thou shalt not" part?

According to Yael Shahar's article "The Ten Commandments" on the Ha'aretz website and Gerhard Von Rad's book *Studies in Deuteronomy*, thoughts put forward by modern commentators (not listed) and Jewish sages such as Rabbi Hanina Ben Gamaliel (Mekhilta d'Rabbi Yishmael) liken the first commandment to the start of a covenantal treaty — "covenant" meaning a type of contract. They interpreted the first commandment as a way of introducing why the rest of the text should be taken seriously.

In other words, this statement could be taken as, "Yo, I'm about to lay down some heavy laws on you. Don't think this is just some yokel rambling on nonsense because, dude, I'm a pretty important being. I'm the One who freed you and brought you out of Egypt, man."

Second Commandment (Exodus 20:3-6)

"You shall have no other gods before Me. You shall not make for yourself any graven image, nor any manner of likeness, of any thing that is in heaven above, or that is in the earth beneath, or that is in the water under the earth."

"You shall not bow down to them, nor serve them, for I, the Lord Your God, am a jealous God, who remembers the sin of the fathers upon the children unto the third and fourth generation of them who hate Me; and showing mercy unto the thousandth generation of them that love Me and keep My commandments."

Most of the commentaries state that the proper interpretation of the second commandment is: Any Jewish person who worships idols or other gods should be punished.

This one always troubled me. Not the commandment of not worshiping idols, but the reason. God's a
jealous God? Whenever I hear about jealous husbands, I
lose respect for them because jealousy is a sign of insecu-
rity. God is jealous? Does that mean God is insecure? I'd
rather hear another reason to not worship idols. Even,
"Worshiping idols is not very nice" would suffice.

Rashi stated in his commentary that whenever the
word *kanah* comes up in the Torah, it should be interpreted as "zealous," not "jealous." So instead of a jealous
God, this commandment can read, "I am a zealous
God." In other words, God has the zeal necessary to
punish the guilty.

Chizkuni points out that the full commandment
shows God doesn't punish until after the third or fourth
generation in the family perpetuates the same crime of
worshiping idols. On the flip side, if one generation
loves God *and* follows the commandments — I like that
it's both — then the family will be granted mercy for a
thousand generations. It's not a get-out-of-jail-free card,
where one can be as bad as they want as long as they
believe in God; one also must follow the
commandments.

But is it so bad to worship idols? Again, the
full commandment refers to the generations of
those who hate God, not just those who ignore
Him. In my opinion, hating takes action. What
have people done when they hated someone? Spat
in their food? Burned down their house? Killed
their loved ones? At what point would you use

your zeal, your power, to put a stop to such behavior?

In Rabbi Menchem Posner's article "The Ten Commandments" on the Chabad.org website, he points out that the two tablets of commandments, when placed side by side, could be read horizontally as if commandments 1 and 6 were connected, 2 and 7 were connected, 3 and 8 were connected, and so on.

In this case, commandments 2 and 7 could be read as, "When one worships a deity other than God, it is like committing adultery." Comedian John Mulaney said he never understood how a person could even consider killing a human being... until his girlfriend cheated on him.

Loyalty, love, and commitment are important qualities for us to practice. So when I ask myself if it's so bad to worship idols, putting it in the whole adultery context, yeah. I can see it being bad.

Third Commandment (Exodus 20:7)

> "You shall not take the name of the Lord Your God in vain; for the Lord will not hold him guiltless that takes His name in vain."

Growing up, I had trouble understanding the literal meaning of this one. A lot of people told me it meant not to use God's name when cursing. But that seems petty to me. What if it meant more than that? What if it meant not to commit a crime in God's name as a way of justifying the crime?

Though some interpretations say God's name shouldn't be used haphazardly, the commandment is more than just about cursing. Rashi and Or HaChaim (whose full name was Rabbi Hayyim ben Moshe ibn Attar) and others wrote that this commandment refers to using God's name to give credibility to false statements, similar to committing perjury in a courtroom.

We can take it further than perjury.

Many terrorists and politicians have killed innocents, directly or indirectly, "in the name of God." Can you imagine how God responded to such things? God probably said, "If I were dead, I'd be rolling in my grave right now."

Fourth Commandment (Exodus 20:8-11)

"Remember the Sabbath, to keep it holy. Six days you shall labor, and do all your work; but the seventh day is a Sabbath unto the Lord Your God, in it you shall not do any manner of work, you, nor your son, nor your daughter, nor your man-servant, nor your maid-servant, nor your cattle, nor your stranger that is within your gates; for in six days the Lord made heaven and earth, the sea, and all that in them is, and rested on the seventh day. Wherefore the Lord blessed the Sabbath day, and made it holy."

I love this one. It's like if the Almighty catches you working on the Sabbath, you'll hear a loud voice, "Stop working, you numbskull!"

Growing up in a world where there is such a high value placed on a strong work ethic, this commandment seems to counter it.

What's the big deal about working? The big deal seems to be about remembering the Sabbath, and resting is just the prescribed way of remembering it.

So why remember the Sabbath?

There are many interpretations. Or HaChaim cited Midrash Tehilim 92, commentary on psalm 92, and this interpretation is my favorite: Adam sinned on the sixth day and on the seventh day, Sabbath, as an entity, advocated for Adam. Instead of Adam getting executed for his sin, his life was spared. As a result of Sabbath's support of Adam, every one of us is alive today. That's worth thinking about.

For all you scientists out there thinking, "That's ridiculous. How can a day be a creature? How can a duration of time be a being that takes up space?"

Just multiply that duration of time by the speed of light constant and your seconds will turn into meters. You know. Spacetime?

Just sayin'.

In high school, another student told me he thought the U.S. shouldn't involve itself in any wars, and that even getting involved in World War II was a mistake. I almost replied, "I'm not sure who you're talking to, because if it weren't for the U.S. getting involved in

World War II, I wouldn't be alive today."

So, yeah. It's worth remembering how moments in history brought us the gift of life. Even scientists do the same thing. For example, cosmologists seek out the truth of the universe's beginnings as a way to honor the past that gave us life.

Also worth noting is that the Sabbath is often given female traits: the Sabbath queen, welcoming the Sabbath bride.

What's up with that?

Maharsha, whose full name was Rabbi Shmuel Eidels, cited the Midrash (Bereishit Rabbah 11:8) — a collection of Jewish oral laws — to explain that when Sabbath said to God, "Everyone else has a mate. Sunday has Monday, Tuesday has Wednesday, Thursday has Friday, but I have no one." God answered, "The Jewish people will be your mate." So when God said, "Remember the Sabbath and keep it holy," it is as if God said, "Remember My promise to the Sabbath and be sure to marry her, putting your attention on her."

Another interpretation of this commandment, given by Rabbi Shimon bar Yochai in his Zohar volume 2, is that the word "Sabbath" is another name of God. Keep in mind, God didn't create the Sabbath in the book of Genesis; God didn't create Herself. So if the commandment is to remember God and don't forget Her existence, that seems like a fair request.

In addition, the Jewish mystics state there are ten attributes of God. The Zohar and Sefer Ha-Maamarim add that *malchut* which is an attribute of God meaning "royalty," is also referred to the *Shekinah*, the female aspect of God.

So perhaps resting on the seventh day as the fourth commandment states is just a way to invite us to use the time we need to put our attention on our marriage to the *Shekinah*. My first book, The Torah Codes, goes more into the *Shekinah*.

Fifth Commandment (Exodus 20:12)

> "Honor your father and your mother, that your days may be long upon the land which the Lord God gives you."

Hmm. If you honor your parents, you'll have longer days. If you don't honor your parents, you'll have shorter days. I imagine "longer days" means a longer life, but I can't be certain.

In one of my Hebrew school courses, the teacher pointed out that the text does not say you must "love" your parents, only that you must "honor" them. Many people have a hard time loving or forgiving their parents. Honoring them? That's an easier task to swallow. It's like saying, "Mom, Dad, I know you had a lot of difficult experiences while raising us, you probably also had a lot of difficulty dealing with your own parents. I also recognize that though you could have raised me better, you did what you could and that may even have been the best you could considering your circumstances. I honor that, and I respect that."

Perhaps by honoring and respecting how your parents did the best they could, you're able to let go of the anger you harbor within and can now live your life without the stress of dwelling on the past.

In fact, Or HaChaim wrote that the extension of one's life is a natural outcome of honoring ones parents, not a reward. If it were meant to be a reward the commandment would have read, "I will lengthen your life."

So living without anger and resentment is a healthier way to live which can naturally lead to a longer life.

My question is, "Why is this commandment in the first five?"

Most rabbis liken the first five commandments as volume one and the second five commandments as volume two. The first five address one's relationship with God, and the second five focus on one's relationship with others.

Rabbi Menachem Posner's article "The Ten Commandments" puts it this way.

> "The commandments on the first tablet are about spiritual matters, between man and the Creator. The commandments on the second tablet, however, seem to be about material matters, with no apparent connection to G-d or spiritual pursuits. In fact, while every one of the

first five commandments includes G-d's name, His name is not mentioned once in the second set of five."

Additionally, the number of Hebrew words on the second set of five commandments is twenty-six, the same number attributed to God's name "YHWH" (Y = 10, H = 5, W = 6). As a result, one could say that though God isn't mentioned in the second set of five commandments, He is encoded within them. So if you're into numbers, there's that.

When I looked deeper into other commentary, I found this great little story. According to Chizkuni, citing the Midrash Pessikta de Rav Kahane chapter 21, when a wicked Roman governor asked Rabbi Akiva why the name of the Lord was in the first five and not the last five, Rabbi Akiva went to the governor's palace and pointed to the governor's lance, later the rabbi went to the palace and pointed to the shield, still later he went again to the palace and pointed out the armor and weapons.

When Rabbi Akiva visited the palace yet again, he went to the toilet and asked why there were no weapons or armor in that place. The governor said it was disgraceful to bring weapons to such a place. Rabbi Akiva said, "Aha! Then why associate the Lord's name with the last five commandments which list such disgraceful acts as murder, stealing, and adultery?"

Some rabbis suggest honoring one's parents is the same as remembering that without our parents, we wouldn't be alive. Remembering the moments that gave us the gift of life seems to be a common thread among these first five commandments.

Sixth Commandment (Exodus 20:13)

"You shall not murder."

Duh.

Seventh Commandment (Exodus 20:13)

"You shall not commit adultery."

In an interesting twist leaning toward immorality, Rashi cites Leviticus 20:10 and Ezekiel 16:32 to interpret this as only applying to men who sleep with married women. In other words, he says it's cool to have mistresses if those women aren't married. The Ezekiel passage suggests that married women can't sleep with any man other than her husband, whether the man is married or not. Sexist much?

One interpretation is that to claim an unmarried woman required a lot of preparation: providing her a place to stay, providing her with her own servants, etc. However, married women had all these amenities already. Committing adultery with married women was simpler and a more accessible temptation, so it was the more likely scenario. And therefore, needed a law against it.

Keep in mind, in these Biblical times men could have multiple wives, so if they wanted an unmarried woman, they could marry her. Sleeping with women who were already married was forbidden.

Rabbis suggest the order of the commandments suggest a link: honor your parents because they gave you life, don't murder because you're taking away a life, don't commit adultery thinking you are providing the gift of life when, in fact, you are stealing the child's ability to honor her true parents.

Speaking of stealing...

Eighth Commandment (Exodus 20:13)

"You shall not steal."

Rashi says this commandment might refer mostly to kidnapping since it is among other heinous crimes.

Rabbi Ovadia ben Jacob Sforno's interpretation is that breaking this commandment includes deliberately deceiving someone into believing a lie was truth. By deceiving someone, the perpetrator is stealing their mind.

I love that.

A teacher of mine in Hebrew school said that not responding to someone who says hello is breaking this commandment. Think about that. If a homeless person on the street says hello to you, you must respond or else your breaking the commandment, "Thou shall not steal." Why? You're stealing their day.

When I heard this it made so much sense to me. Those moments when I greeted someone and they purposely ignored me, I felt such anger and humiliation. I felt like they ruined my day. Ever since then, if someone greets me I make sure to respond with a similar greeting.

It's these kinds of interpretations that make me appreciate Judaism so much. Just to be clear, there's a difference between what Judaism has to offer in the way of knowledge and what people do in the name of Judaism. That goes for any religion.

Ninth Commandment (Exodus 20:13)

"You shall not bear false witness against your neighbor."

An Aesop's fable, "The Dog and the Sheep," tells a story similar to this commandment.

A dog took a sheep to a court of law. The dog falsely claimed the sheep's loaf of bread was actually his own and the dog wanted the bread back. The dog's lie was supported by a wolf called as a witness. Though the sheep lost the case, the sheep later found the wolf dead in a ditch and drew the moral that this was a result of heavenly punishment of the fate reserved to liars.

Tenth Commandment (Exodus 20:14)

"You shall not covet your neighbor's house, nor
his wife, his man-servant, his maid-servant, nor
his ox, nor his ass, nor anything that is your
neighbor's."

Ibn Ezra, whose full name was Abraham ben Meir,
said that many people have trouble understanding how
they're supposed to control their primal thoughts. Isn't
it enough to not act on them? He pointed out that
there's a middle step. Maybe you've worked with an
attractive coworker and knew in your heart that nothing
would ever come from pursuing a relationship. Maybe
you had a classmate you loved but knew in your heart
that the feeling wasn't mutual so there was no point in
flirting. Maybe you love the Mona Lisa painting but in
your heart you know you can never own it.

Ibn Ezra said this commandment is about knowing
in your heart which pursuits are futile. You can have as
many primal urges as you wish, just be aware of what
relationships or ownerships can never be so that you
don't act on them.

My take away is that it's okay for me to covet my
wife, so I do that a lot.

————

Now that you've read the Ten Commandments, how do

you rate yourself? Are you a good person? Do you fulfill at least five of them? If so, yay! If not, boo!

But perhaps these commandments are rather old fashioned. If we were to ask a Jewish person today what the top ten ways are to be a mensch, what would her response be? Read on to find out!

TOP TEN WAYS TO BE A MENSCH (GOOD PERSON)

By Adrienne Gold Davis, JWRP Israel, Trip Leader from The Village Shul (Toronto, ON). Reprinted with permission of the author and of Momentum at MomentumUnlimited.org.

From as early as I can remember, my mother implored me to 'be a lady'. It was the shorthand for behavioral expectations, in any situation. It implied refinement and dignity, a refusal to 'sink to another's level' and to handle oneself properly regardless of the provocation. My brother was meant to be a gentleman. As family, we had a code of conduct, one which I thought to be ours alone. I came to discover that it was gleaned and anglicized from the teachings of my grandparents who had been raised with what today one might call a *Yiddishe Cop*; people raised to be MENSCHEN.

When I was growing up, I remember hearing a woman I knew use "*Yiddishe Cop*" in a way that was clearly derisive, and most definitely shorthand for a dismissive attitude about non-Jews. When someone whose thought process disturbed or confounded her, when they were unsuccessful in business, when they missed an opportunity, she would say that the person did not have "a *Yiddisheh cop*" (a Jewish head).

Her basic message was that they were foreign or even inferior in sensibility; that they were somehow missing the *seychil* (common sense) that a Jew inherently possessed. I thought of her comments as racist; particularly because she couldn't define what a *Yiddisheh cop* really was. Nor did I think she was 'being a mensch' by commenting on another person's mental capacity. Hers was that elitist Jewish mindset that in my uninformed mind was the reason that 'they all hate us', whoever the 'they' might be. Even though they all wanted a Jewish lawyer or Jewish doctor. Because of that *Yiddishe cop*. Oy.

Fast forward 20 odd years or so, and I became immersed in the study of Judaism. I thrilled to its philosophies and ideologies, became enamored with its behavioral, social and interpersonal demands, and came to believe that its paths were the sweeter and more fulfilling ones. And so as I began my journey down a road less traveled, I came to see as Robert Frost said before me, that this path was well trodden. And it was my choice to travel it that made all the difference.

I decided to attempt to break down the notion of the *Yiddishe Cop*, to understand what by then I had come to understand was actually true. Jews DO think differently than the other nations. Not necessarily better or worse, simply different. I decided to think about what constitutes being a Mensch. The following is a breakdown of the things I think best classify a person as possessing *Menschlichkeit*, of thinking with a *Yiddishe cop*. I will leave it to you to decide which path you chose to tread. All I recommend though is that you first look at the map.

It is interesting to note that in Israel a Mensch is called a *Ben Adam* (a son of man, a human) as if the struggle to be human is a feat only accomplished by elevating oneself above ones human urges and becoming holy. Here we go then: Mensch lessons in shorthand. Each point could be studied and discussed in great length. This is simply my shorthand

The Top Ten Ways to be a Mensch or Raise One

1. Shalom Bayit: Peace in the home/business environment

Learn to apologize even when you are in the wrong. Practice saying 'oops I blew it' or 'wow, I sure got that wrong' to prepare yourself for the moments you'll really need to say them. Know that sometimes you can *win the battle but lose the war*. Valuing peace over the moral superiority of being right is a gift you give yourself. *Apologizing does not always mean that you're wrong and the other person is right. It just means that you value your relationship more than your ego.*

2. **Kavod HaBriyot: Respect and show kindness to all creation**

We are ultimately obligated to show respect and honor to all creatures, while we have a *mitzvah* to love all Jews, love occurs in concentric circles. Even the swarming bees have rights. Teach yourself and your kids to feed your pet before themselves in the morning. We have an obligation to answer to their needs first as they are incapable of delaying gratification with self-talk.

3. **Bal Tashchit: Respect the environment and don't destroy or waste**

Environmentalism in not a new political agenda: rather it is deeply Jewish concept. Genesis (*Bereishit*) shows us the model of our relationship as humans with the rest of creation, and our obligations to tend, repair and protect the world. Consider the laws of Shabbat apply to the land as well, the biblical concept of *Peah* (the corner of the field) the concept of *Shmitah* (the land resting).

4. **Tzedakah: Pursue justice or righteousness (charity)**

The obligation to give between 10% and 20% of your net income is a righteous obligation, not a charitable emotional response. The implication of this is that there is an imbalance in the world and the Jews obligation in justice and righteousness is to correct this imbalance.

5. **Don't Speak Lashon Hara: Avoid hurtful language and gossip**

It is *Lashon Hara* EVEN and ESPECIALLY if it is true. Actually, only one type of *Lashon Hara* (lit. "evil speech") reflects lies. Speaking lies (slander) is called "*motzi shem ra*" – literally spreading a bad name. It's pretty easy to imagine how lies, and even exaggeration, can unfairly damage someone's reputation. There are two commandments that explicitly prohibit lying: *Lo tisa shema shav* – you shall not utter a false report. (Ex. 23:1) and *Midavar sheker tirchak* – from a false matter you shall distance yourself. (Ex. 23:7)

Learn the laws together and reward verbal sensitivity.

6. **Don't rationalize:**

We learn that "The Hebrew word for sin is *chet,* which is derived from an old archery term used when an archer 'misses the mark'. This helps inform the Jewish view of sin; all people are essentially good and sin is a product of our errors, or missing the mark, as we are all imperfect". Pick up the bow and shoot again. Do not tell yourself Rational Lies.

7. **Gemilut Hasadim: Perform acts of kindness to help others**

Jews do not practice random acts of kindness; rather we follow the requirement of righteous behavior in an entirely non-random way. This insures that regardless of your mood, or whether you are moved to action, you will act nonetheless. Teach the kids (and do this your-self) to be searching for opportunities to do kindnesses. Carry band-aids, aspirins, chewing gum, subway tokens, loose change, candy or any other things that people 'need' on a regular basis so that *you* can be the one to provide it.

8. Talmud Torah: Emphasize Jewish Learning

Jewish learning as it pertains to ethics, morals and ideals is more important to praise than marks in academics. If your child's honesty, inclusion of an annoying sibling or kindness to a grandparent garnered the same praise as an A on their report card, the child will feel a self esteem not tied to their intellectual learning style. Raising a mensch means teaching them what Judaism says about what it means to be a good person.

9. Rodef Shalom: Be a Pursuer of Peace

For kids this opportunity plays out daily in the school yard or cafeteria, or Facebook or through text. If you or your child searches out opportunities for peace-making they will become righteous themselves and a true gift to their peers. Being the peacemaker amongst peers (for kids and adults alike) can deepen our ability to see two sides of a story and offer perspective in problem solving.

10. Tefillah: Prayer

Prayer can begin in an informal way as an expression of gratitude. Gratitude and humility diminishes entitlement and teaches us to feel deep appreciation for all the gifts we have. While Jewish standardized prayer is exquisite and every word carefully chosen, remember God understands all languages and wants to 'hear from us'. And remember, sometimes the answer to your prayers is 'no'. No is also an answer.

Bio

Adrienne Gold Davis was a Canadian television personality specializing in fashion, style, and beauty for almost two decades before becoming a senior lecturer and community liaison at the Village Shul in Toronto, as well as an international Jewish educator. Adrienne has appeared on all major Canadian television networks and has served as the event host for dozens of charities and organizations. Adrienne and her husband live in Toronto and have two sons.

A GOOD PERSON VS. A BAD PERSON

In Judaism, there are clear laws on how to live one's life in a proper way. Each law is a *mitzvah*, often mistranslated as a "good deed" because many of them are seen by non-Jews or non-religious Jews as optional. For example, giving charity is considered a mitzvah in Judaism, and many would agree that giving charity is a good deed. Judaism, however, disagrees. The word for charity in Hebrew is *tsedakah*, whose root word, *tsedek*, means "justice." Judaism sees charity as not only a law, but an action that is required for accomplishing justice.

While calling charity a form of justice is a nice idea, is that really meant to be taken seriously?

Here's the cool thing. Whenever a word mentioned twice in a row in the Torah, it isn't interpreted as God stuttering. It's interpreted as an extremely important part in the book. Two words in a row in the Torah functions as God's highlighter, God's text in a bold font, God's ALL CAPS. Using two words in a row is God's way of shaking the reader's shoulders and saying, "WAKE UP! THIS PART'S IMPORTANT!"

There's a line in the Torah (Deut. 16:18) that says, "*Tsedek, tsedek tirdof*," which translates to "Justice, Justice you must pursue."

The point is that justice is considered a big deal in Judaism, and one way to serve justice is to give charity. Charity is a law, not just a good deed.

So let's start with the most prominent laws in the Torah. God gave the Ten *Mitzvot*, the Ten Commandments, to the Jewish people. They were God's way of saying, "Hey, folks. Do these ten things. It'll make you a better person."

But "Ten Commandments" sounds a little like they belong to a Top Ten list, like "Top Ten Sauces for Your Salad," or "Top Ten Ways to Get a Career in Yacht Kissing." If the Ten Commandments were the "Top Ten Ways to be a Better Person," then I wonder what are the other ways?

According to the Talmud (Tractate Makkot 23b), the Torah has 613 commandments within its pages.

That's impressive, isn't it? Six hundred and three extra laws to follow, just in case you weren't satisfied with just ten. In my opinion, each of these laws are presented with the unstated intent of helping one determine how to be a good person.

Actually, there aren't quite 613. The number 613 came from Rabbi Simlai, according to the Talmud. Rabbi Simlai said that there are as many positive (thou-shall) laws as there are days in the year (365) and there are as many negative (thou-shall-not) laws as there are bones in the body (248), and that's how he came up with the total of 613. But if you do the actual counting, you get about half that much depending on what one considers a commandment.

What are these laws? Important laws. Laws like, "Don't embarrass others," and "Don't sleep with your daughter," and "Don't walk more than 2,000 cubits outside the city boundary on the Sabbath day."

Okay, so maybe some of them seem unnecessary on the surface. Laws like, "It's okay to eat locusts, but don't eat beetles," seem very odd. You'd think that people like me, people who consider some laws to be more important than others, would make a chart of all the laws that take priority and the other laws would have a shrug factor:

"Is it absolutely forbidden to walk more than 200 cubits outside the city boundary on the Sabbath?"

My response: *Shrug.*

But dismissing some of the laws in the Torah is not the way of Judaism. Many Jews consider every law to be of equal importance. As a result, rabbis got on the bandwagon and wrote the Talmud, a sixty-book series of commentaries and interpretations that include many more laws. In much of the text, the rabbis looked at the original laws in the Torah and interpreted the intention of each law and how to properly execute it.

For example, one of the laws in Leviticus says, "Don't boil a lamb in its mother's milk."

The rabbis came up with all sorts of interpretations

to this law: it's cruel to kill an animal in the milk of its mother, or do not use a symbol of life as a way to kill, or do not practice this ancient fertility ritual since it is an extension of practicing idolatry.

When it came to how to follow the law, the rabbis generally took the safe route. Maybe their reasoning was something like this:

"What if we boil a lamb in another lamb's mother's milk, is that breaking the law?"

"Okay, let's just not boil a lamb in goat milk, mother or not."

"What if we boil a lamb in cow's milk, is that breaking the law?"

"Okay, let's just not boil a lamb in any milk."

"What if we boil a calf in goat milk, is that breaking the law?"

"Okay, let's just not boil any meat in any milk."

"What if the milk isn't boiling, but it's still hot and we mix it with meat, is that breaking the law?"

"Okay, let's just not mix meat in hot milk."

"What if we're out in the cold weather and the milk isn't hot but it's warmer than the cold day?"

"Okay, let's just not mix meat in milk, hot or cold."

"What if we drink milk, it warms in our stomach, and then we eat meat which then sits in the warm milk in our stomach?"

"Okay, let's just not eat meat or milk in the same meal."

"What if we eat a meal of meat and cheese? Cheese has milk in it, right?"

"Okay, let's just not eat meat and dairy products in the same meal."

"What if we eat cheese off a plate and later use the same plate to eat meat? Don't they mix then?"

"Okay, let's just have different dishes for dairy and for meat."

And that's how practicing Jews today follow the law of "Don't boil a lamb in its mother's milk."

Wow, right? Being cautious about not breaking the laws in the Torah has led to pretty extensive extra laws.

Keep in mind, the Talmud didn't just address laws as quirky as "Don't boil a kid in its mother's milk." The Talmud also provided framework on the laws vital to understanding how to behave properly in society, such as how a man must have consent when requesting sex from his wife.

Not to be outdone by the number of laws in the Torah and Talmud, Jews practiced additional laws passed down by word-of-mouth. These are found in the following books: Mishnah, Rabbanan Sevurai, Geonim, Rishonim and Acharonim. In those tomes, Jews added many more laws.

So how many total laws are there in Judaism? Let's see: add the three, add the seven, carry the one... A whole lot!

Actually, to get an exact number would require starting another tome of rabbinical interpretations discussing what counts as a law. There is no exact number.

Is it actually worthwhile to have so many laws, especially ones that don't seem to do any harm if broken? I mean, really. Who — besides your taste buds — is going to be harmed if you eat a beetle?

There's something I like about having laws that come across as ridiculous rules. If someone wants to break the law, I believe that typically the first law they break is an insignificant one. I think a criminal doesn't start by committing a felony. I think they often starts with misdemeanors before working up to major crimes. So a rebellious practicing Jew might walk around the streets without his head covered and not give charity before the idea of stealing a candy bar even pops in his head.

When California had to vote on legalizing marijuana, I had two reasons to vote against it: One, having a law against smoking marijuana put in place something a rebellious teenager could break without harming anyone, as opposed to rebelling in a more destructive manner; two, I hated the smell. The reason I voted to legalize marijuana was because the main purpose of enforcing the marijuana law was to lock up black males who were too poor to buy expensive drugs, like cocaine. The law was used as a way to imprison them and legally take away their rights under the U.S. Constitution's thirteenth amendment.

You might say, "That's just a ridiculous paranoid conspiracy," and if you were right, I'd agree with you. (See the documentary "Thirteenth" on the thirteenth amendment)

An argument might be that since marijuana users

broke the law, they deserve to be locked up. Imagine if your country enforced all Jewish laws and locked up anyone who ate non-kosher chicken or carried a wallet on the sabbath day. Neither of those laws harm other people; they are laws offered on how to be a good person to yourself or how to have a good relationship with God.

The takeaway from all this is that some laws are designed to improve the person-to-person relationships and need to be enforced, laws like, "Don't commit murder," and "Don't steal." Other laws are designed as a way to be good to yourself and, in the case of Judaism, to have a good relationship with God.

I want to move on to a law that not only is harmless if broken, but is harmful if followed. "If a man lies with another man, it is an abomination, and he should be put to death."

This law in Leviticus bugs me to no end. I'll not hide it, I support gay rights. At the same time, I believe God authored the Torah so that's put me in a tough situation. Should I support what I believe is right or should I support what the Torah states is right?

A gay friend of mine who respected my love for Judaism asked me, "You say you support gay rights. Doesn't that make you a hypocrite?"

I replied, "I'd rather be a hypocrite than hurt people."

My father, who was in many ways a right-wing democrat, hated the idea of homosexuals practicing their urges.

As a teenager, one night at the dinner table, I asked my father, "What's wrong with someone being gay?"

"It's against the law in the Bible."

"But why?"

"Because it's an abomination!"

"But what does that mean?"

He stopped, looked down at his plate, took in a deep breath and let it out. "Being a homosexual is very hard. Society doesn't accept you, your religion doesn't accept you, and you hide it from everyone feeling like an outsider."

Man, I think that was the moment I loved him most. He understood the emotional pain gay people went through, even if the idea of people being gay disturbed him.

I pursued any reasonable interpretation I could find for the Torah's anti-gay law. One person told me the problem was the spilling of sperm. Indeed, Judaism follows the tradition of Monty Python's song, "Every Sperm is Sacred." Even male masturbation is against Jewish law. Let's see all those pro-life males stand behind *that* law with vim and vigor! So with that interpretation in mind, the Torah isn't stating that there's anything wrong with being gay, what's wrong is not using the sperm for the purpose of trying to conceive a child.

I didn't care much for that interpretation of the anti-gay law because, first of all, I'm a big fan of masturbation. Pro-life men, I'll never judge you for breaking that anti-masturbation law. Second of all, if a guy doesn't masturbate, the sperm comes out in his pee stream anyway. Then what, don't pee?

Another interpretation of the anti-gay law was that homosexual sex acts used to be a way to worship other gods. Worshiping other gods is such a big no-no in Judaism, the law against it is one of the top ten commandments! I can actually sit comfortably with that one. The law wasn't against being gay, the law was against worshiping other gods.

To me, the treatment of the LGBT community has been horrendous. The epitaph of Leonard Matlovitch, a gay Vietnam War veteran, put it succinctly: "When I was in the military, they gave me a medal for killing two men, and a discharge for loving one."

In Judaism, as I stated in The Ten Commandments essay earlier, most rabbis agree that all the Torah's commandments are divided into three types: the relationship one has with one's self, the relationship one has with others, and the relationship one has with God. All of the commandments are stated with the intention of guiding the way toward being a good person. However, only the ones that involve the treatment of others seem to be worth enforcing via a state or federal law. The others — choosing what to eat or smoke, choosing how often and when to pray — ought to be left to the individual, in my opinion.

When it comes to laws that punish perpetrators in a fashion that can be seen as harmful if followed — like anti-gay laws and anti-abortion laws — I believe a common ground can be found. For example, it's my understanding that most pro-choice women are not anti-life and do not see abortion as a form of contraception; they see abortion as a last resort toward saving a child from a horrible and traumatizing upbringing. Also, it's my understanding that a large number of pro-life women are not anti-choice; though they may never allow themselves to have an abortion they do not feel it is fair to take away the right of that difficult decision from others.

Similarly, my father, though against the idea of letting people practice their homosexual orientation, understood how taking away their rights was not a solution.

When it comes to understanding how to be a good person, Judaism doesn't skimp on providing commandments to follow. Sometimes, though, in my personal opinion, the commandments don't always help guide a person into being good. More on that in the next essay on redemption.

ON REDEMPTION

Okay. You know how this goes. First the essay starts with a dictionary definition of what redemption is, and then the essay goes into specifics, or diverts from the definition, or, at best, explains why the dictionary's definition is totally wrong.

The Merriam-Webster definition of redemption is "the act, process, or an instance of serving to offset or compensate for a defect."

We can define "defect" rather loosely. If we consider a neo-Nazi who shouts out racist and anti-Semitic remarks as someone with a defect, then yes, when that neo-Nazi takes a step to put an end to his racism, he is taking a step toward redemption.

Take Christian Picciolini, for example. A former neo-Nazi skinhead, he once blamed Jews for a white, European genocide; he blamed blacks for the crime, violence and drugs in his city; and he blamed immigrants for taking American jobs.

While in high school, he got in a fistfight with the school's black security guard, Mr. Johnny Holmes, and had to be taken out of school in handcuffs. It was the second time Christian was kicked out of that high school.

Years later, after he had time to reflect on his past behavior, he became an employee for IBM. When he found out he had to install computers at that same high school, he became terrified. Sure enough, Mr. Holmes was still there. Christian froze, not sure what to do, but felt compelled to do something. Perhaps without even realizing it, he felt the need to pursue redemption.

Christian found Mr. Holmes in a parking lot and ran up to him.

"I tapped him on the shoulder. And when he turned around and he recognized me, he took a step back because he was afraid. And I didn't know what to say. Finally, the words came out of my mouth, and all I could think to say was, 'I'm sorry.' "

Christian wasn't told to go out and seek forgiveness. That is what is so wonderful about this moment. He just did what came naturally: he acted from his heart. What followed is what I think solidified Christian's need to change his life:

Mr. Holmes hugged Christian, forgave him, and encouraged him to forgive himself.

That Mr. Holmes was one special man. I think if it were me, I'd mumble some excuse to leave, anything to get away from Christian as fast as possible.

Christian's TED talk on his experience seems to

reveal that his biggest offense as a juvenile was his physical assault against Mr. Holmes and maybe against others. Now he is taking steps toward redemption.

In Judaism, redemption comes from a combination of "*teshuvah, tzedakah,* and *tefillah.*" Often translated as "repentance, charity, and prayer," many rabbis will say that's an inaccurate translation. *Teshuvah* is not repentance where Bob feels bad and works to be a better man, *teshuvah* is when Bob has strayed from his life of being a good man and now returns to a more righteous path. The idea of *teshuvah* is that every person has room to grow and even good people need to narrow their path to find the true thread of righteousness to follow.

Tzedakah is not charity, it's pursuing justice by following one's obligations. In Judaism, *tzedakah* is providing for others from a place of necessity, not to feel good about one's self. When Alice gives money and gives people what they need, she does so because she feels it is her role, not out of an act of kindness.

When I was a kid, I gave my entire Lego® set to my cousin who loved playing with it. Since he seemed in love with the building blocks more than I was, I felt I had a duty to give the set to him. My parents were rather shocked. They were used to seeing me as the self-centered artist I was and in many ways still am.

Yeah, I'm still narrowing my own path of righteousness.

It's a never-ending task.

As for *tefillah,* the word means more than just prayer. It means the work one does to feel a connection with God. Certainly prayer is one way to do that. One of the meanings of the root of the word *tefillah* is "to think." For me, writing these Jewish thrillers is my own method of self-reflection and building a stronger connection to both God and Judaism.

Is it impossible to ever be redeemed? When committing an evil so great that no amount of apology or action can lead to redemption?

In Exodus, chapter 21, the Torah says, "An eye for an eye, a tooth for a tooth, a hand for a hand, a foot for a foot, a burn for a burn, a wound for a wound, a bruise for a bruise," which many people think is a rather primitive way of life. If Bob accidentally pokes Alice's eye out, is justice really served by poking out Bob's eye? Isn't that just committing the same crime, except on purpose?

Historically, the Jewish people never poked out an eye of someone who had done the same. Overall, the offender would have to pay the equivalent of the victim's loss monetarily. You poke out the eye of someone? You need to pay the amount the judges deemed equivalent to the profound loss of the victim's quality of life. You cut off the finger of a musician? You'd have to recompense the musician for not only the reduced quality of life but also for the financial losses that musician must face.

But there's an exception.

If you take away someone's life, if you murder someone, you cannot pay them back for the life they're missing. That's the one situation where you must pay in kind, your life for theirs.

And that's how the U.S. punishes murderers, for the most part.

Ironically, and thankfully, Israel does not enforce a death penalty.

In the Torah, there are crimes listed that deserve the death penalty. Anything from murder, to adultery, to gay sex, to idol worship, to cursing God, to picking up objects on the Sabbath. Just to be clear, for all those people who cite the Torah as their source for why gays should be put to death, gays are just as guilty as anyone who breaks the Sabbath by, say, turning on a light switch. That's right. In the Torah, murder and working on the Sabbath get equal punishment.

Sound ridiculous?

Yeah, that's what the rabbis thought. That's why the Talmud promoted the idea of keeping the death penalty, but made it difficult to enforce. The Mishnah, an oral tradition of Jewish law, took the enforcement of the death penalty one step further: Any court that executed a person once in seventy years was considered destructive.

As a result, Israel rarely applies the death sentence. The two times the Israeli courts have gone through with it was to execute a senior Nazi SS officer and a man believed to be a traitor. And yes, this does not take into account the military operations of targeted assassinations of terrorists. On the other hand, the terrorists brought to court end up in prison if found guilty and are never executed.

What other ways are there of determining proper redemption? How can people know when they've done all they could to redeem themselves?

As novelists and writing teachers, my wife and I steep ourselves in story. In many typical Western story-telling styles, the end of the story fulfills the protagonist's character arc by resolving his or her inner issues.

For example, if the protagonist feels awful for having traumatized his younger brother, by the end of the story the protagonist finds a way to help his younger brother overcome that trauma and the younger brother forgives him.

If the protagonist fears she'll never be good enough to win the approval of her mother, by the end of the story, the protagonist has an experience that teaches her not to care what her mother thinks of her.

If the protagonist murders the parents of a five-year-old girl, by the end of the story the five-year-old girl has now grown into a woman and has a daughter of her own. The way for the protagonist to redeem himself is to protect the woman and her daughter from severe danger and, in doing so, sacrifices his own life.

Storytelling has its own set of rules. How about real life?

As portrayed in the movie Gandhi, I was always impressed by how Gandhi addressed Nahari, a man who begged for forgiveness. In that scene, Nahari's son had been killed by Muslims. To get revenge, he killed a

Muslim child. When he went to Gandhi saying how the guilt made him feel like he was in Hell, he begged forgiveness. Gandhi replied, "I know a way out of Hell. Find a child, a child whose mother and father were killed, and raise him as your own. Only be sure that he is a Muslim and that you raise him as one."

What's so amazing about this is how we get to see an option other than death. Someone can murder another and still find a way to be redeemed without sacrificing his own life. In fact, his life becomes a vital part to helping his community.

It was this scene that inspired my whole interpretation of redemption. I came to see redemption as just doing the opposite of the crime that had been committed, filling the hole that had been made by the crime.

To illustrate what I mean, here's a story from my life.

When I stayed with my sister in the city of Katsrin in northern Israel for a year, I spent my mornings learning Hebrew at Ulpan, a free language school. Most everyone in my class came from Russia, Jews seeking out a safe, democratic country.

I became friends with Helena since she was the only one who spoke English, and I soon met her husband David and her son. After our free Hebrew school finished, I continued to see my former classmates on occasion and asked how they were.

In late November, one classmate who now worked as a janitor swept the floor with angry strokes. He told me what bothered him in broken Hebrew, but I understood.

"Dead. Helena and David are dead."

My gut contracted into a stone.

A man named Dan, while drunk, drove his wife with Helena and David in the backseat. He crashed the car. Helena and her husband were dead, and the driver's wife survived. The driver? He now stayed at home drinking in the dark.

Helena was twenty-three years old, her son — now an orphan — was two.

After visiting Helena's grave and grieving, I wrote a letter to Dan the driver and had a friend translate it to Russian for me.

Here's what I wrote:

Dan,

I am an American who knew Helena and I am worried. I'm worried that the tragedy you experienced will cause you to sit in front of the television and drink your life away.

Every man has an obligation to contribute something to his community and today, the world needs you more than ever. Your task is especially important because you need to fulfill three obligations: one for Helena, one for David, and one for yourself.

For Helena: You must stop drinking. If it is difficult, there are places that will help you with this task. One place is the Marcaz G'milah Cohal. It is in Haifa and they speak Russian. Their number is 04-867-04-50.

For David: Work or volunteer your time at an institute such as the Marcaz G'milah Cohal. By doing so, you will help people and save lives. It is written that if you have saved one life, it is as if you have saved the world.

For yourself: That is up to you. Whatever work you do or enjoy doing will be a constructive contribution to the community.

There is one final thing you must do, and that is to enjoy life. Take your wife to the movies and out for dinner. Go hiking, go river-rafting. Be good to yourself because you need to enjoy all the things life has to offer for three people now: Helena, David, and yourself.

But for now, these pleasures can wait. Now is a time for mourning. And when the New Year comes, so does a new beginning. You have a difficult journey ahead of you, but it's accompanied with the respect and support of Helena's and David's souls.

Be strong. I know you can get past this.

-Ezra

The note was delivered in late December and at the end of January, I spoke with someone who knew Dan. She said, "Dan spends his days just walking around, no job. However, he is now clean and sober. His wife walks on crutches but will be off them soon. And Helena's son lives with his aunt and is very happy."

Hearing that put a lift in my step.

So I believe redemption can come in many forms. The form which works best will depend on the individual.

SADISM

I once attended a meeting whose purpose was to explain BDSM to those who were intrigued or perplexed by it. I fell in the latter category, wondering why there was an appeal by many into that lifestyle.

BDSM is a clever acronym combining Bondage and Discipline (B & D), Dominance & Submission (D & S), and Sadism and Masochism (S & M). It should be noted that though these behaviors are often expressed sexually, they are not solely sexual.

At the meeting, the speaker explained some aspects of BDSM and then I asked the question, "Why don't people who have the desire to practice BDSM go to therapy to work on why they have those desires?"

Apparently, by the sounds of the grumbling coming from the ones practicing a BDSM lifestyle in the room, I hit a nerve. The speaker was great at calming them down and responding calmly.

I don't remember what his response was, but I remember that I didn't feel like my question was answered.

After the meeting, a man spoke to me about his background. Growing up, he said, he was ashamed at having thoughts of wanting to physically hurt others. He had the desire to cut and hit people.

Why did he want to hurt people? What happened in his life to make him have these desires? Was it out of a need to get revenge for some past incident? No. He grew up in a loving household and his relationships had always been positive. So why have these thoughts of harming others?

He knew it was wrong to commit such acts, and so he sank deeper into shame.

Then, he confided his shame to a friend and his friend said, "Relax. You're not interested in emotionally traumatizing anyone, you only want to cause sensations of physical pain. Understand the difference."

That was an epiphany to him. He told me that from that moment on, he was able to accept himself and his inner needs.

Upon hearing this, I remembered how a friend told me she grew up wanting to follow orders. Long before she was old enough to have sexual thoughts, she found a deep sense of joy playing games like Simon Says. Now, in her adult life, she has taken her joy of submission to the bedroom. I later met a man who also enjoyed being submissive, so these roles are not gender-based.

Speaking with the self-proclaimed sadist, I realized

why my question in the BDSM meeting was so offensive. I may as well have asked, "Why don't people with blue eyes go to therapy to work on their need for having blue eyes?"

It's not a choice.

Sure, there may be some instances where people have BDSM tendencies as a response to a hurtful moment in their lives. But the BDSM community encourages those individuals to seek therapy rather than start a BDSM lifestyle for the wrong reasons.

As for the sadist who spoke with me after the meeting, he told me he found a wonderful woman who identifies with being a masochist, one who enjoys receiving physical pain the same way people get a rush from parachuting or bungee jumping. The two of them, as a couple, worked out beforehand what their limits are and how to communicate if the sadomasochistic session was approaching a point outside their limits.

I found a deep appreciation for this open exchange of needs and limits. As far as I know, couples not involved in the BDSM lifestyle often don't communicate their needs and limits, making the resulting relationship strained with secrets, uncommunicated desires, and resentment.

As to whether tendencies toward a BDSM lifestyle are a product of nature or nurture, most people involved in the lifestyle have expressed evidence of it always being a part of who they were. Examples include someone who enjoyed being captured in a game and made to sit in a corner; another who got thrills from being dared to do things; another who had fun being the captive and getting tied up in games. All of these personal pleasures took place before any interest in sex entered their lives.

When a sadist was asked if he got more satisfaction from inflicting pain on someone who enjoyed it or on someone who didn't, he responded that his pleasure came from giving pleasure, not from how bad he could make someone feel.

One therapist involved in the BDSM lifestyle explained that while cutting can be a symptom of borderline personality disorder (BPD), it is not the main diagnostic criteria. In fact, the therapist said the reason she enjoys being cut is because she finds it to be the ultimate form of putting complete trust in one's partner.

Though cutting rarely shows up in the BDSM life-style, I find that quality — the desire to put one's trust in another — a relatable trait. In fact, if the Biblical story of Abraham and Isaac story is true, I imagine Isaac had complete trust in Abraham when he lay on the altar and Abraham raised the knife over him for the sacrifice.

I know. Strange comparison.

The point is that the relationship focuses on trust. Specifically, the BDSM motto is, "Safe, sane and consensual." After reading or watching *Fifty Shades of Grey*, many people falsely believe they understand BDSM and men who then call themselves doms commit unethical, if not illegal, acts and the relation-ships can become abusive.

The point is that most sadists don't choose to have sadistic desires; those desires are a part of who they are. Lastly, like everyone else, their desires aren't what makes them bad or evil, it's how they choose to act on those desires that defines if they are a good person or not.

ARE YOU GOOD OR EVIL?

Judaism considers three categories of relationships: your relationship with yourself, your relationship with others, and your relationship with God.

Let's look at each category one at a time:

Your Relationship with Yourself

In this category, the Jewish interpretation of *inclination* matters most. The good inclination — the *yetser hatov* — and the evil inclination — the *yetser harah*. The good inclination is what we want to do, our long-term goal, whereas the evil inclination is what we feel like doing in the moment.

Rabbinic texts explain the difference of good and evil inclination this way:

If you want to be a movie star, it's a good idea to take acting classes. But you may feel like watching "Game of Thrones" instead. If you want to live to be a hundred years old, it's a good idea to eat healthy and exercise. But you may feel like eating potato chips while watching "Game of Thrones." If you want to become a millionaire, it's a good idea to study how to invest money and practice by starting with small amounts while leading up to larger amounts. But you may feel like watching "Game of Thrones" instead of studying.

The solution? Focus on the steps you need to take to reach your long-term goals. Either that or destroy all recordings of "Game of Thrones."

Judaism proposes an alternative solution called *tshuva*. *Tshuva* is the act of returning, returning to the path of righteousness. If you've gone astray toward the path of temptations, return to the path of righteousness by providing yourself with a good life, taking into consideration both your short term and long-term goals.

Your Relationship with Others

On the question of how to know if you are a good person to others, the nutshell answer is that there's no perfect way to know.

Consider such attitudes as sexism, racism, homo-phobia and other forms of prejudice. One may be enlightened enough to notice when they make unfair generalizations when they think of a group of people. If so, I commend them for noticing. That's the first step to improving one's self. I, myself, have gone through that first step.

If, on the other hand, one believes that they have no qualms with any group of people, and they are good to all people equally, they have a chance of being correct. I'd say statistically, though, they are more likely to be wrong and need to reflect on their attitudes.

There are plenty of topics that could come into play in the category of "Your Relationship with Others," but I'm going to hone in deep on just one:

As of this writing, the United States has detention centers to hold illegal immigrants. Congresswoman Alexandria Ocasio-Cortez and others have called the detention centers "concentration camps."

On the surface of it, calling such detention centers — places where there is a concentration of a group of people — satisfies the dictionary's definition of what qualifies as a concentration camp.

But here's why calling the detention centers "concentration camps" is anti-Semitic behavior.

Calling the immigration detention cages "concentration camps" is a microaggression.

Yes, many people commit microaggressions often, for example, when they say things like "I'm not racist. I have black friends," and "I'm not homophobic. You're just too sensitive." But lowering ourselves to such a level of saying such insensitive things by calling the detention cages concentration camps is not a good strategy for the goal of defending human rights.

In the thoughtco.com article, "What is a Microaggression? Everyday Insults With Harmful Effects," Elizabeth Hopper explains: "Unlike some other forms of prejudice and discrimination, the perpetrator of a microaggression may not even be aware that their behavior is hurtful. While microaggressions are sometimes conscious and intentional, on many occasions microaggressions may reflect the perpetrator's implicit biases about marginalized group members. Whether intentional or not, however, researchers have found that even these subtle acts can have effects on their recipients." (https://www.thoughtco.com/microaggression-definition-examples-4171853, last updated Nov. 1, 2018)

Professor Derald Wing Sue and others put microaggressions into three categories: microassaults, microinsults, and microinvalidations. Microassaults are done intentionally (i.e., "You're a pretty good member of Congress for a woman," he said with a sneer); microinsults are often unintentional insults toward a group (i.e., He cheered, "It's so great seeing two black men speak so eloquently about astrophysics!"); microinvalidations are a disregard of the experiences a group had (i.e., "Black lives matter? All lives matter!").

Additionally, environmental microaggressions exist, like having a government made up of only white men.

Calling immigrant detention cages "concentration camps" is specifically a microinvalidation. Doing so invalidates the attempted genocide of my ancestors.

Trevor Noah put it best when discussing reparations for blacks as opposed to reparations for all poor people. Deciding about whether poor white people should be given reparations or not is "a completely separate conversation." If you're "not careful," he said, you could "combine everybody's suffering in the same bowl and make it seem like all injustices have the same weighting. And they don't." ("Reparations & White Privilege - Between the Scenes," The Daily Show, March 2019)

To say, "All people with socio-economic challenges should be given reparations" is to infer that all struggling poor people were once slaves. It diminishes and denies the true experiences black Americans had.

To say, "All lives matter" is to infer that all unarmed people have to walk the streets with the fear of possibly being shot by police. It diminishes and denies the true experiences many black American males have.

To call the immigrant detention cages "concentration camps" is to infer the U.S. is collecting immigrants for the purpose of committing genocide, putting the immigrants in gas chambers and incinerating their corpses in ovens. It diminishes and denies the true experiences the Jewish people faced.

I realize these microaggressions may seem petty.

They're not.

When a Congressman stated Trump couldn't be racist because he has a black woman working for him, Rep. Rashida Tlaib — love her or hate her — quickly recognized the microaggression and rightly called him on it. She said, "Just because someone has a person of color, a black person, working for them, does not mean they aren't racist."

At that moment, whether or not Trump was racist didn't matter. The point Rep. Tlaib addressed was that using racial employment was not a good metric for determining if the employer was racist, and the Congressman was at fault for saying otherwise.

I think Alexandria Ocasio-Cortez's intentions were good; she wanted to end the heinous conditions the immigrants were experiencing. She wanted to push people's buttons to raise awareness of the detention cages, but in this case, do the ends justify the means? Could there have been another way to raise public awareness without diminishing and denying the Holocaust?

I think so.

I like how the organization "Never Again Action" took a stand against the immigration cages. On their site home page, they said, "As Jews, we were taught to never let anything like the Holocaust happen again. We refuse to wait and see."

By phrasing it this way, Never Again Action is making a clear distinction between what happened in the Holocaust, and what has the *potential* of becoming as horrific as the Holocaust.

The point is that when it comes to how I speak to people, I've been educating myself on the different kinds of microaggressions, and I'm still working on improving myself to avoid making them.

Will that make me a good person to others? No. I imagine there are other factors besides avoiding microaggressions.

Will that make me have better relationships with others? I hope so.

Your Relationship with God

There are many different opinions on how to know if you have a good relationship with God. I see the evaluation of this relationship as more of a spectrum.

On one side, God has presented in the Bible what one needs to do to be a good religious person, and the Talmud has expanded on that just in case you're the kind of person who can never have too many commandments to follow. According to the Bible, if you're not following these laws on how to worship God, you're straying from that relationship.

On the other side of the spectrum, your relationship with God is between you and God. Everyone's relationship is different and each person's relationship is personal to them. For example, one might choose keeping Kosher as their way of putting their attention on their spiritual relationship. If you feel your connection to God is strongest based on your own decisions on how you show your appreciation, then that's the best way for yourself. Even if your decision is that God doesn't exist, your relationship with a non-existing God becomes the best way for you to live.

Which side of the spectrum is the "correct" side?
shrug
Which side do *you* lean toward?
All I know is that I land somewhere in the middle, and I'm comfortable with that.

ALSO BY EZRA BARANY

The Torah Codes

What if you were stalked by a secret society?

36 Righteous; A Serial Killer's Hit List

What would you do if your beloved were on a hit list?

Deborah's Number: A Bank Heist Mitzvah

When your spouse is kidnapped, there's nothing more inconvenient than being held hostage at a bank heist.

6 Short Stories of Suspense

Six authors come together to put their skills of suspense in six short stories.

Plan Your Novel Like A Pro: And Have Fun Doing It!

Co-authored by Beth Barany.

Get excited to plan your novel. The tools shared here are designed to spark your muse and give you confidence when you sit down to write your story.

ABOUT THE AUTHOR

Ezra Barany loves riveting readers with his thrillers, but by order of the DMV must place a warning on every book cover, "Do not read while driving." His first two books in *The Torah Codes* series were award-winning international bestsellers. In his free time, he has eye-opening discussions on the art of writing novels with his wife and book coach Beth Barany. A high school physics teacher, Ezra lives and writes in Oakland with his beloved wife and two cats working on the next book in *The Torah Codes* series. His wife edits the book, his cats chew on it.